DIANE CHAMBERLAIN

is a multiple *SUNDAY TIMES* and *NEW YORK TIMES*
bestselling author, beloved by readers around the world
for stories that are rich with emotion, laced with secrets
and that inspire thoughtful conversations. Born and
raised in New Jersey, Diane obtained a master's degree
in social work in San Diego. She then worked in hospitals
before opening her own private psychotherapy practice,
focusing primarily on at-risk teenagers. This background
as a psychotherapist has given Diane great insight into the
secrets that families hold beneath the surface and how
destructive they can be when they come to light. She has
observed firsthand the ability of those under tremendous
pressure to tap into their inner strength – a resilience that
inspires her most-loved characters.

Diane Chamberlain has written twenty-eight bestselling
novels, and her books have been published in more than
twenty languages. She makes her home in North Carolina
with her partner, photographer John Pagliuca, and her
Shetland Sheepdog, Cole.

Also by Diane Chamberlain

DIANE CHAMBERLAIN

secret lives

REVIEW

First published in 1991 by Harper Collins
Published in 2014 by Pan Books

This edition published in 2020 by Headline Review
An imprint of HEADLINE PUBLISHING GROUP

Cataloguing in Publication Data is available from the British Library

ISBN 9781472271303

Offset in 9.77/13 pt Scala by Jouve (UK), Milton Keynes

Printed and bound in Great Britain by Clays Ltd, Elcograf S.p.A.

Headline's policy is to use papers that are natural, renewable and recyclable
products and made from wood grown in well-managed forests and other
controlled sources. The logging and manufacturing processes are expected
to conform to the environmental regulations of the country of origin.

HEADLINE PUBLISHING GROUP
An Hachette UK Company
Carmelite House
50 Victoria Embankment
London EC4Y 0DZ

www.headline.co.uk
www.hachette.co.uk

In memory of
DIANE MARY MCCRONE

1

Eden Swift Riley was good at pretending. That would get her through this interview, her first in many months. She stood at the edge of her Santa Monica living room, watching the television crew shove her sofa this way and that, and breathed slowly, deeply. She would feign calm. The viewers would marvel at her composure, her dignity. She was the master of make-believe. Ironic. It was for that very reason that Wayne had left her. "You're always on," he said. "Always acting. Always playing a role."

Nina walked across the room to stand next to her. "God, you look good," Nina said as she straightened the collar of Eden's blouse. "I haven't seen you look this terrific since . . . in a long time."

"You look pretty cute yourself," Eden said. Nina was wearing blue jeans—she was not your typical Hollywood agent—a red T-shirt, and a purple scarf tied at her throat which set off her gamin-cut, jet-black hair. She was only thirty-four, one year younger than Eden, and she did indeed look adorable.

"They're trying to move your sofa so they'll get a view of the ocean through the windows behind it," Nina said.

"Uh huh." What they were really trying to do, she thought, was to make this living room look as though it belonged to a star, someone worthy of a Monika Lane interview. Well, her house should come as no surprise to anyone. She was not known for her pretensions.

Nina shook her head. "They're making a mess of your rug."

"I don't care." She didn't. The crushed dents in the toast-colored carpet seemed insignificant. Since Wayne left, this house had no pull on her. The thought of moving had been slipping in and out of her mind the past few weeks. Someplace where there'd be more kids Cassie's age; someplace quieter, away from the beach. Lately she'd found herself longing for trees, for something undeniably green.

Finally the crew was satisfied with the room, and Monika Lane settled her elegant self onto one end of the steel-blue sofa and nodded for Eden to join her. Eden sat down at the other end. She pictured the scene through the camera's lens, the way she and Monika would balance each other. Monika with her dark, dark hair. Eden with her blond. But they were more alike than different, she knew—two self-made women who'd worked their way to the top with ambition and integrity.

Eden curled her legs beneath her. Her feet were bare. She wore white silk pants, a soft, full white blouse open at the throat. It was her favorite outfit for difficult situations. It comforted her. It was like being wrapped in a cloud. Her hair was down today, although lately she'd taken to pinning it up. And there was a single braided gold chain at her throat. She wore very little makeup. No one would expect her to.

Someone handed her a mug of coffee, which she cradled on her lap between her palms.

As soon as the interview started Eden knew Monika was going to be gentle with her, at least more gentle than usual. Monika knew her audience would not appreciate her ripping apart the beloved and betrayed Eden Riley.

"This is one of the best periods for you professionally, Eden," Monika said, "but one of the worst for you personally."

"It's been difficult," Eden agreed. "But I'm surviving." She should say more. Take control of the interview, as Nina would say. She imagined Nina standing against the wall, muttering to herself, and the thought gave Eden some pleasure.

"Your marriage survived a long time by Hollywood standards."

"Fifteen years."

"It was thought to be one of the most stable marriages around."

Eden sat up straighter. Monika wasn't going to let her off as easily as she'd thought. "Well, a marriage can look healthy on the outside and be loaded with problems inside."

"Was yours loaded with problems?"

Eden looked down at her mug to think her answer through. She hadn't known there were problems. She had been as shocked as anyone when Wayne walked out.

"I think there were problems I was unaware of. I worked long hours, he traveled a lot, and I guess our communication suffered along the way. Wayne's been made to look like the bad guy, but a marriage is a two-way street."

"You don't blame him?"

"He no longer wanted to be married to an actress. I can't blame him for that." For other things, yes. But not for that.

"He's remarrying soon, is that right?"

Eden nodded. "Next month. A woman in Pennsylvania." As if Monika didn't know. As if the world didn't know she'd been traded in. A schoolteacher, Wayne had crowed. You can't get much more down-to-earth than that.

"And your daughter. Cassie. You'll have joint custody?"

Eden felt a jab of pain behind her eyes, so quick and sharp she'd had no time to prepare for it. Cassie was the one topic that could throw this interview, turn her into a wailing fool. But she caught herself, smiled broadly. "Yeah. She'll be a bicoastal kid."

"How old is she now?"

"Four. This year's actually been good for me in a way. I haven't been working much and it's given me time to be just a mom."

"You've also been hard at work on your pet project."

"The Handicapped Children's Fund. Yes."

"You were so wonderful as Lily Wolfe in *Heart of Winter*." Monika changed the subject abruptly. She probably thought talk about the Children's Fund would put the audience to sleep.

"Thank you."

"What was it like for you, after years of making films that appeal to the under-thirteen crowd?"

"Freeing. And frightening. I wasn't certain how seriously I'd be taken in that type of film."

"Your Oscar should put that concern to rest. Did it surprise you to win?"

Eden uttered something modest—humble words that poured from her mechanically and that she would forget moments later. The truth was, she had not been surprised by the Oscar. She'd gone to the premiere of *Heart of Winter*, more anxious about what she would see on the screen than she'd ever been before. But once the film began, once she saw how thoroughly she'd become Lily Wolfe, she knew she'd done something extraordinary. When it was over and the audience sat hushed and limp for a few seconds before breaking into wild applause, she knew that they knew it too.

"Why were you so adamant about not doing a nude scene?" Monika asked.

Eden shifted on the sofa, wishing she had a place to set the mug of now cold coffee. "It seemed too great a leap," she said. "You know, one minute I'm playing the heroine of ten-year-olds, the next I'm rolling around naked in bed with a guy."

"And that guy was Michael Carey."

Eden felt the color rise in her cheeks.

"You're blushing, Eden." Monika grinned, delighted.

"Everyone's blown our friendship way out of proportion."

"Is that all it is? Friendship?"

"Absolutely." She thought of Michael watching this interview. He'd heard these words from her dozens of times. Maybe he'd finally believe her if she said them in public. "I like his company, but I'm not rushing into a serious relationship with anyone."

Monika shook her head in disappointment. "You two seem so very right for each other. I don't think I've ever, despite the fact that you were clothed the entire time, seen a more erotic love scene in a movie than that hotel room scene between the two of you."

Eden smiled, felt the color rise again. "There was chemistry between the two characters. That doesn't mean there's chemistry between the two actors." Oh, God, did she really say that? Sorry, Michael.

"Your childhood, Eden. It's the one topic you steadfastly refuse to discuss in an interview."

Eden kept her smile in place. "And I'm not about to change my policy on that now, Monika." She discussed her childhood with no one, not even herself. She felt as though someone else had lived her life before she moved to California.

"Well, let me just summarize a little. You're the daughter of the extremely successful children's author, Katherine Swift, who died when you were quite young. Do you think being Katherine Swift's daughter had anything to do with your success as an actress?"

Eden nodded. "It got my foot in the door. It helped me get parts in the films that were based on her stories. But after that I was on my own."

"You coauthored the wonderful screenplay for *Heart of Winter*. Did you inherit some of your mother's writing talent?"

"I hope so. That was new for me and something I'd like to do again."

"Are you at all like her in other ways? I mean, she earned the reputation of being an eccentric of a sort—an odd, reclusive woman who kept people at a distance."

Eden ignored the urge to come to her mother's defense. She laughed. "Do you think I'm odd and eccentric?"

"Certainly not on the surface."

"Not below the surface either," she said, with a hint of bravado, but she heard Wayne's voice in the back of her mind. "Who the hell is the real Eden Riley? I don't think I've ever met her. I don't think you've met her either."

"What's next for you, Eden?"

She knew Nina's ears would prick up at that question. Nina was fed up with her. She'd turned down one offer after another. She told Nina none of them were right for her. The roles were too earthy; they would cost her her fans. But the truth was that since Wayne left she'd had no motivation. No steam. No energy.

She looked at Monika's carefully made-up eyes. "I don't want to dive into something I'm not sure of," she said. "The next thing I work on will have to be a project I can throw myself into whole . . ." The image of her mother slipped into her mind: Katherine Swift sitting at her desk, bending over her typewriter in the candlelit blackness of the Lynch Hollow cavern.

"Eden?" Monika raised her eyebrows.

Eden leaned forward. "You mentioned my mother. I've been thinking of doing something on her life, perhaps." She sounded as though the idea had been percolating in her mind for months rather than seconds. She could actually sense Nina at the side of the room, standing straighter, tilting forward. What the hell? Nina would be thinking. "I could make her more understandable," Eden said. Her palms pressed against the mug in her hands. "More sympathetic."

"You mean you would make a movie about your mother?"

"Yes. I'd like to write the script myself. And play her as well." The words were flowing and she had no idea of their source. She felt a dampness under her arms, a prickling at the nape of her neck.

Monika grinned. "What a terrific idea!" She continued her questioning with new enthusiasm, and Eden offered answers, but her brain burned now with the images—the cave, the lush green valley of the Shenandoah, the clapboard house of her childhood in Lynch Hollow. Her aunt and uncle lived in that house now. Lou and Kyle. Would they see this interview? What on earth would they think? She imagined them turning to each other with incredulous eyes.

She would have to film in summer, when the heavy, breath-stealing greenness would fill the screen. But she knew next to nothing about her mother. It would take an enormous amount of research, and she would have to spend time in Lynch Hollow. Could she do it? Her heartbeat pounded in her ears with excitement. And with fear. Because Lynch Hollow was real; as real as the cave, as real as the river. She would not be able to pretend there. She would not be able to make believe.

2

Eden parked the car on the shoulder of the road and set out on foot through the woods. Although more than two decades had passed since she last walked through this forest, and although it was dusk and the woods were thick with shadow, she knew the way.

Fireflies hovered in the damp June air, and her blouse was stuck to her back by the time she reached the cavern. It looked just as it had the last time she saw it, when she was eleven years old and knew no home other than this hollow in Virginia's Shenandoah Valley. The mouth of the cave was still blocked by the two enormous boulders Uncle Kyle and some of the neighbor men had rolled into place. But above the pale gray boulders was a black triangular opening. Eden stepped closer. She didn't remember that opening. Perhaps a rock had broken loose from it sometime in the last twenty-four years. She wondered if Kyle knew the cave was open to bats and field mice. She wondered if children ever tried to squeeze through that space, if they dared each other.

"This is the cave where Katherine Swift wrote her stories," they'd say. "This is the cave where she died."

And perhaps they heard the staccato clicking of the typewriter keys on the cool draft of air that slipped through the opening, just as Eden heard it now, as if her mother were still inside, writing, oblivious to the darkness.

Eden walked back to the car, slowly, arms crossed in front of her. One month had passed since the Monika Lane interview and in that month the idea of making a film about her mother had consumed her. Two studios were interested, but she was holding everyone off, much to Nina's chagrin. She could not be rushed in this. She needed to be in complete control.

"This is fantastic," Nina had said when she saw the enthusiasm Eden's idea had generated. "Who could make a better film about Katherine Swift than you?"

But Eden had been barely four years old when her mother died. Her memories were wispy and thin. The sketchy biographical material that existed on Katherine Swift portrayed her eccentricities as something close to insanity and perpetuated the myth that she was a cold woman who chose to live the life of a hermit.

The articles on her mother always began with "the peculiar Katherine Swift" or "the eccentric Katherine Swift," or, as in the review of her latest rerelease: "It is remarkable that Katherine Swift wrote of her young characters with such warmth when it is well known she scorned the company of others throughout much of her short life."

Maybe Eden could alter the tiresome view the public held of her mother. She herself was living proof that her mother had had at least one loving relationship. Eden's father, Matthew Riley, died shortly before she was born. Yet Eden liked to imagine his brief marriage to her mother as vibrant and passionate. It would have taken a special sort of man to pull Katherine from her shell.

On the flight from Los Angeles to Philadelphia that morning, Eden had come up with a title for the film: *A Solitary Life*. The word "solitary" had no particular negative connotation attached to it. It didn't indict her mother for the choices she'd made. That would be her theme for the movie—that the world was wrong in its analysis of this woman who was both writer and archaeologist. She was not cold. She was not crazy.

Eden had rented a car in Philadelphia and driven with Cassie the thirty miles to Wayne and Pam's house. Cassie still did not seem to understand, despite lengthy discussions on the subject, that she would be spending a month with her daddy and his new wife— and without Eden. Eden had been relieved to find Wayne alone at his new suburban home when she and Cassie pulled up. She knew immediately that he was in his element. He was pruning the rosebushes, dirty-kneed, his hands callused from the clippers. There were tears in his eyes when he bent down to embrace his daughter. Then he squeezed Eden's hand.

"Two months with Lou and Kyle, huh?" He smiled. "I can't believe you're doing this, Eden. But I think it's good. And we'll be fine here." He looked down at Cassie, who was still clutching Eden's hand.

As she pulled out of Wayne's long driveway, she allowed herself just one look back at her daughter. That was a mistake. Cassie stared after the car, her eyes wide and glassy with disbelief, and Eden felt a fresh pulse of guilt surface in her chest.

The drive from Philadelphia to Washington was a blur, but then Virginia's rolling wooded hills cradled the road and brought her back to the purpose of this trip. Maybe the film should open with an aerial view of these hills. Or, she thought now as she stepped from the forest onto the road, maybe the camera should slip through the woods during the opening credits, smoothly, silently, until it reached the mouth of the cave. Relax, she told herself. She would come up with hundreds of ideas for the opening of the film over the next few weeks. She didn't need to make any decisions now.

She got back into the car and drove carefully along the narrow road, hunting in the darkness for the turn that would take her through the forest to Lynch Hollow and the house of her childhood, the house where Kyle, Katherine's brother, had retired after leaving New York. She had initially recoiled at Kyle's suggestion that she spend the summer with him and Lou while she did her research. She had seen them as little as she could get away with since leaving home at the age of nineteen, and those visits were always strained and awkward. The thought of spending an entire summer with them overwhelmed her, but she felt as though she had no choice. Kyle knew more than anyone about Katherine. So for the next couple of months she would live in the house of her early childhood, awakening memories buried deep and wisely.

She spotted the boulder marking the driveway to the house and the little carved wooden sign above it. Lynch Hollow. She turned onto the driveway and was surprised to see it was now macadam. The last time she'd been on this driveway she'd been eleven years old, riding in the back of a black car with her step-grandmother, Susanna. She remembered how her eyes burned as the orange dust from the driveway seeped through the car windows. Who was driving that car? She couldn't remember. A relative of Susanna's, most likely. She'd had no idea as they drove away from the small white house that day that she would not see it again for twenty-four years. "Just a ride," Susanna had said. "We're just going for a little ride." That had struck Eden as odd. Spontaneity was not in Susanna's nature, and Susanna was still coughing badly, her face pale from weeks in bed. The ride dragged on and on and Eden grew bored. When they pulled up in front of the square brick building that stood alone in a field, she was relieved that they had finally arrived someplace. It was another hour before she realized Susanna intended to leave her there, with the black-cloaked nuns and children she didn't know. And it was days before she realized that Susanna meant to leave her there forever.

The two years Eden lived at the orphanage did indeed seem like forever. But when she was thirteen Kyle and Lou tracked her down and took her home with them to New York City, where she spent the rest of her teenage years. Since then she had avoided New York as resolutely as she avoided Lynch Hollow.

The little house looked different in the darkness. The woods surrounding it seemed thicker, the trees taller, bending to shelter the roof. The edges of the house were more sharply defined than in the fuzzy one-dimensional image in her memory.

The house was not the same and that filled her with courage, but when she stepped from the car she flinched at the overwhelmingly familiar scent of honeysuckle and boxwood, sweetness and musk.

The front door opened and light streamed onto the porch. The tall frame of her uncle filled the doorway and sent a shadow that touched her toes.

"Eden!" Kyle stepped onto the porch, letting the screen door slam shut behind him. He walked across the yard and she worked at returning his smile. It had been a year and a half since she'd last seen him, when he and Lou flew out to California at Christmas to fuss over Cassie.

Kyle gave her a quick hug. "Luggage?"

She opened her trunk to expose two suitcases and a portable word processor.

"Lou inside?" She heaved one of the suitcases out of the trunk.

Kyle nodded, smiling as he set her word processor on the ground. She thought as she had many times before how warm this man was, how she wished she could return his warmth.

Inside the house everything had been transformed. Urbanized. The front door still opened awkwardly into the kitchen, but that room had been gutted and updated. Eden would never have recognized it. The counters and appliances were set low to accommodate Lou's wheelchair, and a skylight was carved into the ceiling above the table. The choppy little hallway between the kitchen and the living room was gone, and the north wall of the living room was now entirely made of glass.

Lou's easel stood in front of the glass wall, and a Prokofiev piano concerto poured from the huge stereo speakers standing in the corners of the living room.

"You've done wonderful things with the house," Eden said. She stood in the middle of the living room, hands on hips, and looked around her. "You've brought New York to Lynch Hollow."

Lou wheeled toward her to hand her a glass of iced tea. "Kyle had to make a few concessions to get me to move down here," she said. "I hope we haven't ruined it for your research."

"No." Eden leaned down to kiss her aunt's cheek. "I love it." She watched as Lou slipped easily from her wheelchair to the couch, making the fact that she had only one leg look inconsequential. Lou was close to seventy and beautiful, her skin dewy and smooth on her high cheekbones and across the sharp line of her jaw. Her eyes were blue, huge and heavy-lidded under expressive brows. She wore her hair, a dramatic blend of black and white, pulled back in a bun, a style that on another woman might be deadly, but that made Lou look aristocratic and proud. Wearing a black scoop-neck jersey and a long green skirt, she could pass as a retired ballerina, and it was true she had once loved to dance. Every Saturday night when Eden was a teenager, Kyle took Lou dancing. But thank God it had not been her profession. Eden remembered Kyle's relief when, just weeks after losing her leg, Lou was back at the easel.

Kyle set a chocolate cake down on the coffee table, one burning pink candle jutting from the icing. "Happy birthday, Eden. A few days late."

"Thank you." Eden sat down on the love seat. She turned to Lou. "Did you make the cake? It's beautiful."

Lou shook her head. "I don't do much baking anymore, dear. There's a good bakery in Coolbrook. Go ahead." She motioned toward the cake. "Make a wish."

Eden blew out the candle, guilty because the first wish that came into her head was that her work here would go quickly and she could escape from her aunt and uncle sooner than planned.

Lou cut the cake and handed her a piece.

"We put you in your mother's old room upstairs," Kyle said. "It's barely been touched by the remodeling, so hopefully you can still get a feel for her in there."

Eden nodded. That was the most logical room for her to have. The first floor had only the master bedroom and one smaller bedroom which had originally belonged to her mother and Kyle, and later to her. The second story, added on shortly before Eden's birth, held one large bedroom and a smaller room across the hall, where Katherine wrote when it was too cold in the cavern. After Katherine died no one used the upstairs. There were no boulders in front of the stairway, but Katherine's room had become as sealed from the rest of the world as her cave.

"These came for you today." Kyle carried a vase filled with two dozen red roses into the living room and set them next to the cake.

Eden plucked the card from its holder, although she was certain who had sent them. I miss you already, Michael had written.

"Michael Carey?" Lou asked.

"Yes." Obviously Kyle and Lou were up on the latest Hollywood gossip. Eden set the card on the table and picked up her plate again.

"He's very handsome," Lou said.

"Yes, he is."

"Has quite a reputation, though," Kyle said. "You don't have to rush into anything."

Lou laughed. "Ky, she's a grown-up."

"Okay, okay." Kyle smiled. "Old habits die hard."

"Michael's cleaned up his act, Kyle. He's being very solicitous because he hopes to play Matthew Riley in the movie. But we're really just friends, so you don't need to worry."

"Two dozen roses to a friend?" Kyle asked as he ducked back into the kitchen.

Eden sighed and looked at her aunt. "How come I feel like I'm eighteen again?"

"You never stop worrying, Eden. So how's Cassie? We can't wait to see her."

"She's just fine."

"I bet you'll miss her this month."

Eden shrugged. "She'll have a great time with Wayne and Pam and Pam's kids." She felt the tears threaten and took a long swallow of iced tea to stop them. Why do you have to go, Mommy?

"We saw *Heart of Winter* three times, Eden." Kyle stood in the doorway of the kitchen, sipping his iced tea. "We're real proud of you, honey."

Kyle was, how old now? Sixty-four? His neatly trimmed white and gray beard lent him dignity, but the laugh lines carved into the skin around his clear blue eyes were evidence of his good humor. He was wearing jeans and a blue plaid shirt, and he was lean without being gaunt. When he spoke, the remnants of his Shenandoah Valley accent still softened his words, although he'd spent most of his adult life far from Lynch Hollow. He was still a handsome man, quite remarkably so for his age. She'd noticed that for the first time just a few years ago. He'd been in L.A. at an archaeology conference and wanted to take her out to dinner. Spending an evening alone with Kyle had been unthinkable, so Eden asked Nina to join them. At the restaurant Eden had barely gotten seated before Nina dragged her into the ladies' room.

"Your uncle's gorgeous," she'd said. "Is he married?"

Eden had stared at her in disbelief. "He's nearly old enough to be your grandfather, Nina."

Nina leaned toward the mirror to apply a fresh layer of mascara to her already thick lashes. "He's old like Paul Newman's old, like Sean Connery's old. Know what I mean?" She leaned back, blinked her lashes at her reflection. "So, is he married?"

Eden spent the rest of that evening observing Kyle's deft, effortless evasion of Nina's seduction, and she realized with a jolt that this was something he was accustomed to doing, something he had most likely done all his life.

Here at Lynch Hollow she could see the signs of age creeping in. He was moving a little more slowly and Eden watched him grimace as he sat next to Lou on the sofa.

"Arthritis," he said. "Finally catching up to me." The wheelchair had been a part of Lou's countenance for a long time, but Eden hadn't expected this change in Kyle. It sent a quick, unexpected sliver of fear through her.

Conversation sagged as it always did between the three of them. Not once during the years she'd lived with them as a teenager had a conversation between them taken flight. She knew it was her fault, as it was most likely her fault now. With most people she could keep up an easy superficial chatter from behind her Eden Riley mask. But she could only play herself with Kyle and Lou, and that was the one role for which she could never memorize the lines.

Kyle suddenly set his tea on the coffee table and stood up. "I have something for you." He left the room and reappeared a few minutes later with a thin gift-wrapped package about the size of a magazine. He put it on the table and took his seat again next to Lou, who edged closer to him. "Birthday present," he said. There was reluctance in his voice, as if this was a gift he was not certain he wanted her to have.

Eden opened the wrapping to discover a dark clothbound notebook. She looked up at Kyle.

"Part of your mother's journal."

"What?" She set her hand on the notebook. "She kept a journal?"

Kyle nodded. "I meant to give it to you long ago, but . . ." He shrugged. "Your mother was so misunderstood. I didn't want you to misunderstand her too."

Lou set her hand on Kyle's arm.

"Even now, I'm hesitant," he said. "Selfish, I guess. I was the only one who knew about it."

"My father didn't know?"

Kyle hesitated, his eyes on Lou's hand where it rested on his wrist. "Matt knew. But he never read it." He straightened his spine with a great sigh. "So. I'll give them to you—there are more notebooks, about a dozen, and I know Kate wanted you to have them. But I plan to mete them out to you, one by one, because I don't want you to skip ahead. She was a complex person, your mother. A complex woman. And if you don't understand her at age thirteen"—he leaned forward and held up the notebook—"you'll never understand her at thirty-one."

Eden sat back. Thirteen to thirty-one! The journal would make her research a snap. She probably would not need the whole summer here after all. Still, she felt more trepidation than delight at the thought of reading her mother's words about her life. There would be little room for interpretation, for bending the facts to fit her theme. And it was too close. She would have to read with a distanced eye.

"You don't need to worry," she said. "I've always felt she was misrepresented. I'm tired of seeing her portrayed as cold and detached."

Kyle stood up and turned to face the wall of glass, hands in his pockets, shoulders tensed, and Eden wondered if she'd said the wrong thing.

"Kate wasn't cold," he said. "She chose isolation because it was safer for her." He turned to face her. "I'll help you in any way I can, Eden. But I don't want any filming in the cavern. The cavern stays sealed up."

"That's fine." She had expected that, and in a way it relieved her. She was a little frightened of the cave. "We can find another cave or re-create that one."

"I hope you're not going to be disappointed," Kyle said. "A story about a woman who spent ninety-five percent of her time in a cave could be pretty dull."

"Well, it probably won't be for everyone, but I don't plan on it being boring."

"You must be exhausted after your drive, dear," Lou said.

Eden set her plate down on the table and stood up with a false weariness. She'd lost three hours of the day flying east and she was not actually tired, but it would be a relief to be alone again. "Yes, I really am. I guess I'll go to bed early."

Kyle picked up the notebook and held it out to her, like a dare. "Maybe you'd like to do a little reading before you go to sleep?"

She took the book from him.

"I'll speak to my partner, Ben Alexander, about showing you the archaeological site tomorrow." Kyle walked with her toward the stairs. "You should get a feel for it so you can understand why Kate was so fascinated by it."

Eden nodded. Kyle had her research well planned out for her.

Her mother's room was spacious and welcoming with its old pine furniture and double bed. A blue wicker rocker faced the north window, a small pine desk sat in front of the south. She viewed it all with a practiced eye, picturing the way the room would look on the screen. She imagined Katherine rocking in the rocker, sitting at the desk.

She began emptying her suitcase, setting the picture of Cassie on the dresser. Cassie was on a swing at the park, her brown hair flying straight out behind her. She wore her usual devilish grin. Eden looked around the room for a phone, but there was none. Good. It would make it easier to resist constant calls to Pennsylvania. She was not used to this, having no one to tuck in, no one badgering her for another story, a glass of water, an extra good-night kiss. She'd never been this far from her daughter. Even when she had to travel to a film location, she'd taken Cassie with her. The separation this summer was the product of the liberal visitation the judge had ordered for

Wayne after the hideous court battle. She would never forgive Wayne for his attempt to disparage her as a mother. He and Pam could offer Cassie a normal life, he'd told the judge. "My daughter's been in the public eye since her conception," he said truthfully. "I don't want her to grow up thinking Hollywood is the real world."

Eden had brought one other picture with her. This photograph was unframed, dog-eared and yellowed. The woman in the picture knelt in a corner of a rectangular archaeological pit, smiling up at the photographer. She had beautiful straight white teeth. Her thick honey-colored hair, the same color as Eden's, hung over her shoulder in a long braid. She wore khaki shorts, a white shirt open at the neck. She looked about twenty-five or—six. It was one of Eden's few pictures of her mother, one she shared with the rest of the world since it was the publicity photo most often used on the dust jackets of Katherine's children's books.

Eden propped the picture up against the lamp on her night table. She pulled a pendant from her makeup case and set it next to the picture. The pendant was an oval of white porcelain with a delicate lavender flower painted in the center. It had been her mother's. Kyle had given it to Eden for her sixteenth birthday, but she had never felt comfortable wearing it. She wasn't certain even now why she had brought it with her.

She changed into her short white satin nightgown and got under the covers, looking over at the journal on the night-stand. The cover, probably once a dark green, was now nearly black with age. The book didn't close flat because the edges of the pages were wavy, as though they'd spent too many years in the damp. Eden opened the cover and saw her mother's neat handwriting, blue ink on yellowed, lined paper. She closed the book again. No, not tonight. Not yet.

The squeal of brakes and the sound of metal grating against metal woke her. Eden sat up in the darkness, heart pounding. It took her a minute to figure out where she was. Lynch Hollow. And it had only been a nightmare. The nightmare. It had been a long time since she'd had it, but every detail was the same. The darkness, the sickening grating, crunching sound that went on forever. She'd turn around in slow motion to see the white sedan and black station wagon fused together under the surreal glow of a streetlamp. At least this time she'd awakened before the screaming began.

She got out of bed and walked to the window. The thin moon was the only light and she could barely make out the place where the yard turned from grass to forest.

Only a dream, she told herself. You're awake. You're okay.

She'd known this would happen, hadn't she? She couldn't be in the same house with Lou and Kyle and not have that nightmare.

God, Lou, I would give anything if I could change what happened.

She turned on the night table lamp to chase the shadows from the room and sat in the rocker next to the window. She wouldn't go back to bed until her head was clear of the dream. She rocked, and the motion soothed her. Her eyes rested on the old green notebook. She sighed, turned her chair so the light was over her shoulder, and reached for her mother's journal.

3

April 4, 1941

I'm in trouble again. Ma found the dictionary Mrs. Renfrew gave me and burned it. I saw her take it out in the yard and light a match to it. And when she finds me I'll get the strap again for sure.

My hand is shaking as I write this, so excuse the wobbly letters. I always get scared when I know a beating's coming because I'm never sure how far she'll take it. I practically have callusses on my legs and backside from the razer strap, so I guess I should be used to it by now, but I can't stop shaking. I'll lie about the dictionary and tell her I found it so I don't get Mrs. Renfrew in trouble.

I didn't think Mrs. Renfrew liked me, but besides the dictionary she gave me this notebook. She said I should write in it like a diary, only not just what happens each day, but what I think about what happens too. I laughed when she said that because I'd get in worst trouble than usual if she knew what I was thinking. She must of read my mind, because she said, "Kate, this journal is only for your eyes. You don't have to show it to me or anyone else."

That stopped my laughing and gave me a good feeling, like I have a secret friend I can tell anything to. I have to hide this book good though, because if Ma ever found it she'd kill me and Mrs. Renfrew, too. I might let

Kyle read it though, specially as he suggested where to hide it. (Under the loose floorboards beneath my bed.) Ma don't hold with writing or reading. When she watches us write, she says it looks like devil scratch and when Kyle read out loud from the bible the other night, she says he must have it memorized, that no boy of fourteen could read that good.

Daddy has some books hid for us in the spring house so Ma don't know about them. He pulls them out sometimes and lets us read instead of doing chores. Then he does the chores hisself so Ma don't know. He has done this since we was little, so Kyle and me read better than anybody round here.

Kyle says since Mrs. Renfrew is so nice to me I should stop doing the things I do in class that upset her, like pretending to pick imaginary bugs out of the air while she's trying to teach or playing like I got out of control hickups. I told Kyle I can't help it. It's like something comes over me and the things just happen. Maybe Ma's right that I got the devil inside me. I wish one of her beatings would knock it out of me once and for all.

Kyle is sitting next to me as I write this, helping me spell. We are sitting on a wide branch of a giant old elm tree in our yard. From here we can see the house and a little ways into the woods, but nobody can see us.

Kyle says I should write about how crazy Mama is. We didn't know Mama was crazy til a few years ago when we heard the other children at school talking about her, saying things I guess they heard their Mamas say, like maybe she should be put away. She should be locked up, they said. Til then I thought all mothers talked to people who wasn't there and washed the sheets every day and the same clothes she washed out the day before. Once she got me out of my bed in the middle of the night to change my sheets though she done it already just that morning.

Mama is also afeard of indians and until Kyle convinced me that there wasn't any indians around here I was afeard myself. Some nights I wake up and hear the rocker going real slow on the porch. It creaks forward, then stops, creaks backward, then stops. I know if I tiptoe to my window, I'll see Mama in the rocker, her mouth part open like she's about to pray, her eyes wide and staring off, and acrost her chest the shotgun. She stays up like that all night sometime, watching for indians.

Mama cooks us dinner when she remembers but most often Kyle or I cook. Daddy gets angry if there ain't nothing to eat when he comes home from the mill and even though Daddy won't hit, his anger is worst than

Mama's. Kyle says that's because it's real anger, not crazy anger. All I know is, when I'm in the back room where Kyle and me sleep and I hear the floorboards creak outside the door, my heart beats so hard it hurts and I hold my breath, waiting for Daddy to throw the door open and holler or Ma to race in with the strap.

If Kyle didn't live here too I would run away.

Last year Mrs. Renfrew had us write about a person we loved and most everybody wrote about their mother or father. Kyle and me wrote about each other. I said how when we was little he held my hand when I was learning to walk. (Mrs. Renfrew said that is unlikley—he was not even a year older than me and could barely walk hisself, but I remember this clearly.) I wrote he was a calm person and nice and he wrote I was fun but did things before I thought about what might come from them. Mrs. Renfrew said sometimes it's hard to believe we're from the same family.

We live out farther than most of the other children at school so Kyle and I mostly just stick with each other. That's fine with me since I don't like our classmates. I tell Kyle it's because they're stupid, but really I don't know what to say to them. Seems like when I finally say something, they just look at me like I'm as crazy as Mama. They like Kyle, though, and sometimes after chores he goes off with one of them, fishing or whatever. This is happening more and more lately and he always asks me to come along, but I don't want to. I just go home and sit in the tree, waiting for him. But once he gets there I pretend like I hardly notice he's come.

I can't let Kyle read this journal after all.

April 5, 1941

Kyle told Mama the dictionary was his.

We was in the kitchen eating the chicken I fried for dinner when Mama said as soon as dinner was over I would get my due. That's when Kyle said it was his, that he left it on my bed the day before. Kyle's eyes was hooked fast on Mama's face, his jaw was stiff like the day he told me Francie, our dog, died. I couldn't talk. The chicken felt catched in my chest.

Mama pushed her chair out with an awful scraping sound. Then she stood up and went to the pantry where she hangs the razer strap. Kyle looked right scared sitting there.

Daddy coughed and pushed out his chair and though his chicken was only half ate he took the shotgun and went out the door, deserting us like he always does when Mama takes a fit.

Mama come back in the room with the strap held between her hands and stood next to Kyle's chair. She told him to stand up and he lifted his chair a little off the floor as he pushed it back so it didn't make that scraping sound.

"Drop your pants," Mama told him.

A red rash crept up Kyle's neck to the lobes of his ears. "Can we go in the other room?" he asked.

She hit the strap acrost his hands where they set on his belt buckle. "Now!" she hollered.

I tried to say, "Mama, it was mine," but the words came out only like a moan.

Kyle's hands was shaking as he undone his pants and lowered them to his knees. Mama pushed on his back til his elbows set on the table and his white backside stuck out and I hated her for embarussing him that way. I stood up and grabbed her hands.

"Mama, it was mine. The dictionary was mine!" I said.

She pushed me away and hit Kyle with the strap. His body jerked and I could already see the red squares on the back of his legs from the strap. I ran at her again, trying to pull the strap out of her hands but she took ahold of my shoulder and pushed me and I fell into the corner.

Tears was already starting down Kyle's cheeks. "You're making her angrier, Kate," he said.

I looked at Mama's eyes and they was hot and firey, like a crazy dragon's eyes. He was right. I was making it worst for him, so I ran outside and knelt in the garden with my hands over my ears. But I could still hear the strap and I counted to eleven before I vomited up the chicken. And she was still hitting him and he was screaming. I wanted her to die, just to drop dead right there in the kitchen. I hate her so much.

After Ma and Daddy was in bed, I fetched some aspirin for Kyle. He was lying on his stomach and though he was in bed since supper I knew he hadn't slept a wink. I knelt next to him while he arched his back to drink the water. It was cool in our room, but he was covered only by his sheet because he said the blanket hurt too much.

I thought I should look at his legs, maybe paint them with iodine, but he said no. He didn't want me to see what she done to him in the whipping that was sposed to be mine.

I sat on the floor watching his face in the moonlight coming through the window. He looks like me, only people say he's handsome and they don't say much about me, cept for how beautiful my hair is. Our hair is the same color, like wheat, and its real thick. But mine is very, very long, way past my waist. Mama trims just a little off it each time the moon is full to make it grow faster. People touch it sometimes like they can't help themselves, but they never say much about my face. Kyle and I both have blue eyes and too many freckles that look better on a boy than a girl, and we both have real long eyelashes. I sat there on the floor of our room, staring at Kyle's eyelashes while he fell asleep. They was wet and clumped together into four or five little points that made me cry. I stayed there next to him, my head resting against the edge of his mattress til I saw the first little glimpse of dawn out the window, and I knew I better get back in my own bed before Mama come for the sheets.

May 1, 1941

Today Mrs. Renfrew read one of my stories out loud and then she said, in front of everybody, that I was one of the most intellagent students and the best writer she ever taught. Everybody stared at me and my face got hot enough to set my hair aflame. At recess, Sara Jane called me teacher's pet and everyone started saying it til they got tired and went off without me, the boys to throw the ball around, the girls in their little circle to talk about whatever it is they talk about. I took one of the books Mrs. Renfrew keeps in the classroom and sat on the step, reading. This is the way it is every recess.

After school, I ran home, not wanting to hear them call me teacher's pet again. I clumb into the tree, where I'm writing this right now, waiting for Kyle to come home. He took his fishing pole today, though, so he's probly at the river with Getch.

May 7, 1941

Today Mrs. Renfrew talked to me after school to tell me she's not coming back next year. (There is a rumer she's having a baby.) She said we'll have a new teacher, Miss Crisp, and that Miss Crisp will not put up with me. "She will not tolerate your antics as I do, Katherine," she said. She told me I don't need to get in trouble to get the attention of other students, that I could get it in good ways, by writing my stories, by being a good student. I wanted to tell her she's too old to understand. I wanted to say that when she reads one of my stories to the class or says something nice about me, they hate me more. I hope the new teacher won't think I'm so good and will punish me when I'm evil. Mrs. Renfrew gave me another book, this one on grammar and punctuation. I thanked her and then took a deep breath and told her I lost the dictionary. She looked at me funny but didn't say anything, just got up and handed me her very own dictionary, the big one from her bookshelf. It has her name, Madeline Renfrew, written on the inside cover. I promised her that nothing would happen to this one. All the way home I worried that I couldn't fit both books plus my journal beneath the floorboards, but sure enough, they fit perfectly, like that space was just waiting for them to come fill it.

July 22, 1941

It is hard to describe how I feel tonight. I am writing this by lantern light in a cavern I found this afternoon. No one knows where I am, not even Kyle, and I'm afeard to go home. Home is more scary to me than whatever might be hiding in this cave.

I woke up early this morning with a strange ticklish warm feeling between my legs and when I touched down there my fingers come up covered with blood! I jumped out of bed and saw a round red stain on my sheet that had gone clear through to the mattress. A large red stain was acrost the back of my nightdress. I thought I was dying, that maybe I had a tumor.

I shook Kyle to wake him up and told him about the blood and showed him the stain on my nightdress and by then I was crying. I always thought that if I died, I died. But suddenly I thought about the dark nothingness of death and I was terrified. Kyle set me down and told me I wasn't dying. He said he knew what was happening to me and that it was normal. I still have trouble believing this as I sit here with blood soaking into the rag down there. I sure hope he's right. He said I am ministrating (I'm not sure of that word. He wasn't either and I can't find it in my dictionary). He said it happens to every girl once a month (!) so's she can have babies. He knows this from talking to Getch, who has three older sisters. I am sposed to wear a rag down there for a few days til the bleeding stops. Kyle said he thought I knew about this and I said how would I know? Mama would never talk to me about such a thing and I have no friends.

"You ought to have friends," Kyle said. "You deserve to have friends. But you have to try harder."

He's been saying this a lot lately and I wish he would quit and we could go back to the way things were before he started getting popular. I don't want to be bleeding! I don't want no babies. And every month! This is a life sentence as unjust as I've ever heard.

As Kyle was talking to me about friends, Mama come in our room for the sheets. We buttoned our lips and when she saw my sheet she let out a scream like she was bit by a snake. She quick pulled the sheet off the mattress and run out the door and we watched her from the window, running off the porch with the sheet bundled up against her chest. She carried it into the yard, set it in a crumpled heap near the tiger lilies and lit a match to it.

"If the blood's normal, why is Mama burning my sheet?" I asked, calm as ever.

But Kyle was at the dresser, pulling out my overalls and a shirt and stuffing them into my arms.

"Put these on and get out before she comes back," he said.

"I need a rag," I said. Blood was trickling down the inside of my leg and two small red circles of it was on the floorboards where I stood. Kyle stopped what he was doing and looked at the floor.

"Lord, Kate, I didn't think it would just pour out of you."

I started to cry again but he was ripping up one of his old shirts, pressing the pieces of cloth into my hands. I folded the cloth between my legs and leaned my hand on Kyle's shoulder as I stepped into one leg of my drawers, then the other. I pulled my nightdress over my head without thinking that it's been a long time since Kyle has seen me undressed, that my body has changed, the changes so slow that I had to look down at my own chest to see what he was staring at. He blushed and I come near to laughing at his embarrassment but I knew I had no time to waste laughing.

Mama bust in the room again afore I could get out but she didn't seem to notice me and Kyle was even there. She caught ahold of one corner of the mattress and drug it off the bed and out of the room. We heard it thumping down the porch steps and when I looked out the window she was dragging it out in the yard, with the round bloodstain already darkening in the sun. Daddy ran out of the house and grabbed ahold of her hands when she tried to set a match to the mattress. I was shamed that Daddy would know what was happening in my body. He took the matches from Mama and went back into the house while Mama sat on the ground and cried into her hands.

By this time Kyle was helping me climb out the window. "I'll meet you at the mill," he said. (Kyle and I are working at the mill this summer.)

I walked into the forest, looking for a path that would not hurt my bare feet because I left so fast I forgot my shoes! I knew I could not go to the mill today, not bleeding like this and in bare feet. I was in a part of the woods I knew well (the place where the woods drop down to the field by Ferry Creek), so I was surprised when I come acrost the cavern. All my life it's been here and I just now found it. I saw a squirrel disappear back of some bushes and when I got closer I saw that the bushes blocked the entrance to a cave. I pulled out one of the bushes with my bare hands and there it was, a hole stuck in the side of the hill. I walked inside as far as the sunshine would let me see and the air was wonderfully cool. I called "Hello!" and the sound echoed all around the walls.

After a bit, I went back home. Ma was gone, and Daddy and Kyle was at the mill so I took my time picking fruit from the bowl, from underneath so Ma wouldn't likely realize it was missing. I got my shoes and a lantern, the dictionary and grammar book and this journal and came back to the cave. My cave. When I first looked around the cave with my lantern, I felt rich. It is like the caverns the tourists visit at Luray though much littler. The first part is long and narrow with a pitched floor that takes you down to the main part, which is one enormous great room. I can see a little tunnel shooting off the back. This great rooms got reddish colored rocks coming out of the ceiling and floor. I know they are called stalactites and stalagmites because I learnt that when I been to Luray. In some places *the ceiling is real high and the stalactites that come from it is broad and the stalagmites that climb towards them just as great. In some places the stalactites and stalagmites (writing them words makes my hand tired) meet and make walls that look like fancy velvet curtains and there is also a pool that reflects about a million baby stalactites from the ceiling above it and the water is so still that I couldn't at first tell if it was a reflection or a million little stalagmites coming out of the ground. I don't think I ever seen a more beautiful place than this cavern. Some folks think of paradise as green and full of growing things, but today I found my own Garden of Eden.*

I made two more trips back to the house and now I have here my mattress, turned over so the stain don't show and some candles, which I set all round the cave on rocky ledges. I also brung a blanket and some rags from the rag bag for my female problem. Kyle didn't say how long this ministrating will last. I wisht I understood it better. What part of me is bleeding? And what has the blood to do with babies? I could believe as easy some spirit has taken ahold of me as I can believe what Kyle's telling me.

I'm going to spend the night here in my garden, though I wish now I left a note for Kyle. He'll be worried since I didn't show up at the mill neither. I am a coward, afeard of going to my own home. The strap scares me worst than ever.

I'm going to turn out the lantern now and lie here in the darkness. I'm not scared here. Nothing in my garden can hurt me.

July 23, 1941

I went back to the house real early this morning and snuck into my window. I woke Kyle with my finger to his lips and when he opened his eyes I saw they was red and I felt terrible for the worry I caused him.

"Where you been?" he asked. He sounded angry but I knew it was really worry I heard.

"I had to stay away," I said.

"No you don't," he said. He looked excited. "Mama said yesterday you're a woman now, you're too growed for her to whip."

I knew Kyle wouldn't lie to me but it was hard to believe Mama would say that. Kyle swore she did, that she was real calm after her fit yesterday.

"Please stay, Katie," Kyle said. "I promise I won't let her whip you."

I was real nervous and I just set on the chair in our room waiting for breakfast time to come.

I showed up for breakfast like nothing was different. I was so scared I couldn't touch my eggs or grits and no one said a word til after Daddy left for the mill. Then Ma stood up and begun clearing the table and finally she spoke.

"I'm glad you had the decency to get rid of that wicked mattress, Katherine," she said.

I was afeard to turn around and look at her and I could hear her clattering the pans in the basin.

"You're growed now," she said. "Too old to whup."

Kyle smiled at me, but then I saw his eyes get big, his lips go flat. He leaned back in his chair and hollered, "Ma, no!" Before I could turn to look, Ma took ahold of my hair and snapped my head back and then I heard the sound of the scissors as she worked them right close to my scalp and in seconds my hair lay in a thick shiny yellow pile on the floor.

Ma set the scissors on the table, calm as you please, and walked out of the room. For a minute I stared at the hair on the floor and felt tears trying to push out my eyes. Then all of a sudden, I didn't care. I looked at the hair and didn't feel a thing. I touched the spikey, hacked off ends of my hair close to my scalp and felt nothing at all. Kyle jumped from his chair and grabbed up the hair from the floor. He held it to my head as though he could attach it back on some how.

"Leave it be," I said. "I want to show you something. A place I found."

"But, Kate, your hair." Kyle looked upset I wasn't crying or mad like he thought I ought to be.

I stood up. "Come with me," I said.

Before we reached the cavern I made him swear he would never tell nobody what I was about to show him. I pulled aside the brush I set against the entrance and led him inside and when I lit the lantern he let out his breath in a long whistle. I could see he was amazed and I felt proud.

"I can get away from her here," I said.

He walked around like I did the day before, touching the stalagmites, staring into the reflecting pool.

"You can't stay out here," he said.

"Just sometimes," I said, though I had been thinking how good it would be to sleep here on hot summer nights.

"We have to get to the mill," Kyle said.

I touched the back of my hair and the ends of it felt like broom bristles against my palm. "I'm staying here," I said.

I spent the rest of the day turning the cavern into my hide-a-way. The Smiths' house has been deserted since last year when they left for West Virginia, so I took a chair and a table from there and drug them back here. I found more candles there too and a lap desk filled with pencils and paper. There's a long rock above the reflecting pool—sort of a ledge that makes a perfect bookshelf for my dictionary and grammar book. Now they can stand upright like they is sposed to be. High above the place where I lay my mattress there is a deep hole in the wall and this is where I'll keep my journal.

4

Ben Alexander sat on the bed in his cabin high above Lynch Hollow, a small battered address book on his knee. He took another swallow of whiskey from the bottle on the floor and stared at the name on the page in front of him. Valerie Collins. She was the last one. Over the past few months, he'd called everyone he'd ever known. Valerie was his last hope.

She used to send him cards at Christmas. She'd address them to both him and Sharon, but he knew they were directed to him alone. The cards were always a picture of Valerie with her salukis. As the years wore on she'd taken on the look of her dogs, sleek and long-limbed. Her nose grew thinner and more pointed, her hair longer, silkier, blacker. Sharon laughed as she followed Valerie's transformation from woman to canine, never catching the meaning behind the cryptic messages: Hope to see you soon, or Love you. He knew Valerie meant the singular you. She didn't know Sharon and didn't care to.

He took another taste of the whiskey and moved the phone from the apple crate he used as a nightstand to his bed. Surely Valerie would want to hear from him.

The phone was army green, cracked and held together with

masking tape that threatened to break with each turn of the rotary dial.

"Hello?" Her voice was soft. If a saluki could talk . . .

"Valerie?" He sat up straight.

"Who's this?"

"It's Ben Alexander, Valerie."

There was that heavy silence he was growing accustomed to. The name would register, the newspaper images of his face, bearded then and lined with fatigue, would race through Valerie's head.

"It's late, Ben. I'm on my way to bed."

He shot ahead in desperation. "I was wondering if we could get together? I'm living in the Shenandoah Valley now, but I could drive up to D.C.—it's been a long time—I'm divorced now. I don't know if you knew that."

Silence again. Then a sigh. A drawing in of breath and courage. "Ben, the honest truth is I don't ever want to see you. You must have really changed over the years to do what you did. Please don't call me again."

He jumped when she slammed her phone down, and it was a moment before he set his own receiver back in its cradle.

He sat on the edge of the bed with his hands folded in his lap for many minutes. The light behind the open door of the bathroom pulled at him seductively, and he pictured the bottle of Valium on the edge of the sink. He'd gotten the prescription filled months ago, but he hadn't taken a single pill. Twenty still in there. They would do the trick. How long would it take Kyle to find him? When he didn't show up at the site in the morning, Kyle would assume he'd overslept or had some urgent errand. But by afternoon Kyle would start to wonder. And by evening maybe he'd take a drive up here and find him. Ben would leave him a note, thanking him for being the one person who believed him, for offering him the job at the digs when no one else would hire him, for being a friend. Ben shuddered. He couldn't do that to Kyle.

He took another drink. Drinking too much these days. And alone. Little option there. The only people who would condescend to drink with him were not the kind of people he wanted as friends. People who looked at him knowingly, who winked as though they understood how a man could do what he'd been accused of doing.

He'd hoped that here in the Valley he could escape the knowing eyes. But one or two people knew and they'd told others. Sometimes he felt as much a leper here as he'd been in Annapolis.

The phone rang and he had a brief flutter in his chest at the old fantasy: somehow Bliss had stumbled across his phone number, and when he picked up the receiver he would hear her five-year-old voice, perplexed, asking, "Daddy, aren't you ever coming home from this trip?"

He lifted the phone to his ear. It was Kyle. "Sorry to call you so late," he said, "but my niece arrived tonight."

Ben said nothing, still caught in the fantasy of his daughter.

"Ben? Remember? She's working on a film about her mother?"

"Yes. Right." Eden Riley.

"She'll need to get a feel for the site. It was so much a part of her mother's life, and you can use an extra pair of hands this summer, can't you?"

Ben pictured the Valium and turned his back on the gaping bathroom door. "Does she know anything about the site?" he asked.

"Nothing, but she'll learn fast. You have no objection, do you?"

"No, of course not." He wanted to ask, so he could steel himself for meeting her, "Does she know about me?" but he couldn't. He would know by the look in her eyes if Kyle had told her or not. "Sure, it's fine. Just send her over in the morning."

He hung up and carried the bottle over to the sofa. He turned on the TV, made a quick tour of the channels, and turned it off. He lay back on the sofa and stared at the brown water stain on the wood-plank ceiling.

He hated being alone. He'd managed to avoid it most of his life. He and his older brother, Sam, had been inseparable as kids and close to their parents. He'd never gone through the usual adolescent rebellion. His parents flowed too easily with the punches. But they'd been dead five years now, and he was glad they hadn't lived to see this past year and a half. He liked to think they would have been certain of his innocence, but he wasn't sure. It was better not to know, to imagine they would have stuck by him as Sam and Jen had done. Sam and Jen had been his life support during the trial. They still saw Bliss, calling him after each visit to say how cute she looked, how unscarred she seemed to be. "She's fine," Jen would tell him. "And she asks about you." He wondered if she still did, or if Sam and Jen just told him that. It had been a long time, and kids' memories . . . well. Plus she had a new dad now. Jeff. Did she call him Daddy, with the dimple on the second syllable he always used to watch for?

Sam and Jen had begged him to stay in Annapolis after his stint in prison. "You need to be near us," Sam said. Perhaps they knew what he hadn't known then. The ostracism he would face. Shunned by expeditions, he applied for openings at half a dozen universities but was turned down by all of them. And then the call came from Kyle.

"Why didn't you let me know?" Kyle admonished in the familiar soft voice Ben knew from the years as his student, the years as his friend. "I heard about it through the grapevine. But I wanted to hear it from you."

So Ben told him as calmly as he could about the accusations, the trial, the tide of evidence he felt helpless to stem as it mounted against him, the prison term. Then he told Kyle about losing his job, not being able to find work anywhere.

"I know you like a son, Ben." Kyle's voice was sure, full of conviction. "I wouldn't care what evidence they showed me, I could never believe you were guilty. I can offer you a job here—the arthritis doesn't give me much time in the pits anymore. I know it's a pathetic offer after what you're used to. Please don't be offended."

"No, that'll be great." Just that day he'd been turned down to muck out stables.

At first he stayed close to Kyle and Lou. He was so relieved to feel trusted and he knew their sympathy was genuine. The three of them went to see *Heart of Winter* shortly after his arrival, when he was still numb from the months in prison. That movie changed his image of Eden Riley. She was known for her portrayal of angels and earth mothers and, Bliss's personal favorite, the beautiful witch in *Child of the North Star*. But now he could picture Eden only in that hotel room scene with Michael Carey. One sexy scene in an otherwise unsexy movie. One sexy departure from a tenaciously unsexy career. He couldn't scrape from his mind the image of Carey undressing her from the inside out. Expertly. Slip, stockings, panties, bra, leaving her in a silky black dress open just enough to tease the camera with a glimpse of her breasts.

Ben had been keenly aware of Kyle and Lou sitting next to him, watching the woman they'd raised through her teen years, the woman they adored and rarely saw, making love to the rakish Michael Carey. He heard Lou's muffled "Oh, my" and Kyle's chuckled response before he was swallowed up by the images on the screen. There was a hushed stillness in the theater, an electric tension that seemed rooted in his loins. After months of feeling nothing at all he was stunned by the aching in his body, by the yearning in his chest that went far beyond the sexual. And for a few brief moments he kidded himself into thinking that life might still hold something for him, that perhaps he had not lost everything in that Annapolis courtroom.

Then he'd returned to his cabin, to the silent telephone, the numbing emptiness. Kyle and Lou had their own lives to live and he could not spend every evening with them. He tried his old friends one by one and their rejection of him stung. No one bothered to feign politeness. He was not even worthy of common courtesy in their eyes. He'd become a vehicle for their disdain about everything that was wrong in the world.

He saw no way out of his loneliness. The whiskey had become an escape for him, but he took no pleasure in the taste or the burn or anything other than the temporary oblivion it offered. The pills could provide something more permanent.

But he'd promised Kyle a favor. He'd help Eden with the digs, show her what to look for, how to catalog what she found. It was the least he could do for Kyle.

5

"I called Ben," Kyle said as he poured milk over the granola in his bowl. Lou still made her own granola, just as she had when Eden was a teenager, long before granola was a household word. "He's expecting you this morning. I'll walk you over there after breakfast."

"I remember the way," Eden said. The site was in the field between the cavern and Ferry Creek. She'd rather walk there by herself, rather not have to make conversation with Kyle.

"The grant's up the end of this year," Kyle said.

"Then what?"

"Then we fold." Kyle shrugged as if it didn't matter to him, but Eden knew better.

"Isn't there some way to get new funding?"

He shook his head and swallowed a mouthful of granola before he answered her. "Too much competition. It's hard for a little site in the Shenandoah Valley to survive. I can work there on my own, but the site won't have much credibility without the money."

Eden sipped her coffee, watching Lou dart around the kitchen in the electric wheelchair. Refrigerator to toaster to coffeepot and back to the table again, where she set a plate of toast in front of Kyle.

"I'm ready for the second notebook," Eden said.

Kyle raised his eyebrows above his coffee cup. "Always were a fast reader. What do you think so far?"

She had fallen asleep last night thinking about how much of Kyle's life would be exposed to her in the pages of her mother's journal. Suddenly she could picture him as a young kid in this very kitchen, bent over the table, sparing Katherine a beating by accepting it himself. She understood his reluctance to share the journals with her. They would tell his story as well as Katherine's. She thought of thanking him but returned her attention to her cereal instead. Had she ever thanked him for anything?

"You were a nice kid," she said.

His smile was quick and surprised. "And your mom?"

"I'm not thinking of her as my mother right now. I'm trying to stay objective as I read."

"Hmm." Lou tapped her coffee cup with her fingertips. "I wonder how long you'll be able to do that."

"Long enough to get the screenplay written, I hope." Eden ignored the challenge in Lou's words, although if she was to be honest with herself she knew her objectivity was already slipping. "I never realized how difficult her childhood was."

"No harder than yours," Kyle said.

"Well"—Eden poured cream into her coffee, dismayed to see the tremor in her hand—"I'm here to think about my mother, not myself."

"I'm not sure you'll be able to do one without the other, honey," Kyle said.

"The journal's amazing," Eden said. "I can see her writing style emerging already."

Kyle let her change the subject. "She read constantly. Our father—your grandfather—was always sneaking her books. I never did figure out where he got them."

"I have to think about who should play her as a child. And we have to find someone to play you, too." She had given no thought to whom she could cast as Kyle, as either child or adult. Until last night she had not realized how significant his role would be.

"I wouldn't object to having Robert Redford portray me as an adult."

Lou laughed. "He's not randy enough to play you, Ky."

Eden raised her eyebrows. "Kyle? Randy?"

"You don't know your uncle very well, dear," Lou said.

"I'm not sure what age Katherine will have to be before I can play her. I'm already five years older than she was when she died."

The phone rang. Kyle stood to answer it but he turned to Eden before picking up the receiver. "You could pass for eighteen, sweetheart." He spoke into the phone for a few seconds and then covered the receiver with his hand. "It's for you, Eden. Your friend, Michael Carey. You can take it in the living room if you like."

She sat on the love seat in the living room and waited for Kyle to hang up before speaking into the phone. "Michael?"

"'Morning." He sounded half asleep.

"God, Michael, what time is it? Is the sun up there yet?"

"I'm calling you from my bed." He yawned. "Wish you were in it with me."

She had never been in his bed, nor he in hers. She could picture him, though. The dark wavy hair against his pillow, the long-lashed brown eyes that drove women crazy. "The roses are beautiful," she said.

"I can't function without you, Eden," he said, his voice syrupy with sleep. "Went to Sophie's party last night and left at eleven. Eleven. The women were beautiful and I couldn't have cared less. Had no interest in getting high either. Everybody said I was a wet blanket. You've ruined me."

She smiled. "I miss you."

"Well, shit. Did you really say that?"

She could hear him moving, perking up, and she wished she could take back her words. It was not really Michael she missed. It was the safety of him, of the role she played with him.

"I don't know. You'd better not give much credence to anything I say right now." She turned her back to the kitchen door and spoke quietly into the phone. "I'm trapped in the boonies with two people I thought I'd escaped from years ago."

"Hey, it's all for a good cause. Keep your goal in mind, baby. And as soon as I get a break I'll join you, okay?"

They had discussed this without resolution. He could help her, he'd said. He could do some of the research on Matthew Riley himself. But she could not picture him here. She'd have to do a balancing act between him and Lou and Kyle. "I don't know, Michael. Let's talk about it again in a few days, okay?" She steered him into a conversation about Sophie's party and safer ground. It was a world she knew well, a world that welcomed her and honored her status. She had built it with no help from anyone and she couldn't afford to lose it. Without it she was uncertain of her next step.

The trail through the woods was narrower and more primitive than she remembered. She imagined the camera following young Katherine as she walked along it barefoot and frightened. The trail seemed to go on forever and Eden was beginning to think she'd taken a wrong turn when she reached the steep, wooded embankment that led down to the cave. There was a fresh path zigzagging down the side of the hill. That was new. They would have to cover it up when they filmed. When she was small she just slipped and slid down to the cavern and the field below. But Kyle, with his arthritis, would need this trail now.

She passed the sealed cave entrance and stepped out of the woods into the field. It ran between the embankment and wide Ferry Creek, stretching from the dirt road to the Blue Ridge foothills, perhaps a mile away. The section of the field directly in front of the cavern formed the archaeological site first discovered long ago by her mother. There were three pits open now, each about five feet wide by ten feet long, at varying distances from the cave. She'd been lucky the night before she hadn't fallen into one of the pits in the darkness.

The site had a deserted, somber feel to it. She hadn't known that the grant would be up in December. For as long as she could remember, Kyle had talked about reopening this site after his retirement, spending the rest of his life sifting comfortably through his roots after the intensity of his work in South America. Losing the grant would put an end to his dream. Already the quiet, barren pits had the look of being abandoned.

She walked slowly past the first pit. It was deep and empty, the bottom level, the sides square and straight. The floor of the second pit had been carved into different levels, large wafers of earth covered with sheets of plastic.

As she neared the third pit, she saw that the site was not deserted after all. A man knelt in the far corner, engrossed in something on the ground. His back was to her and she watched him for a moment. He wore earphones attached to the tape player on his belt, and he was humming along with the music. His hair was brown lit with gold—Cassie's color—and a little too long in the back. He wore a blue T-shirt and jeans. His feet were bare, but his sandals were set neatly on the scarred grass at the rim of the pit. A white pickup truck Eden assumed to be his was parked in the shade of an elm over near the creek.

His partner, Kyle had said. She'd expected someone closer to Kyle's age, someone content to spend his last active years in a small, quiet site. She hesitated a few yards from the pit, staring at the faint snow-angel pattern of sweat on the back of his T-shirt, the faded-to-white denim covering his thighs. Even from this distance she felt something long buried, at once compelling and dangerous.

Snap out of it. She lifted her chin and walked toward the pit, relieved as the old, familiar armor closed protectively around her.

"Are you Ben?" she asked when she'd reached the edge of the pit.

He jumped to his feet, pulling the earphones from his head as he turned to look at her.

"Sorry I startled you," she said.

"No . . . no problem." He looked up at her, the pale gray of his eyes holding the sunlight, and she let herself stare for a moment, unnerved. This was ridiculous. She was surrounded by attractive men in L.A. and felt nothing. Then she meets this sweaty, scruffy guy in a hole in the earth and she . . .

"Have a seat," he said.

She lowered herself to the edge of the pit, her knees at the level of his shoulders. He looked away from her, adjusting the tape player on his belt, and she sensed his discomfort. She was used to it. People often squirmed when they met her. She reached out her hand. "I'm Eden. Kyle's niece."

"I know." He wiped his hand on his jeans but she still felt the warm layer of dust against her skin as he pressed his palm to hers. "You're doing research on Katherine Swift for a movie."

"Yes. Kyle said you could show me around."

He nodded. "We can start right here." He motioned toward the ladder and she climbed into the pit, feeling him watching her from below.

"I'm at the four-thousand-year level here." Ben knelt down where she'd first spotted him and pointed to a foot-wide plateau carved into the bottom of the pit. "About two thousand B.C. These are pieces of pottery." He touched a few tiny lumps of dirt resting on a piece of newspaper.

"They are?" She knelt next to him.

"Nothing fancy. They didn't do anything fancy back then, just functional. They look like dirt right now, but they won't disintegrate like dirt when they're washed. You'll see."

He showed her how to dust the ground for the clay fragments. He seemed relieved to have the work to focus on. Shy, perhaps. These scientific types often were. She didn't want to intimidate him. She asked him questions, hoping to boost his confidence and get him to look at her—she wanted to feel the pull of his eyes again. But he answered her with his eyes on the ground.

"You can work here and I'll start in the back corner of the pit," Ben said.

For the next hour neither of them spoke. At first Eden was fascinated by her hands, imagining the camera on them as they swept, as the fine tan earth began to coat her fingers. But her shoulders grew stiff as she dusted layer after layer of earth and came up with nothing. She began to understand why those little lumps of clay seemed so precious.

"Are you having any luck?" she finally turned to ask him.

He laughed but didn't turn around. "Bored already?"

"Is this usual? I mean, not finding anything?"

"Think of it as examining a space, so it's just as significant if there's nothing there as if there's something there." He turned now and smiled at her. "You are the first person to touch that dirt in over four thousand years. Does that help?"

She laughed. "Not really."

Ben sat back against the side of the pit. "Your mother never got down this far. She'd be amazed by what we're finding now."

"Where are all the artifacts she found?"

"In the museum in Coolbrook, for the most part. Kyle has the rest of the collection. He keeps it in the old springhouse." He suddenly grinned and shook his head. "I can't believe I'm digging in the dirt with Eden Riley. You look like a regular person. I don't think I'd recognize you if I passed you on the street."

"Good. I'd like to be incognito here for as long as I can get away with it."

Ben picked up a clump of earth and studied it for a moment before crushing it between his fingers. He looked at her. "What did Kyle tell you about me?"

She shrugged, surprised by the question. "Just that you're his partner."

"Partner? That's what he called me?"

"Yes. Isn't that what you are?"

Ben shook his head. "Jesus, he's amazing. I'm his employee. I was a student of his and we did some work together in South America. That's all."

It suddenly fell into place for her. She remembered letters, remembered hearing his name. And she remembered a jealousy she'd had no right to feel. "You're the guy Lou and Kyle used to write me about," she said. "You traveled with them, didn't you? You've known them a long time?"

"I met Kyle shortly after you . . . left them."

Eden smiled. "I'm sure that's not the term he used to describe my going to California."

"He said you ran away. But you were nineteen, right? Old enough to make your own decisions."

"I thought so." She brushed the dust from the front of her shorts and looked up at him again. "Ben Alexander. I remember now. They wrote about you all the time. I was jealous. I guess I wanted them to mourn when I left, and instead they seemed to adopt you. You replaced me."

He shook his head. "That wouldn't have been possible. They adored you. And they mourned you all right. If that's what you were after, you got it."

She felt her cheeks flame as she turned back to the square of earth. "Well, I'd better get back to work on this old dirt," she said. No doubt about whose side this guy was on.

She knew it was another minute before he turned around himself.

The soft bristles of her brush caught on something. She slipped them over the earth again and again, and a small, hard mound, about the size of a dime, began to form beneath the bristles. "Ben? There's something here."

He sat down on the ground next to her and watched as she swept the earth away from the object. "Go easy, now," he said. "You don't want to lose anything that might be around it."

"Maybe you'd better do it." She held the brush out to him.

"Uh uh. It's yours. You're doing fine."

He was so close she could smell the sun on his skin. She edged away from him, closer to the cool earthen wall of the pit. She was not accustomed to men like him. All the men she knew were actors, predictable in the personas they'd adopted. They were either gay, blood-and-guts macho, or strong and slickly sensitive, a facade Michael had perfected and others copied. They were like comic book characters. What could be safer than a paper-thin man?

When she thought of the men in her life she did not even include Wayne. He didn't count as a man. Sorry, Wayne, but it was true. That was one reason she'd sought him out so long ago. His asexuality. His harmlessness. She'd been just a kid then, looking for someone safe to lean on. But the man next to her right now seemed anything but asexual, anything but safe. He was mercurial—self-conscious one minute, brazen the next. She watched him run his fingers over the earth in front of her. She couldn't categorize him. He was a different type of man than Wayne or Michael. Entirely different.

The mound was now the size of a silver dollar. "Is it pottery?" she asked.

"Yes. And it looks like it's going to be the biggest piece I've seen in this pit."

She looked at him in apology. "I'm sorry."

"Don't be silly." He motioned her to continue.

The mound grew until the bristles of her brush finally caught on an edge. By that time the rounded piece of clay was larger than her hand.

"Beginner's luck," Ben said. He stood up to take a clipboard off the rim of the pit and drew the location of the pottery on a chart. Then he carefully slid his fingers beneath it and lifted it out. He held it in front of her. "It's part of a bowl. Would have been about ten inches in diameter." He ran one dusty finger across the curved surface of the clay. "They started mixing the clay with vegetable fiber around that time. The deeper we go, the less pottery we'll find. It'll be replaced with stone bowls." He wrapped the pottery in a piece of newspaper and set it on the rim of the pit.

It was nearly noon. She wanted to get to the archives in Winchester before they closed. "I'll come here in the mornings, if that's all right with you," she said. The work in the pit would give her time to digest what she read in the journal.

"Stay for lunch," Ben said. "I have two sandwiches."

"I don't want to take your lunch."

He patted his flat stomach. "I really don't need two sandwiches."

They climbed into the bed of the pickup truck and sat under the shade of the elm. Below them, Ferry Creek slapped against its banks, and Eden could hear the groaning of the suspension footbridge that spanned the width of the creek. She'd played on that bridge as a child. Cassie would probably love it.

Ben threw her a beer from his cooler and handed her a cheese sandwich. She peered inside at two orange slices of American cheese, iceberg lettuce, mayonnaise, and catsup and bit her lip.

"It's the catsup, huh?" he asked.

She nodded. "A little odd."

He handed her the plain piece of bread from his own sandwich.

"Music?" He turned on the tape player still attached to his belt. The music was fast, full of accordion. The lyrics were in French. She looked at him questioningly.

"Zydeco."

"Interesting."

"It's happy music. I have no idea what they're singing about, which is fine with me. You don't speak French, do you?" He looked worried until she shook her head. "Good. It'd wreck it if I knew what they were saying. This way I can pretend they're singing about whatever I choose. Make it up to suit my mood."

She smiled at him. Had she really thought a few hours ago that he was intimidated by her?

He leaned back against the side of the truck. "I read most of your mother's books when I was a kid. They were full of adventure."

"I'm afraid my mother's only adventures were in her mind."

"I tried reading one of them to my daughter, but she'd rather watch the movie. Typical kid, I guess. She's a big fan of yours."

So, he was married. She wasn't sure if she felt relief or disappointment.

"I told her I sort of knew you," he said.

"Now you can tell her you really do. I'd be happy to meet her, if you like."

"Well, I don't get to see her that often. She lives with my wife."

"Oh. Where does your wife live?"

"Annapolis." He stretched his legs out in front of him. "Your daughter's about the same age as mine. Cassie, right?"

"Do you know about her from Lou and Kyle?"

"Everybody knows about Cassie, don't they? Including all the personal details of how long you tried to get pregnant, how you spent the last three months of your pregnancy on bed rest, et cetera?"

She made a face. Wayne had said he was sick of people learning the most intimate details of their lives while waiting in grocery store lines.

"How do you tolerate having so little privacy?" Ben asked.

"Sometimes I don't tolerate it very well." After *Heart of Winter*, her face had been on so many magazine covers that she'd lost count. That had been fine until Wayne left. Then she'd wished she could have disappeared from the public eye altogether.

"So how do you go about writing a screenplay?"

"The research comes first. I thought I'd have to pick Kyle's brain, since he's the only person still living who knew Katherine well. But last night he told me she kept a journal. It would make my work much easier, except that it's written in a dozen notebooks and Kyle plans to feed them to me one at a time."

A smile broke slowly from Ben's lips. "He wants to keep you here as long as he can. He was so excited you were coming."

"I don't know why. I didn't give him the most pleasant years of his life. Anyhow, I don't want to work strictly from the journal, because I have a specific idea of how I want to present her . . ." She cocked her head to look at him. "How do you think of her? I mean, as someone who only knows about her from the media?"

He swallowed a bite of his sandwich. "As an isolate," he said. "A woman who valued solitude above anything else. That's something hard for me to understand. I'd rather get hit by a train than spend my life alone."

"Exactly," Eden said. "No one understands her because of the way she's been presented in the past. I want to normalize her. I want people to see this film and be able to relate to her, not think, oh, here's that weird Katherine Swift again."

"How old was she when she started the journal?"

"Thirteen."

"What does a thirteen-year-old have to write about?"

"Plenty. She was feisty and impulsive. And lonely. The other kids didn't like her. She got into a lot of trouble. She got her first period and her mother—my grandmother—was so crazy she cut off all Katherine's hair. So she ran away. That was when she found the cavern."

Ben looked in the direction of the cave. "Do you remember what it was like inside?" He almost whispered the question, as though he understood that the cave was a subject to be treated with reverence.

Eden stared across the field to the wooded embankment. She could just make out the dark patch through the trees where the boulders marked the entrance to the cave.

"I was four when they sealed it up," she said. "My memory's very cloudy."

"Close your eyes."

"What?"

Ben set down his sandwich. "My brother's a shrink. Whenever I can't remember something he tells me to close my eyes, and gradually the picture comes into my head."

Eden obediently closed her eyes and leaned back against the cool metal side of the pickup. At first she could concentrate only on the sound of Ferry Creek rushing below them. But then she heard it, the clack, clack, clack of the typewriter keys, muffled by the cotton her mother had put in her ears. She felt cool air on her arms. The cave was dimly lit by lanterns hanging from the walls and by candles set here and there on the floors and rocky ledges. The room was filled with shadows. Eden was playing with her friends, the stalagmites. She'd forgotten about them, the cold, grotesquely shaped formations that in her four-year-old imagination took on human form.

Her mother sat on a wooden chair, an enormous black monster of a typewriter on the table in front of her. Sheets of paper were scattered on the cave floor around her chair. Her face was blurry. Eden could see only her hands, the skin silky and smooth, the fingers slender, the nails trimmed short. Her hands never paused. Clack, clack, clack . . .

Eden opened her eyes. Ben was watching her, gnawing his lip.

"I was afraid you got stuck back there," he said.

"I remembered the stalactites and stalagmites. Tites and mites, my mother called them. They fill the cavern. They were my playmates. I'd play with them while she typed, and when she was finished for the day she'd cuddle me on her lap and read to me." Her voice had softened, thickened, betraying her. She'd forgotten what it felt like to be held that way, with no strings attached to the love.

Ben leaned forward to touch her knee. "This film's not going to be easy for you to make," he said.

She shouldn't have said so much, been so open. With every word she'd made herself more vulnerable. "I don't think it will be that difficult." She stood up and jumped out of the truck, relieved to have the heat of his fingers off her knee. "I'd better get going. Thanks for the sandwich."

"Could you show me how to do that?" he asked.

"What?"

"Turn off your feelings that quickly." His eyes were narrowed.

"I don't know what you mean."

"I think you do. One minute you're sad, next minute everything's right with the world."

She sighed, giving in. "To be honest, I'm usually better at it." She put her hands on her hips and looked toward the cave. "My defenses are down out here. Usually I can pretend everything's fine until I actually start to believe it myself."

"Whew. I'll teach you to dig if you'll teach me how to do that. How about over dinner tonight? Just something casual. Just, you know, platonic." He grinned. "I mean, I know about you and Michael Carey."

She groaned. "Michael and I are just friends. And why do you want to have dinner with me if you already know everything about me?"

He ignored her question. "I'll pick you up at seven."

She wanted to go. It would be easier than having dinner with Kyle and Lou. "Maybe I could meet you somewhere." She'd be in control then. No chance of being stuck with him longer than she could handle.

"Seven at Sugar Hill," he said. "Kyle can tell you how to get there. Don't forget to take your pottery with you to impress him."

She walked across the field to the pit, picked up her pottery, and headed toward the embankment, feeling his eyes on her the whole way. What was his game? She would meet his daughter. He didn't have to take her out for that to happen. He could write to the folks back home and say he went out with Eden Riley. Hopefully he had no illusions that she would sleep with him. Maybe he wanted to get on Kyle's good side to get a boost up the career ladder. He had to be bored in this confining little site. Or could he possibly just be lonely? It didn't matter what his motives were. She knew as she walked through the woods toward the house that it was her own neediness she had to fear, not his.

6

Sugar Hill was Ben's favorite restaurant in the area. He liked the rustic atmosphere, the woody smell. It was always dark inside, which helped him feel anonymous. There was a dance floor in the center of the tables, and the bar stretched the length of one wall.

He sat at a dark corner table, watching the door, trying to recall if he'd eaten dinner with anyone other than Kyle and Lou or Sam and Jen in the last year and a half. He had not. Unless he counted prison, but his dining companions in jail had hardly been his choice.

So he was justified in feeling nervous. He stood quickly when he saw Eden at the door. She hesitated, adjusting her eyes to the dim light. He walked toward her. She wore her dark blond hair pinned up, as she had that morning. Her throat was long and slender, like the rest of her, but she had a solidity that appealed to him. Probably because it was the antithesis of Sharon's fragility. She looked as if she could handle whatever might come her way. She would not spook easily.

Again, he was struck by how unrecognizable she was. Good. He didn't want to draw attention to himself in here.

Eden smiled when she saw him and took the hand he held out to her. He led her to the table, got her seated with a menu.

"What would you like from the bar?" he asked.

"Wine," she said. "Something white."

He ordered Eden's wine and his beer at the bar. As the grinning bartender handed him the drinks he winked at Ben and said, "She's a little old for you, isn't she?"

Ben turned away without comment. On another night he might have said something in return, something sharp to defend himself. But he didn't want to start this evening that way. Ignore it, he told himself. Don't let it get to you.

But by the time he'd set Eden's wine in front of her and taken his own seat, his knees were shaking. That one line from the bartender had thrown him off balance. He was not as anonymous in here as he would have liked. He sipped at his beer, wondering if all eyes in the room were focused on him and Eden.

"Do you come here often?" Eden asked.

He nodded. "In a rut, I guess."

The older waitress, Ruth, appeared at their table, her orange lipstick creeping outside the line of her lips. "You want your regular?" she asked Ben.

"Uh, no." He was in a rut. "I'll have the crab cakes tonight."

He felt hot and knew the color was rising up his neck to his cheeks. If the bartender knew about him, Ruth must as well.

"I'll have the stuffed flounder." Eden smiled innocently up at Ruth.

He was certain Ruth gave him a curdling look of disgust as she headed back to the kitchen. He never should have brought Eden here, should have suggested someplace farther out where no one knew him. But there was dancing here. Nearly every night he watched other couples dance, wondering if he'd ever have the chance to hold a woman in his arms again.

"Do you like to dance?" he asked.

"Love it."

"The band will start up in a little while."

She nodded, lowering her eyes as she sipped her wine.

"What did Kyle think of your pottery?"

"He thinks you planted it for me to find."

"Did he wash it off for you?"

"Yes. And I painted the little numbers on the back."

He swirled the beer in his glass, annoyed at his discomfort. He'd felt fine with her this morning, once he realized Kyle had not told her about him, but he could not shake the feeling that his every move here was being scrutinized by the other diners, by the staff. He would have to keep any conversation on her and off himself.

"You look deep in thought," she said.

"I was trying to think of a question to ask you that I don't already know the answer to."

She laughed and the diamond she wore at her throat shimmered in the light from the dance floor. "Tell me what you know and we can work backward."

"Well, you split up with your husband nearly a year ago." His cellmate had been reading the *National Enquirer* and there it was on the front page. A picture of a dark-haired man arm in arm with a redheaded woman, the caption in capital letters proclaiming something like EDEN RILEY CRUSHED BY HUSBAND'S AFFAIR WITH PENNSYLVANIA TEACHER. There was a small picture of Eden in the lower-right-hand corner, her face contorted with emotion. Probably something they pulled out of one of her movies and stuck, out of context, in the paper. Sitting there on his bed in his cold cinder-block cell, he felt sorry for her. He knew what it was like to have your life picked apart by the masses.

"A year next month," she said. "How about you? How long have you been divorced?"

"We separated about a year and a half ago and were divorced this past January." He couldn't let her question him. "Your husband was a lawyer, right?"

"Uh huh."

"You're lucky you got custody."

"He put up a valiant struggle."

"I'm sure he did. Lawyers aren't my favorite people." He stared at his beer. God, he sounded like an idiot. "You must know people around here from when you were a kid," he said.

"Not many. No one I'd care to see."

"How old were you when you moved in with Kyle and Lou in New York?"

"Thirteen."

"And your grandparents took care of you before that, right?"

"My grandfather and his second wife. You do know my life story, don't you?"

"Kyle and Lou brag a lot. And they're in love with Cassie."

Her face brightened and he knew he had found the right topic. Her beautiful white teeth flashed in a smile as she told him about her daughter. Only problem was, he couldn't listen. It was too hard to hear about a four-year-old girl. He wanted to say, Bliss does that too, or, Yes, I know exactly what you're talking about, but he couldn't. Instead he tuned out her words and focused on the warm blue of her eyes.

"Cassie will be here in July," she said. "Will your daughter visit you this summer? They could play—"

"Shhh!" He quickly covered her hand with his as Ruth set their plates in front of them, and he held her silent with his eyes until the waitress walked away. "Sorry," he said as he took his hand away and picked up his fork. "No, not this summer." Not any summer.

Eden frowned at him. "Is something wrong?"

"No." He cut a wedge of crab cake, neatly, with great concentration. He couldn't look at her, and he was relieved when she finally lifted her own fork and began to eat. How had he managed to kid himself into thinking he could ever have a normal relationship with a woman again? And Eden Riley? Christ, Alexander. He'd thought about her all afternoon, hoping there could be something between them— something short, a brief connection. He wasn't asking for much. When she said she and Michael Carey were just friends, wasn't she telling him she was interested? Fool. This woman was an Academy Award-winning movie star. Every person in this restaurant would recognize her name. She wore an enormous diamond around her throat. Her daughter went to what sounded like an exclusive day-care program. She lived in a beautiful house on the ocean. He could picture it—hot tub, parties in the balmy California air. He saw her again in that hotel room scene with the darkly handsome Michael Carey. How ridiculous that he'd thought she could be interested in him. At one time he might have stood a chance, but not now. He made barely enough to keep a head of lettuce and some cheese in the refrigerator and a leaky roof over his head. He wanted to tell her about the house he and Sharon had owned, the one he'd designed himself. He wanted to tell her he'd had a job that earned him the respect of the entire archaeological community. But then he'd have to explain why he'd lost it all.

She had eaten a third of her flounder when she set down her fork. "Ben, I'm not sure what's going on here but you look as though you'd rather be just about anywhere but here with me. We don't have to drag this out, okay? Let's call it a night."

"No." He grabbed her hand again, panicked. "I'm sorry. I have a lot on my mind, but I don't want to leave yet." The band was starting to play. He liked this band. Old rock and roll, of a sort. They made every song sound as if it had a little country in it, but that was okay. He watched another couple walk onto the dance floor. "Let's dance," he said, getting to his feet. If they moved they wouldn't have to talk.

The band played an old Doobie Brothers song. It was fast, and Eden moved easily with him. He was glad to see her smiling again as they spun around the floor.

The next song was slow and Eden didn't object when he pulled her close. The musky silk of her hair brushed his cheek as she moved her arms from his shoulders to around his neck, surprising him, scaring him. He shut his eyes against the stares of the other diners. During this past year he'd wondered if he'd ever make love again, if any woman would consent to have him. He was not even certain he still had the physical ability. He never would have guessed that an affront to his sexuality could take such a toll on him. Could he ever feel normal again? Could he ever touch or be touched without shame and guilt, no matter how unreasonable those feelings were?

Maybe Eden . . . God, she smelled wonderful. Entirely too good. He tried to think about the pottery she'd found that morning, the shape of Sugar Hill's bar, the words of the music—anything to keep his erection in check. But when he feared it had grown firm enough for her to feel, he pulled away from her, abruptly, leaving her staring at him as she lowered her arms to her sides.

"What's the matter?" she asked.

"Let's sit down." He led her back to the table, his hand light on her elbow.

She sat down and reached for her purse. "I think I'd better leave."

"No, Eden, please don't."

"Do you think you have to entertain me because I'm Kyle's niece?" Her cheeks were red.

"No!"

"That's what I think. You don't seem to want to be here with me. That's fine, but please don't use me to make points with Kyle, or to show me off, or . . ."

"That's not what I'm doing." He felt wrongly accused. It was a feeling all too familiar.

"I'm going to leave. I'll see you at the site in the morning."

"Let me walk you out." He didn't want everyone to see her walk out on him.

At her car he set his hand on her shoulder and turned her toward him. "This was my fault," he said. "It's been a long time since I've been out with a woman and I wanted it to go well so much that I screwed it up."

"I'll see you tomorrow." She got into her car and sprayed gravel behind her as she made her escape from the parking lot.

He drove slowly up to his cabin. He undressed and then, because it smelled like Eden, laid his shirt on his pillow before getting into bed. He'd forgotten to turn off the bathroom light and he thought of the pills on the sink, but he was too tired to do the idea of suicide justice tonight.

In the faint light from the bathroom he could see the photograph of Bliss stuck in the frame of his scratched dresser mirror and he rolled over to face the wall, away from the picture, away from the past.

7

October 2, 1941

Mama is dead.

I look at those words and can't believe they're real. Kyle found her and I know it was bad for him. We both heard the shot. It was late last night and I was sleeping so deeply that I thought I was dreaming. I thought Mama finally shot herself an Indian but then I heard Kyle get out of bed and run into the hall. I got up slowly, like something was holding me down, telling me it was for my own good not to rush. By the time I got to the parlor Kyle was blocking the door to keep me out. He seems to have grown overnight and his shoulders nearly filled up the doorway. His lantern glowed from the room behind him and his face was shadowy, but the little moonlight there was in the house was all in the white of his eyes and they were big and round and scared.

"What happened?" I whispered, trying to push past him into the room, but he held my arms.

"Don't come in," he said. "It's Mama. She shot herself."

"Dead?" I asked.

Kyle nodded and stepped aside because Daddy came into the hall then and wanted to get into the parlor. We listened to hear his reaction but there was none. A more silent man there's never been than Daddy.

I wanted to see her to know for sure she was dead, but Kyle wouldn't let me past.

"It's her head, Kate," he said and I noticed Kyle was not looking in her direction neither. I couldn't imagine what the shotgun would do to someone's head.

I guess I am not a good person because I wanted to laugh. It shames me to write that, but it is the truth and this is the only place I can tell the truth. It was hard for me to keep from laughing. Only Kyle's scared eyes kept me from doing it. I wanted to say, "Oh Kyle we're free!"

Then Daddy came out. He stood in the hallway, his head hung down, then he looked over at me.

"She's never been right since the day you come to us, Katie."

I was shocked, but I could see he wasn't angry with me. His voice was soft and he actually touched the side of my head, something he never done before.

"Don't blame yourself, girl," he said. "Weren't your fault. It's best she done this. Now she has peace. Now y'all have peace."

Kyle and I stayed home from school, but I came here to my cave and Kyle did whatever needed to be done in the parlor. I asked could I help, but he said no, he didn't want me to. He came here a while ago and told me everything he saw and it is all too horrible to write here. The destruction she did to herself is not fitting to put on paper. But I made myself listen to Kyle because he said he just had to talk about it. He sat on the settee he helped me cart from the Smith's house and his voice was one tone, never rising or falling, just steady, telling me one horrid thing after another. His eyes looked changed from seeing what he did and I wished Daddy had not said it was my birth that brought all this on because I felt to blame for the sorrow in my brother's face.

October 3, 1941

I got a terrible shock last night. After I left the cave I found Daddy sitting on the stoop of the house and I asked him what he meant, saying Mama wasn't right since I come along. He was holding the whiskey bottle and he took about five long swigs before he spoke.

"Mama weren't your real Mama," he said. He went on to explain that

Mama had a sister, called Sissy, and that she was my Mama! She killed herself a few days after I was born because she wasn't married. Mama took losing Sissy real hard and Daddy and Mama took me in. "We adopted you," Daddy said. "Figured we'd bring you and Kyle up brother and sister."

"You're not my real Daddy," I said.

"I'm your Daddy every way but one, girl, and don't you go thinking anything else." He was part angry and part sad and I thought I better not ask him any more questions.

At first I wasn't going to tell Kyle. But last night I was crying in bed and just couldn't stop and he came over and put his arms around me. He thought I was crying about Mama. But then I told him what Daddy told me and he kept saying, "It can't be true, it can't be." But I said I knew it was. I was holding onto him tight because I was afraid he'd start to feel different about me and maybe never hug me again. But then he said, "Kate, I don't care who your Mama was, you'll always be my sister."

October 20, 1941

Daddy talks more these days. At the dinner table when he's done eating, he pushes his chair back and talks about the mill, or work that needs doing round the house. Mostly he talks about Mama and I am surprised how much he misses her. I think it is not really the Mama I knew that he misses, but the woman she used to be long ago, before I come along.

"She was so beautiful," Daddy says, looking out the window. "And she could sing."

I try to picture Mama singing but it's impossible.

"Dance too," he says and smiles. "I bet you never thought your Ma could dance. She was like a winged angel on the dance floor, free and light. Always smiling, she was." Daddy looked down at his empty plate and I tried to recall the last time I saw Mama smile. I couldn't.

"What was my Mama like, Daddy?" I asked.

"Sissy? Pretty as a flower petal. All the boys liked your Mama, which was part of the problem, I reckon. She was shamed when she had you, not being sure who your pa was and all. People was mean to her. Guess she didn't think she had much of a life left after that. But Mama wanted to take you in. She wanted babies more than anything," Daddy said. "When

you was born, Kyle, she'd cuddle you and kiss you and sing to you. She felt fine. She was up right away after you was born, happy as ever I seen her. Eyes glowing all the time. She'd take you to the market to show you off. Then when Sissy kilt herself and you come to us," Daddy said and looked at me, "she took sick. Something in her chest. I thought at first that was the reason for her mood. She'd be up all night, coughing. That was your lullaby, Kate, Mama's cough. She didn't have the strength to hold you much. Then she started seeing things that wasn't there, imagining things. I thought it was cause she weren't sleeping enough. She just changed from night to day. She took no pleasure in Kyle, neither, after that."

"I'm sorry, Daddy." I could hardly look at him.

"No, Kate," he said. "Don't go blaming yourself. Maybe it was having to look after two babies so close in years, right on top of her sister's passing. Too much at one time for anybody."

Daddy stood up and took his plate to the basin and I stood up too, wanting to get to my cave where I knew I would feel instantly better. Daddy turned to look at me.

"Don't know where it is you spend all your time, girl," he said.

I just looked at him, my insides churning.

"You safe there?" he asked.

"Yes, Daddy."

"Go on, then."

I feel so sad tonight. There was a woman who was my mother that I never knew. Pretty as a flower petal and shamed by my birth. And Mama. Seems like she was a normal mother before I came along. A happy cheerful person. I guess I ruined two women's lives.

December 1, 1941

Miss Crisp thinks I am a good writer, just like Mrs. Renfrew did. I wrote a story about a girl who discovered a treasure (precious jewels) in a cave and Miss Crisp read it out loud to the class. She reads in a breathy voice with pauses in places I would never think to pause and it makes my little story sound like poetry. I got real nervous when she read it and could hardly breathe. Then she said, "You have bona fide talent, Katherine." She pronounced bona fide "bona fi-dee" and everyone turned to look at me. I heard Sara Jane whisper something to Priscilla and Priscilla giggled. I hate Priscilla. When school started this year she asked me why I cut my hair off. She said it was the one pretty thing about me and I went and did away with it. I know I am the ugliest girl in the class. They all have long hair and they wear ribbons in it and Sara Jane has dimples that Kyle keeps bringing up in conversations that have nothing to do with anything. When he talks like that, admiring Sara Jane or some other girl, I feel about to have a heart attack. Truly there is a pain in my chest and one day I'm going to drop dead away at his feet.

Kyle sits in my cave at night (we wrap up in blankets now because it's right chilly, though warmer in the cave than out) and asks me who do I think is prettiest? Who's nicest? This is all Kyle thinks about these days. Sometimes lately Miss Crisp will call on him and he has no idea what she's asking him about because he is so busy staring at the black braids running down Lucy's back.

We are all changing in that class. Our bodies, I mean. Getch's forehead is covered with pimples. William has fine black hair on his upper lip. Sara Jane's breasts have grown so big that the buttons of her blouses stretch the buttonholes. I have come to realize that breasts are very powerful things. Kyle sometimes turns to jelly when he stares at Sara Jane's breasts, which is often and even I have felt the power of my own breasts. They are much smaller than Sara Jane's but if I pull my shoulders back when I walk past Getch or William I can feel their eyes on me and I know I have power over them. Also, when this happens, I feel an odd tingling in my breasts like Getch and William's eyes are actually touching me. Sometimes my breasts ache to be touched, and sometimes in bed at night after Kyle's asleep, I touch them myself. I am amazed that anything can feel so good.

This is all very much on my mind tonight because of a talk Kyle and I had earlier here in my cave. Kyle is by far the handsomest boy in our class. He is tall—just fifteen and already near six feet. His hair is very straight and thick and always shiny and his teeth are beautiful and white (I have the same teeth). He is broad acrost the shoulders and wearing Daddy's shirts now.

Anyhow, tonight he asked me if sometimes at school I tried to imagine how the boys look without their clothes on! I said "No!!! Why would I want to make myself sick?"

Then he looked worried and I realized he was imagining how Sara Jane and Lucy looked naked and he thought he wasn't normal. Is he? Is that normal? I don't know.

I heard Sara Jane and Priscilla talking about their "friend" and I know they mean ministration. I wish I could ask them questions about it because I still don't understand the purpose of this monthly misery, but as soon as they figured I was trying to listen in on their conversation, they stopped talking.

December 7, 1941

The Japanese attacked Pearl Harbor today. Before today I'd never heard of Pearl Harbor. I know about the war—everyone does, but I never realized we were in any danger. All day that's all anyone is thinking or talking about and Daddy sits quietly by the radio, just listening. The president will ask for a declaration of war. We are in it now.

When I reread all the silly things I wrote the other day, about breasts and ministration, I wish I could erase it all. It seems so unimportant when you think that people are dying, that many more people will probably die before it's over. Kyle says he wants to fight. He is only fifteen! Daddy says he's got to finish school first, but that's two years away and surely this won't go on that long. I'm hoping it's over by Christmas.

January 6, 1942

I went to school drunk yesterday. I don't have a good reason why. I just wanted a taste of Daddy's whiskey and didn't stop when I should of. I stayed all night before last in the cave, drinking and reading Jane Austen, wrapped up in my quilt. It was warm in there compared to outside. Kyle came to get me for school but I told him I was too tired, to go on without me. Then I showed up later. I thought maybe the walk would sober me up, but it didn't. I took my seat and Miss Crisp said, "Katherine, are you ill?" and Priscilla said, "No, she's drunk. Can't you smell her?"

I said, "You smell all the time" to Priscilla. Then I said to Miss Crisp, "I don't believe Priscilla ever takes a bath."

Priscilla started crying and Sara Jane said, "You are so rude and disgusting" to me and Getch said, "Hey, Kate, you got any more of that stuff for me?" and Miss Crisp started walking towards me. All I could see was her big head getting closer and closer. Suddenly Kyle yanked me out of my seat by my arm and dragged me outside. He pushed me against the wall of the building and held me there.

"What are you trying to do?" he yelled at me.

I couldn't speak. His hands pressed my shoulders into the wall and his hips touched mine and I felt real dizzy.

"How do you ever expect to make friends with anyone when you do things like this?"

"I don't need friends," I said. "I've got you as my friend."

Kyle backed away from me like I'd sprouted thorns all over me. "I'm glad I'm not your brother," he said. He might as well have hit me, but then his voice went real quiet. "Go home," he said. "Can you get there all right? Do you need me to walk you?"

I shook my head, feeling ashamed. I made a promise to myself right then and there I will never do anything like that again. I won't embarrass him again in front of the other children. I won't make him ashamed to be my brother.

June 6, 1942

Getch's older brother Pete, who lives in Washington, is home for a visit and took us (Getch, Kyle and me) to the library in Winchester. I wasn't going to go, one, because I don't like going into town—it makes me real nervous for some reason—and two, because of Getch being along, but the library! How could I resist?

I felt funny being the only girl. Pete who is twenty three years old and more handsome than Kyle (in a way) said he was pleased to have such pretty company in his car and "I'm not talking about my brother or yours," he said to me. I don't think there's a person in the world who has ever called me pretty and at first I thought he was making fun of me but I could see by the look on his face that he meant it. Pete left us at the library and drove off to do some errands. I left the boys and the first thing I looked up was menstruation. (I have been spelling that word wrong for a long time.) It was also the last thing I looked up because I got so interested in what I was reading that I never got around to anything else.

There were pictures in the book and explanations and now I know exactly why I bleed each month. I am amazed that my body knows to do this and that someday a baby could grow in my uterus. I only wish I didn't have to have a husband to make that happen.

On the drive home I found myself staring at Pete's trousers, remembering what Kyle said about imagining the girls at school without their clothes on. I was amazed I was doing it too. I was too obvious though because when we got to our house, Pete chased Getch and Kyle out of the car and then he took my hand and set it right on the bulge in his trousers and said, "Is this what you want?"

I pulled my hand away and tried to open the door but he caught my arm and the next thing I know his hand was up my skirt, his fingers pressing hard between my legs. The shameful thing is that I wanted to hold his hand there instead of pushing it away, but luckily pride got the better of me and I set my mouth to his shoulder and bit him hard til he let go of me. I got out of the car and ran all the way to my cave where my legs almost gave out on me. I was shaking all over. I kept thinking about my Mama. My real Mama, how she was loose with the boys. For the first time I can understand how a girl could come to be that way.

I lit just the one candle on the ledge near the reflecting pool. Then I undressed in the cool darkness of my cave and lay down under the quilt on my mattress and touched myself where he had touched. My fingers seemed to know what to do, and very quickly a feeling came over me, like the river rushing towards the falls. And then I cried out, my voice a surprise to me as it echoed around my walls. I hoped nobody could hear me. They would of thought I was in pain, but it was not like any pain I ever felt before.

June 7, 1942

Kyle and I were studying for our exams last night in the cave when I realized he was staring at me. When I asked him why he was looking at me that way, he said, "You are pretty. I never noticed til Pete said it. But you are."

8

Eden got out of bed before her alarm rang and pulled on her robe. No use lying awake staring at the ceiling any longer. Her mind was too full to let her sleep anyway. She wished she could call Cassie, but it was far too early. She walked downstairs and stood at the glass wall of the living room, watching the forest change from gray to green as the sun rose from behind the trees.

Lou's easel stood next to her and Eden stepped back to study the painting. It was typical of Lou's work—ramshackle houses made of mud and tin set against a vivid blue, cloud-flecked sky. Some little village in South America, no doubt. Lou and Kyle had spent most of the last decade traveling in Ecuador and Colombia, Kyle completing his research, Lou taking photographs to use in her painting. She had an eye for irony, for contrasting the poverty of man against the richness of nature.

Eden turned at a sound from the kitchen, and in a moment Kyle walked into the living room and handed her a mug of coffee.

"Thanks." She took the mug from him and sat down in the Barcelona chair by the fireplace. She felt awkward with Kyle this morning. There were things he hadn't told her, a world of things she hadn't known.

"You're up early." He lifted his own mug to his lips.

"I didn't sleep very well." She'd lain awake the night before thinking about Ben. What a disastrous evening. She'd finally concluded that Ben was a manipulator. He'd probably never accomplished what he'd hoped to as an archaeologist. He'd gotten this job from Kyle and was now going to kiss up to him for connections so he could move on to something grander. She'd grown so irritated thinking about him that she finally got up to read the journal, and after that it had been impossible to sleep. That was probably just as well. Sleep was not a friend these days. It was just the waiting period between nightmares.

"Why didn't you tell me you're not my uncle?" she asked, the words blunt, reproachful.

Kyle stiffened. "What do you mean?"

"I mean no one is who I thought they were. My grandfather was not really my grandfather. You're my . . . what is it, second cousin?"

"Ah, I see." Kyle sat down on the sofa and rested his mug on his knee. "I think it would be first cousin once removed."

"Why didn't you tell me?"

Kyle ran a hand over his beard. "When you first came to us, Eden, you were so withdrawn. I thought it would make it harder for you, more confusing. I didn't think it was that important. Then later . . ." He smiled. "Well, you were not the easiest adolescent to talk to."

She found herself smiling back. She was having a hard time holding on to her indignation. "No, I guess I wasn't."

"Maybe Lou and I just didn't know how to raise a teenager."

Eden sighed. "I think it was my fault, Kyle, not yours. I hope Cassie will be a little easier to deal with than I was." The tenderness in her words surprised her.

"So." Kyle lifted the mug to his lips. "How was dinner last night?"

"A little strained. I don't think we'll ever be the best of friends." She waited, expecting him to say something nice about Ben, something to endear him to her.

But Kyle leaned back on the sofa. "Well, that relieves me somewhat. It's probably best for you and Ben just to work together at the site this summer and keep things impersonal."

She was surprised. And curious. "I thought you liked him."

"I love him. Like a son. But he's the wrong person for you to get involved with right now."

"Why?" She was right in her assessment of Ben after all, but she felt disappointed all the same.

Kyle shrugged and looked into his mug.

"I thought he might be using me. For my money, or his ego. Or to get more from you," she ventured. "Connections or something."

Kyle's eyebrows shot up and he laughed. "No, honey, you're way off. Ben has more connections in the field than I do at this point. And he's no schemer. He had a very messy divorce, that's all. He's not over it yet. I'd love to see you with someone outside of Hollywood, Eden, but it should be someone who has his life in a little better shape."

"But why is he working here for . . . I'm sure with your loss of funding you can't pay him much." She suddenly realized that Kyle was probably paying Ben out of his own pocket.

"You'll have to ask Ben that question."

"Where did he work before coming here?"

"University of Maryland. He taught there. He was vice-chair of the department."

She sat forward. "Then why is he here at such a tiny enterprise?"

Kyle shrugged.

"You're not going to tell me, are you."

"My advice to you regarding Ben is to treat him kindly but keep your distance."

She sat back again, wrapped her hands around the mug in her lap. This entire exchange seemed familiar. Kyle sounded just as he had when she was a teenager and getting in with the drama crowd at school. She had finally belonged. But Kyle didn't like her new friends. His admonishments were always gently offered but unyielding. Softly masked authority that made her want to slug him. The kids were on drugs, he'd say. The boys would use her. "They're no good, honey, can't you see that? The only thing they're good at is acting, and they can charm you into doing things you'll regret. They can only hurt you in the end."

From her adult perspective she knew Kyle had been absolutely right. But she had been getting attention from her peers for the first time in her life. She'd experienced a confidence on stage she'd felt nowhere else. She could pull a role over her head like an article of clothing. But the drama crowd had been wild and she'd been ripe for the attention of the boys. Their long hair and earrings intrigued her. They plied her with their grass and poetry, those unrhyming verses that always had a sexual overtone to them, so that when they stopped reading and started touching her it seemed to be the natural progression of things. She learned to slip into a role, into someone else's skin, and do things the real Eden might not want to do. She convinced herself that seventeen was a magical age. No one could hurt her anymore, and her life suddenly filled with excitement, with a joy she'd thought she would never know. She couldn't understand back then how Kyle could ask her to give that up.

And now she felt something of that old teenage rebel in her at his words about Ben. Ben was not trying to use her. That was the most important thing. He was troubled, yes, she could see that. But someone could give him the same warning about her, couldn't they?

"Are you ready for the next notebook?" Kyle asked.

"I guess," she said. Last night's notebook had left her so drained she wouldn't have minded if Kyle slowed down a bit in dealing them out to her. She looked around the living room and added quietly, "This is the room where your mother killed herself."

He nodded.

"Finding her must have been terrible for you, Kyle." The words slipped out easily, but even so she knew it was the first empathic thing she had ever said to him.

"She was sitting in a rocking chair right where you're sitting now," Kyle said. "My father burned the rocker. It was caked with blood. There was blood on the ceiling and the floor and pieces of her head back there." He pointed toward the wall behind her. "Nothing I saw later in the war compared to what I saw in this room that night."

She looked up at the ceiling. It was painted a clean white, crossed with huge oak beams.

"She left you and Katherine to raise each other."

"We'd already been doing that for years."

"Katherine seemed a little sexually precocious for fourteen." She shifted uncomfortably in the Barcelona chair. She'd meant to change the topic but hadn't expected those exact words to come out of her mouth.

"Did she? Seems to me the only thing any of us had on our minds in those days was sex."

"Was she really that nasty to other kids?"

"Worse." Kyle laughed. "She makes herself look like a saint in her journal. But she was nasty in self-defense. The other kids weren't very nice to her either."

"You were all she had. Didn't you resent her dependency on you?"

He leaned forward and rested his elbows on his knees. "I was dependent on her too. It doesn't come across in the journal—maybe Kate never realized it. I talked a good line about wanting her to be with other people, but later on, when she became friends with Matt, I was pretty jealous."

"The journal's not as easy to read as I thought it would be," Eden said. "It's harder to stay objective than I expected. Katherine's become so real to me."

He nodded as though he'd fully expected that to happen.

"What will this be like for you, Kyle? I mean, the film. Seeing yourself—the actor who plays you—finding your mother after her suicide, coping with all you had to cope with. Can you stand it?"

"It was a long, long time ago, Eden. All I ask is that you present the past honestly, that you don't exploit it."

"When I finish the first draft of the script I'd like you to read it," she said, surprising herself again. "I want to be sure you're okay with it."

"I'd like that," he said.

Eden squeezed the mug hard between her palms. "Kyle, I understand why you've waited so long to tell me about the journal. I know I'm reading your story as well as Katherine's. I just want you to know I appreciate it."

He nodded slowly, a thoughtful smile on his lips. Then he stood up and walked to the door. "I'm glad you're here, Eden," he said. "It's time."

*

She called Cassie from the phone in the kitchen before leaving for the site.

"I'm brown as a strawberry, Mommy," Cassie said. Eden heard Pam's laughter in the background. "Just a plain berry, Cass," Pam said. "Brown as a berry."

"Oh. I'm brown as a berry, Mom."

"Don't get burned, honey." She pictured Pam standing next to Cassie, pretending to be engrossed in some chore as she listened in on this conversation. "Does Daddy have some sunscreen for you?"

"Pam does. We have a raft for everybody! Mine's blue."

"Your favorite color."

"Yes, and you know what?"

"What?"

"That's April's favorite color too!"

"I miss you, Cass."

"And you know what else? Tomorrow we're going to Hershey Park!"

"That's wonderful, Cassie." She struggled to get some enthusiasm into her own voice, which sounded depressingly flat to her ears. "I'll call you tomorrow night to hear all about it."

"Okay."

"I love you, honey."

"I love you too, Mommy." Eden listened as Cassie planted a dozen messy kisses on the mouthpiece. Then she heard Pam's voice in the background.

"Oh Cassie, that's disgusting. Other people have to use that phone too, you know."

Eden heard the click of the phone being hung up. She listened to the silence for a few seconds before hanging up herself. Then she climbed the stairs to her room and made it all the way to the wicker rocking chair before the tears started.

9

Ben woke up the same way he'd fallen asleep: angry with himself. His shirt was still beneath his head on the pillow, but it had lost Eden's scent overnight. Time to step out of fantasyland and back to the real world.

The phone rang and he raised himself up on one elbow to answer it. "Hello?"

"Ben? This is Alex."

For a moment he said nothing. He'd called Alex Parrish twice since he'd gotten out of prison, and the last time Alex had asked him not to call again. "I'm surprised to hear from you," he said.

"This is business, Ben. Do you remember Tina James?"

"Sure." Tina had been one of his most promising students.

"She's applying for a position with Stanford and wanted me to ask you if you'd write her a reference letter."

So that was it. Poor old Alex had no goddamned choice but to call him. "I think a letter from me will do her more harm than good, don't you?"

"I talked to her about it. Her thinking is that no matter what you did in your personal life you still have a name in the field and—"

"Yeah, I'll do it." He picked up the pen and a pad of paper from the apple crate. "Give me her address and I'll mail her a copy."

"Well, she said maybe you could just mail it to me and I'll send it on to her."

Ben sighed. She wanted a reference from him but didn't trust him with her address. "Whatever," he said. "So, are you teaching this summer?"

There was hesitation on the other end of the line as Alex debated whether or not to prolong this conversation. "Yes. Just one class."

"How's Leslie?"

"Fine."

"And my goddaughter?" Ordinarily he would refer to Alex's eight-year-old daughter as Kim, but he wanted to remind him of just how close they'd once been.

"She's okay."

"Her birthday's in a couple of weeks."

"God, you have an incredible memory. I'd forgotten myself."

"Alex . . . I wish you'd see me."

"We've been over that."

"You've only heard things from Sharon's perspective. Give me a chance to talk to you."

"I can't, Ben."

"Could you at least talk to Sam? Let him tell you . . ."

"I've spoken to Sam. I know he thinks you're innocent, but frankly I don't know what he's basing that on other than brotherly love."

"You've got some legal background. You might be able to help him figure out a way to—"

"Forget it."

"How long have we been friends, Alex? I really think you owe it to me."

"I don't owe you anything." Alex's voice had a nasty edge to it. "I'll tell Tina you'll get that letter out within a week or so?"

Ben clenched his teeth. "Right," he said, and he hung up the phone.

"Good morning."

Ben looked up from the pit to see Eden shading her eyes against the morning sun. He was relieved to see her. He stood up. "I was afraid you might not come back after last night," he said.

She climbed down the ladder into the pit. "I wanted to see what else I could find."

She's been bitten, he thought. Like her mother. Like himself.

"Plus I have the feeling Kyle can use all the help he can get before the grant's up."

"Yeah, you're right. He had a couple of graduate students, but they left about the time I came." Actually, the two women had left the day after his arrival. Kyle made up some excuse for their abrupt departure, but Ben knew that he was the cause of their flight.

Eden lifted the plastic from the square of earth she'd been working on the day before and picked up her brush.

"Eden," he said.

She raised her eyes to him.

"I want to apologize for last night. It's been so long since I've been out with anyone. I was nervous. Sorry."

"It's all right," she said. She wasn't saying, It's all right, we can try again. She was dismissing him. I'll forgive you, but you blew your chance.

He sat down on the ground at the other side of the pit and began working. The silence was intolerable to him. He could feel her behind him, content to work quietly. Maybe Kyle had told her last night. Maybe she'd gone home and said to Kyle, "That guy's really screwed up," and Kyle nodded and said, "Yeah, well, he spent six months in prison, you know."

"I'm finding some little clumps of stuff," she said suddenly, and he turned around to see her examining the soil in her hand. "But I swear they're just dirt."

He moved next to her, and she set the little brown lumps on his palm.

"They're pottery all right. Probably pieces of that bowl you found yesterday."

They worked together quietly for the next hour, dusting the ground in front of her, charting her finds on the graph paper. It was close to eleven when he stood up to stretch.

"Want some O.J.?" he asked.

She looked up at him. Her lips were dusty and beautiful. "That'd be great."

He got two bottles of juice from the cooler in his truck and returned to the pit. She sat with her back braced by the corner of the pit, twisted off the cap and took a long drink. She no longer looked the Hollywood actress. Brown dust coated her calves and traced the line between her temple and jaw.

He lowered himself into the opposite corner and took a swallow of juice. "So, what's your mom up to these days in her journal?" he asked.

Eden stared at the toes of her tennis shoe as she spoke. "Well, her mother committed suicide, the Japanese invaded Pearl Harbor, and she learned to make love to herself."

Ben smiled at her candor. Kyle must not have told her after all. "I guess when the world's crumbling around you the only way to survive is to comfort yourself," he said.

She looked up at him. "I hadn't thought of it quite that way." She pulled a pad and pencil from her shorts pocket and wrote something down.

"I didn't know Kyle's mother killed herself."

"She was crazy." Eden fingered the crumbs of pottery lying next to her on the newspaper. "She did crazy things. She hallucinated. She beat my mother and Kyle. She shot herself in the head. Kyle found her. He was only about fifteen."

"Jesus. That must have been horrendous. Did you know before you read the journal that she was crazy?"

Eden nodded. "I got teased a lot for being the daughter of a woman who lived in a cave and the granddaughter of a lunatic. The kids at school used to jump rope to this song." She shut her eyes and began to recite.

> "Old Lady Swift was crazy as a loon,
> Washed her clothes from night till noon,
> Ate bugs for breakfast and bats at night,
> And blew her head off when the time was right."

Eden opened her eyes and looked at him. "No one cared that my mother had published twenty-six books. I learned to talk about my father even though I'd never known him, because he was respectable. He started the *Coolbrook Chronicle*."

"I didn't know that." He was completely certain now that Kyle hadn't told her. She would never speak this openly to him if she knew.

"But anyway, I learned that my grandmother was not actually my grandmother after all. Katherine and Kyle were cousins. Kyle's parents adopted her after her own mother killed herself."

"A lot of early deaths in your family. A lot of suicide."

"They say it runs in families."

"Have you ever felt that way?" he asked.

"Like killing myself? No. You?"

"The thought ran through my mind after my marriage broke up."

She set her juice down on the ground between her feet. "What ended it, Ben? Or is that too personal?"

"Sharon ended it because . . ." He hesitated a long moment. He could think of no lie he was willing to tell her. Omission was one thing, lying another.

"It is too personal." She let him off the hook. "Sorry I asked. Kyle told me you used to teach. That you're well known as an archaeologist. Why are you here in a failing site?"

"Kyle didn't tell you?"

"He just said your divorce was traumatic."

Ben nodded. "It was bad. And I . . . couldn't keep up with my job, really." Well, okay. So there it was. The lie. Not bold-faced, exactly, but now she probably assumed he'd had a nervous breakdown. Still, that was preferable to the truth.

"Kyle heard about my problem and rescued me."

She smiled. "That's his hobby, rescuing people. He rescued me a couple of times too. Will you be ready to go back to teaching when the grant's up here?"

He looked at the streak of dirt across her cheek, at the strand of blond hair that had fallen free to rest against her throat, and wished he could be as open with her as she was being with him. "It's a little more complicated than that," he said.

Eden stared at the blank screen of her word processor, trying to concentrate on her mother but able to think only of Ben. The morning with him had been thoroughly comfortable. She'd worn no mask and she'd survived. She hadn't meant to spill quite so much to him, but he'd treated her words with interest and respect.

His sadness touched her. He's harmless, Kyle. He'd sat there in that pit with the body of a football player and the aching vulnerability of a little boy. God, he was attractive. He lacked Michael's polish, and perhaps that was what pleased her. Nothing stirred inside her when she was with Michael. The fact that he'd been voted *People* magazine's sexiest man of the year had no impact at all on her body. He thought she was exercising herculean willpower when she refused to sleep with him, but the truth was, she found him extremely easy to resist.

Could she resist Ben? Would he ever give her the opportunity? She liked the feel of his gray eyes on her as he drank his juice in the pit this morning. The cut of his jaw, the dark hair on his chest where it curled ever so slightly above the neck of his green T-shirt, the splay of his dusty fingers as he swept them across the earth ... She had no desire to play a role with him, and that scared and excited her at the same time. If he ever touched her again she wanted it to be Eden Riley the woman, not the actress, he touched.

But he hadn't come near her today. She'd felt her body longing for it, just for his fingers on her knee. She smiled at the thought of her mother, whose breasts ached when she passed the boys at school. Katherine was so real to her now, so very human. She switched on the word processor and began to write.

10

September 9, 1942

Kyle begun courting Sara Jane this summer. He goes to her house about two evenings a week, and on those evenings I write and write and write to keep from thinking. Sara Jane is my enemy and I don't understand why Kyle likes her so much. At first he asked my advice about what to say to her and how to ask her out. He'd say, "What would you think if a boy said 'Would you like to go to a movie with me?' or 'Can I come to your house this evening?'"

I was amazed he trusted my opinion to be like other girls', and I tried to answer like other girls might, saying "I'd be pleased to have your company," etc, not at all sure what words Sara Jane would use. I realize how little I know about these things.

He dresses pretty to go out with her and stops by the cavern to ask "How do I look?" and I tell him how handsome he is and how thrilled Sara Jane will be by the very sight of him and I can see the excitement in his eyes. I asked him the other night if he's kissed Sara Jane yet.

"Sara Jane loves to kiss," he said and I was sorry I asked. I believe Sara Jane is trying to be nicer to me. She offers me sweets and tries to talk to me before school, but I ignore her. She thinks if she is nice to me, Kyle will like her even more.

The other girls are jealous of her. She and Kyle hold hands or tip their heads together to share a secret. Kyle is no longer off with the boys at recess and lunch but now is with Sara Jane. They sit on the bench close together and talk. The girls make their circle without Sara Jane, but their eyes are always in the direction of the bench and I wish I could hear what they say. I sit on the stoop, reading as always and watching. I'm beginning another school year the way I ended the last one, reading, writing, and watching the world go by. Only this year is worse in a way because I feel real nervous in school, like I'm going to pass out or get sick. I can't wait for that bell to ring at the end of the day.

Daddy has a new lady friend, a real young woman from Strasburg. One day a couple of weeks ago he said at the breakfast table, "I'm thinking of gettin' married again. How would y'all feel about havin' a new ma?"

Kyle and I looked at each other. We were doing fine without a ma and Daddy could tell we were not too pleased with his idea. He cleared his voice and said, "Well, she wouldn't be your ma, exactly, but I could use me a wife. Y'all wouldn't deny me that, now would ya?" He was grinning a grin I'd never seen on his face before.

"No, Daddy," said Kyle, but my heart was pounding. I didn't want some stranger in my house.

"Her name's Susanna Cody," Daddy said. "She's a little young, but—"

"How young?" I interrupted.

"Nineteen. Nearly twenty."

"Nineteen!" Kyle said. I was too shocked to say anything. Daddy is thirty-five!

"That's too young for you, Daddy," Kyle said.

"You presume to be tellin' me my business, boy?" Daddy said. He was not really angry. Actually, I have not seen Daddy angry since before Mama died.

So last Saturday, Daddy invited Susanna Cody to dinner. Of course I had to do the cooking, which was fine with me since it gave me something to do while Kyle and Daddy entertained Susanna in the parlor. I was wondering if she knew that was the room where Daddy's last wife blew her head off.

Susanna is near as tall as Daddy and very pretty. She is not too talkative which makes me wonder what she and Daddy have to say to each other.

She has nearly black hair that she wears short and curled and she looks no more than eighteen, I think. She looks like she should be with Kyle instead of Daddy, but she took no interest in Kyle whatever. She only has eyes for Daddy. I don't understand it. Daddy's not bad looking but his face is lined and his hair's shifting back from his forehead. Still, she's smiling at him all the time and calling him Charles which is new to our ears. Ma always called him Daddy. Anyhow, Susanna seems like a nice enough person if she'll just leave us alone. Daddy announced at dinner that they'll be getting married in November.

November 7, 1942

Most of the time, I don't feel lonely, even when I'm alone in the cavern. Or maybe least of all there. There is something living about the tites and mites. They are my company, along with my stories. And you, my journal.

But today at the wedding I felt lonelier than ever before. The wedding was held in a little chapel in Strasburg. Hardly a soul was there. Just Susanna's mother, who is a widow and would probably make a more fitting bride for Daddy than Susanna, considering age anyhow, Susanna's friend and the friend's boyfriend, and Susanna's older sister and her husband. Kyle brought Sara Jane, and he and I fought about this, I'm ashamed to say. We were in the cave and he said he's tired of me criticizing Sara Jane and being cruel to her. "She tries to talk to you and you ignore her," he said. "The other night she was talking to me about it and she cried, she felt so hurt."

I was outraged. "What about all the times she hurt me?" I said.

"When we were kids maybe. I know she was mean then. But she's different now. She'd like to do things with you. You could go shopping or just talk or do whatever most girls do when they're together."

"I'm not like 'most girls,'" I said.

"Well, I wish you were," he said. "Look at you. You live like a hermit in this stupid cave. You don't care how you dress or how you look or—"

"I'd like you to leave my cavern now, please," I said, very calmly. I wasn't about to sit there and listen to his insults. His cheeks were red and he turned on his heel like a soldier and left the cave. After he was gone I made a decision to treat Sara Jane more kindly. Otherwise I'll lose Kyle.

So I was determined to be nice to her at the wedding. I sat on one side of Kyle, Sara Jane sat on the other, and as I sat there I tried to think of things I could say to her after the ceremony but my mind was blank as a sheet of new writing paper. A panicky feeling come over me and I thought I would die if I didn't get out of that church and into the air.

As we left the church, Sara Jane said to me, "Your Daddy looks so happy."

I tried to say yes, but no words came out, and I tried to nod but my neck was stiff and wouldn't move. I wanted to get away from her so I could breathe. Truly, I have never felt so close to suffocating.

It is not just Sara Jane. Susanna's ma came up to me and took my hand and said, "We're family now," and I felt ready to pass out.

This is what I mean about feeling lonely. I wanted to be nice and social and instead I felt like the time I accidentally got locked in the pantry when I was five. I couldn't breathe right, my eyes got all blurred up, and my heart thumped like I would die. I can't even explain it to Kyle because he would just say I'm not trying hard enough, but I don't know how to try any harder.

January 5, 1943

Susanna had a brother, John, who died at Pearl Harbor. He was just seventeen, a year older than Kyle. When I try to imagine what it would be like if Kyle died I get that heart attack pain in my chest again. I look at Susanna and wonder how she can smile, how she can go on at all.

I wish the war would end before Kyle finishes school next year because he is bound and determined to fight. He talks about it being his duty and now he talks about "avenging John's death." And I say what if he dies too? But Kyle doesn't seem to think that's possible. He has this attitude that nothing bad can happen to him, that he is protected in some way. I never have that feeling. Instead, I am certain my death is waiting for me around the next bend in the road. Every morning I am surprised to wake up alive.

11

Seventy-six miles per hour. Eden kept her eyes riveted on the speedometer as Lou bore down on the gas pedal with her one foot, the foot that would also have to work the brake. There was little traffic on 81, but Eden clutched the armrest with a damp hand nevertheless.

They were on their way to a doctor's appointment in Winchester. Lou had asked Eden to go with her, and Eden had agreed, thinking Lou might need her help. She offered to drive, but Lou laughed at the suggestion. "It takes practice to drive this thing," she said, pointing to the van. Eden watched Lou's effortless operation of the lift that swung her chair into position behind the steering wheel, and as they flew down the curved roads between Lynch Hollow and the highway, she knew that Lou had not asked her along for her help.

Kyle had handed Eden the next notebook as she climbed into the van. "Maybe you'll want to do a little reading while you're waiting for Lou," he'd said. Now the notebook rested on her knees, along with a script Nina had sent her to consider.

Eden watched the waves of heat rising from the road as the usual silence stretched between her aunt and herself. "Hot," she said after they'd driven a few miles.

"It's going to be a real scorcher of a summer," Eden said. "It's probably hotter in New York, though. Do you miss it?"

"Not really," said Lou. "Too much traffic up there. I like to cut loose in a car."

"I noticed."

"We go up about once a month. See friends, do the theater, go shopping. I always knew we'd end up back here eventually, though. Kyle's roots have a strong pull on him."

There were a few other patients, mostly elderly, in the waiting room of the doctor's office.

"Geriatrics," Lou whispered to Eden as she wheeled herself into the room. "He specializes."

Eden took a seat next to her aunt's chair and set the journal once again on her lap. She'd left the script in the van. Nina was pushing her, as usual, but Eden couldn't think about another film right now.

There were some whispers from across the room, a twittering that let Eden know she'd been recognized. In a moment a frail-looking little woman left her seat and came over to sit next to her.

"You're Eden Riley, aren't you?"

Eden smiled. "Yes, I am."

"I knew it! I was just sitting there reading this article in *People*"— she held up the magazine, open to a picture of Eden with Michael Carey—"and I looked up and there you were in the flesh."

"Well, you have a very keen eye. Not everyone recognizes me. Would you like me to sign that picture for you?"

"Oh, yes. My granddaughter worships you. She'll be thrilled."

Eden set the magazine on top of the notebook in her lap. She had seen this picture, taken at the opening of *Heart of Winter*, many times before. She and Michael were arm in arm and dressed to kill, he in a tux, she in sequins. They'd given birth to an abundance of rumors that night.

She personalized the autograph to the woman's granddaughter and signed it, the witch of the North Star, Eden Riley. The woman looked far less frail as she hopped back across the room with her new treasure.

"You do that very easily, don't you, dear?" Lou asked. "Switch into the professional Eden Riley?"

"It becomes second nature after a while." It was switching out of that role she found difficult.

The receptionist peeked out of her glass room. "Good morning, Mrs. Swift," she said. "How's Mr. Swift doing?"

"He's fine, thank you, dear."

"Has Kyle been ill?" Eden asked.

"No, not at all. Just the arthritis, which irritates the hell out of him. But when you reach a certain age you realize that even under the best of circumstances you don't have that much time left. So, Kyle's fine, but he feels every little ache and pain and it makes him think about what's important to him, what he wants to accomplish with the rest of his life."

"The site?"

Lou closed the magazine in her lap. "The site means a lot to him, but you're more important to him than anything else," she said. "You and Cassie. That's why he's so happy you're with us. He wants to . . . set things right with you. He always regretted not taking you in as soon as Kate died. He wishes he could make it up to you. He thinks this is his chance, helping you with the film."

"Kyle's already done enough for me," Eden said.

Lou glanced over at her. "Do you know that, dear?"

"Yes." She looked down at the journal, her cheeks hot. Kyle had done plenty for her, but in one crucial way Lou had done more.

"Maybe one of these days you could find it in your heart to tell him that."

A nurse led Lou into the back office, and Eden stared at her hands where they rested on the notebook. She knew Kyle had wanted to take her in after Katherine died, but her grandfather wouldn't let him. Granddaddy disliked Lou, and he told Kyle that his traveling would be no good for a child. So Eden stayed in Lynch Hollow with Granddaddy and Susanna. Her grandfather all but ignored her. He said Katherine had spoiled her beyond repair and now he had to set her right. Susanna ran hot and cold, and it was never safe to turn to her for anything. Eden remembered trying to climb into Susanna's lap for a hug just a few weeks after Katherine's death. Susanna pushed her away, telling her she was too old to be cuddled, and Eden never bothered trying again.

Her grandfather died when Eden was ten. His death was a surprise, something to do with his heart. Shortly after that Susanna developed pneumonia. The house filled with her cough. The roof started leaking that year, and Eden set buckets and bowls on the floor of the living room whenever it rained, while Susanna lay in bed, pale and wheezing. Susanna finally got so bad her family took her in. But they refused to take Eden, wanting nothing to do with the daughter of the woman who'd lived in a cave. Susanna never told Eden her plans. Instead she had bundled her off to the orphanage. Once the initial shock wore off, Eden wasn't surprised to find herself there. She'd learned not to grow attached to anyone, too fond of anyone, so there could be no surprises and no hurt.

She lived at the orphanage for two years, surrounded by children whose lives had been even more devastating than her own and who therefore had nothing with which to taunt her. But it was too late. Eden wasn't going to risk getting close to anyone, and the other children quickly gave up on her. She devoted her time to her homework and reading. Then one of the nuns began taking them to the movies, and Eden found her passion. The movies stayed in her mind for weeks at a time, and she imagined herself starring in her favorite roles. She'd sneak into the communal bathroom in the middle of the night to practice in front of the small mirror above the chipped porcelain sink. Once she was caught in the midst of her tearful portrayal of Ingrid Bergman learning she had tuberculosis in *The Bells of St. Mary's*, and she had a terrible time explaining what had devastated her so.

The day after her thirteenth birthday Eden was summoned to the director's office. She was afraid of Sister Joseph, the diminutive, razor-tongued director, and by the time she reached the office she was trembling. Sister Joseph was dwarfed by her big mahogany desk, yet she looked formidable to Eden with her bushy black eyebrows and thin white lips. There were two people sitting in the chairs in front of Sister Joseph's desk, but it wasn't until they stood to face her that Eden recognized them as Kyle and Lou. She felt an old, nearly forgotten joy that they'd come to visit her, and dread at the knowledge that they would leave her again. It was always that way with Kyle and Lou. They had stopped in at Lynch Hollow from time to time between trips to South America, but they never stayed long. So Eden had no expectation that this visit would be any different. Her dread locked horns with her happiness, and she allowed no emotion whatever to show on her face. That was nothing new. The only times she cried these days, the only times she laughed, were during her hours of escape in front of the bathroom mirror.

Kyle hugged her while she stood rigid as stone in his arms.

"I'm sorry, sweetheart," he said. "We didn't know about Susanna, and when we found out, we had trouble tracking you down. We never would have let you stay here."

They were not just passing through this time, she thought. Kyle meant to take her away with him and Lou. Still, she didn't let her happiness show. She could be wrong. She could be back here within a week.

Sister Joseph took Kyle aside, and Eden knew she was telling him she was too withdrawn, too sullen. She heard it from the nuns herself all the time. But Kyle left the office with determination in his smile. He put one arm around her, the other around Lou. "We'll take good care of her," he said to Sister Joseph.

Eden was an adult before she understood the sacrifice Kyle and Lou had made for her. They had intentionally had no children so they'd be free to travel, to pursue their careers. When she moved in with them Kyle took a teaching position at NYU to put an end to his traveling, giving up his first love to create a stable home life for her.

They'd lived in New York, a block from Washington Square in Greenwich Village. The kids in New York had read all of Katherine Swift's books, so at first they were impressed with Eden. But her accent earned her the label "hillbilly," and soon the teasing started again.

Eden learned to keep her mouth shut. Kyle and Lou did all they could for her, buying her dance lessons, piano lessons, speech lessons, trying to scrape every last trace of Lynch Hollow from her. They would have bought her friends, too, if that had been possible.

Eden remembered her life in that apartment as a string of television shows. She stayed up late watching old movies, sneaking again, because Kyle didn't approve. Once she overheard Lou and Kyle talking about her voracious appetite for movies. She was just like Kate, Kyle said, living her life through the lives of other people. The apartment was nothing more than her cave.

The cave. Eden's eyes rested once again on the notebook in her lap as the receptionist broke the hushed stillness of the waiting room by calling another patient. She really should see the cave. She wished Kyle were not so adamant about keeping it closed. But would she go in if he'd let her? She would have to. She was missing something, missing the atmosphere that had comforted her mother and would color this film.

Eden picked up the journal from her lap and began to read.

October 11, 1943

Kyle is seventeen now but he acts like twenty-five. He thinks he is all grown up.

Yesterday was his birthday and Sara Jane took him into Winchester for dinner. I was in my cave when he got back and he had whiskey with him. I could tell he'd already had plenty to drink because his tie was undone, his shirttails were loose outside his trousers and his hair was hanging straight and blond in his face. He sat on the settee with a blanket around his shoulders and asked me to read the story I was writing aloud to him.

"Give me some of that whiskey first," I said.

He came over to the mattress and sat next to me and handed me the bottle. I drank til my ears burned. I wanted to get drunk fast. I've been drunk two or three times and I like it because for a few hours I feel as though I have no worries at all.

We passed the bottle back and forth for a while and I was enjoying Kyle more than ever because he was at ease and grinning and not as serious as usual.

"I need your sisterly advice," he said, and I could see he was trying to look serious with his out-of-focus eyes. "Your help as a girl, I mean."

I was confused and obviously not as drunk as he was.

"See," he continued. "Sara Jane and I have decided to make love." He raised his eyebrows at me, waiting for my reaction.

I wanted to tell him he shouldn't do that until he was married, but I'm not too sure I believe that myself and I sure don't want to put any notion in his head about marrying Sara Jane. "How can I help?" I asked.

"Well, I don't know what to do. I mean I understand basically what to do but ..." He started giggling uncontrollably. I just stared at him in amazement because I never saw him act silly before. Once he finally stopped giggling I asked him, "How far has it gone already?" I loved that he was drunk enough that I could get away with being nosy about this.

"Just above the waist," he said, all straight-faced now. My breasts started that weird aching that I knew would only go away if they were touched.

"She's getting impatient," he said. "But I don't know how to touch her ... below the waist. I mean, I'm not even sure what's there."

I couldn't believe Kyle was saying all this without even blushing.

"I mean, the only girl I ever saw was you and you were only about five years old."

Kyle and I used to inspect each other down by Ferry Creek where we could take off our clothes and let the water run over our bodies.

"Well," I said. "Let me show you now." I started to unfasten the straps of my overalls, but Kyle was not drunk enough for that! He leaped from the mattress as though someone goosed him.

"Kate!" he said. "Don't you dare!"

"All right." I shrugged. "I'll draw you a picture instead."

So I drew it the best I could. I drew pictures of the inside, too, the uterus and tubes and all and explained to him everything I'd learned about menstruation. I wasn't about to just teach him what felt good to a girl without making sure he had some respect for her body. He sat with his head on my shoulder, watching me draw. Then I pointed out the place he could touch to make her crazy with longing for him.

He grinned and told me Sara Jane was already crazy with longing for him.

"No, this is different," I said. "If you touch this place, just kind of rubbing, but real easy—well, you'll be amazed what will happen." I set down my pencil, thinking what a favor I was doing Sara Jane.

"How do you know all this?" he asked.

"I do it to myself," I said.

"Really? I thought only guys did that."

That was a surprise to me, because it never occurred to me that guys could do this too. But I suppose that makes sense.

We talked a little longer, but Kyle was slowing down. I managed to half walk and half carry him to the settee before he passed out. I told him he'd be right sick this morning (and he was). Then I lay down on my mattress, all of my body burning from our conversation, and spent the rest of the night with my own loving hands.

October 22, 1943

Sara Jane and Kyle are closer than ever. I watch them at school, sitting on the bench, not noticing anything but each other. They touch by drawing their hands slowly across each other's skin, like some gluey substance connects them.

The other children are more respectful of me these days and I'm sure it's because I'm Kyle's sister and Kyle is looked up to more than anyone in our school. I want to know if my anatomy lesson helped him, but I know it would embarrass him if I asked. I'll have to wait til the next time he's had some to drink.

Yesterday Miss Crisp had a long talk with me. My stories have improved, she said, and my writing is "wise and touching."

"But your characters are more alive than you are, Kate," she said. "You always have your nose buried in a book, and while I certainly don't want to discourage you from reading, there are other things in life."

"I'm happiest when I'm reading or writing," I said.

She looked at me like she didn't believe me and I am not too convinced any more myself, but that is the type of happiness I'll have to settle for. There are parts to life I'll never have: a best girlfriend, a boyfriend. I'll never have children. I myself will be my only lover. I'll never see other parts of the world. The only place I can breathe easy is in my house or my cave.

Susanna took me shopping for clothes yesterday and I felt nauseous the whole time, so bad that when I'd twist or bend to try things on I would start to retch. The streets in town looked wavy and made me dizzy. I was afraid to be with Susanna alone because I couldn't think of anything to say *to her. She is nice and I feel bad about this. I always thought the reason I had trouble talking to people was because they were idiots, like at school. Now I know it is something about me, not them, that is the problem.*

Lou wanted to stop at the bakery in Coolbrook on the way home from the doctor's office. "Some rolls for supper," she said.

"We have that wheat bread," said Eden. There was still at least half a loaf from last night's dinner.

"Oh, yes. Then muffins for breakfast." Lou seemed determined to go to the bakery. She raced down the sidewalk in her chair while Eden struggled to keep up with her.

An enormous round-faced woman dressed in white stood behind the counter in the bakery. "Hi there, Lou!" she said. Her mouth was a tiny red rosebud in a sea of white chins. Her curly white hair was cut far too short for the enormity of her face. "What would you like today?"

"Half a dozen muffins," Lou said. "Three blueberry, three bran."

The woman started to reach into the case for the muffins but froze when her gaze fell on Eden. She stood up straight. "Lord, you have got to be Kate's girl. Eden Riley, right?"

Eden smiled. "Yes."

The woman laughed. "Kate's girl, all grown up. Lord, if you aren't the spitting image. And just as pretty in person as in the movies."

Lou looked up at Eden, cocking her head so she could wink without the woman seeing. "Eden, this is Sara Jane Miller, an old friend of your mother's."

"And your Uncle Kyle's," Sara Jane said.

Eden's eyes widened and Lou squeezed her hand to help her stay in control. "It's nice to meet you." Eden reached across the counter and Sara Jane gave her hand a pulpy shake.

They made small talk while Sara Jane put the muffins in a paper bag. Then Eden held the door open for her aunt, who barely made it outside before she started laughing. "Every time Kyle sees her he says, 'If only I hadn't met you, Lou, all that could have been mine.'"

Eden stopped walking and looked down at Lou. "You know exactly where I am in the journal, don't you?"

Lou nodded. "Yes. Does that bother you?"

"I don't know." Eden started walking again, slowly. "It feels strange, as though I'm being observed every step of the way as I learn about my mother."

"And what are you learning about her in this notebook?"

"That her isolation was not as much a matter of choice as I'd thought. That she was phobic of people, of leaving Lynch Hollow."

"You're right. Kate was afraid of the world to such a degree that it paralyzed her. Her fears crippled her far more than this old leg cripples me."

Eden set her hand lightly on her aunt's shoulder. She felt the bones through the thin blouse. "You get around so well, Lou. It relieves me to see that."

Lou patted her hand. "Yes, sweetie, I'm fine."

The atmosphere in the car on the ride back to Lynch Hollow was no longer strained. Eden felt freed by something—Lou's little plot to introduce her to Sara Jane Miller perhaps, or maybe it was just that Lou's leg had ceased to become an unmentionable between them for the first time. Whatever the cause, Eden felt safe enough to ask Lou's opinion of Ben.

"Ah, Ben." Lou smiled and nodded as though she'd been wondering when Eden would get around to asking that question. "Ben was always a favorite of mine, of all Kyle's students. He traveled with us in South America, you know. I guess the more important question is, What do you think of him?"

"I don't know. Kyle tells me he'd like to see me with someone outside of Hollywood, then he throws me into a pit five feet by ten feet with a good-looking guy and tells me, 'But I don't want to see you with this someone.'"

Lou laughed. "Well, he's right. Ben needs to get his own life in order before he can do justice to sharing it with someone else. But that doesn't make him any less a dear." She turned onto the road toward Lynch Hollow, lifting her foot briefly from the gas pedal to negotiate the first curve. "My favorite story about Ben was the time we had dinner in a little seafood restaurant, somewhere in Ecuador, I think it was. It was just the three of us—Ben, Kyle, and myself—and we had a table right next to the tank where they kept the live lobsters. Well, all the lobsters looked bored and resigned to their fate. But there was this one that was constantly on the move, trying to engage the others in, I don't know what you'd call it, playing or fighting or whatever. He wouldn't give up and we watched him through our entire meal. When it was time to leave, Ben bought him. He thought he was special—a survivor—and shouldn't end up like all the others, as somebody's supper. Then we had to drive about thirty miles out of our way so he could set him free in the Pacific."

Eden stared at her aunt. "That's the most ridiculous thing I've ever heard."

Lou smiled. "If that's what you think, dear, then I doubt Ben's the right man for you."

12

He drove his truck into the Valley as the sun crested the hills, warming the cornfields with its pink morning light. He parked on the shoulder of the narrow road, got out, and began running toward Coolbrook. He had not run in a long time. It used to be a passion. In Annapolis he'd leave the house early in the morning before Sharon and Bliss were up and run along the river, not even counting the miles. It had been thinking time, and back in those days all his thoughts were good.

He'd run a little during his first few weeks in prison, when he still thought he could find a way to survive the experience without losing his spirit. He would stay in shape, he had told himself. Read the classics, study Spanish and French. But the numbness settled in so quickly he wondered if the food was drugged. He'd never watched much TV before, but soon he knew the story lines from the soaps and his dreams were full of game-show drivel. Any extra energy he could dredge from his depression was devoted to keeping his fellow prisoners from learning what he was in for, and for protecting himself when they did. His was not a respected crime.

It was a good sign that he felt like running now. He was coming back to life, like a drowning man surprised to find himself on the surface of the water. It had not taken much to put him there. Just a few simple conversations with a woman who treated him like a person rather than a criminal.

He wouldn't see her for two days. She was working at the archives in Winchester, and tomorrow she would meet with the Children's Fund volunteers in Richmond. She'd told him she visited local Children's Fund headquarters every chance she could, and she'd invited him to go with her, but he'd declined. He could just imagine her introducing him to a bunch of people who work with children. Surely one of them would recognize his name, and that would be the end of that. She'd told him she'd nearly lost her job as spokesperson for the Children's Fund after her role in *Heart of Winter*. "They said I was tampering with my wholesome image," she'd said. Being seen with him wouldn't do her wholesome image much good either.

He arrived in front of the Coolbrook post office and took a minute to stretch and catch his breath before going inside to check his mailbox. There was a large envelope from Sam. Once back on the street he caught his reflection in the mirrored glass of the post office. Christ. He ran his hands through his hair. He looked like an aging hippie.

He stopped at the barbershop, where a small, gray-haired man took great delight in cutting his hair shorter than he requested, and then walked across the street to Miller's Bakery. He bought a doughnut and coffee, which he carried for another block until he reached the park outside the Coolbrook Museum. He sat on a bench, took a swallow of coffee, and opened the envelope.

There were three copies of journal articles and a short note from Sam. He peered into the envelope to see if he might have overlooked a picture of Bliss. Sam sent them sometimes, even though he had to do it behind Jen's back: she thought it would only make things harder for him. How much harder could they get?

He glanced at the title of the first article: "Discrediting the Child Witness." He shook his head and slipped it back into the envelope. He'd told Sam to forget that tack, but Sam seemed determined to leave no stone unturned. The second article was on the same general theme. But the third was a study done by two social workers—"In the Child's Best Interest: The Healing Power of Visitation."

"Yes," Ben said out loud. He took a bite from his doughnut and read the article through, then turned to Sam's note. He wasn't having much luck with the lawyer, Sam wrote. An appeal seemed out of the question at this point. The best they could hope for was supervised visitation and they might get a chance at that in January. Only thing was, they'd have to get approval for it from Judge Stevens. Ben groaned. Stevens had hardly been able to keep the grin off his face when he pulled the future out from under Ben's feet in the courtroom. Ben shouldn't worry, Sam wrote. The evidence that visitation would be the best thing for Bliss was everywhere. He just had to compile it and find a few expert witnesses and they'd be all set.

And by the way, Sam added in a P.S., Sharon and Jeff told him that someone was calling the house and hanging up. They suspected Ben, and they were thinking of getting an unlisted number. So if by some chance it's you calling them, bro, slow it down a bit.

Well, okay, he'd have to give up that little ploy. It hadn't worked anyhow because Sharon always answered. He'd called about once a week, hoping that Bliss would answer. He wouldn't talk to her—he wasn't crazy. He just wanted to listen to her voice. He'd asked Sam and Jen if they could tape a conversation with her and send it to him. He hated that her voice was lost in his memory, that he couldn't recall her tone or the way she strung her words together. She probably sounded different now, anyway. He wanted to hear. "I don't think that's a very good idea, Ben," Jen had said. "You don't need any more reminders of her."

Sam and Jen called him once a week, on Sunday nights. Sam would get on one extension, Jen on the other, and they'd tell him how their adoption plans for a baby were proceeding, how well-adjusted Bliss seemed the last time they saw her. They'd ask him questions about his work. He hadn't told them yet this job would be up in December. He didn't want to worry them. He didn't want to think about it himself.

Sam called him sometimes during the week. At those times Ben knew his brother was playing shrink. "How are you sleeping?" Sam would ask. "How's the appetite?" Once, a long time ago, Sam asked if he felt like killing himself. Ben had managed to laugh that question off in such a way that Sam apologized for even thinking such a thing. It would only worry Sam if he knew the truth. Or, God forbid, he'd try to stick him in a hospital. The last thing he needed. When he thought about doing it, when those pills started calling to him from the bathroom, it was often the thought of Sam that stopped him.

This morning that bottle of pills was ten miles from his body and a thousand from his mind. He stood up and leaned against a tree to stretch his calves. They'd tightened up from sitting. He'd probably have to walk most of the way back to his truck. And he shouldn't have eaten that doughnut. But he started a light jog, and as the diminutive shops of Coolbrook fell behind him and the cornfields took their place, he broke into a run.

13

November 8, 1943

There is a new boy in our class named Matt Riley. He is Kyle's age, seventeen. He and his mother just moved here from Richmond to be closer to his grandmother who is ailing and he is the talk of the class as it's been forever since we had a new face. Kyle particularly likes him. They spent all Saturday fishing together while I wrote.

November 16, 1943

Something shocking happened today.

I usually sit in the great room of my cavern where I have my mattress, the settee, an old rocker and a couple of straight-back chairs. This great room is about the size of a small church but the space is broken up by the different rock formations and the stalactites and stalagmites. The ceiling is low near the entrance, but as you walk farther into the room, towards the reflecting pool at its rear, the ceiling is very high and decorated with stalactites.

Off this room is a tunnel. In all the time I've had my cave, I've never gone into it more than a few feet. Today I was writing a story about a girl who explores a cave. She crawls through a tunnel to discover a spectacular cavern that's been turned into a shrine of some sort.

So I thought, why am I writing about this when I've never even bothered to see where my own tunnel leads? So I took my lantern and stepped into the tunnel. It was spooky! I am not afraid of such things yet the closeness of the walls and ceilings was difficult to bear. At first it was high enough for me to walk upright, but then I had to hunch over. The floor rose steeply and at times I nearly lost my footing. The lantern only lit a few feet in front of me and I felt like I was walking into a black emptiness.

Finally I reached the end. Instead of finding myself in the grand shrine of my story, I was in a huge cave with a low ceiling that had long stalactites dropping from it like spikes and long thin stalagmites growing from the ground to meet them. They met at the level of my waist, forming stone columns, so that to walk through this room I had to twist and turn and I felt like I was in the middle of a giant taffy pull. The lantern knocked into the rocks as I walked and I was trying to keep a sense of direction so I would be able to get out.

Then I saw there was a break in the maze, a small, open area with no tites or mites. Lying on the cave floor was—at first I thought I was wrong and I held my lantern very close—a human skeleton! I screamed so loud my ears hurt from the echo. I backed into the maze again and in a panic tried to find the tunnel. It took me minutes and by that time I was partly crying and partly laughing and the skin on my legs and arms was scraped from the rocks. I got through the tunnel as fast as I could and ran outside the cave and didn't stop running until I reached the far end of Ferry Creek where Kyle and Matt were fishing. I grabbed Kyle's arm. "You've got to come with me!" I said.

"What are you doing with that lantern?" he asked.

I was still carrying the lit lantern, out in bright daylight. "Just come with me!" I said.

Kyle sighed like I was a terrible bother and started reeling in his line. "Let's go see what she wants," he said to Matt.

"No!" I said. "Matt can't come."

Kyle looked at me with his mouth hung open like he couldn't believe I could be that rude, but I didn't care.

"Kyle," I said in a voice too low for Matt to hear. "It's the cave."

Kyle turned to Matt who was pretending not to be interested in any of this. "I'll be back as soon as I can. You can use my pole too."

Matt nodded without looking at us—he is strange, but I have no time to write about that just now.

I explained what I'd found on the way back to the cavern so he was prepared by the time we got to the little maze room. We each had a lantern now and I was shivering from the cold and my nerves. The tites and mites cast shadows everywhere that we moved as we walked through the maze.

I expected the skeleton to be gone because by now I'd convinced myself it was only my imagination that I'd seen it at all, but there it was, laid out like its owner had died in his sleep.

Kyle's face went white as he knelt down next to it. "God," he said, looking from the skull to the toes and back again.

"I screamed like a girl when I saw it," I admitted.

"You are a girl," Kyle said, still staring at the bones. "And Matt's noticed that. He likes you."

"I don't like him," I said.

"Look how small this is." Kyle stretched his six foot body down next to the skeleton. He was nearly twice as long as the bones. "It must of been a child."

That made me feel sad. "How did it get here?" I asked. "When did it get here?"

Kyle shook his head. "We should tell someone about this," he said as he stood up.

"No! They'd come in my cave."

"Kate, this was a human being. We can't just act like we didn't find it."

"We're not telling," I said. "It's my cavern and I say we don't tell."

November 20, 1943

I named the skeleton Rosie. I haven't returned to the maze room to look at her and at first I was uncomfortable in the cave, knowing she was at the end of the tunnel. But now that I've given her a name I feel more comfortable in her company. I wonder sometimes what killed her. An accident? Murder? Disease? I guess I'll never know.

I am more envious of Matt Riley than of Sara Jane. Kyle spends so

much time with him. They are like brothers and at times they joke with each other in a way that leaves me out. When they see I don't get it, one of them explains the joke to me but by then it's no longer funny.

Matt's grandmother died last week. He has been red-eyed since. He is a very soft boy and feels things too sensitively. He looks young and girlish compared to Kyle, who can pass as a man these days.

Kyle is begging me to let Matt into the cavern. I've decided to let him, not because I want Matt there but because Kyle visits so infrequently these days and this is the only way I can think of to get his company back.

14

Eden needed to tell Ben about the skeleton. At least that's what she told herself when she called for an invitation up to his cabin. He'd sounded pleased as he gave her directions. "It's hard to find after the sun's down," he said. "Do you want me to meet you somewhere instead?"

She thought of their grisly date at Sugar Hill. "No, I'll find it."

The moment she hung up, Michael called. It had been only a few days since she'd last spoken to him, yet it seemed like months. Nina was upset about her, he said. She wanted to know what Eden thought of the script she'd sent.

"Haven't looked at it yet," Eden said.

"She says she has a few more for you to see if you don't like that one. She wants to know if you ever plan to work again."

"Tell Nina to relax."

"She doesn't like having you three thousand miles away from her. Out of her control, you know?"

Eden grinned into the phone. "Well, I like it."

Michael was silent. "You like being that far from me, too?"

"I just needed a break from the whole scene. From L.A. I didn't even realize it till right now. Don't take it personally."

"You sound like you're getting a hillbilly accent or something."

Did she? "I'm getting in character early, I guess." She glanced out the window at the dusky woods. She wanted to get to Ben's before dark. "I've got to run, Michael."

"Where are you going?" He sounded hurt.

"I need to see a friend of Kyle's."

"Call me when you get back?"

"I'm not sure what time that'll be."

"Doesn't matter. I'm not going out. Parties aren't the same if I'm not getting high. Or if you're not there. Aren't you proud of me? Three weeks straight."

She had told him that one reason she could not consider a serious relationship with him was his cocaine use. "That's great, Michael."

"Have you found out anything about Matthew Riley?"

"My mother writes in her journal that he's overly sensitive and girlish."

"Whoa! If you want me in that role, you'd better bend the truth a little."

"We'll see. Gotta go now."

"Eden? Don't forget I'm here, okay? I love you."

She cringed. "'Bye, Michael. Thanks for calling."

She took pains with dressing, finally deciding on khaki pants and a plain white shirt. She let her hair down and actually sneaked out of the house. Kyle and Lou knew where she was going, but she didn't want them to see how she looked. Her appearance would give her away tonight: they would be able to see in her face that this evening meant something to her.

She drove first to Coolbrook to pick up fried chicken and biscuits and then headed back past Lynch Hollow and into the hills. Ben's cabin was about seven miles above Lynch Hollow. There was no address, only landmarks to guide her. The car filled with the smell of fried chicken as she passed the big oak, the farm by the creek. She pressed the gas pedal harder.

What was she doing? She'd been cold, practically rude, to the man she'd been seeing for months because she was anxious to see a man she barely knew. A man who rescued lobsters from seafood restaurants. Well, she needed to tell him about the skeleton. Ha! If she had not read about the skeleton in the journal she would have had to invent a reason to see him tonight. She hadn't seen him in two days. She'd spent all of yesterday at the archives in Winchester and most of this morning in Richmond, giving a pep talk to the Children's Fund volunteers. Then she'd had lunch with Fred Jenkins, the dynamic blind director of the Virginia Children's Fund. By this afternoon she could no longer remember the shape of Ben's hands or whether his eyes were blue or gray, and that mattered to her in a way that nothing had mattered in a long time.

She almost missed the cabin. It was tiny, tucked so thoroughly into the trees that all she could see from the road was the amber light of the two small front windows.

"I like it," he called from the open front door before she had even gotten out of her car. "Your hair down."

"Thanks." She handed him the bag of chicken. "You got a haircut. Looks good."

"What's that?" He pointed to the notebook in her hand.

"Part of the journal. There's something I want you to see in it."

He pushed the door open for her. He wore jeans and a T-shirt that had once been red or purple but had faded to a mauvey pink that looked good against his tanned arms. "Sorry it's so hot in here."

It was hot. The cabin was the size of her bedroom in Santa Monica and purely functional. The floor was bare wood. The tiny kitchen in one corner held a small refrigerator, a two burner stove, and a sink. A sofa and chair, both upholstered in an industrial-strength brown plaid, sat in a second corner next to a wood-burning stove. Newspapers and books littered the heavy wood-plank coffee table, and a fan in the window above the stove blew hot air across the room. The third corner housed a small closet or, more likely, a bathroom. Ben's bed was in the fourth corner, in front of one of the two front windows. The bed was somewhere between twin size and full, with no head—or footboard. It was covered by a blue-and-white quilt which stood out in the room for its handmade beauty. In the center of the room stood a round table with spindly legs and four wooden straight-backed chairs.

"Sorry this place is so small." Ben looked around him as if he'd just noticed the size of his cabin. "And primitive."

"It's rustic," she said, her tone complimentary. She looked at Ben. Despite his rugged demeanor he did not belong in this bare little mountain cabin.

"It's a little cooler outside," he said. "Why don't we move the table out there to eat?"

They set the table and two of the wooden chairs in the small clearing in front of the cabin.

"You're really isolated up here," she said. "It must be scary at night."

"Not scary. Just lonely." He had brought a bottle of wine from the cabin and he poured it into plastic glasses. "Sorry about the plastic cups."

"If you apologize for one more thing I'm leaving." She took the wine he offered, hoping it would loosen his tongue a little. She thought of Kyle drunkenly asking Kate for her help in his plight with Sara Jane and began to laugh.

"What's so funny?"

"I'm learning more about Kyle than I ever wanted to know. Do you know the bakery on Main Street?"

"The Millers'?"

"Yes. Do you know Sara Jane Miller?"

"Is she the heavyset woman?"

That he would be so kind in his description of Sara Jane said a lot about Ben, she thought. "Yes. Well, she was Kyle's first."

"First . . . ?" He looked confused for a moment. Then his face broke into a warming smile. "Oh, you mean his first."

She nodded.

Ben set down his glass and laughed. "You really shouldn't tell me things like that. Does Lou know?"

Eden told him how Lou had manipulated her meeting with Sara Jane.

"I should have guessed," Ben said. "Lou and Kyle don't have many secrets between them."

Just one, Eden thought.

"Lou's one of a kind," Ben continued. "She inspires me. When I'm wallowing in self-pity, I think of what she's accomplished with her positive attitude. She's never let her handicap hold her back."

"No, she hasn't." Eden thought of changing the subject, but she wondered how much Ben knew. "Did she tell you how it happened?"

"Car accident. You were with her, right?"

She amazed herself by considering the truth, but settled for the lie. "Yes."

"She said she was going too fast and a station wagon plowed into her."

"She makes it sound like it was her fault."

"She drives like a maniac," Ben said. "You were lucky you weren't hurt."

Eden sipped her wine. "She likes you very much," she said.

"Lou and Kyle have been wonderful to me. They've gone way beyond the call of duty."

She picked the fried crust off her chicken. "What stuns me is that Kyle hasn't censored the journal in any way. If I were him I would have wanted to pull out a few pages here and there."

"Maybe he did want to, but he's an archaeologist. He'd never tamper with an artifact. Besides, he said your mother wanted you to have it, right? She knew what was in it."

"Yeah, but the truth is my mom was a little kooky. She wouldn't care what I learned about her." She leaned forward and rested her elbows on the table. "Tell me about you, Ben. I'm not sure what to ask you because I get the feeling some questions aren't safe to ask."

"Some aren't." He smiled. His eyes were gray, a true gray, pale as mist. "I was born in Maryland. Bethesda. Thirty-eight years ago. I have a brother, Sam, who's a psychiatrist and rich and successful. My father was a doctor, my mother a nurse. They died a few years ago within a couple of months of each other."

"Oh, I'm sorry."

Ben took a bite of chicken before he answered. "Well, it was lousy for Sam and me," he said, "but really best for them in a way. I couldn't imagine one of them living without the other."

"Did you always want to be an archaeologist?"

"Since I was a teenager. I like examining the past. It's safer than the future. Not too many surprises."

"Do you miss teaching?" she plowed ahead. He was still talking, still comfortable.

"Yes, I guess I do." He tossed a shred of his biscuit to a squirrel at the edge of the clearing. "I liked standing up in front of people, trying to make what I had to say entertaining enough so they'd get something out of it. I liked working with really bright students who showed a lot of promise." He shrugged. "But, you know, it's nice to be in the field, too."

"Do you miss . . . what was your wife's name?" More dangerous ground, but he didn't seem put off by the question.

"Sharon? I miss the life we used to have. We had so many plans, and we'd done a lot together that's hard to just forget, you know?"

She nodded, thinking of her own marriage. She and Wayne had done amazingly little together over the fifteen years they'd been married. Cassie had been their only common thread.

He put down his chicken and leaned forward. "I designed the house we lived in. That had always been a goal of mine, and we did a lot of the building ourselves. Would you like to see a picture of it?"

"Oh, yes."

He wiped his fingers on his napkin and went into the cabin. When he returned he showed her a snapshot of a beautiful cedar contemporary that she had no trouble at all picturing him in.

"It's wonderful," she said.

"It was on a wooded lot that backed to the water. Not huge—we couldn't afford huge—but it was really nice. Lots of glass. We were in it eight years and I never stopped marveling at what we'd done."

He looked up at her. She saw the glimmer of pride in his eyes and felt his loss.

"Is Sharon still in it?" she asked.

He nodded. "With her new husband. She remarried a couple of months ago, probably about the same time Wayne and his schoolteacher tied the knot." His voice was quiet, his pain almost tangible as it hung above the wobbly table.

"Something is terribly wrong," she said.

He looked up, alarmed.

"No, not here. I mean, you've been gypped somehow."

His laugh was bitter. "No kidding."

"You had a special house, a good job. I don't care how vicious a divorce is, people don't lose everything unless they've done something outrageous or . . ."

He shook his head, touched her hand. "You said there was something in the journal you wanted me to see."

She shoved her plate aside and leaned toward him, arms on the table. "Ben, do you understand that I know exactly how it feels to lose a marriage? To have the person you love marry someone else?"

"Shhh. I just need a change of topic, okay?" He pushed his chair back from the table. "Where's the journal?"

It was getting too dark to read outside, so they carried the table and chairs into the cabin. She sat on the plaid sofa; he sat in the matching chair.

"My mother found a human skeleton in the cave," she said.

Ben's eyebrows shot up. "What did she do with it?"

"Nothing, as far as I've read. She was only sixteen when she found it. She wasn't interested in archaeology yet."

"Did you ask Kyle about it? Is it still there?"

"I didn't mention it to him." When she'd told Kyle she was having dinner with Ben tonight he'd shaken his head at her. "You need to be very careful, honey," he said, and she was so bothered by his words that she didn't ask him anything else.

She opened the notebook to the entry from November 16 and read it to him. Ben laughed when she had finished. "Your mother was a pip," he said. "Who's this Matt guy?"

"My father." She smiled. "This is my introduction to him."

"Your mother seems very fond of him." Ben snickered.

"It's only 1943 and I wasn't born until 1955. I think it's going to be fun to see how her feelings for him change. I want her to have one great passionate love affair. Can't you picture it in the movie? The way their relationship will grow as they mature into adults? Great sensual tension. Michael Carey's going to play Matt. How young a character do you think he could get away with?"

"In terms of looks, maybe twenty-one or—two with a little makeup. In terms of behavior, fifteen or so."

She laughed. "You don't like him much, huh?"

"I'm jealous."

"You don't need to be."

He sighed and set the notebook on the coffee table. "I'll ask Kyle tomorrow about the skeleton, but probably it's nothing or he would have told me. If it were any older than a couple hundred years it would increase Lynch Hollow's value as an archaeological site, so surely he would have done something about it if that were the case. Skeletons don't last more than a few hundred years anyhow. Unless it was really dry in that part of the cave. Your mother did say the tunnel was on an incline, huh? It's possible."

Eden was no longer listening. She had spotted a photograph of a little girl on the mirror above his dresser. She walked over to the dresser and plucked it from between the glass and the frame.

"Is this your daughter?"

"Yes."

She carried the picture back to the sofa and sat down again. The girl had long, straight platinum-blond hair with deep bangs above wide gray eyes. "She's adorable. She has your eyes."

"Yes."

"What's her name?"

"Bliss."

"Bliss?" Eden smiled.

"Yeah. We had two girls' names picked out and hadn't decided between them by the time she was born. When I saw her in the nursery at the hospital the name Bliss just popped into my mind. I was thinking that someone with that name could never be unhappy." He rubbed his palms on his thighs. "A little naive of me, I guess."

"You miss her."

"God, yes."

Eden leaned forward. "Is money the reason you aren't having

her visit this summer? You shouldn't let that stop you. You don't need money to love a child. You and she could have such a special relationship out here, something she'd always remember. You can teach her about nature and the site and give her plenty of things nine-to-five fathers with loads of money can't begin to touch."

"Eden." He stood up and took the photograph from her fingers. "I just can't talk about this." He walked over to the dresser and slipped the picture back into the mirror, and she felt a wall go up between them, as it had at Sugar Hill.

"I'm sorry," she said. "I don't seem to know when to shut up."

"It's not you, it's me." He stood in front of the small stereo, hands in his pockets. "What kind of music do you like to dance to?"

"Anything."

He put on a tape of oldies. The first song was slow, and he held out his hand to her. She took it reluctantly. "Are you going to push me away again like you did the other night?"

"No." He drew her against him.

She shut her eyes and an agreeable dizziness filled her head. She drank in the subtle scent of his after-shave, the laundered smell of his shirt. He tightened his arms around her. The pressure of his thigh between hers seemed something more than accidental. Be very careful, honey. She returned the pressure, and he groaned. He lifted her chin with his fingertips and kissed her softly, but she backed away from him, although her arms still circled his neck.

"I'm afraid to get any closer to you," she said. "You won't let me know you. If I get close I'm afraid you'll disappear."

He laughed. "You summed up my insecurities perfectly. I'm afraid if I let you know me, you'll disappear."

"Why would I do that?"

"Other people have."

"What could you tell me that would be so awful?"

"Shhh." He pulled her against him again. "Let's just dance. It's safer than kissing, and definitely safer than talking."

The music quickened and they danced to every song on the tape, sometimes touching, sometimes not. She felt the wine and the heat. She liked watching him move. And she liked to imagine how this cabin would look from outside, from deep in the woods, where the music could just be heard and two shadows moved dizzily in the amber light.

Maybe Sharon had kidnapped Bliss. Parents did that sometimes, ran off with the kids for one reason or another. But Sharon was still in their house, so that didn't fit. What did it matter? She didn't need to know his secret. Let him have it. She would focus on the here and now. Forget the past.

When the next slow song came on she didn't wait for him to reach for her before settling into his arms. She held him tightly, listening to their breathing work out a pattern. The song ended and she looked at her watch behind his head. It was nearly midnight.

"I'd better go," she said without moving, although another song, this one fast, had started.

He lifted her hair and it caught on the damp skin of her neck as he buried his lips just below her ear. She felt his heart beating against her breast and pulled her head back to find his lips. They were warm, and salty from her own perspiration.

"Nice," he said, his mouth on hers.

She thought of the bed, half twin, half full, the beautiful quilt. She wanted him to lay her down on it. She couldn't remember the last time she'd actually wanted a man. Her breasts ached for Ben to touch them. She was her mother's daughter. But there were things to be concerned about these days before you had sex with a stranger. With a jolt she thought of his secretiveness, of Kyle's warning.

"Could you have AIDS?" she whispered.

Ben laughed and took a step back from her. "You really know how to bring a guy back to reality. No, I could not, and where is your mind, woman? I was only kissing you."

She pressed her forehead against his chest so he couldn't see the color in her face. "I don't know how to date," she said.

"Well, that makes two of us. Anyhow, I'm the one who should be worried about getting AIDS. Michael Carey's something of a Casanova."

"That's true, but he and I aren't lovers."

"Right, Eden. What about that scene in *Heart of Winter?*"

"We were acting. We didn't actually do it."

"But after something like that—after you've been that intimate with someone, even if you're only acting—how do you date and not . . . ?"

"I haven't been interested in sex with him." She wondered how much she should say, how vulnerable to let herself be. "I haven't been interested in making love to anyone since Wayne. And I wasn't very interested in making love to him, either."

He was quiet, his face serious, his eyes on hers. Then he kissed her forehead. "I'd better get you out of here before any more slow songs come on."

Kyle was still up when she got home, although it was close to one.

"You waited up," she said, feeling a mixture of annoyance and gratitude.

"No, no." He raised himself slowly from his chair and handed her a notebook. "Just reading your next journal installment. Did you have a nice evening?" She didn't miss the worry in his voice.

"I like him, Kyle, but I haven't completely disregarded your warning." She had almost forgotten that an hour ago she wanted this man to make love to her on his quilt.

Kyle smiled at her. "You know, there was a time many years ago when I thought of fixing you up with him. My favorite two young people. I thought I could send him out to California and you'd fall in love with him and he'd bring you back to us."

She felt a little stab of very old guilt. "I had a dream for myself, Kyle, and I had to go after it."

"I know." He put his hand on her back and steered her toward the stairs. "Ultimately I guess it was the right thing for you. I just wish it hadn't driven such a wedge between us." At the bottom of the stairs he caught her elbow, turned her to face him. "Has Ben told you anything about . . . his marriage breaking up?"

"No, but I've decided it doesn't matter. I'm only here for the summer—I'm not planning to marry the guy. We don't need to know all the gory details of each other's pasts." She started up the stairs and then stopped to look back at her uncle. He hadn't moved. "If I knew, would it change the way I feel about him?"

"There's a good chance of that, honey."

"Then I don't want to know."

15

We have become something of a threesome, Kyle, Matt and I. At school now, when Kyle is off with Sara Jane, Matt sits with me on the stoop to read. He doesn't expect me to talk to him, just accepts me as I am and I like that about him. Although he is still pretty as a girl, with his dark eyes and black hair, in just these few months since I've known him his features have taken a more masculine turn and his voice has deepened to a pitch I like to hear in the cavern. He has the proper amount of reverence for the cave and I have complete trust in him.

I have even read my stories to him. He calls them "children's stories" and I realized he is right about that because although I'm now sixteen and a half, the children in my stories are never older than twelve.

I just reread this and it sounds as if I'm as close to Matt as I am to Kyle. This is not at all true. I don't talk much to Matt, but that is fine because he himself is a quiet person. Often, Kyle and I have conversations with Matt just looking on, smiling at us. Last night Kyle and I spoke about how he keeps Sara Jane from getting pregnant (he uses trojans, which are disgusting but apparently work). Matt said he couldn't believe we would talk about such a private thing and Kyle said there was nothing we didn't know about one another, that we are each other's best friend, now and forever.

April 3, 1944

Matt's mother had a terrible accident last week. A neighbor who had just learned to drive drove them both to the market and the car's brakes went out and they hit a tree. Matt's mother is in the hospital and she can't move her legs. Matt has been quieter than usual this week at school and in class. I watch him stare out the window, or fold and unfold the edge of the paper he's supposed to be writing on til it falls apart. At recess he sits next to me on the stoop, his book on his knees, never turning the pages.

Last night he came to the cavern for the first time since the accident. Kyle was in the rocker and I was on my mattress and we were quizzing each other on our spelling words. Matt sat down on the settee and began to cry. Kyle set his book down and was next to Matt in a flash, asking him what was wrong.

"The doctor said she's permanently paralyzed," Matt said. "She'll never be able to walk again."

I moved to the settee too and Kyle and I both put our arms around Matt while he cried. My arms were around Matt, but my hands were on Kyle's shoulders and I had the feeling, not of comforting Matt, but of holding on to both of them because we are still at war and very soon I will lose my brother and our friend and I cannot bear it. They plan to enlist as soon as they graduate. I didn't realize I was crying too until I felt Kyle wipe the tears from my cheeks with his fingers.

Later, after Matt left, Kyle told me I must be in love with Matt to have reacted so strongly to his crying.

"No, I'm not," I said. "I like Matt but I don't want him or anyone else as a boyfriend."

"He's in love with you too," Kyle said as if I hadn't spoken.

"Kyle, I'm not in love with him!"

"Sure." Kyle smiled at me like he knew more about me than I know about myself and then went off to meet Sara Jane, with his trojans in his pocket.

June 5, 1944

I haven't slept for days. At night, I lie awake in my bed, watching the moonlight as it moves from one side of the ceiling to the other and finally disappears in the dawn. I listen to the sounds: Kyle's breathing from the other bed, a few night calling birds, a few cicadas, though it's still early in the season. In the middle of the night I hear Daddy and Susanna's bed start its rhythmic creaking. Sometimes Susanna cries out but most times she doesn't and I don't feel a thing listening to them. I don't remember the last time I felt the urge to touch myself down there. I know if I try it will be like touching dead wood.

In another week Kyle will be gone. Oh, why must he go? Why did he have to graduate when we are at war? He is excited about leaving. I lie awake thinking of Susanna's brother who died at Pearl Harbor, the other Americans who have died in Europe, and the ones who came back with one leg gone or worse, and I think, selfishly, of what my days will be like working without him at the mill this summer, going to school without him or Matt. I wish I could quit, but Daddy says no.

At least Matt is not enlisting. His mother is home now and he is her nurse. He turns her in bed to keep sores from forming, he gives her the bed pan, he bathes her. It is a horrible existence for him. There is a neighbor woman who cares for her for a few hours in the morning so he can finish out this school year and graduate.

The only other person who is as sad as I am about Kyle leaving is Sara Jane. At school, her nose is always red and she clings to Kyle, but Kyle is unable to offer sympathy to either of us. He won't miss us. He believes he has an adventure ahead of him and maybe he does.

June 13, 1944

Kyle is gone. We had a party for him last night, Daddy and Susanna, Sara Jane, Matt and I. We fed him chicken and cake and told jokes and tried to laugh. I watched Kyle's face and I could see he had already left. His eyes were faraway, full of his new life.

Towards the end of the evening, Sara Jane pulled Kyle outside, where

I'm sure they said their long, sappy goodbye while I cleaned up. I didn't see him again til he came to bed. He sat down on my bed and told me he'd miss me more than anyone. I said I would miss him, too. I was trying hard not to cry. Then he got a real serious look on his face.

"I want you to promise me something," he said.

The only thing I couldn't promise him, I thought, was to become friends with Sara Jane.

"Promise me you'll leave the cave. I mean, leave it. Close it up. It's not normal to spend so much time there."

"I don't care about being normal," I said.

"The cavern's from your childhood and you're not a child anymore. You don't need it."

Yes I do, I thought to myself. But the last thing I wanted tonight was to argue with Kyle.

"All right," I said.

Kyle smiled and leaned over to hug me. I started crying then and he stroked my hair and told me everything would be all right, that he'd be home before I knew it, and all in one piece to boot.

August 22, 1944

Matt is the prettiest man I've ever seen. Last night I watched him as he read in the cavern by lantern light and I wished I was a painter so I could make proper use of his beauty. He always looks like he should be on stage—his eyes are so dark and his lashes so thick that he looks like he's wearing mascara. His lips are very full and in the lantern light, a pale rose color. I was certain that if I touched them with my fingertips they would feel like velvet.

I know Kyle told him to look out for me. He sits in the rocker or on the settee and reads while I write. I want him to be here. I want his quiet companionship, yet I feel guilty because not only am I still in the cavern after promising Kyle I would leave it, but I have made Matt dependent on it as well. If I were in love with him as Kyle thinks, it would be all right. But I am not and Matt should be meeting some girls who would appreciate him better than I do.

For my seventeenth birthday a couple of weeks ago, Matt bought me a typewriter! (I think he has a lot of money saved up from when his father died.) The typewriter is big and black and wonderful. At first I was very reluctant to use it, but Matt gave me a book that shows how to type and now I am good at it. I've got it on a little table in front of one of the straight backed chairs. It echoes horribly in the cave so I put cotton in my ears when I use it, and I only use it before Matt arrives in the evening so as not to disturb his reading.

I can't believe the way my words look in print!

October 3, 1944

School is horrid. I'm more nervous there than ever, like I am when I'm in town. I've moved my seat so it's right near the door because that's the only place I can breathe in there.

Sara Jane brings her letters from Kyle to share with Priscilla. I believe she's gotten more from him than I have and it disgusts me that she reads them to Priscilla. I'm sure Kyle didn't mean his words to be heard by anyone but Sara Jane. Sara Jane is getting fat.

October 15, 1944

There is a large, fast-growing bush next to the entrance of the cavern and every few weeks I hack back its branches to let in the sunlight. Yesterday I decided to dig it up and be done with it once and for all.

It was a hard job and took me most of the morning because the roots went very deep. After I'd pulled out the bush and carried it over to Ferry Creek, I started to fill in the hole. Then I spotted something in the bottom of the hole and lifted it up with my spade. It was an arrowhead, perfectly chiseled and unmistakable for anything else. I dug around a little more and found a second, less perfect than the first but still obviously something that had been carefully made by someone.

When Matt came that evening it was too dark to dig further but we decided to look for more next weekend. I keep thinking about Rosie the skeleton and wondering if her family was connected to these arrowheads. Maybe I'm not the first person to live in this cavern?

December 22, 1944

Matt asked me to a Christmas party at Priscilla's. I was not directly invited, but I don't blame Priscilla for that. She probably figures if she asked me I would say something nasty back to her and there is a chance I might have.

I told Matt no at first and he said he expected me to say that, but he wanted to ask me anyway. Matt understands me. He never demands anything of me.

He said he wished I'd reconsider because he wanted to get out and he didn't want to go alone, so I finally agreed to go. It is tomorrow night and I am nervous.

December 24, 1944

Matt borrowed his neighbor's car to take us to the party. He drives very slowly because he really doesn't know how.

I couldn't think of what to wear because all I have is dungarees and skirts that are only fit for school. Susanna said I could borrow something of hers but she is too tall for me to fit in her clothes.

So I wore nothing. Just my heavy brown coat.

I figured I'd better tell Matt before we got there. In the car he looked over at me and said I looked very pretty. I had tied my hair back with a red bow. I thanked him and then said, "I don't have anything on under this coat."

"You mean, nothing special."

"No, I mean nothing." I hadn't even worn underwear and the lining of my coat felt cold against my bare skin. Now that we were halfway there I was feeling some regret at my decision, but Matt laughed.

"I don't believe you," he said.

I unbuttoned my coat and opened and shut it quickly and he gasped and stepped on the brakes so that we skidded to the side of the road. And there we sat. He stared at me speechlessly and then suddenly started laughing. We both laughed so hard tears rolled down our cheeks. When he could talk he said, "You are the most unusual person in the world, Kate." Then he started the car and we continued on to the party.

I think even Kyle would have turned the car around to take me home to change. Maybe that's what I was hoping would happen.

Of course at the party I couldn't take my coat off and had to be careful how I sat and Matt kept grinning at me over the secret we shared. Everyone from our class was there (I guess I was the only person who hadn't been invited). Plus Getch who graduated last year and what seemed like a dozen of Priscilla's cousins. She has a cousin our age in every town around here.

That feeling of not being able to breathe came over me real fast as I was sitting there trying to be polite. Nobody was talking to me, which was fine because I like the feeling of being invisible. Matt was talking to a boy he knew and I finally had to get up and leave the room. I started exploring Priscilla's house. It is a large old white farmhouse. Priscilla's family isn't rich but you would think so by the size of her house.

The downstairs rooms were all full of partiers so I walked upstairs where I could get my breath easier. It was wonderful up there, dark and quiet like the cave. I started quietly down the hall but stopped when I heard sounds coming from the end of the hall. I let my eyes get used to the darkness and saw that it was a girl and a boy, and it was not so dark that I couldn't tell what they were doing. I got a glimpse of the boy's naked backside before I stepped into an open doorway. I was embarrassed at first and I just stood there shaking, hoping they hadn't seen me.

It went on a long while and I was afraid to leave the room for fear they'd see me. I thought for sure I was going to pass out. Finally I could hear them talking and putting their clothes back in order. Their voices got louder as they walked down the hall, and by the time they walked past the room where I was hiding, they were laughing up a storm. I peeked out—I just couldn't help myself—and saw that the girl was Sara Jane!

I hate her! She may as well have stuck a knife in my side for all the pain I felt just then. My brother is fighting for his country and she is cheating on him.

I jumped out of the room behind them.

"Sara Jane!" I said.

She turned around, but it was too dark for me to see the expression on her face.

"Kate? Is that you?" she asked.

"I saw you," I said.

"Who is that?" the boy with her asked. I recognized him. His name is Tommy Miller and his father owns the bakery in Coolbrook.

"No one," Sara Jane said, not making me feel any more kindly towards her. "Kate, I don't know what you're talking about."

"I saw you fucking." It was the first time I ever used that word, but it won't be the last. I loved the way it sounded when it came out of my mouth and it wasn't too dark to see the horror in Sara Jane's face when I said it. Her face is as big and fat as a pumpkin.

"It's your imagination, Kate," Sara Jane said, right calmly. She turned to Tommy. "Kate writes stories. She has a very vivid imagination."

"Ah," said Tommy, as if that explained everything and the problem was solved.

"Let's go back to the party," Sara Jane said, to both of us. I followed them down the stairs, thinking the whole way about pushing her head over heels to the floor.

Downstairs, I found Matt in the middle of a group of Priscilla's cousins (all girls) who were captivated by his dark eyes. I was shaking and felt sick as a dog. I wanted to ask him if we could leave, but I hated to take him away when he looked as if he was enjoying himself. I was going to tell him I'd wait for him outside, but he must have seen I was upset because he excused himself from the girls and took my arm.

"Ready to go if you are," he said.

Once in the car I told him what I'd seen and he said I should tell Kyle. "If I were in his shoes I'd want to know what she was doing behind my back."

I wasn't sure, and I'm still not sure. It might be better to learn the truth about her when he gets home and has Matt and me to cheer him up. If I wrote to him about it—well, I can picture him opening the letter and having no one to talk it over with. It would upset him. It might affect his concentration just when he needs to be alert and looking out for himself.

16

Rain pelted the thin cabin roof and Ben sat up to look out the window. A downpour. He switched on the radio he kept under his bed and listened for the weather report. Rain until late afternoon, clearing this evening. Damn. That meant no work at the site, no chance to see Eden.

He watched drops of rain falling from the ceiling near the bathroom, a puddle forming on the floor below. He could spend the day working on that leak. Or reading. Maybe write a letter to Sam. He smiled to himself because for the first time in months he had not even considered suicide as an alternative to spending a day alone.

Kyle called just as Ben was getting out of the shower. "Do you want to join us for a barbecue tonight?" he asked. "Just hamburgers and such. Rain's supposed to quit around four."

Ben grinned, tightened the towel around his waist. "Yeah, I would. Thanks."

"And listen, Ben," Kyle continued. "I'm worried about you and Eden. She hasn't been divorced all that long, you know. She puts on a good show—that's her forte—but she's still a little on the shaky side."

"So am I," he said, hurt.

"You have to tell her the truth about your divorce."

"I will, Kyle. But I need some time. It's not the kind of thing you can just blurt out to someone."

"You're not being fair to her."

He didn't want to hear that. "I wanted her to get to know me before I told her, so she'd believe me."

"Sharon knew you for a decade and she still didn't believe you."

Ben flinched as the cruelness of Kyle's remark cut through him.

"I'm sorry," Kyle said when Ben didn't respond. "I'll go to bat for you after you tell her, Ben. I'll tell her I think you were railroaded. But it's only fair she know the truth."

"And I'll tell her." He felt his voice rise and worked to lower it. "Just not quite yet. I'd like to feel like a normal person leading a normal life for a change. And Kyle?" He hoped Kyle would let him change the subject. "She told me about the skeleton in the cave."

"What about it?" Kyle's voice was ice.

"Well . . ." Ben hesitated. He had never felt this awkward talking to Kyle before. "What happened to it?"

"There were three actually," Kyle said after a moment's pause. "I went in to take a bone from the one in the late fifties when radiocarbon dating caught on. I found a couple more back there."

"And . . . ?"

Kyle took a long time to answer. "Two thousand B.C.," he said finally.

Ben stood up. "Why didn't you tell me this?"

"It's moot, that's why. The skeletons are in the cave—the cave is sealed and is going to stay sealed."

"But Kyle, those skeletons could give a whole new meaning to the site." Just yards away from the pits was a chance to save Lynch Hollow.

"The subject's closed, Ben."

Ben was quiet for a moment. He was completely unaccustomed to Kyle's anger. "I was just thinking of the grant," he said softly.

"I'll tell Lou and Eden you're coming tonight?"

"Yes, please." He hung up with a heaviness in his chest. He'd stop by the liquor store and pick up some of Kyle's favorite grape brandy. And he wouldn't mention the skeleton again. But what should he do about Eden? He had to tell her, but he knew what would happen when he did. He'd lose what little he had of her. He'd be alone again. Kyle was right. How could he expect Eden to believe him when even his own wife thought he was guilty?

17

Even in the rain Eden could smell the aroma of baking bread as she climbed the outside stairs to the apartment above Miller's Bakery. Sara Jane opened the door for her before she reached the landing.

"Come on in, Miss Riley. Why, you're soaked right through!"

Eden left her umbrella on the landing and stepped into the small living room, where the yeasty smell filled the air. She felt it settle on her damp skin and lace itself through her hair, and she knew she would carry this scent with her for the rest of the day.

The living room was exactly what she had expected: dark green carpeting, yellow floral wallpaper, family photographs crowding the top of the television. Three children giggled together from behind the toothpick-thin legs of a tall, balding man, and two women—one about Eden's age, the other a little older—sat together on the couch, grinning at her.

"Oh, I hope you don't mind this." Sara Jane swung one helium-filled arm through the air. "But they all wanted to meet you. Janie has her little autograph book out and all. Soon as they say hi, they'll be going and you and I can talk in private about the movie."

Eden smiled. "Well, who's who?" She peeked at one of the little girls, who shrank, giggling, deeper behind her grandfather's legs.

"This here's my husband, Tom." Sara Jane grabbed the elbow of the dangerously thin man and drew him forward.

"Pleased to meet you, Miss," he said as she shook his hand. "We're big fans of yours. No one round here ever misses an Eden Riley picture."

"Thanks," Eden said. "And please call me Eden."

The man nodded. "Well, if you'll excuse me, I'll get you gals some refreshments." He stepped out of the room and Eden lowered herself to her haunches.

"And who are these three?"

Without Tom's legs to hang on to the two smaller girls clung to the arms of the older child, who thrust a blue autograph book toward Eden.

"Grandkids," said Sara Jane. "They belong to Maggie there."

Eden looked over at the sofa where the two women sat. One of them, Maggie presumably, had a wry, bored smile on her face, and she gave Eden a little salute. Eden noticed with a jolt that the woman next to her had no arms, just hands dangling from her shoulders. She kept her smile in place and turned back to the little ones.

"Now come on, Janie," Sara Jane said. "Get your autograph and then you got to be on your way."

Eden signed Janie's book and talked with the two younger girls for a minute before standing again. Then Maggie rose from the couch, stretched, and kissed her mother's cheek. "We'll get out of your way, Mama." She shook Eden's hand, while the little girls latched on to their mother's legs. "*Heart of Winter* was hot." She gave Eden a conspiratorial grin, as if she and Eden were the only people in the room who could understand what she meant. "Is Michael Carey as good as he looks?"

Eden laughed. "I hate to disappoint you, Maggie, but I wouldn't know."

Sara Jane gave her daughter a little shove. "Hush, Maggie, now get out of here. Miss Riley doesn't have all day, I'm sure."

Once Maggie was gone, Eden braced herself and turned to face the woman on the couch. She was strikingly pretty, although her round face was beginning to bloat like her mother's. "I'm Eden," she said. She stopped herself from reaching out her hand.

"This is Eleanor, our first daughter," said Sara Jane. "Say hi, Ellie."

Ellie smiled. "Hi. You're the beautiful witch." Her words were heavy and slurred.

"That's right. Did you like that movie?"

Ellie nodded as Tom returned to the room with a tray laden with cinnamon buns and a teapot.

"Ellie was a favorite of your mama's," Sara Jane said.

Eden started to say, "She was?" then caught herself.

"C'mon, Ellie." Tom tugged at his daughter's shoulder. "Let's give your ma and Miss Riley some privacy." Ellie rose obediently and followed her father out of the room with a foot-dragging gait that put a lump in Eden's throat.

Once they had left the room, Sara Jane let out an enormous sigh, then turned to smile at Eden. "Have a seat, dear." She pointed to the sofa and Eden sat down and pulled her tape recorder from her purse. Sara Jane stopped pouring the tea and her eyes widened. "You're going to tape me?"

"I'd like to. Do you mind?"

"No, I guess not. I'm delighted as could be you want to speak to me. I hope I can help."

"I really appreciate it. I'd like to know about my mother from your perspective. Kyle's is a little biased."

"Oh, your mother was a delightful girl, so pretty and smart." Sara Jane handed Eden her tea. "She could write—even as a young girl. My, how she could . . ."

"Mrs. Miller." Eden smiled. "You don't have to spare my feelings. I want to deal with reality. I don't think anyone thought of my mother as delightful. Plus, I should tell you that she kept a journal from the time she was thirteen, which I have."

Sara Jane's eyes widened. "Does she mention me in it?"

"Yes."

"Oh, Lordy. Well, I'm sure she didn't have anything too kind to say about me."

"But it's obvious that my uncle cared about you."

Sara Jane beamed with pleasure, her skin so flushed that Eden could almost see the blood pulsing beneath it. "Well, you want the truth about your mother? I can give it to you in two sentences. Your mama was crazy. And she was in love with Kyle. She was brighter than the rest of us, and sometimes—well, ignorance can be bliss, you know. I think she had a price to pay for being smart."

"What do you mean, she was in love with Kyle?"

"She had an attachment to that boy that went beyond the typical brother-sister sort of thing, you know? Kyle and I were close friends and—" Sara Jane clamped her little rosebud lips shut and tapped her fingertip against them. "Exactly how much do you know?"

"I know you and Kyle were lovers."

Sara Jane sat up straight, eyes big as angel food cakes. "Oh, my. You don't mince words, now do you? Sort of like your mama. She could be straightforward like nobody else. Well, what I meant about her and Kyle was . . . she wanted to be with him all the time, and he'd sometimes tell me he couldn't go out because he should stay with her, like she was an invalid or something. She was right jealous of me, I know that. I was so glad when Matt—when your father finally came along because she let Kyle go a little."

"What was he like? Matthew Riley?"

"A good match for your ma, that's what. He was smart as she was and bookish like her. Only he was respected where she was just thought of as a little . . . off, you know? When we all found out about the cave, we knew she was even weirder than we'd imagined." Sara Jane bit her minuscule lower lip. "I'm sorry, dear. I'm speaking very rudely to you. But you said . . ."

"That's all right. Go on."

"Of course, when her books started coming out we could hardly believe it was the same girl we knew who'd written them. They were wonderful, but it took me a long time to realize that. I guess I didn't give them a chance at first because I disliked Kate so much. And yet, she had a soft side. That was the most confusing thing about her, something I've never known how to make out. When Ellie was born, and Kate found out about her, about her hands, she came over here to visit. We were about twenty years old at the time, and she rode a bicycle over here from Lynch Hollow. She never went anywhere, so you can imagine my shock when I opened the door and saw her standing there. I didn't trust her a whit. I thought she'd come to make nasty cracks about my baby. But she had an armful of flowers she'd picked for me. And I let her in, mostly because I was too stunned to do anything else. She came in and sat down. She seemed real nervous, but in those days your mama . . . I think she had that sickness where you can't leave your house, you know?"

Eden nodded.

"Anytime I saw her out she had that look, you know, like a scared rabbit, always on the alert for danger. Anyhow, she sat right on that sofa and I brought Ellie out to her and I was ready to tell her if she made one crack about my baby I'd shoot her. But she held Ellie and tears filled her eyes and she let Ellie hold her finger. I'll never forget that. Nobody'd done that, you know, played with Ellie's hands. Everybody except me and Tom avoided them, just pretended they weren't there. I think maybe Kate knew what it was like to be different, you know? She came a time or two after that to visit Ellie, but I think it was hard on her. Once Kyle brought her, but Tom . . . He didn't want Kyle in the house, thought maybe he was trying to start something up with me again." Sara Jane narrowed her eyes at Eden. "Is that going to be in the movie? About Kyle and me being . . . close? Tom knows, of course, but I don't know how he'd like the rest of the world to see it. He was upset last year when Kyle moved back here."

Eden nodded sympathetically, trying not to smile at the thought of Kyle being a threat to Sara Jane's marriage. "I may put it in, Mrs. Miller. I think it's important to understanding my mother's life."

"Oh, Lordy." Sara Jane reached toward the tray. "I need a cinnamon bun."

They talked a while longer, Sara Jane offering a few more anecdotes about Kate and suggesting some people Eden could interview at the *Coolbrook Chronicle* about her father.

"You've been so helpful," Eden said as she stood to go.

"Anytime, dear. I enjoyed it. You want to talk more, just come on over. You don't need to call first." Sara Jane heaved herself out of the chair. "Wait a minute now," she said as she disappeared into the kitchen. She returned a moment later with a bakery box tied with string. "Lemon meringue pie," she said as she opened the door for Eden. "By the way, I admire the work you do with that Children's Fund. I wish they'd had something like that when Ellie was little. Tom and I give money to it every year."

Eden squeezed her hand, touched. "Thank you." She stepped onto the landing and looked up to see a blue sky struggling to break through the clouds. "It's clearing up."

"About time." Sara Jane held the screen door open. "How is your uncle, Eden? I see Lou quite a bit, but Kyle doesn't get into the bakery much."

"He's doing very well, thanks."

"He was something else, your uncle." Sara Jane reddened again. "Now, don't you go telling him I said that."

Eden was lighting the citronella candles on the picnic table when Ben arrived. He stopped first at the grill where Kyle was fanning the coals and handed him a bottle of brandy.

"Peace offering," he said quietly.

Kyle set his hand on Ben's shoulder and Eden wondered what had passed between them that required an offer of peace. She hoped it had nothing to do with her.

Kyle went into the house for the hamburgers and Ben walked over to her. He leaned his head toward hers, and she thought he was going to kiss her cheek, but instead he whispered, "Don't mention anything to Kyle about the skeleton. I spoke to him about it this morning and he nearly snapped my head off."

Ah, so that was it.

He touched her elbow. "Let me say hello to Lou."

She had known, perhaps intuitively, not to talk to Kyle about the skeleton. It was not so much the skeleton that was off limits. It was the cave itself. Kyle had sealed that cave in a fury. He took his anger over Kate's death out on it, and although Eden didn't have her own memories of this, the story grew like a legend that Kyle had single-handedly pushed the largest boulder into the opening while the men from the neighborhood looked on in stupefied silence. No one was to mention the cavern to him again. Somehow everyone knew, then and in the years that followed, to keep their thoughts about the cave to themselves when Kyle was around. Before reading the journal Eden had only partially understood Kyle's sadness over losing his sister. She had not known the bond that existed between them, their dependence on one another. In Kyle's mind the cave had become a living being, responsible for the hold it had over Kate and for making her its victim.

"We have a foursome tonight," Kyle said to Ben during dinner. "You know what that means, don't you?"

Ben caught on immediately. "Tramposo!" he said.

"It's been so long," Lou said. "I'm not sure I can remember the rules."

The men laughed at what was apparently a joke. Ben must have seen Eden's look of confusion. "It's a card game we used to play in Colombia," he explained. "You'll see."

After dinner they sat at the walnut dining room table and played tramposo. Ben was her partner. With his eyes and with his foot beneath the table he cheated shamelessly, letting her know what was in his hand, when she should make a move, when she shouldn't. At first she was uncomfortable. She sent him incredulous stares across the table and did the opposite of what he requested in an effort to put an end to his brazenness. But gradually she realized Kyle and Lou were cheating as well. It was part of the game, a game with no rules. The cheating mounted until the cards themselves were almost immaterial and it boiled down to which team was more skilled at nonverbal communication. It was no contest. Kyle and Lou, with their years of practice at cheating together, slaughtered the competition.

Kyle poured them each a glass of the grape brandy Ben had brought and told her about the first time they'd played tramposo with a few rough sorts in a small Colombian village. They played with three teams: Kyle and Lou, Ben and another archaeologist, and the two Colombians, who upped the stakes by threatening to kill the losers.

"Of course they wouldn't have," Ben said, "but we really weren't sure at the time. They were just trying to get us into the spirit of the game. We cheated like our lives depended on it."

"Desperate people take desperate measures," said Lou.

Eden thought of the few evenings she and Wayne had spent with Kyle and Lou. She had dreaded those visits, and the memory alone was enough to bring on the burn behind her breastbone, the damp palms. It had been nothing more than a duty to visit with these two relatives who had taken her in and from whom she'd fled. The atmosphere on those occasions was always stiff and formal. They would never have played cards. They would never have played a game of any sort. Each of them would have chatted politely about their work: Kyle's latest project, Lou's painting, Eden's movies, Wayne's cases. Conversation that was lifeless, hollow, dry as bone.

Tonight had a completely different quality. She realized now that she and Wayne had set the tone for those evenings, that Kyle and Lou had probably felt the discomfort as keenly as she had. She was jealous of the easy camaraderie between them and Ben. He treated them like peers. Intimates. His love and admiration for them was candid and genuine. She wished she could express her feelings for them so easily.

"Let's move into the living room and have some of that pie Sara Jane sent you home with," Kyle said.

Lou wheeled herself into the living room. "I don't know if I want you to eat any of Sara Jane's cooking, Kyle," she said. "Eden thinks she still has a crush on you."

"'Crush' is the definitive word in that sentence." Kyle laughed as he walked into the kitchen for the pie.

Eden was taking the dessert plates from the china cabinet as Lou started to shift herself from the chair to the sofa. Suddenly the chair slipped out from under Lou's hands, sending her sprawling onto the hardwood floor.

"Lou!" Eden ran to her aunt's side. Lou was struggling to sit up, her skirt up to her thighs and the stump of her right leg flailing the air. Ben was quickly behind her, supporting her back with his arms. Eden pulled Lou's skirt over her knees and helped Ben lift her to the sofa.

"What's going on?" Kyle peered into the room.

Eden opened her mouth to say that Lou had taken a terrible fall, but Ben spoke first. "Lou just took a little tumble," he said. He sat next to Lou on the sofa, his arm across her shoulders.

"Are you all right, Lou?" Kyle asked.

She waved him back to the kitchen with her hand, but she was clearly shaken. Her face was drained of color, and her hand shook violently as she tried to brush the long strands of her salt-and-pepper hair back into her bun. Eden knelt in front of her.

"Are you sure you're okay?"

"I'm fine." But even Lou's voice seemed weakened by the fall.

Ben tightened his arm around her and pressed his lips to her pale temple. "You gave us a scare, Lou," he said. Sitting next to Ben, Lou looked frail enough to break under the weight of his arm.

"Would you like some iced tea? Lemonade?" Eden asked.

"Iced tea," Lou all but whispered as Kyle set the pie on the coffee table.

Once in the kitchen, Eden began to cry. She leaned against the refrigerator and pressed her hands to her face. Her head filled with the image of Lou lying on the floor, her legs thrashing the air in a desperate attempt to right herself. God, she'd kidded herself into thinking Lou didn't suffer.

"Eden?"

She turned to see Kyle in the doorway of the kitchen. He walked toward her. "Lou's okay," he said. "Her pride's hurt more than anything."

"You didn't see it, Kyle. She fell hard. Ben made light of it to spare her embarrassment."

Kyle set his brandy glass on the counter. "I've seen her fall before," he said.

"You mean it happens often?"

"More often than she'd admit to you."

"Maybe she needs a different kind of chair. The Children's Fund makes this chair you can stand up in and—"

Kyle shook his head. "Her chair's fine. I long ago stopped trying to protect her from everything that could possibly happen to her. She doesn't want that, Eden."

Eden's eyes filled again. "I don't want to see her suffer."

Kyle put his arms around her and she didn't resist. For a few minutes she cried softly against his shoulder while he stroked her back. Not since that day in the orphanage a lifetime ago had she let him hold her, and she wondered if he would be holding her now if he knew her part in Lou's tragic loss.

She returned to the living room with the iced tea, but Lou was back in her wheelchair. "I'll take it to bed with me, dear," she said. "I'm tired all of a sudden. I'll just read for a bit."

Kyle wheeled Lou into the bedroom, and Ben looked up at Eden. "You've been crying." He reached up to take her hand. She drew his hand against her leg, and the electricity she'd felt between them the night before shot through her again.

"A little." She looked down at the pieces of pie on the coffee table and shut her eyes. "I'm not hungry."

Ben stood up. "Neither am I. I'm going to go. Walk me out to the truck?"

Cicadas had taken over the night outside, their song rising and falling in gentle waves. The air was still damp from the rain and sweet with honeysuckle. It made Eden feel dizzy. Or drunk. She wasn't sure which and didn't care. When they reached the truck Ben turned her toward him, sandwiching her between the truck and his body.

"I've been waiting all night to do this," he said as he lowered his head to kiss her. She opened her lips, tasted brandy on his tongue. When he finally leaned away from her she was winded, her lungs fighting to pull in the thick, wet air.

"Catch your breath and we'll do it again." He smiled.

She let her head fall back against the cool metal of the truck as he slid his hands from her back to her sides. He raised them slowly until his thumbs rested just shy of her breasts. She wanted more. She felt his hard but uninsistent erection and pressed her hips against him. He drew in a quick, sharp breath, dropping his hands to the seat of her jeans with an intimacy that startled, then pleased her as he pulled her even closer. Her legs turned liquid. She closed her eyes, let her head fill with the sound of cicadas.

"I'm a little tipsy, I think," she said. "Not responsible for what I'm doing."

He laughed. "You know exactly what you're doing. You speak very fluent body language." But then he drew his head away, his hands, his hips, and took a step back from her. "We need to have a talk," he said. "A serious one."

"I don't see why."

"You want to know what ended my marriage and you have a right to know before we . . . before things go any further between us."

She shook her head. "I've thought about it, Ben. I don't see why I need to know anything at all about your past, except what you'd like to tell me. I'm the one who should be talking seriously to you. You have to realize that I live in a different world, and I'll be returning to it at the end of the summer." She had a sudden image of Michael and Nina in her living room in Santa Monica, talking loudly, pushing her, pulling her, and felt a distinct wave of nausea. "Whatever happens between us this summer will have to end."

She couldn't read his face. Then he gave a little nod, a small smile. "Okay. But if you change your mind, about wanting to know, or"—a broader smile now—"about wanting it to end when the summer's over, let me know."

He leaned forward for one small, quick kiss. Then he got into the truck and pulled her hand in through the window. "Tell Lou she better not drink any more of that brandy. And tell her I love her." He cupped all ten of his fingers around her hand. "It's supposed to rain again tomorrow. Would you like to do something? Take a drive? Go to some used-book stores?"

She was suddenly aware of danger, hanging like a scent in the air, mixing with the honeysuckle. Her cavalier speech about leaving at the end of summer might have convinced him but not herself. She shook her head quickly. "No thanks," she said. "I've got to work on the screenplay."

*

Lou was alone in the bedroom when Eden poked her head in the door. "I just wanted to make sure you're all right."

"Come in, dear." Lou patted the edge of the bed. Her color was back. She was propped up by two pillows and she held a hardcover book in her lap. Her hair was loose and hung thick and straight over the shoulders of her pale yellow nightgown. Out of its bun, her hair gave her the appearance of a wise old sage.

Eden sat down on the bed. "You look much better."

Lou took her hand. "I feel like such an old fool when I do things like that. Forgetting to lock the wheelchair. You'd think after all these years it'd be second nature. It's my brain that's the problem, Eden, not my leg."

Eden held Lou's hand as Ben had just held hers, her fingers cupping Lou's protectively. "I know you're trying to ease my guilt about your leg. But you can't. My guilt is here to stay. I'll take it to the grave with me."

Lou stared at her. She can't believe I'm talking about it, Eden thought. "Ben said to tell you he loves you," she added. "And I do too."

Kyle suddenly stepped into the room and Eden looked up to see his surprise at finding her there, holding Lou's hand. "I'm interrupting something," he said.

"We were just having a little chat," Lou said. Her blue eyes had misted over and she blinked to clear them. She smiled at Eden and squeezed her hand.

Kyle stood near the bed, his hands on his hips. "I haven't heard Ben laugh that much in years," he said.

Lou nodded. "And I don't think I've ever seen that look on your face before, Eden."

"What look?" she asked.

"That hungry look." Kyle answered for his wife, and he and Lou both laughed.

Eden felt the color in her cheeks. "Was it that obvious?"

"Yes, but it's also obvious Ben shares your feelings," Lou said.

Kyle let out a great sigh. "I don't want anything to do with wrecking whatever's making the two of you happy. You're both adults. I'm not going to say another word about Ben to you."

She was surprised that his words brought her no relief. She felt a little deserted.

Kyle looked down at his wife. "How're you doing?"

"I'm fine." Lou sounded very sure of herself.

Kyle leaned over and set his hands on Lou's shoulders. He bent low to kiss her lips, and Eden got to her feet. She'd seen affection between her aunt and uncle before, but it had never jarred her in quite this way. This last week had forced her to see Kyle as something other than the solid, simple-hearted man she had always assumed him to be. He was something else, your uncle. He had at one time been an impassioned lover. Perhaps he still was.

She knew by the way Lou looked at him when he pulled away from her that they were still lovers—that tonight Lou would find solace from the evening's trials in his embrace.

19

The next morning was rainy, as promised. Ben looked at his watch. Seven-thirty. Seven-thirty on a Saturday morning. He remembered Saturday mornings long ago, getting up to find Bliss parked in front of the television, a bowl of cereal in her lap, watching cartoons. Why hadn't he thought of that before? She might be the only person up this early.

He reached for the phone and set it next to him on the bed. He took a minute to think this through because he suddenly felt his chances of having her answer were very good. She would answer and . . . what if he spoke to her? He could just say he loved her, he hadn't forgotten her. She had to be confused about his disappearance. How had they explained it to her? He could say . . . But that would be the end, wouldn't it, if he spoke to her? What would they do to him? Jail again? Maybe just a warning? It would be worth a warning. He dialed the number. His pulse throbbed somewhere in his gut.

Someone answered and he sat up in the bed. He heard a metallic click, the static of a tape beginning to play.

The number you have reached has been changed to an unlisted number.

He called again to be certain he'd heard correctly. He had.

He lay down. He was completely cut off from her now. The final blow. It hadn't been much—calling a number, imagining she was in the next room when Sharon answered—but it was all he had. And now he didn't even have that.

If anyone had asked him during the last five years what was most important to him, he would not have had to stop and search for an answer. Nothing—not his career, not his reputation, not his friends, and although he would have balked at having to admit it, not even his marriage—could compare to his attachment to Bliss. He himself had wondered if he was too attached. If anything happened to her he was not certain how he would cope with the loss.

The pleasure he took in Bliss had come as a surprise. He and Sharon had both been absorbed by their careers when they first married, and he'd been comfortable with that arrangement. When Sharon suggested a baby he'd felt indifferent to the idea.

"I have to travel too much," he told her.

"I understand that," Sharon had said. "And I won't expect you to do half the work. You can be one of those daddies who come home on weekends to do all the fun stuff while I wipe runny noses and teach manners."

So they went into childbearing with that agreement, but something changed. He was first aware of the shift in his feelings during Sharon's pregnancy. Every time he returned from a trip, her body had changed again. Her emotions peaked and plummeted, and he felt guilty that he was not with her during the low times and left out when she described feeling the baby move in her belly late at night. He knew she was careful about telling him these things. She had made a bargain with him that she wanted to honor. Still, she was overjoyed when he decided to leave the field for a while and teach so he could be closer to home. He took the job at the university just before Bliss was born.

If anything, the bargain they had struck with one another was the antithesis of what actually happened. With his schedule at the university Ben had more time at home with Bliss than Sharon did. (Yes, they brought this out during the trial, pointing out to the jury just how much time alone he had with his daughter, how he had deliberately arranged his work so as to have that time with her.)

Sharon took on more work for herself at the private high school where she taught, as her comfort grew with Ben's ability to care for Bliss. (She blamed herself later. "Did I push you into it, Ben? I mean, maybe you had those leanings, but if I had been there more often you never would have acted on them.") It was usually Ben who took off work when Bliss was sick. It was Ben who cooked for her, fed her, bathed her. ("Indeed," the prosecuting attorney had said, "your wife was absent from the home much of the time and your little girl was all the company you had. She, in essence, took your wife's place, did she not?")

He was a lousy disciplinarian. Everything Bliss did struck him as endearing. When he did reprimand her he could barely keep the smile off his lips. And she knew. It infuriated Sharon. "She'll be running wild by the time she's a teenager if you let her get away with everything now," she'd said. But he saw no point in getting on Bliss's case over every little thing she did wrong. Save the lectures for the big stuff. The fact was, she never required much discipline around him. She'd often throw tantrums for Sharon, who would turn her over her knee for a spanking, a practice he found barbaric. This was all drawn out of him and Sharon during the trial. Picked apart. How he treated Bliss more like an adult than a child. That was ludicrous, he said. He took care of her, protected her. He just refused to talk down to her. Sometimes the lawyers tried to turn this whole thing into a war between him and Sharon. It was not that. He was not angry with Sharon, only hurt that she wouldn't believe him. He defended her when his own attorney tried to paint the picture of her as an absent, ineffectual mother. And Sharon never, not once, said an incriminating thing about him. But in the courtroom both her words and his were twisted and distorted to the extent that they began to see each other as enemies. Even if he had been cleared he didn't think their marriage could have survived the beating it took in that courtroom.

Ben began dialing the phone again. This phone had become his lifeline in the last six months. His brother answered on the second ring.

"Did I wake you?" Ben asked.

"Not completely," Sam said. "What's up?"

"Did Sharon have her number changed?"

"Yeah. Jeff insisted. Are you the one who's been calling?"

"Occasionally. Not enough for him to get steamed about."

"He gets steamed pretty easily when you're the topic of conversation. Real self-righteous asshole."

"I know you're saying that to make me feel good, but it doesn't work. My daughter's living with him, remember? I'd like to think he's half decent."

Sam laughed. "Yeah, okay, I'll give him that. He's half decent."

"Listen, I want to tell you something but you have to keep it quiet. Is Jen right there?"

"No. She's gardening."

"I'm seeing . . . well, sort of seeing, Eden Riley."

"What? What do you mean, sort of seeing? Is she visiting Kyle? Does she know any—?"

Ben smiled. "Slow down. She's visiting Kyle for the summer because she wants to do a film about her mother and needs to do some research. So I've seen her a few times."

"Define 'seen'?"

"Gone out with. Talked with. Kissed."

"Shit, Ben, you dog!" Sam laughed. "Eden Riley! What about her boyfriend, what's-his-name, that guy she was giving it to in her last movie?"

"I don't think she's particularly enamored by him. Besides, this is just a brief, summer sort of thing." He had to keep reminding himself of that.

"Does she know about Bliss?"

"She knows there's a problem. She doesn't know what, and she doesn't seem to care."

"The woman's made for you. Is she as prissy as her image?"

"No, I wouldn't call her prissy at all." He remembered the hungry pressure of her hips against his last night, and his penis sprang to life beneath the sheet. He laughed. "She's having an effect on me."

"Well, hallelujah. Go for it, bro. Just . . . I mean, I hate to inject a serious note here, but don't get screwed, okay? For my sake if not for yours? I don't think I can handle any more of your traumas."

"Not a word to anyone, Sam. Not even Jen."

He felt courageous after talking to Sam. So much so that he called Eden to ask her if she'd changed her mind about doing something today. He wanted to drive to Belhurst to buy dollhouse furniture for Kim Parrish's birthday. She'd love to go, Eden said, and for some reason he wasn't surprised at her change of heart. She'd been up for hours, she said, and had made a good start on the screenplay. But Kyle had just handed her another notebook and she wanted to read for a while. Would eleven be too late?

Eleven would be fine.

He got out of bed, put on his shorts and running shoes, and left his cabin for a good long run in the rain.

20

March 7, 1945

Last week Matt's mother developed pneumonia and Tuesday she died. Matt blames himself because he thinks he should have gotten her to the hospital sooner, but the doctor told him it wouldn't have made any difference.

He asked me to come to his house last night to help him straighten up. There was not much to do but I think he just didn't want to be there alone when he went through his mama's things.

His mama had taken to reading magazines as she lay in bed, so I sat on the sofa in the living room trying to read Life, *but feeling real nervous at being in the house of a dead woman. Matt was in her room sorting through her things, but I couldn't go in her room at all.*

After a while he came into the living room and sat next to me on the sofa and I knew he'd been crying. Matt cries very easily. "I'd like you to have this," he said, pressing something into my hand. It was an oval-shaped pendant, painted white with a purple flower in the middle. It's the most beautiful thing I ever saw. "She wore it a lot and it always reminded me of you, because it's just one flower, all by itself." He lifted it from my hand and fastened it around my neck and he was close enough that I could see the dark stubble from the last time he shaved. Then he suddenly leaned down to kiss me on the lips and I quickly turned my head away.

"Kate?" he said.

"Don't do that." I knew I needed to explain my reaction to him, so I told him that I care about him, that I even love him in a way. But I am not in love with him. I'm not prudish, I said. I don't believe you have to be married to make love, but I do believe you should at least be in love with the person.

I told all this to Matt and he said, "I only wanted to kiss you."

"But if we kissed you might think I was in love with you."

"Well, you've made it very clear you're not."

He looked sad and I felt terrible. I thought Matt and I understood each other, that we were friends with neither of us expecting more than that.

"I'll walk you home," he said.

"I can go by myself," I said. I wanted to get out of that house. It had suddenly changed everything. Before I set foot in it we were good friends, free to say anything to each other, but now we couldn't look each other in the eye. I turned to the door and suddenly he put his arms around me from behind.

"Kate." He kissed my neck through my hair. "Please don't leave me here alone."

I held perfectly still and after a while he let go of me, walked into his mother's room and closed the door behind him. I left his house and ran back to the cavern, crying all the way. Once I got there it took me a long, long time to catch my breath.

Today I feel terrible. I woke up sick to my stomach and I know it is because I hurt Matt. I should have hugged him and comforted him, but I was afraid he would start trying to kiss me again. Why did he have to try to get so close to me? He's ruined our friendship. I wish Kyle were here to talk to about this because I'm just not sure what to do.

March 12, 1945

Matt hasn't come to the cavern since before his mama died. Next to Kyle, he is my dearest (and only) friend and I have failed him terribly. I know he only wanted my comfort the other night at his house, that he wasn't about to pressure me for more, but I am so afraid of being close to another human being that I had to get away from him. I keep thinking of what that night *must have been like for him, feeling left by his mother and turned away by me.*

Matt needs a better friend than I can be. He deserves a better friend. Maybe I shouldn't let him come here anymore. I should force him to go out and mix with other people.

March 13, 1945

Matt came to the cavern last night, just as I was writing in my journal. He walked in, sat down in the rocker, and said: "Everything's got to be on your terms, Kate, doesn't it?"

"I don't know what you mean," I said.

He shook his head. "Never mind."

I wanted to apologize, to tell him how much I care about him and how sorry I am for hurting him. I tried to find the right words but couldn't, so finally I handed him this journal, opened to what I wrote yesterday, and let him read it. There's no better way I could think of to let him know how I feel.

I felt naked as he read it, more than I did the night of the Christmas party when I opened my coat in his car.

When he looked up, his eyes were wet. "I'm not going to beg you to love me, Kate. But please don't tell me I can't come here anymore. Let that be my choice."

So we sat, and he read and I wrote, just like nothing ever happened.

June 2, 1945

I graduated today and at the ceremony, Sara Jane announced she is marrying Tommy Miller in July. I wrote as gentle a letter as I could to Kyle.

August 14, 1945

Today the Japanese surrendered and we got word Kyle is coming home!

August 21, 1945

I have bound up ten of the stories I typed over this long year with a cover so it looks almost like a book for Kyle to read. Only two days til he gets back. I also have the arrowheads in a box to show him. I'm so excited that I can't sleep at all and can barely eat enough to stay alive. Susanna and I are buying all his favorite food, Matt bought him some new shirts, and Daddy bought champagne!

August 23, 1945

I am so confused. Susanna and Daddy and Kyle and Matt are all in the house celebrating Kyle's return and I am here in the cave by myself. I feel more like crying than writing and actually, I am doing both.

Kyle came home just a few hours ago, around dusk. He was earlier than we expected and I was writing in the cave, trying to keep busy to steady my nerves while I was waiting for him. Suddenly I saw him silhouetted against the entrance to the great room. He was still in uniform, tall and beautiful, and I felt actual pain on the inside of my arms which I knew would only stop once I wrapped them around him.

I jumped up and ran to him but he put his arms out to stop my hug.

"Damn it, Kate," he said. "What the hell are you still doing in this cave?"

I stopped in my tracks to try to make out his expression but it was too dark. I thought he must be joking, so I reached out my arms for him again and this time he grabbed my arm.

"You promised me you'd leave it," he said.

"But I like to write here," I said. I was feeling guilty.

"God, what is wrong with you? This is crazy, Kate. Do you hear me? It's crazy! You're eighteen God damn years old. You're a woman, for Christ's sake." He picked up the book of stories I'd bound for him and threw them across the cave into the darkness. "Screw your writing!" he said.

He grabbed my shoulders then and for a terrible moment I thought he was going to kill me, that maybe his military training had gone haywire and he couldn't stop killing and hurting. "I'm not the enemy," I said, scared as I've ever been in my life.

He let go of me so suddenly I nearly fell. "I expected you to grow up this year," he said, and then he turned and left the cavern.

I waited, thinking he would calm down and come back. When he didn't I crept through the dark forest to the house, just close enough to see the four of them in the kitchen. I wondered where Daddy and Susanna thought I was. I could see Kyle's face clearly and he looks years older. We are both eighteen this month, but he is a man now. His chin has grown square and solid and his face has nothing of a child left in it. I felt about ten years old, standing there watching them. Finally I walked back to the cave.

For the first time I can understand how a person can feel empty enough to kill themselves. I pity my poor mama and her sister for feeling this way so long.

August 24, 1945

I waited until the house was dark before I went back last night. I considered spending the night in the cave but I couldn't bear to be that far from Kyle, whether he wanted me away from him or not. Everything was quiet as I tiptoed through the kitchen and hallway, and when I reached our bedroom I discovered Kyle was not in his bed. I went out in the parlor and there he was, sleeping under a blanket on the sofa. I watched him for a minute and then went to my own bed for a good cry.

I finally fell asleep and when I woke up it was still dark out and Kyle was sitting on the edge of my bed, holding my hand. When he saw my eyes were open he said, "I worry about you, Katie. I'm sorry for the way I acted last night, but what's made this last year bearable for me was thinking that you were out and living a normal life like other girls your age. When I saw you in that cave, I just . . ." He shook his head. "There's a world out there, Kate. I have to get you away from here somehow."

I felt like a burden to him. I sat up and leaned against the wall. "You don't need to worry about me. I'm content just as I am."

He looked like he didn't believe me and shifted on the bed so his back was against the wall too. He needs some new pajamas. Those he was wearing are way too small for him now.

"Why are you sleeping in the parlor?" I asked.

"We can't sleep in the same room anymore. Guys my age don't share a room with a sister. It's not natural."

"That's crazy," I said. "We've done it all these years just fine."

"No, it's not right. It's not done. I'll just stay on the sofa."

I decided not to argue with him just then. I figured in a few days he'd be back to his old self and in a more normal state of mind. We talked awhile longer and then suddenly he said, "Kate, do you realize I'm out a lot sooner than I'm supposed to be?"

"Well, the war's over," I said.

"Yes, but you don't just come home the day after the war's over. I've been discharged. What they call a medical discharge."

My heart just about stopped beating. "Are you hurt?" I asked.

He was rubbing my hand hard and slow, like he was trying to work a cramp out of my fingers. "What I'm going to tell you stays between you and me, right? You won't tell anyone? Not even Matt?"

"No," I whispered.

"They discharged me because I had a breakdown." He lowered his eyes and I didn't really understand what he was saying, but I knew it shamed him.

"What do you mean?"

"You have no idea what it's like, Kate. I killed people. The first time it was hard and then it got easier. You start thinking it's either them or me and damned if it's going to be me. It scares me, how easy it got. I started having nightmares, about things I was seeing in the jungle, or sometimes about Mama the night she . . . you know. The dreams got so bad they finally sent me to the hospital, but I wasn't much better there. Finally the army just figured a loon like me wasn't much use to them and sent me home."

"I'm glad they did," I said. "And you're not a loon."

"I'm still afraid to go to sleep at night," he said.

I sat away from him. "Is that why you don't want to sleep in here? Are you afraid you'll wake me with a nightmare?"

He smiled, the first smile I've seen out of him since he got home. "No. We're not sleeping in the same room anymore and that's the last word on the subject." Then his smile was gone again. "The whole time I was in the hospital I thought of you. All these doctors were trying to get me to talk to *them and looking at me like I was crazy and I was thinking there was only one person in the world I could really tell anything to and who would care about me whether I was crazy or not. I missed you so much, Katie. I don't ever want to be that far away from you again."*

"Well, you're home now," I said. "You're safe. No place safer than Lynch Hollow."

He went back to sleep in the parlor, against my wishes, and this morning at breakfast he was smiling. He said it was the first good night's sleep he'd had in months.

Eden found Kyle in the springhouse. She stood quietly in the doorway for a moment, watching him. He sat with his back to her, his head bowed under the circle of light from a desk lamp, and she knew he was painting the tiny identification numbers on fragments of pottery. Marked fragments covered the surfaces of the three long wooden tables that nearly filled the tiny stone springhouse.

"Kyle?"

The old wooden chair creaked as he turned to face her. "Come in." He motioned to a chair on the other side of the nearest table.

She sat down. It was cool in the room, but not so cool that she needed to hug her arms against her chest, as she did now. He turned back to the desk and she watched his steady hand as he finished painting the numbers on a fragment. The lamp lit the silver frames of the glasses he wore for close-up work. She waited until he looked up at her before she spoke.

"I didn't know about your discharge from the army, Kyle."

"No, not many people do." He put down his brush and pushed his chair a few inches from the desk. "I finally told Matt about it a couple of weeks after I got back. Matt had a way of making you feel sane even if you weren't. You could tell him the craziest thing you'd ever done and he'd act like you were talking about the weather. And I've told Lou, of course. But I don't think there's anyone else who knows."

"Do you want me to leave it out of the film?"

Kyle laughed. "It's the kind of thing you're ashamed of at eighteen, not sixty-four. I don't care who knows now, but back then, I thought I was going crazy—that I'd inherited some of my mother's loony genes." He took off his glasses. "You know, on the one hand I was angry with Kate for not leaving the cave. On the other hand, I was jealous of her. Right then, I wanted to hide away, not have to face what was going on in the world. But I was supposed to be sane and stable. Kate could get away with holing herself up in a cave. I couldn't." He smiled at her and then suddenly sat up straighter, his eyes at her throat. When he spoke again his voice was soft. "I haven't seen that in a very long time."

Her fingers felt the pendant at her throat. "It's the first time I've worn it." She'd put it on just an hour ago, when she'd read about her father giving it to her mother.

Kyle shuddered a little, picked up his paintbrush again. "A little bit of a shock, seeing you in that. You look so much like Kate to begin with."

Eden lifted one of the larger pieces of pottery from the table in front of her and felt the smooth surface with her thumb. "Kyle," she said. "I'd be more than happy to help out with . . . I'm not sure how to say this. Please don't take offense. But I'd like to help with the site. Financially, I mean."

He held the clay fragment closer to the light and slipped on his glasses. "Thank you, honey, but that's not the way I want this site to survive."

"I understand. Let me know if you change your mind." She stood up. "Ben's picking me up in a few minutes. We're going to Belhurst for the afternoon." She waited for his response.

"Have a good time," he said.

At the door of the springhouse she turned back to him. "Will you leave the next notebook out for me?"

"Uh . . ." He leaned back again and turned to look at her. "Wouldn't you like a break from the journal for a few days? I read the next notebook this morning. It covers the semester we were at G.W. together and—"

"At G.W.? What do you mean?"

"Didn't you know Kate had one semester at George Washington University while I was there?"

"No." She hadn't known her mother had spent any time at all away from Lynch Hollow.

"Her journal starts to get sketchy now because she was working on her stories much of the time. And this particular notebook, the one from G.W., is a little disturbing to read. At least it disturbed me to read it. And we're moving into the X-rated material. You sure you can handle it?"

Eden laughed. "X-rated?"

"It might shock you a bit."

"Kyle, I'm thirty-six years old. It's not going to shock me, and no, I do not want a break from the journal. If I had my way I'd read it straight through."

"Okay." He turned back to his work. "I'll give it to you in the morning."

21

She was waiting for him out on the road, sitting on the boulder that marked Kyle's driveway. Her hair was up again and she wore a blue blouse cut high on her shoulders and tucked into white shorts.

She climbed into the passenger seat of his truck. "Hi." She smiled.

He wanted to touch her but locked his hands around the steering wheel instead. "Hi." He pulled back onto the road. "Did you get your reading done?"

"Uh huh." She looked out the window as the road dipped and turned through the woods. "God, I love it here. I wish I could bottle this place and take it back with me."

"Maybe you need to visit Kyle and Lou more often."

"Maybe I do."

"You're in a good mood today."

"I guess I am." She sounded surprised. "The screenplay really started to work this morning. I always feel good when something I'm excited about begins to come together."

"How's Lou doing today?"

"She seems fine. Back at the easel this morning." Eden played with the catch of her watch and then looked over at Ben. The tone of her voice changed, deepened. "What kind of problems has she had because of her leg over the years? Do you know?"

Yes, he knew. Lou's disability had created one problem after another for them when they were in South America. But somehow he sensed Eden's need to be protected from all of that. "She's had fewer problems than you'd imagine. She does fine in that chair, ordinarily. A few times in Colombia we'd hit a restaurant or a hotel that wasn't set up for a wheelchair, but Kyle and I would lift it and it wasn't much of a problem."

"But Kyle couldn't possibly lift her now."

"Well, they're not traveling now either, so it's not really a problem. At one time she tried a prosthesis, but she got so frustrated with it that she gave up."

"I didn't know that. I guess there's a lot I don't know about her. Or Kyle."

"Once she had to be hospitalized," he continued, not sure if he should. "We were in Ecuador then, I think. She had pressure sores, you know, from sitting too long in one spot? I guess she always has to put up with them, but they got infected that one time." He glanced at Eden. She had turned her head away from him, but he could see one tear resting diamondlike on her lower lashes, and he knew he'd said too much. He reached down to wrap his hand around hers. "I'm sorry. You were in a good mood and I brought you down."

She shook her head, still not looking at him. "I asked the question. You only provided the answer."

He liked the connection he felt to her. He'd noticed it for the first time last night when Lou fell, when he recognized in Eden the same concern he felt. The same love. It had been a long time since he'd found himself on the same team with anyone. And he liked her unexpected neediness, the way it made him forget his own.

"Lou's a proud person," he said. "I think what bothers her more than anything else is being dependent, not being able to fend for herself the way she'd like to."

Eden sighed. "I just wish the accident had never happened. I wish I could change the past."

"Oh, yes," he said. "I know exactly what you mean."

*

They reached Belhurst before noon and he parked the truck in front of the dollhouse shop. Once they were inside, Eden's mood lifted. The shop held room after room filled with dollhouses, some of them completed with paint and furnishings, others in the raw wood stage.

"How old is your goddaughter?" Eden asked.

"She'll be eight. I built her a dollhouse just like this one"—he indicated a tall, shingled Victorian—"when she was three, and every year since I buy her something for it." Usually something expensive. This year would be different.

"How did you come to be her godfather?"

"Alex, her father, is my best friend. We went to school together—he was a student of Kyle's too. Then we both taught at the University of Maryland. We got married about the same time and he was my best man and I was his. His wife and Sharon are good friends." It saddened him to recount the closeness that no longer existed. "I haven't seen much of him since the divorce. I guess that happens—people feel as though they have to pick sides."

"Wayne and I didn't have mutual friends to begin with. That was part of the problem, I suppose. We really had no shared life aside from Cassie." She opened the arched door on a little Spanish-style ranch and peered inside. "Did you make a dollhouse for Bliss?"

"Yes. I modeled it after our house. Does Cassie have one?"

"Oh, a little one. Nothing so fancy."

He could make one for Cassie. Slow down, Ben. Besides, the kits cost a few hundred dollars.

He had only enough money to buy a tiny bedroom set if he intended to treat Eden to lunch. He tried not to be obvious about it as he took the bills from his wallet and counted what was left, doing some disheartening subtraction in his head. The little bit Kyle was paying him was fine for a man on a tight budget, but it would not cover dating. He knew he could ask Kyle for a loan and have it granted without question. But he could hardly ask him to support a relationship he viewed as deceptive.

Over lunch Eden told him how she'd like the movie to open. There would be a helicopter view of the Valley, following the Shenandoah for a while, then moving closer to Ferry Creek and the field by the site, finally dipping into the woods and smoothly slipping inside the entrance to the cave until the screen was completely black. Then the title and credits would appear on the black background. "Very dramatic," she said. "All that green. And then the blackness of the cave."

"What's the title?"

"*A Solitary Life.*"

He nodded his approval. "That fits," he said. "But Kyle won't let you in the cave."

"Mmm, I know." She nodded, swallowed a mouthful of salad. "We can fake it. Then we cut back to the house—only, of course, not the way it is now. We'll build one to look like it did when Kate and Kyle grew up in it. Kate's in the elm tree, writing in her journal, terrified that she's in for a whipping because her mother found her dictionary."

"Did that really happen?"

"Yes. Only Kyle said it was his and took the beating for her."

Ben laughed. "Christ. Figures. He started early rescuing people, didn't he?"

Eden touched her napkin to her lips. "My mother gave me such a gift when she left this journal behind. I can practically write from it scene by scene."

"When will you start filming?"

"I'm aiming for next summer."

He felt the most horrendous jolt in his chest and set his fork on the table. He suddenly remembered that he had nothing to look forward to. Life would go on with him or without him, seasons would change with a deadening predictability. Next summer held no more promise for him than this summer. Possibly less. What could be worse than having no future? Maybe in January they would let him go before the court and beg to see Bliss and maybe if he humbled himself the right amount and maybe if Sam could dig up the most persuasive experts and maybe if Bliss still had any goddamned memory at all of who he was, he could . . .

"Ben? Are you all right?" Eden had grabbed his hand, and when he looked at her he saw alarm in her eyes.

"I'm okay." His voice sounded as if he were speaking through a straw. He forced a cough. Took a swallow of water. "Something went down the wrong pipe," he lied. Then he settled back in his chair again, dropping his hands to his lap to hide their trembling. "Tell me more about the film."

22

November 20, 1945

Today Kyle and I had a long talk that's left me as nervous as I've ever been. I didn't know it, but he has been getting information about colleges in Washington, D.C., and now he told me he plans to go in January and he wants me to go with him. He thinks we should study archaeology. I have never seen him as excited about anything as he's been over the arrowheads we've been digging up. He went to the library in Winchester to try to figure who might have made them and he thinks they are from some people who lived here maybe two thousand years ago or more! Matt and I find this very hard to believe. Kyle says we're going about digging things up too sloppily. There are holes all around the front of the cave now. We need to go to school to learn what we're doing. He says we'd need to have jobs, too, to be able to afford our classes.

Well, first I tried to talk him out of this, but I could see he's been thinking about it a long time. Then Matt told me he's going away to school too, in North Carolina, to study journalism. I believe he and Kyle have been plotting. I sat on my mattress in the cave, crying and moaning, because this is a fix I can see no way out of. They sat next to me, one on either side, talking me into it. So I have agreed, although I cannot imagine being able to survive away from Lynch Hollow. But as scared as I am about going away, I am even more afraid of being apart from Kyle again.

January 15, 1946

Kyle and I each have a small room (right next door to each other) in what is called a townhouse in Georgetown, an area of Washington, D.C. Washington overwhelms me and I don't enjoy all the sights as Kyle does. Each time we venture out I am anxious to get back to my tiny little closet of a room, which Kyle calls my second cave.

I am not having an easy time of this and I'm afraid to tell Kyle how bad it is for me. I suffer through my classes even though I love what I am learning. In my room I read and read and do the assignments, but in the classroom I cannot concentrate, cannot breathe. My heart beats so fast I lose track of the rhythm, and I pinch myself to keep from fainting. The inside of my arm has little red marks on it from my nails.

I am taking a writing course and it is my favorite. I sit right next to the door and usually that helps me breathe better and pay attention. I have my typewriter here and my teacher thinks my writing is very neat and creative, but she says I still need to work on my sentences and punctuation.

I'm working as a waitress in a little hotel restaurant down the street from here and it's a nightmare because I'm so nervous that I spill things. Last night I spilled a bowl of stew on a man and he says I burned him. I dread going back, but we need the money badly.

Everyone makes fun of my accent so I talk even less than usual.

March 6, 1946

I quit my math class today because I was about to suffocate in there and I had to walk out. Mr. Sims followed me into the hall and asked me where I thought I was going and I told him I was sick and would be back tomorrow, but I won't be. It's not going to be any better tomorrow than it was today. I can't tell Kyle.

April 7, 1946

I made the mistake of letting Kyle talk me into going to a party with him last night. He goes to lots of them and I usually stay in my room and write or study, but last night I finally said I would go. I'm sure that's the last party he'll ever hound me into going to.

It was at the house of a girl in one of our classes, Julia. She is very wealthy and I've never seen a mansion like the one she lives in.

Things here are just as they were in high school, with everyone loving Kyle. When Julia invited me, she told me that Kyle is "so charming," and I am certain she invited me only because I am his sister. I wore my one good dress, which Susanna forced on me when I left Lynch Hollow and which I despise. I feel like a pig trussed for the spit when I get dressed up in that miserable garter belt and stockings and all. Kyle thinks garter belts are sexy (his favorite word these days). He also thinks Julia is sexy and was looking forward to this party.

I didn't realize it was a dinner party until we got there. If I'd known, I never would have agreed to go. There was a long, long table set with china and crystal glasses and little cards with names on them by each plate. About thirty people were there, some students from our anthropology class and some other students I didn't know and a couple of professors. Kyle's favorite professor, Dr. Latterly, was there. Kyle's little name tag was between Dr. Latterly and Julia, so he took his seat looking like he'd died and gone to heaven.

My name tag was between two students I didn't know from Adam, a girl with bug-eyes and a boy with freckles and red hair slicked down on his head with what smelled like cough tonic. The second I sat down I started having trouble breathing. My hands shook and sweat was running down my back. I could feel it soaking into my dress (which is now in the trash, good riddance). I sat there sweating and shaking while everyone ate some cold white soup I didn't touch, and a salad full of some yellow vegetable I couldn't even look at. Then I thought for sure I was going to faint so I started pinching on my arm out of habit, not even realizing I was doing it. Suddenly the bug-eyed girl cried out, "What are you doing??!!" so loud that everyone turned to look at me. The girl was staring at my arm and when I looked down I could see little red pinch marks all over my white skin. A couple of times I'd drawn blood and not even felt it.

The whole table seemed to have gone quiet, everyone looking at me. I lowered my arm. "I have a little poison ivy," I said, quietly as I could and working hard at pronouncing my words the way they did. For an awful minute no one said anything and I looked over at Kyle. He was frowning at me and I tried to tell him with my eyes how desperate I was to get out of there but he turned back to Dr. Latterly and resumed talking again.

Everyone was talking except me and my eyes started filling up and I pinched my arm harder—I had to—to try to keep the tears back. Then the maid or whatever she is put a plate in front of me that had a big slab of bloody red meat on it and that finished me. My breathing raced up, my heart beat like it was sure to explode. I reached for my water glass and knocked it over and everyone was looking at me again and then the tears just spilled all over my face and I stood up to try to get away from the table. But the chairs were so close together I couldn't budge. The freckled boy had to push his chair out and the girl next to him had to push hers out and I nearly started to retch. Everyone was staring at me with their mouths wide open and I heard Kyle excuse himself from the table as I ran out of the room. I got out the front door before he caught up to me. He was furious. When he talked, it was through gritted teeth, and real slow.

"What . . . the . . . hell . . . is . . . the . . . matter with you?"

"I'm sorry, Kyle." I was crying so much now I could hardly talk. "I'm sick. I can't stay in there. I'll wait out here for you."

"You can't wait out here."

"I can't go back in there either."

"I should have just let you stay home and rot in your goddamned room."

I grabbed his arm. I hate worse than anything when Kyle's mad at me. "I'm sorry."

"Wait here." His teeth were still gritted together like someone poured cement in his mouth.

I stood outside the open front door and could hear him inside talking to Julia, saying he had to leave, he was so sorry and how ill I was, etcetera. And before he stepped outside I heard Julia say, "Tell your sister I hope she feels better," and he answered, "She's not actually my sister. Just my cousin."

It makes me cry all over again to write those words. He pushed out the front door like a bull looking for something to charge and he didn't say a word to me, just walked ahead of me the entire two miles to our townhouse. I had to practically run to keep up with him and after a while I stopped trying to say I was sorry because it was obvious he wanted nothing to do with me. Once I actually did have to stop to vomit and he didn't even slow his pace. When we got back here he walked into his room and slammed the door behind him. I came in here and thought about writing it all down in my journal but I just didn't have the spirit. I fell asleep missing Lynch Hollow.

This morning he went on to breakfast and class without stopping in for me. I can't go to class today. Even if I could breathe in those classrooms, I can't face the other students who were at the party last night. So here I am, in my second cave, longing for my first.

April 8, 1946

It's midnight and I can't sleep, so I'll write. After dinner tonight Kyle finally came to my room. He brought me a chicken sandwich he made from some of his food at dinner. I was sitting on my bed reading our anthropology textbook. "Are you all right?" he asked me, his first kind words in a while.

"Guess that's the last party you're taking me to," I said.

"It's not funny, Kate." Kyle sat down on the end of my bed. "Mr. Sims told me you never go to his class anymore. Then I checked around. Latterly's is the only class you go to, isn't it?"

I nodded. It's the only class I go to because it's the only class I have with Kyle, the only one I can breathe in.

"I guess I want you to be somebody you're not able to be. That's not fair of me. I'm sorry." He moved closer to me then and lifted my hand. He pushed my shirt sleeve up to my elbow and turned my arm over so he could look at it. I looked myself. There must be twenty or thirty little marks, little double crescents from my nails, some of them just pink, some scabbed over with delicate little moon-shaped scabs. I felt like I'd never seen them before, there in the light. It shocked me and I tried to draw my arm away but Kyle held tight to my hand. Then he lowered his head to my arm and set his lips on it and it was a minute or two before he raised his head up. "You'll

have to go back to Lynch Hollow, Kate. It was wrong for me to talk you into going to school. You knew what was best for you all along, and this isn't it."

"But I like learning," I said. "I don't go to class, but I study the books anyway."

"When I get back to Lynch Hollow I'll teach you what I've learned."

"I want to stay here," I said. "I'm fine in the room. And I can still work." *(That is not quite true. A few times lately I've had to leave work early, but I wasn't about to say that just then.)*

"I'm scared for you, Kate. I thought if I could get you away from home, get you around other people, you'd be all right."

"I am all right," I said. *I wanted him to stop talking so sadly, like I was dead.*

"It's been torture for you here."

"I'm fine in my room," I said again.

"All right," he said. "Until the end of the semester."

I feel like the weight of the world's been lifted from me. I can stay in the room all I want, although I do have to work—I will have to force myself to do that—and in the summer Kyle and I can both return to Lynch Hollow. Next year he will leave again but we can cross that bridge later.

May 10, 1946

Kyle brought Julia home with him tonight. We usually study together in one of our rooms in the evening, him teaching me what he's learned that day, but tonight he poked his head in my door to say Julia was here and he would see me in the morning.

He's been grumpy lately and yesterday he told me it was because he hasn't made love to anyone in so long. Hopefully he'll be in a better mood in the morning.

May 21, 1946

I cannot stand the nights Julia is here. She is a nice person and it doesn't bother me so much that she takes Kyle's time away from me because I am fine in my room studying by myself. But once I go to bed, I can hear them. Kyle's bed is directly on the other side of the wall from mine so I am just a few feet from them. They laugh, or talk quietly, though it's rare that I can make out their words. But it's the quiet moments that disturb me most, when I imagine they are kissing and touching each other, and there are times I can hear Kyle's bed rocking and I know he is inside her. I wonder what that feels like, being filled up by a man? I doubt I'll ever know.

Most times, I am grateful for my good imagination. Stories pour out of it and it's like I can actually see everything that happens in them clear as day. But sometimes it's a curse. Like now, when Kyle is with Julia on the other side of my wall and I can see in my head his lips on hers, his hands on her breasts and between her legs. I know this will be one of those nights when I pull my blankets and pillow onto the floor and sleep there to try to still my thoughts.

May 25, 1946

Kyle is no longer seeing Julia. They had a fight and now he is grumpy again. Last night he was so rude while we were studying that I got mad at him. I told him that I'm grumpy too, that he's not the only person in the world who needs sex. I am reading Lady Chatterley's Lover *and it is making me crazy. Kyle doesn't think much of Constance Chatterley. "She's a tramp," he says. "She married that poor guy in the wheelchair in sickness and in health. She should learn to keep her skirt down." I told him if she kept her skirt down it wouldn't make much of a book.*

Some nights I have to chase him out of my room early so I can go to bed and put out the fire by myself. He says I am in "critical need" of a boyfriend and he offered to find me one, saying it wouldn't be hard because I'm so beautiful. He actually said that!

"I'll never have a lover," I said. I am resigned to this.

"You're only eighteen. I wouldn't approve of you having a lover now anyway."

"Julia was only eighteen," I pointed out. "And Sara Jane was just seventeen."

"Yes," he said, "but they weren't my sister."

May 29, 1946

Yesterday we got an amazing surprise. When I got home from work, who should be sitting with Kyle on the front porch of our townhouse but Matt! I was overjoyed to see him and that shocked me because although I've missed him, I have certainly not been pining for him. He has not even been much in my thoughts. But when I saw him sitting there, grinning up a storm at me, my whole heart seemed to expand with happiness. I hugged him like I wanted to break him in two.

He is out of school for the summer already, although Kyle and I have another week left. He's visiting Washington for a couple of days, staying at the very hotel where I work! We stayed up late last night talking and catching up on things. He looks wonderful and has had a few girlfriends this year but no one serious. Kyle says that Matt's still interested in me, so I guess I will have to make it clear once again that all I want is his very good friendship.

May 30, 1946

Matt just left and I'm trembling as I write this. We went out to dinner tonight, Kyle, a girl Kyle likes named Sally, Matt and I. It's rare for me to go out like that, but I felt safe with Kyle and Matt there, like old times. Afterwards we came back here and Kyle and Sally went in his room and Matt came in mine.

We sat on my bed, talking about his school and his studies. He wants to work for a newspaper when he's done with school. We talked for an hour or so and then suddenly he said, "Kate, I want to kiss you, but you're the scariest girl in the world to kiss."

"What do you mean?" I asked.

"The last time I tried you went running off on me."

I said he could kiss me, but that it wouldn't change things, that we had a friendship and that was all I wanted. It was a mistake to let him kiss me, I can see that now. But the truth is, I wanted to do it. I wanted to feel what it was like, and it was wonderful. Better than I ever imagined. I never knew how hooked together everything is in my body. When he kissed my lips, I felt it in my breasts and my stomach. He laid me down so my head was on my pillow and I just couldn't get enough of his lips and tongue. I knew I could make love with him and leave it at that, but he couldn't. He certainly would never settle for friendship after that.

And then he asked if he could touch my breast. I said no and he said, "Just through your blouse. Let me just rest my hand on it."

My breast was begging me to let him touch it. "Just set your hand there," I said. And at first that's all he did, but then he was kissing me again and his hand started playing with my breast, squeezing it, pulling at it, and I actually said for him to touch the other one too. He was groaning, and I might have been too. I never felt so on fire. Then he reached up my blouse and around back to undo my brassiere. My head was saying no and my body was saying yes. I wanted him to touch me everywhere, but if he did what would it mean? Something different to him than to me, I was sure of that.

When he touched my naked breasts, I had a sudden crazy need to tell him I loved him. I managed to stop myself from saying it, but it was like I lost all sense of where I was and who I was. And then he said it. "I love you, Kate," and it snapped me back. I sat up right quick and pulled my blouse down, feeling real embarrassed all of a sudden.

Matt was breathing hard, still trying to kiss me and I held him away. "Oh, Kate, please." He was practically whimpering. I could see the bulge in his trousers trying to break loose and I looked away from it.

"Matt," I said. "Next to Kyle you're my best friend. You know that, don't you?"

He said he did, and I went on to tell him how best friends don't make love, how that kind of closeness led to expectations and changed a relationship forever. I told him I hoped we already didn't do it damage that couldn't be undone.

I went on that way for a while until finally he told me to shut up. That's just what he said. "Oh, Kate, shut up. I've heard this all before from you."

He was sulky for a while, but then we got back to talking and laughing and I think we'll be all right. He left around eleven and said he'd stop in tomorrow before he heads back home to Coolbrook.

After he left and I thought over all that had happened I started getting really shaky. I cannot trust this body of mine. It has a mind all its own.

June 4, 1946

I am nearly packed for the trip back to Lynch Hollow, and I can hear Kyle next door opening and closing dresser drawers. I will be so glad to get home. I long to see my cavern again.

There is a tense silence between Kyle and me tonight that I hope will pass with a good night's sleep. I know the cause. I was getting dressed for dinner this afternoon and I was late. I had put on my skirt but had nothing on up top and I was standing in front of my dresser mirror, brushing my hair. I was, to be truthful, admiring myself. My hair is full and sparkly from the damp air and my breasts are round and white. Suddenly, there was a knock on my door and I knew it was Kyle coming to get me for dinner. I don't know why I didn't answer him. I just kept still, knowing full well that he would open the door. He did and I stood frozen, facing the mirror with my back to the door, my brush in my hair. "Kate," he began and then forgot the rest of whatever he was going to say as he saw my state of undress. I watched him in the mirror as he watched me in the mirror. Our eyes locked for the longest time, neither of us moving or speaking. Finally he took a step backward into the hall and closed my door quietly after him.

He was already at the table when I came downstairs. Just a couple of other boarders are left now, and he spoke to them, not to me. We walked upstairs together after dinner and he said that I could have the larger suitcase if I liked, and that he had a box we could put our books in. His friend, Pete, can drive us to the train station tomorrow, he said, and he hoped they serve us hotcakes for our last breakfast here. He talked all around that moment in my bedroom, made circles around it with his words and never got close enough to touch it. I am not sure if he feels he is at fault for walking in on me or that I am at fault for not warning him. I am not sure if either of us is embarrassed. The only thing I am sure of is that if I could choose over again whether to answer his knock or not, I would not change a thing.

23

Eden spent the morning in her room. Twice she'd turned on the word processor and read what she'd written over the past few days, and twice she'd set her fingers on the keys, waiting for inspiration that never came. Three or four times she lay down on her bed and stared at the ceiling. Now she sat once again in the rocker, studying the picture of her mother. Katherine Swift, the public Katherine Swift, with her thick honey-colored braid and perfect white teeth, smiling broadly up at the camera from her seat in the pit. Eden had always taken this picture at face value, never wondering what lay hidden behind that smile. So much lay hidden. Too much. She felt overwhelmed at how to present it on the screen.

Her mother had described her emotions far too well. As she read the journal earlier that morning, Eden felt herself inside Kate's skin, sometimes to the point that she had to set the journal down and stare out the window to break the mood. She'd pinched the inside of her own arm to see how much pressure it would take before she drew blood. She dug her nails into the skin until tears sprang to her eyes, but she had still barely left a mark.

She started at a knock on her door. "It's one-fifteen, Eden," Kyle said through the door. "Don't you want some lunch?"

One-fifteen? She'd been brooding in her room half the day. She opened the door to face her uncle's furrowed brow. "Are you all right?" he asked.

"Yes. I'll come down."

He walked ahead of her down the stairs. "Lou's out with a friend at one of the scenic overlooks. She goes there about once a week to paint. Not really her favorite subject matter, but she enjoys the company." They'd reached the kitchen and he opened the refrigerator door. "I made some tuna salad. Can I get you a sandwich?"

"I can take care of it, Kyle. Have you already eaten?"

"Yes, but I'll sit with you." He poured himself a glass of iced tea and proceeded to tell her about the woman Lou was out with. She was from Georgia, he said. She had three grandchildren and was a nut for African violets. The chatter was not at all like him. She sat and listened, picking at her sandwich.

After a while he stopped talking to take a long drink from his tea. Then he looked across the table at her. "You're very quiet," he said.

"She needed psychiatric care, Kyle." She hoped her tone didn't sound accusatory. She didn't mean it to be.

He ran his finger down the long iced-tea glass. "Yes, she most definitely did. But it was 1946. Things weren't like they are today and—"

"I know there was a stigma attached to seeing a psychiatrist back then, but God, Kyle, she really needed help."

"It wasn't the stigma that worried me. Kate didn't know it, but I talked to people about her. Stan Latterly, for one. Trying to get advice on what to do for her. Everyone thought there was a good chance they'd lock her up. I wasn't about to let that happen."

"Oh." She hadn't thought of that. "You must have felt so helpless."

"Well." He stroked his beard thoughtfully as though he hadn't considered that possibility before. "I guess that was part of how I felt."

Eden smiled at him. "You certainly had your share of women. I can see what Lou meant about you being randy."

Kyle laughed. "Tame me down a little in the film, okay?"

She'd felt intrusive reading about Kyle and Julia, Kyle and Sally, Kate and Matt. Kate had left nothing to the imagination. But she was writing in a journal meant for her eyes alone. Of course she wouldn't censor what she had to say.

"Her writing was so . . . graphic," Eden said. "Maybe she never meant for anyone else to see it."

Kyle shook his head. "It would never occur to Kate to mince words, no matter who she thought might read them. And I know for a fact she wanted you to have the journal."

"Did she actually say that?"

"Uh huh."

"At what point?"

"You'll have to read on. I think she liked writing that way. Making it graphic, as you say." He drew another stripe through the condensation on his glass, then looked up at her. "After she died, I went into the cave to take the journal out. I knew she kept it on the ledge above her desk. Well, way on the back of that ledge I found a stack of stories that were definitely not written for children."

"Pornography?"

"That would depend on your definition of pornography. I wouldn't have called it that. They were similar to the journal in that they were written in the first person, but the writing was more elegant, like her stories. And they were pure fantasy."

"Maybe they weren't. Maybe she had a secret lover who crept into her cave when no one else was around." Eden could already picture it on the screen—a dark, wolflike man stealing into the cave at dusk, finding himself in Katherine's willing arms.

"I wish that had been the case," Kyle said. "She deserved a little more pleasure than she got out of life."

"Do you still have the stories? They'd be worth a fortune now."

"No. I read them through and then destroyed them. Burned them. Lou was appalled. She said they were works of art, some of Kate's best writing—I didn't even notice the writing. I was afraid they'd get into the wrong hands."

Eden nodded, thinking that Kyle had probably been right to destroy them. The wrong hands were everywhere.

"When does Katherine finally make love to my father?" she asked.

Kyle laughed. "You have no patience at all."

"It's hard to work on the screenplay when I'm not exactly sure where I'm headed."

"That must be a challenge." He obviously had no intention of helping her out.

"I'm struck by how different she and I were at that age. All she wanted was to be able to stay at home, and all I wanted was to run away."

"Oh, I don't know. I think you were more alike than different," Kyle said. "You were both just trying to find a way to feel safe."

He understood, and she felt forgiven. But he had no idea how much there was to forgive. She stood up and dumped the rest of her sandwich in the garbage. "I'd better get back to work."

She returned to her word processor, her thoughts in better order but a lingering uneasiness in the pit of her stomach. She and Kyle had not talked about that last entry in the notebook, his walking in on Kate. She had wanted to say something about it and perhaps he had as well, but neither of them had known what to ask, how to respond, and she wasn't sure if their silence on the topic gave it greater significance or none at all.

24

It was dusk when she curled up on the living room sofa to call Cassie, and for the first time Wayne answered.

"It's Eden, Wayne." She could hear laughter and a few childish screams in the background. Three little girls. She could imagine the giggling, the teasing, the hugging, that filled that house. "I just wanted to talk to Cassie," she said.

"How's the screenplay coming along?" Wayne asked.

"Slowly, but I'm pleased with what I have so far. I still have a ton of research to do, though. How's Cassie?"

"She's having the time of her life. Hold on, I'll get her. She's out in the pool."

Cassie was breathless by the time she reached the phone. "Mommy, you know what?" she asked.

"What?" Eden could picture Cassie in her ruffled pink bathing suit, clutching the phone, dripping on Pam's clean kitchen floor.

"I can hold my breath for twenty whole seconds under water! It's the longest of anybody."

"You're turning into a real fish this summer, aren't you?"

"What kind of fish?"

"Well, I don't know." She usually had an easy rapport with Cassie. Now she was struggling for words. Why couldn't she get her tone right? Why couldn't she sound a little more upbeat? "What kind would you like to be?" she asked.

"Mommy, you're not making any sense."

"Isn't it getting too dark to swim up there?" She looked out the window. The forest was black.

"We've got lights right in the pool, Mom. They make your skin look all white and fat. And the water's real warm. Can you come over and swim with us?"

"I'm too far away, Cassie, you know that." Hadn't Cassie gotten this straight yet? "You'll be coming down here to Virginia before you know it, though, and then we'll have lots of time together."

There was a short silence. She could hear Cassie's teeth chattering. "But April and Lindy won't be there."

"No. But I'll be here and we can canoe together and"—what else?—"we'll have fun and then we'll go back to Santa Monica and you can start nursery school and make lots of new friends."

"Daddy says I have to go there."

"Go where, honey? Santa Monica?"

"He says I have to go to Virginia."

Eden waited for the fierce little arrow of pain to leave her heart before she spoke again. "Don't you want to come here, Cassie?"

"I want to stay here 'cause of the pool and April and Lindy."

God. When would Cassie be old enough to at least make an attempt at sparing her feelings? "But I really miss you. I want to have some time with you this summer too."

"Then come here." There was an about-to-cry quality to Cassie's voice that Eden recognized all too well.

"Sweetheart, that's just not possible."

"But I have a kitten here. Mommy let me get it and I can't—"

"Mommy?" Eden shut her eyes as the arrow struck home again. "Do you mean Pam?"

"Yes, Pam. She let me—"

"Do you call Pam Mommy?"

"Sometimes." Cassie's voice was still a little rough, but the answer was matter-of-fact. She had no concept at all of how her words cut.

"Cassie, I can hear your teeth chattering. You'd better warm up and I'll call you tomorrow, okay?"

"Okay. 'Bye."

"I love—" The phone clicked in Eden's ear. She sat still for a moment, then picked up the small leather address book from the end table and opened it to Alexander. She started dialing without stopping to think.

"Hello?" Ben's voice was anticipatory.

"Can I come over?" She didn't bother to identify herself.

"I wish you would," he said.

She didn't take the time to change out of her shorts and T-shirt, or to fix her hair where it was pulling loose from her clip. She glanced in the dimly lit rearview mirror as she drove up the winding road to his cabin and wrinkled her nose at her reflection.

He opened the door before she knocked. "You're upset," he said.

"I just spoke to Cassie." She looked at him as she walked into the cabin and knew instantly why she had come here: he would understand. "I feel as though I've lost her."

He motioned toward the sofa and she sat down. "Wine?" he asked. "Beer?"

"Wine," she said. "And a lot of it. I want to feel numb."

He poured them each a glass of wine and sat down on the arm of the upholstered chair. He was wearing his mauvey T-shirt again. "What makes you think you've lost her?" he asked.

She took a few sips of her wine and set the glass on the coffee table. "She's so happy up there with Wayne and Pam and Pam's daughters. She doesn't want to come down here. She actually said that. She's adjusted so easily, as though I'm expendable, you know? I don't think she misses me at all. She calls Pam Mommy."

He winced. Oh, yes, he understood.

She curled her legs under her on the sofa. "Then I think, if she's happier with them—they can give her a mother and a father plus two siblings and stability and a normal life—then what right do I have wanting her to live with me? I have to admit she might be better off with them. Where I live . . ." She shook her head, not certain if Ben could possibly comprehend what her life was like. "Wayne says it's all plastic. Fake. The people are fake, and he's right. I'm fake."

Ben scowled. "Bullshit."

"No, he's right. You're not seeing it here. I'm different here. In Hollywood I'm nothing but a caricature of myself. And I'm raising Cassie in that unreal world. The only good reason I have for making her live with me is a purely selfish one: I want her." Her voice cracked. "I can't give her up. It would be like starting over and—" She stopped herself as a look of quiet resolve came into Ben's eyes.

"I'm sorry," she said. "That's what you're doing, isn't it? Starting over?"

"Yes. And you're right to be scared of it. It's hell. But I think you're worried about nothing. You've forgotten the relationship you and Cassie have. She still loves you. Little kids—they just say what's on their minds. They don't mean to hurt anyone. Right this second she might think she wants to live with her dad forever, but . . . What was she doing when you called?"

"Swimming. Wayne got her out of the pool to talk to me."

"There you have it. She's having a great time and you start talking about leaving."

She took another swallow of wine. "Maybe," she conceded. "I really am glad she's happy up there. She's adapted so well."

"You raised a resilient daughter." He swirled the wine in his glass and then leaned forward. "Why do you think you're fake in California and not here?"

Eden sighed. "I'm a good actress, Ben. I can fool people. I can make them think I'm confident and strong and . . . untouched by events in my life. You learn to wear the mask. After you've done that for a while, you get stuck behind it. But I can't fool Lou and Kyle. You can't fool the people you grew up with, the ones who know the real you, warts and all." She looked at him squarely. She could be honest with him. "And I don't want to fool you. It's a relief to feel real around someone for a change. No offense, but part of the reason I feel so safe around you is that I think you're as screwed up as I am." She took a deep breath. "May I have some more wine, please?"

He was smiling, nearly laughing. He shook his head. "No, you may not. I have no interest in making you numb." He stood up then, shoving the coffee table out of the way with his leg, and held his hand out to her. "Come here," he said.

He led her to the bed and sat her down on the blue-and-white quilt. She felt the layers of fabric, the knots and seams, beneath her palms. He sat next to her and unfastened the clip at the back of her head, and her hair fell softly to her shoulders. He lifted it in slow motion to kiss the nape of her neck, and she felt her blood rushing there to meet his lips.

"You have a beautiful neck," he said. "But when your hair is up it makes you look very, very vulnerable."

"I thought it made me look matronly."

"Nothing could make you look matronly." He cupped his hand under her calf and lifted her leg across his lap. He began untying her tennis shoe and she watched silently as his fingers deftly worked the laces. He motioned her to raise her other leg. "You okay?" he asked as he tugged at one end of the shoelace.

She knew he was asking if he should proceed. "Fine." She leaned back on her hands, remembering the elaborate explanation her mother had given Matt to keep him from getting any closer. "In the journal, my poor father is in love with my mother and he's trying to get close to her. They're still just kids. Well, eighteen or so. My mother got spooked. She wants it and she doesn't want it. So she stops him with this long lecture on how sex and friendship don't mix. I feel sorry for her. It's obvious she cares about him and wants to make love to him—she's immensely aware of her own sexuality—but she turned what could have been a warm and passionate moment into a cerebral exercise."

Ben set her shoe on the floor. "Like you're doing now, you mean."

She gave him a defensive stare. "I'm making conversation."

"And you're not going to get spooked?" He reached across her to turn out the lamp and his arm brushed her breasts, deliberately, she thought.

The room dimmed. Only the lamp near the sofa lit Ben's face, and the angle of light altered his features, made him a stranger.

"I might," she said. Her heart was pounding. She had a sudden fear that if they made love it would indeed change things.

He leaned toward her and she set her fist against his chest. "Wait."

She saw the question in his eyes as he pulled away from her.

"Could we talk a little longer?" she asked.

He smiled. "A few more cerebral calisthenics, huh?" He moved up on the bed, pulling her along with him until they were lying face to face, close together on the narrow bed, sharing one long pillow. "You're not alone in being uptight about this," he said. His hand rested on her hip, fingers splayed, his thumb tracing the line of her hipbone. "I felt sexually dead after my divorce. It was like that part of me had died. But the first night you and I were together at Sugar Hill, I discovered it was alive after all." He grinned at her. "That's why I was such a jerk that night. I felt like a thirteen-year-old kid with his first public erection. It took me completely by surprise. I didn't know what to do with it."

Never would Wayne have shared something that intimate with her. Wayne would not even share that sort of thinking with himself. And Michael would have made up some excuse for acting like a fool, something to protect his carefully inflated ego.

"I admire your openness," she said. "You're not at all afraid to be yourself."

"Thanks, but that's not completely true."

"I'd like to tell you why I'm with Michael."

"Now? I'd rather not have him here in bed with us."

"I need to tell you, though, because I don't want you to think I do this easily."

He brushed a strand of her hair back from her face and let his fingers rest for a moment on her throat before returning them to the arc of her hipbone. "Okay," he said. "Tell me."

"I was nervous about seeing anyone after Wayne and I separated. I finally got up the courage to go out with this guy. We kissed good night, that was it, but he spread it all over town that we slept together. I was holding my breath, waiting for one of the tabloids to pick it up. I could just see the headline, I FUCKED EDEN RILEY, across the front page."

Ben frowned. "Do you think I would do something like that?"

"No, no. I didn't mean that. I'm just trying to explain why I'm with Michael. You see, I would lose so much if that sort of thing happened, if my public image deteriorated. If I'm linked first with one guy, then another. I'd definitely lose the Children's Fund. Maybe even Cassie. Wayne would be back in court so fast I wouldn't know what hit me. He'd make me look loose and less fit to have Cassie than he already has. That's where Michael comes in. He cares about me, to the extent that Michael's capable of caring about anyone other than himself, and I can call all the shots. I don't have to worry about dating, being linked with other people, rumors. Michael is very safe for me."

"My God, you really can't live your own life, can you? You can't be yourself."

"It's difficult."

"But you said you and Michael aren't lovers. Don't you need that? Sex?"

"Not this last year I haven't. And even with Wayne, I would never say I needed it. He said I lacked desire." She made a face, lowered her eyes to the quilt. Was there nothing she wouldn't tell him?

Ben laughed. "Well, that's certainly bullshit."

"How would you know?"

"Well, I don't want to embarrass you." He tugged her T-shirt from her shorts as he spoke and slipped one warm hand inside on her back. "But every once in a while I catch you staring at me with a look that says 'I want your body, Ben Alexander.' It hasn't been my imagination, has it? Not just wishful thinking?"

"No, it's not your imagination." She slid the tips of her fingers tentatively beneath the snap of his jeans and heard his quick intake of breath. "I think I'm going to explode if we don't make love right now. Does that qualify as desire?"

She could see his smile in the dim light. "Close enough," he said. He raised himself up on one elbow and kissed her, then lowered his head to her breast. She tugged him closer by the waistband of his jeans and he nibbled her breast through her shirt. She wanted her shirt off, wanted to feel his lips against her skin. She reached for the hem, but he caught her hands.

"Birth control?" he asked.

"Oh." The color rose in her cheeks. She had not given it a thought. She would remember later, no doubt. But that would be a little late. "I stopped taking the Pill when I was divorced. I completely forgot I needed to worry."

He groaned and buried his head against her stomach. Then he grabbed her hands and pulled her off the bed. "C'mon."

"Where are we going?" She scooped up her shoes.

"Drugstore."

"But Ben." It was ten winding miles to the nearest drugstore.

"Do you have another suggestion? I doubt a pregnancy would do much for your image." He grabbed his keys and was pulling her toward the door. She saw he was not angry, not even upset. He seemed to be enjoying this. "I could leave you here while I go but I'm afraid you might take a page from your mother's book and make love to yourself—as you so sweetly worded it—and there'd be nothing left for me by the time I got back with the goods."

She climbed into the passenger seat of his truck, laughing. There was something about his sudden rush of joy, about the caution he would take with her body when she hadn't thought of it herself, that made her want him even more. She sat close to him, resting her cheek on his shoulder, and slowly stroked his chest through the soft cotton of his T-shirt. She felt the springiness of the hair beneath the fabric, the small rigid knots of his nipples, the hard edge of his rib cage. The only sound in the truck was his breathing. He kept his hands on the steering wheel but she felt his chin against her temple.

"Ten fucking miles," he said at about the halfway point. "I knew there was a good reason I should have found a place closer to town."

Thunder sounded in the distance as they climbed out of the truck in the small parking lot of the drugstore. The light inside the store was glaringly offensive and it took them a minute to find the condom display.

"Look at this." Ben shook his head at the rows of condoms. "The last time I used one of these things, there were about two brands to choose from. Do you want something fancy?"

"Just utilitarian, Ben." She turned her face into his shoulder and he smiled at her discomfort.

"Wait in the truck," he said.

She could see him at the cash register from her perch inside the truck. She tried looking at him with objective eyes. He was startlingly handsome. In a rugged way, not like Michael. The young female cashier had to be jealous of whoever inspired his purchase. Ben said a few words to the young woman, and they both laughed. He was buying condoms. What could they possibly be saying to each other? She was glad she'd chosen to wait outside.

Condoms. God. The last time she'd even seen one had been in high school. The drama crowd. The actors, Lou called them. The impostors, Kyle would rejoin, infuriating Eden. She could remember several occasions when she'd sat outside a drugstore waiting for one of them—Tex, or Will, or Bo—to buy cigarettes, Hershey bars, and rubbers. She'd be sitting in a VW Bug then, or a Chevy. Or on Tex's motorcycle, the inside of her thighs building in anticipation as she straddled the leather seat. She shuddered now to remember those days and the constant lies she told Lou and Kyle. She tested their love over and over again, while she ran off with people whose rejection couldn't hurt her because it was so predictable.

She watched Ben push through the drugstore doors. He threw the package up in the air with his left hand and caught it behind his back with his right. She smiled, let the memories fade.

This time when she set her hand on his chest, Ben stopped the truck in the middle of the road and pulled his T-shirt over his head. He dropped it into the space behind his seat and began driving again. He steered with his left hand and reached for her with his right. She turned to face him and his hand traced the shape of her breasts, his fingers light as feathers. A few scattered raindrops dotted the windshield and the thunder sounded again, this time closer and deeper. The roads began to twist so sharply that every once in a while Ben had to take his hand from her to steer. He finally stopped the truck square in the road again and slid both hands beneath the back of her T-shirt, hunting for the hook on her bra.

"It's in front," she said. She reached up and unhooked it for him and he kissed her, cupping her breasts gently in his hands before he began driving again.

The inside of the truck felt like a sauna. Ben's chest was damp beneath her fingers, and when he stroked her breast her skin burned as it had that first day she met him, when he touched her knee.

"Windows are steaming up," he said.

Her own breathing was as coarse and loud as his now, and when he softly tugged at her nipple she dropped her hand to the crotch of his jeans and cupped her fingers possessively around his erection.

Ben suddenly turned the truck into the woods and brought it to a jolting stop.

"What are you doing?" She withdrew her hand as he turned to pull a blanket from behind his seat.

"It's seven more miles to the cabin," he said. "I don't know about you, but I'm not going to make it."

A warm rain was falling and a bolt of lightning lit the woods as they climbed out of the truck. Ben laid the blanket on the ground above a cushion of leaves. He moved quickly, acting as if it were an emergency. And maybe it was in a way. She caught his frenzy as she lowered herself to the blanket. She pulled off her shirt and the loose bra while he tugged her shorts to her knees with one hand and unzipped his own pants with the other.

She felt impatient with kissing. When he moved his hand from her breast to her stomach she caught it and guided him lower. He let out his breath when he slipped his fingers inside her.

"You're soaked," he said.

"I know." She felt her pulse beating where he touched her and she whimpered when he drew his hand away.

"Hold on," he said.

She heard him unwrap the condom but couldn't see him in the darkness. Then his hands were on her knees, easy and unhurried now as he parted her thighs and lowered his head between her legs.

She sank her fingers gratefully into his hair, lifted her hips to meet him.

The rain washed over her face, spiked against her belly. When she was very close Ben raised himself to his knees and entered her. For a moment the momentum was lost and she panicked, thrusting against him in her struggle to find it again.

"Easy," he said, holding her hips, drawing her into a rhythm. The feeling grew again as she rocked with him. "Okay?" he asked.

"Yes."

Lightning struck dangerously close to them just as she peaked, and a clap of thunder shook the ground beneath their blanket. Ben's hands were on her shoulders, holding her, containing her as her body spun out of control. He pressed into her one final time, deeper now, his breath caught somewhere in his throat, and then she felt him shudder and go still. Eden breathed with her mouth open, pulling in warm, wet air. She ran her hands down the length of his back, slick with rain, and he said in her ear, "You really ought to do something about that lack of desire of yours, Eden."

She laughed as he raised himself to his elbow. He leaned down to kiss her and in the darkness found her eyes instead of her lips. "That was pretty dramatic," he said. "I thought maybe you'd been struck by lightning."

"That's what it felt like." She wished she could see him. She reached up and stroked his lips with her fingertips. He caught her hand and turned it to kiss the palm, and in that simple gesture she felt reassured that what she had just done was not a mistake.

"You can have the shower first," Ben said when they reached the cabin. "I'll dig up something for you to wear."

The bathroom was tiny. There was barely enough room for her to turn around. Ben knocked on the door and handed her a towel.

"Oh, and leave Charlotte alone, please."

"Charlotte?"

"She's in the shower stall and she was here when I moved in. She's kind of my roommate."

He shut the door and Eden pulled open the shower curtain to reveal a huge black spider hanging in the corner near the ceiling. She kept her eye on it while she showered in case Charlotte was the jealous type.

She brushed her teeth with Ben's toothpaste on her finger. Then she noticed the bottle of Valium on the ledge of the sink. She lifted it, read the label. Ben Alexander. The date was six months earlier. The doctor's name was also Alexander. His brother, most likely. The label specified twenty pills. She opened the bottle and poured the pills into her palm to count them. Twenty. He hadn't taken any. But they were here, close at hand. She looked at the bathroom door as if she could see Ben on the other side. Poor man. What had he been through?

She jumped at the knock on the door and a few of the pills fell to the floor.

"You ready for some clothes?" Ben asked.

"In a second." She picked up the pills that had fallen and set the bottle back on the sink before opening the door.

"You look great," he said when she finally emerged from the bathroom.

The T-shirt he'd given her was black and, she thought, looked passably sexy on her. The blue drawstring shorts were cinched at her waist but otherwise hung from her.

"How about some dinner?" he asked.

She looked at her watch. Nearly ten. She was starving. "Okay."

"I have some hot dogs and a can of baked beans but that's about it."

"I'll cook while you shower."

"Will you stay tonight?"

"After you feed me baked beans?"

He smiled. "Please?"

She wanted to. "I'll have to call Lou and Kyle."

Ben lost his smile. "Maybe I'd better call them."

"No." She gave him a push. "Take your shower."

She had never seen a kitchen so desolate. The shelf above the stove held a couple of cans of soup, some rice, and a box of cornflakes. The refrigerator was no better with its lettuce and hot dogs, milk and wine and orange juice. She put three hot dogs in a frying pan, poured the can of baked beans into a saucepan and set it on the stove, all the while staring at the green phone on his night table. What was the worst they could say? Ben was not Tex or Will or Bo. They loved Ben.

Lou answered.

"Hi, Lou," Eden said. "It's so stormy out. I'm going to stay up here tonight." She grimaced, and for a moment Lou said nothing.

"You're at Ben's?" Lou asked finally.

"Yes."

"The storm's really letting up."

"I want to stay, Lou." She twisted the cord in her fingers. Lou sighed. "You know how it is, dear. You never stop worrying. Wait until Cassie's a grown woman. You'll see."

"I'm fine."

"Of course."

25

It was still dark when he heard Eden gasp and sit up in the bed.

"Eden?"

"Nightmare," she said.

He tugged at her shoulder. "Lie down again."

"I can't. Can we turn the light on?"

He switched on the lamp on the apple crate. She raised the sheet to her chest and looked around the room, from object to object as though assuring herself she was here, awake. She reminded him of Bliss when she'd awaken from a bad dream and need reassurance that she was in her own room, surrounded by the safe and familiar.

In the circle of light from the lamp he could see rough shadows on her face, fine lines across her forehead. The signs of age in her face touched him, the signs so few people were allowed to see.

"Tell me about the dream." He laid his hand on her back. Her skin was damp with perspiration.

"I've had it nearly every night since I've been in Virginia."

"Really?"

"It's about Lou." She shook her head, smiled as though she felt foolish. He could see the threads of the dream leaving her, falling away. "Can't talk about it," she said.

He did not mind that she wanted to have a secret. It gave him more right to keep his from her. Still, he felt sad that reality was so quickly seeping into this perfect night.

"We can leave the light on." He eased her back to the pillow. She was shivering in spite of the heat, and he tucked the sheet around her shoulders. "Are you all right?"

"I gave myself to you."

"Yes," he said, puzzled.

"I don't mean physically." She looked up at him, her eyes credulous, unmasked. "I mean, I've told you so much. I've let you know the real me. It's always scared me to do that. But it's okay, isn't it? I'm safe."

"Yes," he said, and he felt a lump form in his throat because he knew that she was not safe with him at all.

She sighed and pulled herself closer to him. "Just hold me, Ben," she said, although he already was.

When he woke for a second time, the sun was pouring into the cabin. Eden's head was on his shoulder, and a sinking feeling lay heavily in the pit of his stomach. Kyle would be angry with him, and justified in his anger. The only way he could make it right was to tell her.

He felt the heavy warmth of her in his arms. She stretched, her body lithe and catlike, then leaned back to look at him. She gave him a big smile, a smile that told him she was waking up exactly where she wanted to be.

"Would you consider moving to California?" she asked.

He laughed. "Sure. I could become one of the plastic people."

"I wasn't joking."

He kissed her. "I need to talk to you."

She set the tip of her finger on his lips. "I don't want to hear."

This was not the time or place, anyway, he thought with some relief. Not in bed, for Christ's sake.

She sat up and turned to face him, holding the sheet against her chest as she had the night before. She grinned at him. "We wrecked your bed."

"We certainly did." The sheets had pulled free of the mattress and were twisted like sailors' knots over their legs. In the middle of the night they'd heard one of the bed slats give way under their endeavors but had been in no mood to do anything about it. He had not had a night like this in many years.

Whatever signs of age or fatigue he had seen in her face the night before were gone now. Her skin was smooth and the sun rested like gold on her long eyelashes. He carefully pried her fingers from the top of the sheet and it fell to her lap. He watched her nipples rise under the touch of his eyes. He was about to tell her that he wanted to make love to her in the sunlight, but he stopped himself. He knew he would not be able to. The trap he was in was entirely too clear to him this morning.

Suddenly she stretched over him, her breasts a delicate weight on his chest, her lips on his. He should have told her last night. He had no right to make love to her without her knowing. She set her head on his chest and reached for his lifeless penis with her long silky fingers. He let her stroke him, but he felt nothing. What words could he possibly use to tell her? He ran his fingers down her arm until he reached her hand and drew it up to his lips. "I think we wore it out," he said. "I'm sorry."

"No, I'm sorry. I don't mean to be greedy."

He got out of bed and headed for the shower without looking at her because he had a horrible feeling he was going to cry. I gave myself to you, she'd said. Jesus. He'd had no right to take as much as he did.

When he returned to the room she was dressed and sitting on the edge of his bed, an empty orange juice glass in her hand. She looked up at him with worry in her face. "Are you upset with me?"

"God, no." He bent over and kissed her. "I'm in love with you."

He watched her swallow, watched how quickly her eyes filled. "Oh, Ben," she said.

"But it's absolutely essential that you and I talk about my divorce."

"Okay."

"Why don't I take you out for an early dinner tonight?" Probably not a great idea. Could he tell her in a restaurant?

"Okay. But it's my treat this time. You bought me lunch, and I've been drinking your wine and eating your baked beans."

She was pitying him, patronizing him. He thought of the four dollars he had in his wallet and his body jerked as though he'd touched a live wire. A terrible impotent fury reared up inside him.

"I don't want to live this way any longer!" He grabbed the empty orange juice glass from her hand and threw it across the room, where it hit the wooden wall with a dull crack and fell in pieces on the floor.

She stood up calmly and folded him into a tight embrace. "It's all right," she said.

His body shook beneath her arms; his breathing was raspy, uneven. "I'm sorry, Eden." He clutched the hem of her T-shirt in his fist. "I scare myself sometimes. I don't recognize myself."

Her arms tightened around him. "Money isn't important," she said.

He let go of her and took a few steps backward, sinking his hands into his pockets. "Eden, no matter what happens between us from now on, thank you for last night. I don't remember the last time I felt that completely happy."

"You make it sound as though it has to end."

He felt the happiness slipping away. "I think that will be up to you."

It was nearly eleven when Kyle joined him at the site. He climbed down the ladder into the pit where Ben was working and turned a bucket upside down to sit on. Ben felt the muscles in his chest contract. Kyle wasn't here to work.

Ben stood up to face him. "I guess you have a few things to say to me."

"About January. Do you want me to write to Carl Petrie? He can use some help down there in Florida."

Ben frowned. He'd expected Kyle to talk about Eden. But this was the same thing, wasn't it? "What if I said I was going to try to find something in California so I could be near Eden?"

"Well, I'd say maybe you weren't being too realistic."

"You mean I'm not good enough for her."

Kyle sighed, set his hands on his knees. "If things were different, you'd be the best thing in the world for her. But your situation, Ben . . . I don't want to see her hurt."

"Neither do I."

"She came home this morning all light and smiling—and a little tired." He gave Ben a concessionary smile. "I've never seen her like that. She doesn't trust easily. She's been let down once too often, and I worry that the higher she goes with you, the steeper the drop's going to be."

"Maybe there won't be a drop."

"And it seems to me you're setting yourself up for a lot of grief, Ben. Even if you could work out this one major snag, I can't picture you fitting into her lifestyle. You barely know her. And she certainly doesn't know you."

"I'm going to tell her today," Ben said quietly. "She's bringing something over here later for a picnic."

"Nice timing. You tell her after you sleep with her."

Ben ignored the cut. He looked down at Kyle. "I'm going to lose her."

Kyle shook his head. "You don't have her to lose. The little you have you got under false pretenses."

Ben's throat tightened, and his voice shook when he spoke. "What's happening between you and me?" he asked. "I don't want to argue with you, Kyle. You're just about all I've got."

Kyle rose to his feet. He walked over to Ben and put his arms around him, held him close. "I don't want to argue with you either," he said. He stood back and reached for the ladder, avoiding Ben's eyes. There was something unfamiliar in his face. A helplessness. A powerlessness so alien to Kyle's demeanor that for a moment he looked like a completely different man, and Ben felt afraid for him.

"Kyle?"

Kyle turned back to face him, one hand on the ladder. "I'm going to have to hurt her myself soon, Ben."

Ben stepped toward him, truly frightened now. "What do you mean? You're not sick, are you?"

Kyle shook his head. "No, nothing like that. I can't say just now. I'm only telling you that it's going to happen. I don't want her to feel betrayed by both of us at the same time."

26

August 3, 1947

Last night, on my 20th birthday, Sara Jane gave birth to a baby girl who has no arms. Susanna told me this morning and I guess it is the talk of Coolbrook. This baby has little dangly hands where her arms should be. Much as I had differences with Sara Jane in the past, I feel sorry for her now. Imagine how it feels to carry a baby all those months and be full of hope and joy, only to take one look at it and know it has no chance for happiness. I was trying to work on a story in the cave this afternoon, but I just can't get Sara Jane and her baby off my mind, so I figured I would have to write about it in my journal.

I haven't touched this journal in a very long time. From time to time I come across the notebooks and feel like throwing them out. The journal seems like such a part of my childhood, and there is not too much about my childhood I want to remember. But something stops me from throwing them out each time I have a mind to. I feel awkward writing in the journal now. It's like meeting up with an old friend after too long an absence, having to get a feel for them all over again.

I did do a lot of writing this year, though. More than twenty children's stories—I needed the companionship of my young characters with both Kyle and Matt gone. But they are back now for the summer and Matt is *quitting school to start a paper in Coolbrook. He's taken to wearing suits and smoking a pipe! But when he can, he changes to dungarees and helps Kyle and me dig. We have carved a pit into the earth in front of the cave and are finding arrowheads and pieces of clay. Even though Kyle's going back to school next month, he'll be home weekends to work in the pit. His interest in discovering what lies below the earth will keep him here. As for me, I've decided never to leave Lynch Hollow again. There is nothing for me outside except discomfort.*

I wrote other stories this summer too that would put Lady Chatterley and her lovers to shame. Those I've hidden. They are just for me and they were far more important than my children's stories in helping me survive this last year without Kyle and Matt.

August 5, 1947

Today I met Ellie Miller, Sara Jane's new baby. I woke up this morning after having dreamt about that baby for the fourth time—this time she had no feet, the last time no face—and I knew I had to see her.

I asked Kyle if he would take me and he looked at me like I was crazy. "Leave her alone, Kate," he said. "Let Sara Jane have her grief in private."

But something was driving me. Susanna said I could borrow her old bicycle, and though it's been a few years since I was on one, I had no trouble riding it. I picked a bunch of wildflowers from the field near Ferry Creek, stuck them in the basket, and went on my way.

I've kept so close to the cave this last year that I'd forgotten how bad I feel out in the world. When I reached the part of the road with the cornfields on both sides I felt dizzy, like I would fall off the bicycle any minute. But I made it all the way to Coolbrook and felt right proud of myself. I was still nervous, though, and by the time I got to Sara Jane's door I was trembling.

Sara Jane herself opened the door. She is big as a house and her eyes were puffed out, from crying, I assumed, and I felt sad for her.

"Hello, Sara Jane," I said. "I've come to visit your new baby." I held out the flowers and she took them from my arms and stepped aside to let me in, all without saying a word to me.

Tommy Miller was sitting at the table in the little dining part of their living room and he said "hi" to me, and "thanks for coming."

Then Sara Jane said it was way too soon for anyone to visit the baby—
she was only three days old and there were germs she might catch. But
Tommy said, "Oh, let her see her. Have a seat there, Miss." He called me
"Miss" and I figured he didn't remember who I was.

I sat down on the sofa and Sara Jane disappeared in another room and
came out holding the tiniest little baby I've ever seen, wrapped up in a pink
blanket. She put her in my arms, and I learned something about myself
right then. I want to be a mother. I want to have a baby of my own.

Ellie Miller is adorable beyond words. First she was asleep and looked
like an angel with her pretty face and a little bit of peach fuzz on her head.
Sara Jane had given her to me wrapped up so I couldn't see her arms, but
I was determined. If I was going to spend all my sleeping hours dreaming
about this baby, I wanted to get it right. So I tugged the blanket away with
Sara Jane standing above me, breathing like a steam engine. Ellie has
little hands where her arms should be. Tiny, precious little hands. I know
this baby was put together wrong, but somehow I couldn't see it just then.
She seemed beautiful to me, like maybe it's all the rest of us who are not
formed right. I had a hard time giving her back to Sara Jane, who still had
said next to nothing to me. I thought of what it would be like for her when
she started taking little Ellie out, when people would stare and talk behind
her back, and my heart nearly broke for her. For Sara Jane! When I was
about to leave I said to her, "People can be mean, Sara Jane. Just you don't
listen to them. Ellie is beautiful and you and I both know it." She still said
nothing to me. She probably fainted once I left, not sure what to make of
Kate Swift talking kindly to her.

Kyle was mad when I got home. He says you just don't do that sort of
thing—barge into someone's house when there's a brand new baby—even
if it's a healthy baby that everybody's excited about showing off. I told him
there's never been a time in my life when I've cared about what was proper
or improper and I wasn't about to start caring now.

October 5, 1947

I visited Ellie again today. Why am I so drawn to her? I still dream about
her. The doctor told Sara Jane that Ellie will be "backward." Slow to talk

and walk, he means, and slow to learn things. She'll probably never be able to read and write and that, in my opinion, is the cruelest blow.

"But she can still imagine," I said to Sara Jane.

"What does that mean?" Sara Jane all but barked at me. She still doesn't care much for me.

I tried to explain how being able to dream things up is the most important thing in the world, more important than having arms or being able to add two plus two. I thought I was sounding poetic, but Sara Jane looked at me like she used to in grammar school—like I was too weird to be believed.

October 25, 1947

Kyle is home for the weekend and it is too rainy to dig and too rainy to bicycle over to see Ellie, so I begged him to take me over to Sara Jane's in the car and he finally agreed. I think he had some curiosity himself about the baby.

Sara Jane got all flustered at finding Kyle Swift on her doorstep and it made me giggle inside to see it. I went directly over to the bassinet where Ellie was sleeping and took her out to sit with on the sofa. Meanwhile, Sara Jane and Kyle sat down and tried to think of things to say to each other and I saw right away that Sara Jane still loves him. I recognize the feeling in her clearly—it's the only thing she and I have in common. I watched her watching him. She was thinking how different her life would be now if she'd been true to him, waited for him. She was thinking she could have married him, instead of ending up with a baker who stuffs her with cake and keeps her so fat she can barely get up out of a chair. She was thinking how if she'd stayed with Kyle she might have a child now that was whole, a child no other children would snicker at on the street. She looked at Kyle with such longing. When he moved, when he stood up to come sit next to me and have a look at Ellie, I could see her remembering what it was like to make love to him and I could see more than anything the regret in her eyes.

And what do I see in Kyle's eyes for her? It's not pity, and that surprises me. It's more like compassion. I can see he still cares about her, not as a girlfriend, but as a human being. Despite how she hurt him, despite how, at twenty, she's let herself fall apart, he still cares, which pretty much sums up the kind of person my brother is.

While Kyle and Sara Jane chit-chatted, I had my own little talk with Ellie. I can prop her up on my lap and she looks at me, though her eyes wander off after a minute or two. I played with her, with her tiny perfect hands, but what I longed to do was cuddle her. I wanted to hold her close to my breast. I'm so envious of Sara Jane for being able to nurse her. I got misty-eyed, sitting there, thinking of how I'll most likely never have a baby of my own. I can't imagine getting close enough to a man to allow that to happen. I thought I've been hiding this longing well, joking when Susanna and Daddy talk about me ever getting married or having a family. But Kyle knows. I should have guessed he would. He seems to know the world inside my head. After we left Sara Jane's and were driving back to Lynch Hollow in the pouring rain, he said, "You want a child of your own."

I was startled by the matter-of-fact way he said it, without even taking his eyes off the road to look at me. I said, "I'll never have one of my own."

"Matt would be right pleased to provide you with one," he said.

"I haven't seen it rain this hard in years," I said, and that was that.

September 10, 1948

I have amazing news, but first I have to update this journal a bit. I can't believe it's been almost a year since I've written in it! I used to keep it under my pillow, write in it day and night. Today I had trouble even finding this notebook.

Ellie Miller is now a year old. She is a very quiet child and still doesn't walk, but she has a smile that lights up your heart. I have only seen her a few times this year, when I go to the bakery with Susanna. I stopped visiting her because Susanna had heard from Priscilla Cates that my visits made Sara Jane nervous. Sara Jane can't relax around me, Priscilla said. I have no interest in upsetting Sara Jane, so I stopped coming to see Ellie and in a way I think that's good. Every time I saw her I wanted a baby and the feeling was turning into a painful one. So I've spent this year putting all my energy into writing and archaeology.

Our digs have grown around us. Kyle has been home from school all summer and we have two pits dug in front of the cavern. We've unearthed arrowheads and pottery that date back three thousand years and we have gotten very organized in cataloging them. Much of the day, I am torn between the careful, painstaking work of chipping away at the earth, dusting the years off the old pieces, and writing my stories. I switch from one activity to the other easily and I feel sorry for Kyle with just one interest to consume him. But he seems quite content as well. He has found his calling.

I've thought a great deal about Rosie, the little skeleton in the maze room. We have never gone back to look at her again and we have no way of knowing when she lived and died. But thinking about her gave me the idea of writing a story about a child who lived in the times we're studying from the digs. The story turned out very well. In July, Matt had to go to a meeting in New York, and he took my story with him to read on the train. Here is the great news: when he returned, he presented me with a check for one hundred dollars! He'd sold my story to a publisher, Waverly Books, and next year it will appear as an actual book, illustrated by someone at the publishing house. And they want more! Matt, who had this plan up his sleeve for several months, said they are ecstatic about my work. But they want the stories to be longer and more detailed, so that is what I'm working on now and what absorbs my thoughts much of the time.

July 10, 1949

Kyle graduated last month and he's already talking about going back to school because he wants to get a doctoral degree. I guess I have been hoping he would just settle himself down here now that he's done with school, but I have to face up to the fact that he's never going to settle here. Our digs have a hold on him, but he has too much wanderlust to stay for long. He promises to come home on weekends while he's going to school, so I am not too distressed.

I sold five more books this year and occasionally I write an article for the Coolbrook Chronicle, Matt's paper. No one thought a paper would ever make a go of it in Coolbrook since it's so small, but everyone reads the Chronicle now.

Yesterday, Matt was in the cave with me, reading while I typed and he *finally looked up and said, "You and I might as well get married. We're together most of the time anyway."*

I took the cotton out of my ears and said, "What did you say?" even though I'd heard him very well.

He said we wouldn't have to make love if I didn't want to, that he'd be content just being with me.

"What about all your fancy dinner parties and meetings and such? I could never go with you, you know." I wanted him to see how ridiculous his idea was.

"I don't care. You could stay here. I'd go by myself. I'd just like to be able to sleep with you at night."

When he said that I felt a funny little rise in me, like I'd like that too. I don't want to marry him and I don't want to make love to him—it would confuse things between us too much—but I like the idea of sleeping next to him the night through. I could slip him into my bedroom after Daddy and Susanna were asleep and just feel the warmth of him all night long. I think he probably could sleep with me without touching me. He's never tried since that time in Georgetown, although a few times he's kissed me on the cheek. I think Matt's still a virgin.

July 12, 1949

I told Kyle what Matt said about wanting to sleep with me and Kyle said I should do it if I want to but I shouldn't expect him not to touch me. I said I thought Matt was a virgin and Kyle laughed. "Get your head out of the sand, Kate," he said. He told me that Matt has two sides to him. There's the soft, gentle side he shows to me and to most of the girls he goes out with. And then there's his "animal side", Kyle called it, and this he shows to a few select girls. There is one in Luray, Kyle said, another in Strasburg.

I was shocked. "Matt?" I said. "Matt Riley?"

Kyle said, "It's you he really wants. He gets all steamed up around you and he has to have someplace he can let it out."

I can't look at Matt quite the same way now. He sits in here—as a matter of fact, he's here right now—reading, with those big innocent brown eyes that are not so innocent after all. I will not be sleeping with him anytime soon, but I'm glad to know this about him. I used to feel guilty, like I was depriving him of something. Now I find he's been getting that something all along.

October 29, 1949

Kyle has been home every weekend since school started. He is driven. He's interested Dr. Latterly—who he calls "Stan" now—in his "backyard dig." He got Dr. Latterly to come down here to visit Lynch Hollow and a more comical scene I'd never witnessed. It was a Saturday two weeks ago, and Kyle and the professor came to the cave. This man did not know what to make of a woman typing with cotton in her ears and a gentleman (Matt) reclined, reading, and smoking a pipe on the settee. Kyle and Matt and I treated it all as normal. Dr. Latterly was a little shaken, I think, but he was impressed with what Kyle and I have done here, so now he's gearing his work with Kyle to our specific needs.

Easter Sunday, 1950

Matt brought the woman he is seeing to Easter dinner. He has been dating quite a few lately, and making no secret of it to me. Trying to get me jealous, I suppose, and it's not working. Matt is viewed as one of the most alluring young men around, as is Kyle, although Kyle is not here enough to take advantage of that status. Kyle says he's not even dating much at school, which I find hard to believe, but he is very caught up in his professional pursuits these days, so I guess it's possible.

Matt's lady friend, Delores, is thoroughly in love with him. I was fascinated, watching her watch him. She tried to anticipate his every desire. It was revolting. I know Matt doesn't return her love and adoration. I wonder if she knows about the hussy he sees in Luray? A few months ago I told him I knew about his sordid little side interests. He was at first mad at Kyle for telling me and then pleased, I think, that he could speak more openly with me about the women in his life. Our friendship is the best it's ever been. I know he would like more from me, and I know it is his caring about me that prevents him from getting serious with anyone else, but I've told him we will never be more than friends. I believe he's finally come to accept that.

November 10, 1951

Yesterday my tenth book was published and Kyle and Matt and I drank champagne in the cavern until we were punchy. I felt warm and satisfied and I started talking, saying way too much. I said what a lucky person I was to have four loves in my life when many women must settle for one, or less.

Kyle and Matt set down their glasses to listen to me and I began ticking off my four loves. "My writing," I said. "The digs. My brother." Kyle held his glass up to me in a salute. "And my cavern."

Well, I was quite satisfied with my little speech and we finished the bottle and it wasn't until the buzz of the champagne started to wear thin and we could feel the chill settle into the air of the cave that I realized Matt had not spoken. There was hurt in his eyes and I nearly vomited when I realized why: I had left him out. How could I have been so mean? It would not have hurt me to say I had five loves and included him. I do love him as my dear friend, but the truth is that it never occurred to me to name him, and it was certainly too late to add him on as an afterthought.

"It's cold in here," he said finally, standing up. "I'm going home."

"Not yet," said Kyle. I could tell from his face that he also knew what was bothering Matt. "We can all sit in the house for a while."

I should have said something then. Oh yes, Matt, come sit in the house with us. But instead I got down on the ice cold floor and began picking up the scattered pages from the story I was working on.

"I have an early day tomorrow," Matt said from behind me. I heard his footsteps on the floor of the cave and then silence as he entered the forest.

I couldn't move from my place on the floor. I stared at the pages resting there, thinking of how hurtful I could be without even trying. Then Kyle knelt next to me. "Come on, Katie," he said. "Let's go in the house."

"I didn't mean to hurt him," I said. I think I was crying. Kyle smoothed my hair behind my ear. "I know. He'll be all right."

"I should have thought before I spoke."

"Shh." Kyle sat on the ground behind me and hugged me into his arms. He told me he'd talk to Matt for me tomorrow, tell him how bad I felt, how it was an oversight, nothing more. He kept talking like that, his breath

sweet with champagne, but after a while I stopped listening. My back was against his chest, his cheek soft on my hair. Cold as it was, I could have sat like that all night.

So today Matt informed me that he is now engaged to Delores Winthrop. He told me this by note, because he is so much like me, best able to express himself on paper. He wrote,

Dearest Kate,
I have been foolishly hiding from the truth. For so long I have kidded myself into thinking that you love me, or at least had the potential to love me. It is something I wished for so desperately, you cannot know. I admire you so—your beauty, your spirit and ambition. I could easily put up with your "unusual" ways. I am charmed by them.

I can't be angry with you because you have never tried to deceive me about your feelings. The idea of you loving me has been my own fabrication and you can't be held responsible for what occurs in my tormented imagination. Last night as you described your four loves and I was not among them, I knew I must finally abandon my hope of having my love returned. Therefore I have proposed marriage to Delores. She is clearly my second choice, although I trust you will never tell her that.

I am nearly twenty-six and need to settle down. I truly hope, Kate, that you find someone who can unleash the loving woman I know is within you. I am sorry to have failed in that task.

All my love, Matt

I wept as I read his note, but I know this is best for him. I will miss his company so much. I am certain he will never bring Delores to visit the cave with him. I could see her looking down her nose at the suggestion, but she will make a fine wife for him.

There will come a day when Kyle will also want to marry. I hope she will be someone I can tolerate, not a silly girl like Sara Jane or a holier-than-thou sort like Julia from Georgetown. I'm not going to be jealous. She may share his home and his bed but she can never steal from me the life-long closeness I've had with him.

December 12, 1951

Kyle is to be Matt's best man and Delores's sister Vanessa will be her maid of honor. Matt is being swept quickly into their plans and every evening he comes to tell us more. He seems to have no control over what's happening to him. The wedding is planned for January 5th. I am less enthusiastic now about his getting married because I can see he's not happy about it. He looks like a man being sucked into quicksand. I want to speak—or perhaps write—to him about this. I want to tell him not to allow himself to be trapped in this way, but I know it is hardly my place and it would be very unfair of me.

December 23, 1951

Matt broke off his engagement to Delores. He came to the cavern last night and spoke very frankly with Kyle and me.

"I don't love her as I'm capable of loving a woman," he said. "She's put me off as a lover, saving herself for marriage as if she's some great prize. I can respect that, I suppose. I'd even be appreciative of it if I were truly interested in her, but I'm not even excited by the prospect of sleeping with her."

Kyle and I sat very still while he spoke because we'd never heard Matt speak with such candor.

"I'm dreading our wedding night because I'll be making love to Delores, but thinking of you, Kate." His face took on such color that he probably didn't even notice it in mine.

"I haven't been able to concentrate on this wedding or work or anything because I'm so obsessed with thoughts of you. If I married Delores I would lose you for good. I can't bear to have that happen. I'd rather have the little bit I have of you than nothing at all."

A long silence stretched between the three of us. I wanted Kyle to break it but knew he was looking at me and I had no choice but to speak.

"You have me on a pedestal, Matt," I said. "I'm never going to be a wife, to you or anyone else. I don't think you should marry Delores if you're so unhappy about it. But don't avoid marrying her on my account." All the

while I was speaking my heart was galloping. I am selfish straight to the core. I was glad of his decision. I want Matt here in the cave, but on my terms. That's what he said a long time ago. "Everything has to be on your terms, Kate." He was right.

27

She made chicken salad for their picnic supper, taking her time, savoring the simple domesticity of the task. She set the salad in the basket along with a bottle of wine, a couple of peaches, crusty rolls from Miller's Bakery, and two brownies Lou had baked that morning. Her actions were slow and deliberate, and she knew she was putting off seeing Ben, putting off hearing whatever it was he needed to tell her. Finally she could procrastinate no longer. She put on a blue sundress—Michael Carey's favorite—and set out for the site.

She'd spent the afternoon working on the screenplay and it had gone very well. She could see Michael clearly as Matt, especially now that she knew her father had a little of the rake in him. She would have to ask Kyle to tell her more about Matt's pursuits in Luray and Strasburg, how he had quenched his thirst for Kate in the arms of other women.

She was perspiring by the time she reached the site. Ben knelt in the third pit, in much the same position as the first time she'd seen him. She stood still for a moment in the burning sunlight, watching the muscles in his back contract beneath his blue T-shirt as he brushed the ground. There was a stirring in her body, a warmth that had nothing to do with the sun.

She called to him as she walked toward the pit and he waved and climbed up the ladder. The front of his T-shirt was soaked with sweat and he wiped his arm across his forehead. "How about up on the bridge?" He nodded toward the footbridge that crossed Ferry Creek. "Maybe there's a breeze up there."

They walked to the center of the bridge and sat with their legs dangling over the edge. The water below was black and silent as it cut through the forest to the hazy green mountains beyond. Eden clung to the suspension wires as the shivering of the bridge, and her vertigo, subsided.

"I used to play up here when I was a kid," she said as she unloaded the basket. The bridge had seemed as long as the river then. She remembered running across it, alone as always, stopping in the middle to pump her legs and make it sway. "You know how kids love to get dizzy." She handed him the bottle of wine and a corkscrew.

He stared at the distant hills, holding the bottle in his hand as though he had no idea why she'd given it to him, and she realized he had said nothing to her since leaving the pit.

She touched his shoulder. His shirt was damp beneath her fingers and his body felt rigid, unfamiliar. She drew her hand away. "Ben? Could you open the wine?"

He licked his dusty lips and turned to look at her. "Let's talk first and eat after, okay?"

She didn't want to talk. She didn't want to know what was draining the life from his face. And it was too hot out here. She pressed one of the napkins to her face, her throat. "I'm famished," she said. "I'd just as soon eat—"

"Eden." He shook his head at her and she knew she was making it more difficult for him.

She lowered the napkin to her lap. "Is it that serious?" she asked.

"It's extremely serious."

She put the bowl of chicken salad back into the basket and closed the lid. "All right."

He looked out at the stream again. "I don't know how to say this to you. I wish I knew a way to pretty it up." He set the bottle of wine down on the bridge and drew in a long breath. "The reason I'm divorced, the reason I lost my job, and the reason I can't see Bliss is that I was convicted of molesting her."

She frowned at him. "You molested your daughter?"

"No." He glared at her, then dropped his eyes. "I don't mean to yell, I just . . . No. I didn't do it. I was convicted, but I'm innocent."

Her body shrank away from him, ever so slightly, but he didn't miss it. She saw him working at control, the muscles in his jaw tensing, releasing.

"I didn't do it, Eden."

"Why would anyone think you did?"

He sighed and wrapped his hands around the edge of the bridge. His knuckles were white, the skin stretched taut above them. "There was evidence . . . It was enough to convince them that I had . . . Damn." He turned his head away from her, ran a shaky hand through his hair. "This isn't going to work. I don't know what to tell you to make you believe me. Everything I say is going to make it look worse."

She wanted to stay calm, to still the gallop of her heartbeat. She rested her hand on his arm. "Just tell me the truth, Ben. Who do you mean by 'them'? Was there a trial? With a jury?"

"Yes."

She pressed her fingers to her lips as the night before disintegrated in her memory. Had she actually slept with him? "Twelve people heard evidence and decided beyond a reasonable doubt that you were guilty?"

He turned to her. "I swear to you, Eden, I'm the last person on earth who would hurt Bliss."

"But you must have done something to make them think you did it."

He looked toward the hills again, and when he spoke he sounded very tired. "I didn't do anything. Doesn't matter though. Whenever someone finds out about it, they turn their back on me. I was hoping that wouldn't happen with you."

She remembered his joyful run to the drugstore for condoms, the thunderous lovemaking in the woods. He was a man who rescued lobsters from restaurants, who protected spiders in his bathroom. He couldn't possibly have molested his own child.

"I don't know what to think, Ben," she said quietly. "'There's nothing you could tell me you'd done that would disgust me quite as much. I think I'd be less horrified if you told me you'd been convicted of killing someone."

He gritted his teeth. "I didn't do it."

"Whether you did or not, I wish you'd told me about this sooner."

"You didn't want to know."

She thought of last night again. She'd felt listened to. Safe. Loved. Or had she just been used by a man no one else would have? If he'd told her sooner she never would have slept with him. I fucked Eden Riley. The muscles in her arms contracted; her hands curled into fists. "I had no idea it was anything like this," she said, her voice rising.

"You're right," he said wearily. "I should have told you sooner. I could have saved both of us a lot of grief."

She looked down at the water. "Last night was so nice," she said. "I felt . . . hopeful. I felt . . ." She bit her lower lip to stop its trembling, then turned to face him. "If you'd only been accused, Ben, I might feel differently. But a conviction." She thought of the little blond girl in the photograph and tears sprang to her eyes. "What did they say you did to her?"

He didn't answer. Instead he turned around so quickly she had to grab the guy wires to keep her balance. He packed the wine into the basket and pushed it closer to her. "Go," he said, his eyes a cold, hard gray. "Please just go."

Kyle and Lou were eating chicken salad sandwiches at the kitchen table when Eden returned to the house. She set the picnic basket on the counter and took a seat at the table.

"I wish you'd told me about Ben," she said to Kyle. "It's not as though he was caught shoplifting a candy bar."

Kyle put down his sandwich. "I tried to warn you off him, honey, but I didn't think it was my place to tell you the whole story. And frankly, I never expected the two of you to be interested in each other."

"You don't believe him?" Lou asked.

"I don't know what to believe. Of course he's going to deny it—who wouldn't? But he was convicted, Lou."

Kyle shook his head. "I think he was wrong not to tell you right off the bat, but I understand his thinking. Everyone who knows about him has taken off in the other direction as fast as they could run. I had a couple of graduate students working with me before he came, and when they found out it was Ben Alexander I'd hired to help out they quit on the spot. Everybody thinks like you do, Eden, that if he was convicted he must be guilty. But I'm as sure as I can be that he's not."

"How can you possibly know that?"

"Because I've known him for sixteen years. I watched him grow from an enthusiastic but very young student into a well-respected archaeologist. Do you know he didn't even have to apply for that professorship? Universities were soliciting him. He had his pick. But he's lost all that now. At first there was a lot of disbelief among his colleagues. Then it turned to disgust and now he's pretty much become the butt of their jokes."

"Kyle." She shook her head at her uncle's naïveté. "Profession has nothing to do with it. Neither does skill or enthusiasm or anything else. You can't possibly know who's capable of molesting a child by those things."

"We traveled all over with him. Shared hotel rooms. Spent weeks together without ever being out of each other's sight. There would have been a clue, something, that he had a problem."

"He hung himself at the trial," Lou said. "They were going to put his daughter on the stand to testify against him and—"

"A four-year-old?" Eden interrupted. She tried to picture Cassie in a courtroom, telling a roomful of adults the terrible things that had happened to her, and her heart broke for that blond wisp of a child on Ben's dresser mirror.

"Yes," Lou said. "Ben couldn't stand to see her up there, so he pled guilty, right in the middle of the trial. He told the judge he wasn't really guilty, but that he wanted to spare his daughter going through any more torture."

"He was a fool to do it," Kyle said, "but I guess you don't think straight under those circumstances. The judge ordered a recess and Ben's lawyer talked him into sticking it out, but the damage was done because the jury heard him say it. I think they should have started over with a new jury, but then I wasn't the judge."

Eden sighed. "I don't know, Kyle. I can't imagine why he'd blurt out he was guilty if there wasn't something to it."

"I've watched him with Sharon and I've watched him with his daughter," Kyle said. "He was a real family man. He was as content as he could be with his marriage and his life."

"That's what convinced me he was innocent, if nothing else," said Lou. "If he had admitted he hurt Bliss, all they would have done was slap him on the wrist and put him in a counseling program and he could have had his family back. But he couldn't admit to something he hadn't done. So instead he was locked up for six months and told he could never see his daughter again. He would never have made that choice unless he saw no way out of it."

In spite of herself, in spite of the revulsion that still festered in her stomach, she felt sorry for him.

"When he first moved down here, we talked about it for hours and hours," Lou continued. "We sat right here at this table and talked. You should let him tell you, Eden. I don't think you can listen to his side of the story and still think he's guilty. They twist things in a courtroom. He made a grave tactical error, and the prosecution had a better lawyer. That's what it boils down to sometimes."

Kyle leaned away from the table and shook his head. "He was in bad shape when he first got here. I think he sometimes wanted to kill himself. Scared us, didn't it?" He looked at Lou, who nodded. "We made him stay here a few nights because he got so upset talking about it we were afraid to let him go back up to his cabin. He never came right out and said he was suicidal, but he'd talk about wishing he were dead, not seeing much point to going on. It was hard to argue with him. Everything he'd worked for and cared about was gone."

She remembered the photograph he'd shown her of his house in Annapolis. His pride. His loss. She thought of the way he'd told her to leave him alone, the coolness in his eyes. The Valium in his bathroom.

"I had a couple of nightmares when he first got here," Kyle said. "I dreamt that I'd go up to the cabin and find him sitting in a rocker—though he doesn't have one up there—with a shotgun in his arms and his head splattered all over the wall behind him."

"I don't think he'd use a gun," she said quietly. "He has some Valium."

Kyle narrowed his eyes. "Was he upset when you left him?"

"I think so."

"Maybe I'd better go up and check on him."

"No." She stood up. "I'll go."

Lou caught her hand, squeezed it hard. "You're wise to be leery of him, Eden," she said. "He's going to carry that conviction around with him for the rest of his life. You're a public figure and a mother—you wouldn't be able to shake it. If you want to end your relationship with him, do it on those grounds, not because you think he hurt his daughter."

28

Ben wanted to get to his cabin, to the whiskey, before the jagged teeth of his memories had a chance to do their damage. But they caught up to him at his front door, and by the time he had the top off the bottle, by the time he felt the liquid burn his throat, he was theirs.

The moment that had changed his life forever had come on a cold January day, one week into the spring semester. He had stopped at the public library on his way home from the university, as he did at least once a week, to pick up some books for Bliss's bedtime stories. When he arrived home he found Sharon sitting at the kitchen table, her hands folded in her lap. Her strawberry-blond hair was up in a ponytail and she wore her usual jeans and sweatshirt, but there was something peculiar in the way she sat, in the way she looked at him. It was six-thirty but there was no sign of dinner, and the house was strangely quiet, no customary wild greeting from his daughter. He set the books on the counter and loosened his tie.

"Where's Bliss?" he asked.

"At Alex and Leslie's."

He frowned, trying to remember. Were he and Sharon supposed to go out tonight? Had he forgotten something?

Sharon was so still that he shuddered. He took a step closer and leaned down to kiss her, but she turned her head away. "What's the matter?" he asked.

She looked up at him as though he should know.

"Is it your father?" Her father had been sick for months.

She shook her head and then stood up. "Pat Kelley and Joan Dove spoke with me when I picked Bliss up today."

"About what?" Pat Kelley was the director of Bliss's day-care center and Joan Dove, Bliss's teacher.

"She said they've noticed a change in Bliss's behavior. She's irritable and she cries a lot and she's more fearful than she used to be."

"Same as at home," he said. Bliss had started sucking her thumb again and crying at bedtime. A few times recently she'd wet the bed.

"Joan said that during naptime yesterday Bliss was masturbating and trying to snuggle up to Jason Peterson. Joan thought it was a little odd but didn't say anything to her except to move her away from Jason." Sharon was watching him carefully, waiting for him to piece the puzzle of her words together. But he had no idea where she was going with this. "Then yesterday during her nap Bliss wet herself. I'd taken Joan a change of underpants a few weeks ago in case Bliss had an accident during the day. When Joan changed her she noticed a rash." Sharon put her hand to her mouth and tears filled her eyes. "I noticed it during her bath yesterday, but I thought it was just from wetting herself. I never asked her about it."

Sharon looked so guilty that he put his arms around her, but she jerked away from him.

"You know what I'm talking about, Ben, don't you?"

He frowned, shook his head. "I have no idea."

"Joan asked Bliss how she got so sore down there and Bliss said you did it."

"What?"

"She said you put your finger inside her."

He stood very still. He could feel his heart beating. "Why would she say that?"

"You tell me."

"Joan must have misunderstood her."

Sharon shook her head. "I thought so too. But on the way home in the car I asked her myself. I said, 'Ms. Dove says you have a rash around your vagina,' and she said, 'She said I can't put a Band-Aid on it.' And I said, 'How do you think you got a rash there?'—I was careful, Ben. I didn't want to lead her—and she said, 'Daddy put his finger in my vagina.' She said it just like that, every word clear as a bell, and then she said, 'I wish he'd stop that. It hurts sometimes.' I started crying and I had to pull over. That scared her, seeing me fall apart like that, but I couldn't help myself."

A wave of nausea passed through him and he sat down at the table. "Sharon, I never touched her. I would never hurt her."

"Then why would she say you did?"

"I don't know. Could she have dreamt it?"

Sharon shook her head. "Joan says there's too much evidence that she's been molested. The fearfulness, the wetting, the seductive stuff with Jason. You don't dream up a rash. And she's been masturbating so much lately. I thought maybe she irritated herself." She looked at him hopefully.

"That must be it." He heard the flatness, the uncertainty in his voice.

"But why would she say it was you?"

"I don't know. Look, let's go pick her up and talk to her. If I can talk to her I'm sure—"

"No! I don't want you talking to her."

He frowned at her in disbelief. How dare she tell him he couldn't talk to his own daughter? But he spoke calmly. "You can be there too. I'm sure if—"

"You can't, Ben. She has to stay at Alex and Leslie's tonight. I told them we were going out. I couldn't tell them the truth." Sharon sat down again. Her hands shook as she rested them on the table, and she lowered them once more to her lap. "Look, Pat and Joan wanted to call the child protection people right away but I persuaded them to wait until tomorrow so I could talk to Bliss myself and talk to you . . . At that point I really didn't believe it. I told them you were the best father imaginable . . ." Sharon's voice broke. "I defended you. I rattled on. I gave them examples of how you take her places with you, read to her, give up your own activities for her. They kept nodding, and Pat finally said that it's often the fathers who seem most sensitive and caring about their children who are the abusers. I wanted to hit them. I felt they were so wrong about you."

"And now?" He watched her face, and in the silence that followed he could hear the quiet ticking of the clock on the wall behind him.

"Now I don't know what to think," she said finally. "But I had to promise them to keep you away from Bliss tonight. That was the only way I could get them to agree to wait on the call."

"This is insane!" He pounded the table with his fist and stood up. "She's my daughter! Nobody can tell me I can't see her."

Sharon bit her lip and looked away from him.

"Look, I'll go in and talk to Joan and Pat in the morning," he said.

"It's not that simple, Ben. They have a legal responsibility to call."

"Sharon." He looked down at her. "How long have you known me?"

"Nine years."

"Have you ever known me to lie to you?"

"No."

"Then I'm asking you to believe me now."

She started to cry again. "It's my fault," she said. "Things haven't been good between us since the surgery." He sat down again, moving his chair next to hers so he could hold her. He understood what she was saying. A year ago she'd had surgery on her back, and for a long time afterward they couldn't make love. When her doctor finally gave his okay she seemed to have lost interest. But he'd viewed it as a phase. Marriage was cyclical. Eventually sex would be good again. It was true, though, that the lack of physical closeness had spilled over into the rest of their relationship. And it was true that he looked forward to seeing Bliss in the evening more than he did Sharon.

He pressed his lips to the smooth, freckled skin of her neck. Her skin was warm, her scent comforting. "I didn't do anything to Bliss." He lifted his head. "But even if I did, it wouldn't be your fault. I know you haven't felt like yourself this past year."

She looked up at him. "I'm so scared, Ben."

He felt none of her fear, though looking back later, he knew he should have been terrified. He was naïve, a true innocent who trusted that everything would work out. He kissed Sharon and was surprised by the heat in her response. He led her to the bedroom and they made love, hungrily, the way they had when they were new to each other. He was inside her when she came, her body reaching, arching. But then she began to sob and her muscles fell limp, her arms slack on the bed, her legs lifeless when only a few seconds earlier they'd been gripping him. And he couldn't go on, not with her like that, her face turned away from him in disgust. He pulled out of her carefully, went into the bathroom, showered, dressed, and came back to sit on the edge of the bed.

She'd pulled the spread over her and she lay on her side, weeping into a tissue. Her ponytail was coming loose and he gently tugged out the rubber band and smoothed her hair over her throat. "Let's go get Bliss," he said. "Let's straighten this whole thing out before it goes any further."

"Oh, God, Ben." She rolled onto her back to look at him. "Why would she say you did it if you didn't?"

He felt a fury in his chest, like something trying to escape, to explode. "I did nothing!"

She stood up and pulled the spread around her. Her chin quivered; her wet cheeks glistened in the light from the bathroom. "I love you so much, Ben, but I . . ." She shook her head. "I can't sleep in here with you tonight. I'm sorry, I just . . ." She pressed her hand to her face as though she might be able to hold back her tears.

"Sharon." He reached for her, but she stepped away.

"I'll sleep in the guest room," she said, and he watched her gather the spread around her shoulders and turn her back on him.

He was tempted to drive over to Alex and Leslie's and talk to Bliss himself, but he thought better of it. Later on he would berate himself for not going. That had been his only chance, the last time he wasn't helpless to save himself. Could he have talked to Bliss, understood what she was trying to say? Could he have turned the entire tide of this nightmare right then? If he'd been able to see the future, he would have gone to see Bliss that night. But he never dreamed the devastation that lay ahead of him.

*

He had nearly finished teaching his two o'clock class the next day when he spotted a police officer in uniform standing outside the open door of his classroom. He tried to slow things down. The dismissal bell rang, but still he talked to the class, droning on as the minutes passed. His students shifted in their seats, their books piled on their desks, ready to make their escapes. They looked at each other, asking with their eyes, What's Alexander up to? Finally he let them go. Then he sat down at his desk and waited.

The officer identified himself and said, too loudly, "You are under arrest for the sexual abuse of your daughter." He read Ben his rights and, although Ben said he would go quietly, handcuffed him. He was led out that way, through the interminably long hallway of the science building, past openmouthed students, many of them his. He wanted to smile at them reassuringly, offer a joke or two, but his throat was dry. He kept his eyes focused on the stream of sunlight pouring through the door at the end of the hall.

The policeman pushed him into the backseat of the car with a growl of disgust. Everyone was taking this very seriously, and for the first time he thought that maybe something had happened to Bliss. If that was the case, it had to have been someone other than him. He trembled in the backseat of the car. His wrists burned where they were cuffed. He could not tolerate the thought of anyone touching her.

He ran down the list of people Bliss spent time with. Joan Dove. Sam and Jen. Alex and Leslie. Bliss's occasional baby-sitter, the elderly Mrs. Blayton. None of them fit. What about the kids in the neighborhood? There were a few older kids that were pretty rough with the younger ones. Maybe when Bliss was playing at another child's house? Someone else's daddy? Or maybe the young maintenance man who worked at Bliss's day-care, that ferret-eyed, seedy kid that Ben had never liked to see around the children. It would all have to be looked at, wouldn't it?

He used his one phone call to reach Sam at the clinic. Sam was in a session with a patient, but Ben told his service it was urgent, to interrupt him, and he sounded desperate enough that the woman put him through.

"I've been arrested," Ben said. "I need you to post bail."

Sam was quiet on the other end of the phone. What could he be thinking? Ben in jail? Ben, who had never even had a parking ticket?

"Why are you there, Ben?" Sam's voice was quiet, gentle. Ben pictured Sam's patient sitting in the brown leather chair, imagining that Sam was talking to another patient, a fellow sufferer.

"I don't want to go into it over the phone. How soon can you get here?"

"I have one more patient and then I'll see you." Sam chose his words carefully. "About six-thirty. And Ben?" There was no euphemistic way for Sam to ask this question. "How much do I need?"

"One thousand." Ben shut his eyes. Sam could afford it, but that didn't make the asking any less humiliating. "I'll pay you back tomorrow when I can get to the bank."

"No problem. See you later."

He sat in the passenger seat of Sam's Mercedes, staring at the streetlights, their white glow blurred by a freezing rain. He'd told Sam he couldn't go home, that he wanted to go to Sam and Jen's instead. But he didn't tell him why. He didn't tell him he was not allowed to be in the same place as Bliss. "If you want to stay at home, your daughter will have to go into foster care," they'd told him. That hardly left him a choice.

He was quiet as they drove, dreading the moment he would have to tell Sam the truth. He didn't want to see the same revulsion in Sam's face that he saw in everyone else's.

Sam pulled up at a red light. He looked over at his brother. "C'mon, Ben. Get it out."

Ben met his eyes. "They think I hurt Bliss," he said. "Molested her."

Sam's jaw dropped and Ben quickly resumed staring out the window. "Jesus," Sam said.

"I didn't do it."

"Of course you didn't." Sam started driving again. "I can't believe anyone would think you did."

"Even Sharon thinks I did."

Sam nodded. "Well, that's good. That's healthy. Bliss is her baby. She wants to protect her at all costs to herself. She can't think straight about you right now. What evidence do they have?"

"A rash. But it's worse than that—Bliss told them I did it."

"What?" Sam looked at him and Ben thought he saw a glimmer of doubt about him in Sam's green eyes.

"I didn't do it, Sam." His jaw ached. He was close to tears.

Sam shook his head. "She's such a happy-go-lucky kid."

"She used to be. She's changed, though. Sharon and I noticed it but we didn't make much out of it till now."

"She seemed fine when we saw her last weekend. The only problem with spending time around Bliss is that it upsets Jen, she's so hungry for a baby."

"How's the adoption process going?" Ben thought of the hours Jen and Sam had spent having their lives scrutinized to see if they'd make suitable parents. He wondered now if he'd be a liability for them.

Sam sighed. "Another year or two of waiting. I'll be forty by the time we get the baby. Forty!" He shook his head.

"I hope this doesn't screw anything up for you," Ben said. "I mean, if the adoption agency discovers you have a brother who—"

"Shut up, Ben. We're calling a lawyer friend of mine the second we step inside the house. You'll come out of this thing smelling like a rose."

Even Jen believed him. At least she did until she drove over to his house to get the clothes Sharon had packed for him. When she came back she was very quiet. A few times he caught her staring at him. Just before bed she hugged him and said, "It's hard for me to believe you could do it, Ben, but even if you did, you can get help. Sam knows people who could help you. And we'll stick by you no matter what happens."

He backed away from her, disappointed. "I didn't do it, Jen." He turned and walked into the guest room to spend the first of many nights alone.

29

It was dusk when she reached his cabin. Darkness already filled the forest and was spilling into the clearing, and the stillness of the air sent a shiver through her. She slipped the picnic basket over her arm and knocked on the door.

Several minutes passed and she knocked again. Ben's truck was parked in the clearing, so he was here. She thought of the Valium in his bathroom and put her hand on the doorknob, but it turned in her hand as he opened the door.

He looked at her without interest, as though he was neither surprised nor pleased to find her there. He still wore the sweaty blue T-shirt he'd had on in the pit, and in the dusky light she could see a smear of dirt across his cheek.

"Can I come in?"

He stood back to let her into the room. The smell of whiskey, faint but unmistakable, teased her as she passed him. There were no lights on in the cabin, but in the triangle of gray light from the open door she saw the stony mask of his face. She knew that mask. She'd seen it in the mirror any number of times.

"I've been worried about you," she said.

"I don't want your charity."

"Kyle and Lou think you're innocent."

He sighed, and she heard anger in the sound. "Fine."

"Ben . . ." She spotted the open whiskey bottle on the apple crate by his bed and didn't finish what she'd started to say. "I'd like to use your bathroom, please."

He shrugged and closed the door. "Be my guest."

The Valium was still on the sink. She poured the pills into her hand and counted them. Twenty. She dropped them back into the container and left the bathroom.

"I brought some food with me." She nodded toward the basket. "You probably haven't eaten yet."

He picked up the bottle of whiskey and sat down on the bed, his back against the wall. "Why are you here?" he asked.

She took the bottle from his hand, screwed the cap on, and set it on the crate. "I want to hear your side of what happened."

Even in the failing light she could see his cheeks redden as he leaned forward. "What gives you the right to come here and tell me that I can't drink and I have to spill my guts to you? Do this, Ben, do that. Jump through this hoop and then maybe I'll believe you."

Eden spoke quietly. "Because I need to believe you. I trusted you. I let myself feel something for you and I haven't done that in a very long time."

Ben looked down at the blue-and-white quilt and smoothed his hand across it. "I thought by some miracle you might say to me, 'Ben, I know you couldn't possibly have done it.'"

She sat down on the edge of the bed. "Please tell me everything, Ben. Please convince me you're innocent."

His laugh was bitter. "I couldn't even convince my lawyer I was innocent."

"Maybe I have a bigger investment in believing you than your lawyer did."

"Well, Sharon certainly had an investment in believing me and even she . . ." He shook his head.

"She thought you did it?"

He screwed up his face. "I never did figure Sharon out. I felt sorry for her. I know she loved me and I think deep down she believed I was innocent. I'd watch her on the stand and she'd say nice things about me. But every good thing she'd say would be turned around by the so-called experts until I looked like the biggest pervert that ever walked the earth. The evidence was very convincing. I would have been convinced myself, so I can't blame her for assuming I'd done it."

He'd had a good marriage once, she thought. There was still caring in his voice when he spoke about Sharon. "Tell me everything." She moved next to him on the bed. She could just make out the line of his nose, the white of his eyes.

And he began to talk.

His voice was quiet as he described the change in Bliss's behavior, the day-care teacher's suspicions. It was hard for him to get the words out, and pauses stretched between his sentences like silent bands of pain.

"The thing I feel guiltiest about is that her teacher picked up signs that we completely missed. Like the masturbation. We thought it was best not to make an issue of it. What would you do if Cassie started masturbating a lot?"

"Same as you did, I guess," she said. "I don't know. Cassie never does, as far as I know."

"Well, the teacher got out of Bliss that I put my finger inside her, and that was that. I was arrested, I got out on bail and stayed with my brother and his wife for a few months while we were waiting for the trial. I wasn't allowed to see Bliss at all. At first I thought she must have dreamt it. Sometimes I would snuggle with her when we'd read a story together before she'd fall asleep. I thought maybe she imagined it."

"Could the teacher have planted the idea in her mind somehow?"

"I wish I could answer yes to that, but I think she was careful. I think she's a bright lady who knew what she was dealing with and knew she had to proceed cautiously. But they'd just had a program at the day-care center on bad touching and good touching, and I've wondered if maybe Bliss got confused and thought something happened to her when it didn't. I hope to God that was it, because I can't stand the thought that she actually was molested." He shook his head. "She was able to recount it all in such detail, though. The story the social workers finally got from her was that on a few occasions—

they figured it happened more than once, but probably not more than two or three times—Bliss would wake up in the middle of the night and I—her daddy—would be lying behind her, holding her very tightly and rubbing against her. Her pajama bottoms would be off and he'd have his finger inside her. He'd tell her this was a good thing to do, that Daddy did this to Mommy and Mommy liked it. He'd say it was a secret, that she shouldn't talk to anyone about it. She told the social workers that she was scared and that it hurt."

Ben looked out the window into the darkness for a long moment, and Eden's heart pounded hard against her ribs. She was sitting shoulder to shoulder with this man. She thought of him making love to her the night before, his fingers stroking her, slipping inside her. Kyle and Lou believe him, she reminded herself. They know him very well and they believe him absolutely.

"Ben," she said. "I don't think a four-year-old could make some-thing like that up."

"No, I guess I don't either. It's so inconceivable, though. She said it was dark, she never actually saw the man, and he was behind her. But she said she knew it was Daddy. She called the man Daddy and he answered her. I've wondered if it might have taken place somewhere else and she was confused and thought it happened to her in her own room. Or maybe making the man me in her mind made it less scary for her. I lay awake night after night trying to figure out what might have happened. I still do sometimes."

"Who else could have done it?"

"I have no idea. I've suspected everyone at one time or another. Even my brother, Sam, and my best friend, Alex. Even Sharon's poor old cancer-ridden father. The maintenance man at Bliss's day-care is my top candidate. But why would she say it was me? Why would she say it happened in her own room? Unless he told her to say that." He sighed. "It's crazy-making, Eden. I've spent this last year and a half trying to figure it out. But even if I could, no one would listen to me." He suddenly pounded his fist into his thigh and she jumped. "They wouldn't let me talk to her. I thought if I could just have a few minutes with her, I could figure out what was going on."

"Ben . . . could you possibly have walked in your sleep or—"

"No, God damn it, I couldn't have walked in my sleep." His voice was still calm, but the anger was real.

"I'm sorry."

"It's all right. I have to admit I wondered about that myself. As the trial got rolling I felt such hatred building against me. In the jury, in the courtroom. In the whole community. It was hot stuff in the papers. I was guilty in everyone's eyes. And everyone was waiting for Bliss's testimony. I couldn't believe they'd put her on the stand. She was barely four years old, but they said she knew the difference between truth and falsehood, she was bright, articulate. A prosecutor's dream child, my attorney said. She—my own daughter—was going to hang me. All I could think of was her being up there in front of all those people, being scared, having to answer questions that would make a grown-up squirm. I knew what Barbara—my lawyer—would do to her when it was her turn to question Bliss. She kept telling me not to worry, that she was going to tear Bliss's story apart. Confuse her. But that was my little girl she was going to shake up. I couldn't stand to think of Bliss going through all that."

"Kyle said you pled guilty."

"Yeah, I did." He laughed. "Temporarily. Temporary insanity. I don't think I had a clue how serious things were. People kept telling me I was in deep shit, but I knew I was innocent and I figured the truth would eventually come out and I'd be okay. I was never as scared for myself as I should have been. But I was terrified for Bliss. The day she was to testify, I was falling apart. I was sitting next to Barbara. Sharon was on the other side of the courtroom. Bliss came walking out, holding the hand of a woman, a social worker, I guess. She was clutching the stuffed monkey that she carried around with her everywhere. She was so, so tiny. She'd always been tall compared to other kids her age, but she looked unbelievably small in that room with the huge witness stand and all those grown-ups. My heart just about broke, Eden, looking at her. I hadn't seen her in months. She looked over and saw me and her face lit up. She waved. She pointed me out to the social worker and I could see her mouthing the words, 'That's my Daddy.'" Ben was quiet for a long moment. "Can I have my whiskey, please?" he asked finally.

She handed him the bottle. He unscrewed the cap, then screwed it back on without drinking. "Anyhow, I felt as though I would fall apart if I had to sit there while they questioned her. So I pled guilty, right then and there. I said I wasn't really guilty, but I wanted to spare Bliss from going through the whole mess. I caused quite a stir and I absolutely didn't care. I just wanted her out of there. I wasn't thinking about the consequences at the moment. After Barbara gave me a talking-to I recanted, but I'd done myself a whole lot of damage. The judge refused Barbara's request for a mistrial. He told the jury to ignore my 'outburst,' as he called it, but they were twelve human beings and they all had ears. How could they forget they'd heard me say I did it?

"So the trial went on, confusing the hell out of Bliss. She really was beautiful, though. She had as much dignity as a four-year-old can have. Everyone was in love with her. And no one could possibly have thought she was making any of it up. I would have convicted me too if I'd been on that jury. It seemed so obvious that someone hurt her, and it looked like I was the only possible candidate. That's what kills me. If it really did happen, there's only one other person besides me who knows for sure that I'm innocent, and he's not about to come forward. And he might very well still be around her. It makes me crazy. There's no one to protect Bliss because they think they've got the culprit put away. I've talked to the protective services people about it, asking them to watch out for her, and they just tell me to forget it, the case is closed."

"You haven't seen Bliss at all since the trial?"

"Right. It's been one long, lousy year. Barbara said if I got into a counseling program for abusers she could fight to get me supervised visits with her. So I tried. I went to the counselor, but it was a catch twenty-two. I told her I was innocent, she said 'Right,' and then she told me that until I was willing to admit to her—and to myself— what I'd done, she couldn't help me. She said I wasn't cooperating. I considered playing along, acting like I'd done it so I could get to see Bliss, but I just couldn't. So they said I was a danger to her." He laughed and shook his head. "I was a danger to her, so they locked me up and told me I could have no contact with her until she's eighteen."

"My God, Ben."

He stood up and set the whiskey bottle on the table. "I lie awake sometimes wondering what she thinks about not seeing me . . ." His voice cracked. "Wondering if she thinks I don't love her anymore and that's why I went away."

"They must have explained it to her."

"Yeah. They told her Daddy can't see you anymore because he hurt you."

He was innocent. He had to be. She stood up and put her arms around him, but he felt wooden beneath her touch and she knew he was a different man from the man she'd slept with the night before. Different, but not dangerous.

She leaned her head back to look at him. "Ben, I'd like to stay over tonight."

He pulled away from her with a shrug. "That's probably not a great idea. Talking about all this makes me depressed as hell." But then he smiled at her. "It doesn't do much for my libido either. My sex life was examined under a microscope and it doesn't matter that I'm innocent, I'm still left feeling like there's something wrong with me. I don't know how I managed last night."

"You managed very well."

He looked at her, reached over to touch her arm lightly. "I'd like you to stay. But I don't want you to have expectations."

I don't," she said. "I just want to be with you."

Ben was quiet as he ate the food Eden brought. She didn't seem to mind his silence. She cut his roll for him and sliced his peach, then cleaned up the kitchen while he showered. And later they talked about Kyle and Lou, the site, the screenplay, as though the topic of his conviction had been dealt with long enough. It wasn't until she was nearly asleep, her arm across his stomach, that he forced himself to ask her, "Do you believe me?"

She sighed, raised herself up on one elbow to look at him. "I must," she said. "Or I wouldn't be here with you. But there's one thing I keep pushing to the back of my mind because it bothers me so much."

"What's that?"

"That you pled guilty. I'm sure I love Cassie as much as you love Bliss. Yet I would never have said I was guilty if I wasn't."

He nodded, pulled her head back to his shoulder. "I agree. When I'm rational, it doesn't make a bit of sense."

He felt her fall asleep. Her breathing slowed down, her arm grew heavy on his stomach. He felt drained. It was remembering the trial that exhausted him, and now the image of Bliss walking into that courtroom would not leave his mind. It was the last time he'd seen her.

They'd had some kind of booster seat for her and she'd climbed up, still clutching her monkey, a long-ago gift from Sam and Jen. They attached a small microphone to the collar of her dress and the prosecutor asked her her name.

"Bliss Azander." She never could get that 'I' in there. The courtroom was quiet for the first time during the trial. Someone coughed and the sound bounced off the walls as the prosecutor continued with his gentle questions. Bliss was trying hard to please him. Someone had explained to her how important this was, how she had to tell the truth. A question—an easy one—confused her. Ben could see the fear in her eyes even from where he sat.

He leaned toward Barbara. "I can't stand this," he said.

"Shhh." She patted his hand with her cool, patronizing fingertips.

"No, I'm serious." A drop of perspiration ran from his temple to his chin and he wiped it away with his handkerchief. "Call it off," he said. "I'll say I did it. Just get her off the stand."

"She's fine, Ben. She's doing—"

He stood up. "Your Honor, I'm innocent of these charges but I want to plead guilty to prevent my daughter from going through any more of this."

Judge Stevens stared at him while Barbara jumped to her feet. "I'd like to request a recess, Your Honor," she said.

"Good idea," said the judge. He was a sixty-year-old man whose own daughter had been raped as a teenager; his life as a man and a magistrate would always be colored by that crime. "And please advise your client of the gravity of his action."

"I don't need a recess," Ben said to Barbara. "It's over. I want this to be over." His hands shook on the table in front of him while the tittering mounted in the jury box. Bliss looked frightened.

"Daddy?" she said into the microphone.

He was breathing hard and fast, almost choking on the air. He watched Sharon push through the crowd to get to Bliss. He watched her lift Bliss up and carry her out, and he felt enormous relief that this was over for her. It's over, baby, he thought. You don't have to go through any more of this.

"Ben?" He felt Eden next to him in the darkness. "Are you all right?"

He wrapped his arms around her. She was wearing one of his T-shirts and the fabric warmed his hands. "I want you to understand why I pled guilty," he said. He rolled onto his back, holding on to her, holding tight. "When I was five and my brother was seven we had a baby-sitter. Randy. He sat for us often, at least once a week. He would take us into the bathroom, one at a time and make us . . . do things we didn't want to do. He told us if we told anyone—even each other—he'd kill our mother. So I never even talked to Sam about it, though I'm sure the same thing was happening to him. Every night after Randy baby-sat I'd spend an hour or so throwing up. My parents eventually questioned me." He laughed. "They asked me if Randy was giving me candy or something. I finally said he touched me. I remember thinking that if I just told that little bit, maybe he wouldn't kill my mother. But my parents didn't believe me because Randy was such a nice boy from such a nice family. They asked Sam about it, and Sam was so scared he said he had no idea what I was talking about. But I kept getting sick, and finally my parents took me to see a shrink. Then the police. I can't remember what I did yesterday, but I remember that whole experience vividly. All the questions. I kept changing my story, getting trapped in my own lies, because I thought if I told the truth Randy would hurt my mother. When I'd finally gotten the whole story out no one believed me. Randy would pass me on the street and laugh at me. I'd wake up in the middle of the night and sleep outside my parents' door on the floor in the hallway, thinking I could protect my mother somehow if Randy came to get her."

Eden didn't speak, but she nudged closer to him, set her cheek against his shoulder.

"They tore me up with their questions," Ben continued. "Then they left me feeling crazy and scared. I remember so clearly how that felt, and there was no way I could watch Bliss go through it. She'd already been questioned and interviewed and picked apart enough. But I think what really terrified me was having to watch it, to feel myself going through it all over again through her. So I guess ultimately it was myself I was looking out for, not her."

He ran his fingers through Eden's hair. "Sharon's the only other person I've ever told about Randy. Even Sam and I have never talked about it."

"Sharon knew and she still didn't believe you?"

"Well, you have to understand that by the time I pled guilty, things had already fallen apart between Sharon and me. Plus, Sharon had read somewhere that men who were sexually abused as children stood a good chance of becoming abusers themselves. My experience had the exact opposite effect on me. I could never hurt a child the way I was hurt. Never."

Eden sat up and pressed her back against the wall. She held his hand in her lap. "You haven't had a very easy life," she said.

He laughed. "You must think I'm totally screwed up now. But honestly, Eden, between the ages of five and thirty-seven I was dynamite."

She smiled at him, drew his hand to her lips. "Tomorrow morning I'm going to call Michael," she said. "I need to tell him that I'm seeing someone else." She lowered his hand, leaned forward to kiss his cheek. "I need to tell him I'm in love with someone else."

30

One week later Ben and Eden beat Kyle and Lou at tramposo for the first time. No one said it out loud, but Eden knew it was a milestone. Tramposo measured the quality of a relationship, the intimacy, the teamwork. So when Ben grabbed her in the kitchen for a kiss and said, "We beat the shit out of them, Eden," she knew he was talking about more than a card game; he was telling her they were solid now.

They had fallen into an easy routine, so easy that she'd forgotten the risk she was taking in this relationship. Mornings, she worked with Ben at the site. In the afternoons, she pored over old newspapers at the archives in Winchester or interviewed the few elderly neighbors still living in the area. Or worked on the screenplay. She wasn't reading the journal. "You need a rest from it," Kyle said in his "I know what's best for you" voice, and she didn't fight him.

She and Ben spent several evenings that week with Lou and Kyle, whose company she looked forward to in a new way. They made dinner for the older couple on a few occasions, followed by the heady games of tramposo. One night Kyle showed slides from their trips to South America, and it was like watching strangers, people she was just getting to know and care about, a family she wanted to belong to. Ben's hair was longer, scruffier in those old slides, and he wore a beard. "I shaved it off after the trial," he said. "I was too recognizable."

She was thoroughly convinced of his innocence. There was nothing mysterious about him. Nothing suspicious. And nothing kinky, although he was certainly a far more intriguing lover than Wayne had been. Well, she was not the same woman she'd been with Wayne either. "You inspire me," Ben said to her one night. She doubted she had ever inspired Wayne.

When she woke up these mornings, sometimes in her mother's old room, sometimes in Ben's cabin, she had the feeling of being perfectly safe. The nightmares had vanished. The only missing piece in her life was her daughter, but at least their phone conversations had improved. Ben suggested she tell Cassie about the things they could do when she came to visit—King's Dominion, the dinosaurs, Luray Caverns—and Cassie was finally looking forward to coming.

Ben was building Cassie a dollhouse. "It's from Kyle and me," he said the first time Eden saw the pieces spread out on his table. "Kyle's the financial backer." She watched him put it together, a huge Victorian with lacy gingerbread trim, and thought of what his own daughter was missing out on and would continue to miss.

"Are you allowed to give her gifts?" she asked as he glued a tiny window frame in place.

"No contact," he said. "That would constitute contact."

"But even if you were guilty, isn't totally depriving her of her father more damaging?"

"You and I are the only people who seem to think so. And Sam. Sam's doing what he can to try to get me supervised visitation, but I'm not optimistic. Her counselor says it would confuse her. It's not in the best interest of the child." He stood back to look at the house slowly taking shape on his table. "What color do you think I should paint it?"

As open as he was, there were times he could not talk about Bliss, and she learned when to back off. When he did speak of her Eden felt his helplessness and his rage.

"I can't stand the thought of Jeff being in my house, sleeping with my wife, reading Bliss Green Eggs and Ham, and tucking her in at night. One day I had a wife and child and the next day Jeff strolls in out of nowhere and takes over. Finders keepers."

"How did Sharon know Jeff?"

"The school where she taught. He teaches history."

"Could Sharon have set this up somehow?" she asked, carefully. "Maybe she wanted you out of the picture."

"No, I don't think Sharon knew Jeff very well back then, and our marriage was okay. Besides, even if she despised me she wouldn't use Bliss that way."

The phone call to Michael had been more difficult than she'd anticipated. She was surprised at how much it hurt her to hurt him. She cared about him more than she'd admitted to herself.

"Is this just a summer thing?" Michael had asked. "I mean, how serious is it?"

"I'm not sure," she'd answered. "I'm taking it one day at a time."

Michael hesitated. "Have you slept with him?" he asked.

"Yes."

He gave a pained laugh. "You've been going out with me for nearly a year and I get a good-night kiss if I'm lucky. You've known this guy a couple of weeks and . . . Christ."

"Michael, I'm sorry. But I never led you to believe there would be more between us."

"I know."

"I still want you to play Matthew Riley. The more I get to know about him, the more I realize you're perfect for the part. You even look like him."

Michael said nothing.

"Michael? You'll still do it, won't you?"

"As long as you're still playing your mother and we get some juicy scenes together."

She smiled. "I care about you a lot, Michael. Please, let's stay friends. And don't let this . . . set you back." She could see him going out tonight, getting high, licking his wounds. She thought of asking him not to spread this around, but that would hardly be fair.

"I need to see you," he said. "I feel like you're changing into a different person."

"I am changing, but not into a different person. For once, I feel like myself."

She got off the phone with Michael's question sounding in her ears: How serious is it? This relationship was a mass of impossibilities, most of which she was not ready to face.

One afternoon, she let Ben up to her mother's old room to type a reference letter for a former student. She sat on the bed and watched him hunt and peck his way across the keyboard of her word processor. He was wearing a gray-and-white striped cotton shirt and his hair was damp from a shower. He looked beautiful, and she felt sure of what she was about to tell him.

"Ben?"

He pushed the print button and turned to face her.

"I want to start taking the Pill again."

She watched his face as her words registered. "Does that make sense?" he asked. "It won't be effective for a couple of weeks, right? And you won't be here that much longer."

"Maybe I won't leave at the end of the summer."

He looked at her blankly for a moment. "Eden, you really need to think through what you're doing. You told me you were with Michael Carey to keep people from linking you with anyone else. You said you had to protect your public image. I'm about the riskiest person in the world for you to get hooked up with—you know that, don't you?"

"Who's going to know what I'm doing as long as I'm out here in the boondocks?"

He stood up and came over to the bed, put his hands on her shoulders. "I'm not going to argue with you. I'm not that anxious to get rid of you." He reached into his jeans pocket and pulled out a wrapped condom. "Might as well use these up."

She laughed. "You're carrying them around with you?"

"I like to be prepared for anything." He leaned over to kiss her but she held him away.

"We can't make love here. Kyle and Lou are downstairs." She remembered with a clarity that pained her the times she'd sneaked one boy or another into her bedroom in New York. Tex, usually. Bo on one occasion. They would do it on the floor to keep the bed from squeaking and waking up Kyle and Lou.

Ben walked to the door and closed it quietly. "I can't tell you how many times I had to listen to the two of them going at it—those Colombian hotels had paper-thin walls." He sat next to her and kissed her softly.

"We have to be very quiet," she said.

"Like snowflakes," he whispered, and he stood up to unbuckle his belt.

At the breakfast table on the morning after the tramposo upset she asked Kyle for another notebook.

"I'm begging you, Kyle, let me have it. I'm stuck in the screenplay because I don't know how Matt finally gets Kate to surrender."

Kyle carried his plate to the sink, then stood behind Lou's chair. He rested a gentle hand on his wife's shoulder, and Lou reached up to cover his fingers with hers.

"What's your hurry?" he asked Eden.

"I'm curious. Just let me read ahead a little, please?" He shook his head. "Sorry, honey. It'll be over soon enough. Don't rush it."

His words shook her. This was not a game. It was a real life she held in limbo inside her word processor, a real life that would end all too soon.

"I'm sorry," she said. "It's just that writing a screenplay still doesn't come naturally to me. I get nervous when I'm not sure where I'm going with it."

"You always were an excellent writer," Lou said. "Even as a child."

"I never wrote anything as a child."

"You wrote papers in junior high and high school. You always brought home As."

Eden laughed. "Your memory's inflated my grades over the years."

Lou looked up at Kyle with a question in her round blue eyes, and he nodded. "Come in the bedroom, dear," Lou said. She wheeled herself down the hall with Eden and Kyle following.

Kyle disappeared inside the walk-in closet of their bedroom and returned carrying a dusty cardboard box.

"Your pack-rat uncle," Lou said as she shifted from the chair to the bed. Eden sat next to her, and Kyle set the box on Eden's lap. She lifted the top. The first thing that met her eyes was yellowed typing paper: "The Pros and Cons of Legalizing Abortion," by Eden S. Riley, January 7, 1970.

"Oh, my God." She laughed. "I'd forgotten I ever wrote this." She leafed through the stack of papers. History, science, book reports. Kyle had kept everything. And they were indeed all As, except for the Cs from her senior year.

"I can't believe you saved all this stuff," she said. At the bottom she found a stack of report cards held together with a cracked rubber band that broke when she removed it. She glanced through them. All As and Bs until her senior year. That year she'd even failed a couple of subjects, and the teachers' comments were consistent.

"Eden needs to realize that her involvement in the Drama Club this year is hampering her academic performance," Eden read aloud, her nose wrinkled.

"They can eat their words now," Lou said.

"I loved reading your papers because it was the only way we had of knowing what was going on in your head," Kyle said. "You never shared much with us."

"I didn't bring you two much pleasure," she said quietly. She felt herself moving toward them with baby steps of intimacy.

Kyle laughed. "What teenager does?"

"I was testing you. I wanted to see how much obnoxious, despicable behavior you'd put up with before you got rid of me. I was always afraid you'd send me away."

Lou stared at her. "What did we ever do to give you an idea like that?"

"Nothing. But everyone around me died or shipped me out. I figured it was just a matter of time until that happened with the two of you."

"I wish we could have reassured you somehow," said Lou.

"You did everything you could. You made enormous sacrifices for me. I know I appeared ungrateful at the time, but deep down I was so thankful I had both of you. It was just hard for me to tell you that." She returned the report cards to the bottom of the box and looked at her uncle. "I feel as though I stole those years from you and gave you very little in return."

"Don't ever think that, honey," Kyle said.

Eden moved the box from her lap to the bed and stood up. "Well." She smiled at both of them. "I just hope Cassie gets around to telling me she appreciates me before she's thirty-six."

The four of them went to New York for a few days early in July. This followed a painful discussion during which Eden persuaded Ben to let her pay for their train tickets and the hotel. Money was the sorest point between them, and she had to address the topic with great care.

They got rooms with a connecting door at the Sheraton Centre. They watched the fireworks from a bench overlooking the East River, visited the Museum of Modern Art, and saw two shows on Broadway. Whenever they waited in line they played games— something Ben, Lou, and Kyle were obviously accustomed to doing. Ghost, Botticelli, Twenty Questions. The three of them were quick with each other, taking esoteric shortcuts through the games that left Eden dazed.

The trip was fun, but Eden couldn't shake the feeling of dread she had at being in New York with Lou and Kyle again. From each point in the city she was acutely aware of how far they were from the intersection of Twenty-third and Park. It pulled at her from the seventeenth-story hotel window, and although the view was blocked by a mile of skyscrapers, in her mind's eye she could see that intersection clearly. She wondered if it had changed, if the streetlights still formed a spotlight in its center. She wondered how many other accidents had happened there.

On their last night in New York, the four of them went to dinner in a small Italian restaurant in the Village, not far from where she had lived with Kyle and Lou as a teenager. They'd spent the day shopping, and by the time they were seated behind the red-and-white checkered tablecloth, they were hot and hungry. Eden and Lou told the men what they wanted and left for the ladies' room.

The rest room was cramped and dirty, with one narrow stall.

"It's not wheelchair-accessible," Lou said. "I'll need your help, Eden."

Eden supported Lou as she hopped from the chair to the toilet, where she struggled to lift her skirt and pull down her underpants. Eden's arms shook with the strain as she lowered Lou to the seat. She stepped outside the stall and held the door closed.

"What do you do if you're someplace like this and don't have another woman around to help?" she asked.

"Kyle comes in with me. We holler first to get the women out and apologize to anyone who walks in on us. But most people are very understanding."

Eden closed her eyes and leaned against the wall. She pictured the corner of Twenty-third and Park. Could Lou ever pass through that intersection without remembering?

"I'm ready, dear."

She helped Lou back into her chair and turned it toward the sink just as a woman entered the rest room. Eden gave the stranger a quick smile while she waited for Lou to wash her hands. The woman stood in front of the closed bathroom door, making no movement toward the stall, and Eden assumed she was waiting for the sink. She watched the woman from the corner of her eye. Her greasy blond hair was hacked off chin-length. Her once white sweater was ratty and gray with a long mustard-colored stain down one arm. She wore gold polyester pants over doughy legs. There was something peculiar in the way she stood motionless, speechless. Something that made Eden's heart pick up its beat.

"Excuse us," Eden said as she grasped the handles on Lou's chair.

"You ain't going nowhere till you give me your pocketbooks," the woman said. Her eyes were big and brown, her stare unnatural and riveting.

"We have to get back to our table," Lou said. "I'm sure our husbands are wondering where we are by now."

The woman reached slowly, calmly, into her own purse and drew out a knife, a steak knife with a cheap plastic handle and a serrated edge.

Lou made a sound of disgust and opened her purse. "How much do you need?"

"The whole pocketbook." The woman's teeth were brown and crooked. "Hand it over."

Eden thought of the contents of her own purse. Credit cards, driver's license, check-cashing cards, keys. All those things that were a nuisance to replace, and all those things that identified her as Eden Riley. This woman would think she'd struck gold. And then there were the pictures of Cassie, starting with the baby picture taken at the hospital.

The blade of the knife caught the yellow light from above the sink, and Eden handed over her purse.

"Money," Lou said. "That's all you get from me." Her voice was strong, but as she opened her wallet Eden saw her hands shake. It took her a few seconds to grasp the three bills and hand them over to the woman, who took them without protest.

"Now why don't you give this young lady her purse back, dear," Lou said. "Take the money but let her have the rest. I'm sure she has pictures of her family in there that are irreplaceable."

"It's all right, Lou." Eden set her hand on Lou's shoulder. "Just let us out please."

"Stay back!" The woman held the knife in front of her menacingly, and Eden drew Lou's chair back as close to her as she could. Then the woman spun around, pushed the door open, and ran into the hall.

Suddenly more furious than afraid, Eden pushed her way out of the room. She spotted the woman running down the long, dirty linoleum hallway toward the back door of the restaurant, the gold polyester pants straining over her bulbous rear end. "That woman stole my purse!" she screamed.

A couple of workers darted from the kitchen and took off after the thief. Eden heard them laughing, saw their grins. It must have been a boring night for them.

She went back into the rest room to find Lou shaking almost convulsively. "I'm a little dizzy," Lou said.

Eden wrung a paper towel out in cold water and laid it on the back of Lou's neck just as Ben pushed the door open. "What's going on? Are you two all right?"

Eden explained what had happened, and Ben left to call the police. She knelt in front of Lou's chair. Her aunt's face was gray, her hands clammy and cold. "Put your head down, Lou," she said.

Lou obeyed and Eden put her arm around her, pressed her cheek against Lou's forehead. "You were so brave," she whispered.

Lou chuckled and lifted her head. "I'm an old fool, that's all. Let's get out of here. No air in here."

Two police officers met them outside the ladies' room, and the gleeful cooks turned Eden's purse over to her intact. She leaned against Ben's back to write them each a check for a hundred dollars, while Kyle pulled up a chair and sat down next to Lou.

"It's fucking Eden Riley!" one of the cooks said as he looked from the check to Eden's face and back again.

"Shhh." Eden pressed her finger to her lips. "Our secret, okay?"

The cooks walked away, shaking their heads and patting each other on the back, and Eden turned her attention back to Lou. From the distance she heard a siren, getting closer, louder, and she realized someone had called an ambulance. No. Her stomach churned.

Lou heard it too, and there was panic in her eyes as she gripped Kyle's arm. "I'm all right," she said. "Tell everyone just to leave me alone."

The siren wound down to a low moan as the ambulance stopped outside the restaurant. Eden felt dizzy herself. Nauseated. The dim light in this dirty hallway, the clatter from the kitchen, the questions and commotion from the police, made her head spin.

Two uniformed paramedics, a young man and a younger woman, joined them in the hallway.

"I don't need you," Lou said, trying to wave them away. "False alarm."

The young woman ignored her. She wrapped the blood pressure cuff around Lou's arm and set her fingers on her wrist. Then she told the other paramedic to get a stretcher.

"She should go to the hospital for observation," she said to Kyle.

"I'm fine," Lou insisted, although her face was still chalky, her eyes glazed and a little wild.

"I'll go with you, Lou," Kyle said.

Lou clutched his shirt in her fist. "No, please, Ky. I don't want to go to the hospital. Please, no ambulance."

"It's all right, hon." Kyle squeezed Lou's hands. He looked up at the young woman. "No ambulance. I'll take her back to our hotel in a taxi. She'll be all right."

"You're taking responsibility?" the woman asked.

"Yes," Kyle said.

"We'll drive you," one of the police officers said.

Eden leaned against the wall as she watched Kyle wheel Lou out into the hot evening air. Ben put his arm around her.

"Come on," he said. "They just put our food on the table."

"I can't eat. Could we please just go back to the hotel?"

"That really shook you up."

"I'm sorry," she said. "But I really want to leave."

Once they were outside, Ben slipped his arm around her waist. "I'm sure Lou's okay," he said. "She looked as though she just needs a good night's—"

"Eden Riley!"

She looked up quickly as a man darted onto the sidewalk from out of nowhere and flashed a camera in their faces.

"Thanks!" he called behind him as he took off down the street. She never even saw his face.

"Damn." She scowled.

"What was that all about?" Ben asked.

"I don't know," she said. "I guess we'll find out when and if that picture ever sees the light of day."

The sound of screams and grating metal woke her. She bolted up, her own scream caught in her throat.

Ben sat up and put his arms around her. "You're all right," he said. "You're here with me."

She pressed her fingers to her eyes. "It seems so real."

"Was it the same dream you had that night in my cabin?"

She nodded. "They'd stopped. But I guess it's being here in New York with Kyle and Lou. It brings it all back to me." She looked toward the window and felt the odd electric pull of Twenty-third and Park again. "It's Lou's accident. I see it playing out in front of me in slow motion. And I feel so helpless."

"Why do you call it Lou's accident, as if you weren't with her?"

She wanted to tell him the truth. "I wasn't with her. But I saw the whole thing. It was sickening."

"They told me you were in the car with her."

She shook her head.

Ben was quiet. He slipped his fingers between hers, locked their hands together. "Maybe it would help if you told me about it."

"I can't."

"But look what you know about me. You know everything."

"Yes, but you're innocent. I'm guilty."

"Of what?"

She didn't answer.

"Whatever it is happened a long time ago."

"You won't be able to look at me the same way once you know."

"There's nothing you can tell me you did at eighteen that could change the way I feel about you now."

"I was nineteen."

He laughed. "Oh, that's different."

She had never told a soul, not even Wayne, what had happened that night, but she knew she was going to tell Ben. She would have to start way back, have to explain it all, or he'd only be able to see the ugliness in what she was about to say.

She lay down next to him again, settled into his arms.

"I lived for Kyle and Lou's visits when I was little," she said. "They were like folk heroes around our house. Bigger than life. They dressed differently than anyone I knew, and talked and acted differently. They only made it to Lynch Hollow once or twice a year, so their visits were a major event. In between visits they'd send me wonderful gifts." She told him about the huge rocking horse they'd sent her from South America, brightly painted as if it came off a carousel, with real horsehair as its mane and tail. "The only times I felt loved after my mother died were when they were around.

"The happiest memory of my childhood was when I was about eight. Kyle and Lou came to the States and took me to Washington, D.C., for the weekend. We went to the zoo and the natural history museum and a puppet show. I fantasized that they might take me with them and I wouldn't have to go back to Lynch Hollow, back to Susanna and my grandfather. We had a hotel room with a double bed for them and a twin for me. The last night we were there, they thought I was asleep and they were talking about me, about how unhappy I seemed, and I thought, oh God, they hate me. The next day I tried to act happy and perky—I wanted them to like me so much they'd keep me, but of course they didn't." She stopped, bit her lip. "I'm sounding pathetic."

Ben ran the back of his fingers up her arm. "You had a lot to overcome."

"Once I was in the orphanage, I gave up completely. But when Kyle and Lou found out where I was they took me in after all."

"You must have been very happy."

"I was afraid to be happy. I thought it wouldn't last, that they'd send me away one day. I know now that wasn't ever their intention, but I never could relax. I was a good kid up until my senior year when I finally got the courage to join the Drama Club. I was in my element then, and I stopped caring about anything else. I met a lot of people and suddenly had friends and a social life. There were a few guys in the club who were pretty rowdy. They smoked a lot of dope and played around with other drugs. And they were very attentive to me. It didn't take much to seduce me back then because I was dying to be held and loved and"—she sighed—"whatever. I starting sleeping around. Kyle knew what was going on. These guys would come to pick me up, and they'd be polite as hell to him, but he could see right through them." She laughed. "After reading the journal I know why. He wasn't so different himself. So my grades started slipping, and Kyle finally said that as long as I was living under his roof I couldn't go out with these particular guys any longer. I started sneaking around. Lying all the time. And then I got pregnant."

"No," Ben said.

"I didn't even know whose baby it was, but I told the guy who was the most likely candidate—his name was Tex—and he said I had to get an abortion. I didn't want to abort that baby"—her hand moved to her stomach—"but I couldn't see any way out. I felt like I was abandoning my own child, the way I was afraid of being abandoned myself." Her eyes filled. "Kyle and Lou don't know about any of this."

"They would have understood. I don't think you needed to go through it all without them."

"Oh, God, we weren't getting along at all then. I was a bitch. I'd swear at them, tell them I hated them. I was determined to hurt them before they could hurt me. After I graduated, I went to NYU and lived at home, but I was still seeing Tex. He was an extremely attractive psychopath." She tensed at the memory of how easily she'd been drawn in by him. "He had long blond hair and he wore all white and rode a big black Harley."

"Strange."

"One day he asked me if I'd like to go to California with him. That was my dream, California. I wanted to be a movie star and I knew I had to be there to make that happen. So I said yes. Kyle and Lou thought I hadn't seen Tex in months, but I'd actually seen him every day, and had an abortion to boot. Well, Kyle was out of town . . ." She shivered and Ben pulled the spread up from the foot of the bed and tucked it around their shoulders. "I packed my toothbrush and a change of clothes. I waited until Lou was asleep; then I called Tex to come get me. I left Lou a note. I wrote that I was going to California with Tex and that I'd let them know when I got there. I left the note on the kitchen table. Lou must have heard me leave. She found the note and—in her nightgown and robe—got into her car to follow us."

"Oh, Jesus," Ben said. He knew where this was going now.

Eden rolled onto her back and looked up at the dark ceiling. "She caught up with us at the first stoplight. She honked the horn and started to get out of the car, but Tex took off again and she took off after us. I thought she was crazy to do that. I thought she was so angry with me she was going to this insane length to catch up to me so she could kill me. It never occurred to me then that she was afraid for me, that she wanted to keep me from making a huge mistake, wrecking my life. Tex was laughing, going faster and faster, zipping around corners, and Lou was keeping up with him. At first I wanted to get away from her, but then I got scared. I started worrying about her. We were moving way too fast.

"Then all of a sudden there was a crashing sound behind us. Tex stopped the bike and I jumped off. The sound—the crashing metal sound—wouldn't stop. At least in my memory it goes on for minutes while Lou's car and a big black station wagon tie themselves together in the middle of the intersection. Then Lou started screaming. Tex said, 'Let's get out of here,' and I said no and he took off without me. I ran over to the car. The guy in the station wagon was dead, but I didn't know that till much later. I didn't even notice him then. I just wanted to get to Lou. I opened her door and started to pull her out, but her legs were pinned. There was a chunk of metal slicing into her leg and blood all over her robe and the floor of the car. She was screaming for me to help her." Eden stopped. She felt sick again, as she had in the Italian restaurant earlier that evening. She swallowed hard against the nausea. Next to her Ben was so still that she couldn't even feel him breathing. "The police were there very quickly, and an ambulance. Sirens everywhere. Just as the cops pulled up the other car burst into flames, so they had no choice but to pull Lou out with that piece of metal cutting into her leg, practically cutting it off right there." Eden covered her ears with her hands. "I'll never forget her screaming. I got sick to my stomach and the police thought I'd been in the car with her. And that's what we told them. And Kyle."

"Why would you tell Kyle you were with her?"

"I rode with Lou in the ambulance, and all I could think about was what Kyle would say when he found out I'd caused all this by running off with Tex. I held Lou's hand and I kept saying to her over and over again, 'Please don't tell Kyle.' It was the most selfish thing I've ever done. And she kept my secret. She let him think we were both in the car, going to the store. She was in her nightgown and I was going to run in and get whatever it was we needed. We had to keep talking about what a miracle it was I wasn't hurt. When Lou got out of the hospital I moved into the dorm. I couldn't stand to see her struggle to get around and know it was my fault. But it still wasn't far enough away, so the first chance I got I left for California. That time I didn't bother with a note." She closed her eyes. "I didn't even say good-bye."

From far below them Eden could hear the sound of traffic. Car horns. Brakes squealing. She wished Ben would say something. She put her hand on his chest. "Ben?"

He squeezed her hand and set it on her hip. "I need to get up." He stood up, and the cool air hit her side for a second before the spread fell back over her. He was so quiet. He pulled on his jeans, zipped the fly, and snapped them closed. Then he sat down in the chair next to the window. Cool white moonlight caught the edge of his jaw and spilled onto his bare chest.

She sat up, hugged her knees. "What are you thinking?" she asked.

"Just stunned."

"It's an ugly story."

"Lou loved you very much."

"And I repaid her by avoiding her. Avoiding both of them. I married Wayne practically the day after I met him so I'd feel safe out there, like I had a home and didn't need to come back to Lou and Kyle. And I think I also married him so that when I did visit Lou and Kyle I wouldn't ever have to be alone with them. This visit—this is the first time I've been alone with them in all these years."

Ben's arms were folded across his chest and he stared at the corner of the bed. The minutes ticked on without either of them speaking, and she knew she had said far too much.

She tightened her hands around her knees. "Are you coming back to bed?" she asked.

He looked over at her and she wished it were light enough to read his face. "I can't imagine what it's been like all these years for Lou to keep the truth from Kyle. The strongest thing in that relationship has always been their honesty and openness."

"I know."

"It would be a wonderful gift to her. If you told Kyle."

"Ben, I can't. It was so long ago. I'm trying to make it up to them in the present. I'm really trying. But I have to leave the past alone."

He looked back to the window and after a minute she lay down again, pulling the spread up to her chin. She closed her eyes, wondering if he was going to sit in the chair the entire night and leave her with only her guilt as a bed partner.

She woke to find the bed awash in sunlight. She turned her head to see Ben sleeping next to her, his forehead lined with a frown. In the light of day she felt exposed. The room was filled with the secrets the safety of the night had drawn from her. She should have kept it all to herself, as Lou was doing. Kept it their shared burden. Now she had made it Ben's as well. On this sun-filled morning, she felt defined by this one act in her life. She was selfish, ungrateful, cowardly.

She had a sudden longing for Santa Monica, for her simple house on the ocean, for the ability to pull a role over her head when she got out of bed in the morning. If she had one of the scripts Nina had sent her, she would start reading it right this second. She would give anything to be able to make believe.

She got out of bed and into the shower. Her head was lathered in shampoo when Ben stepped in beside her and took her in his arms. "I woke up and you were gone," he said. He pulled her head onto his shoulder.

She was glad he couldn't see her face so she didn't have to fight the tears. "You said if I told you it wouldn't change your feelings about me," she said. "But it has, hasn't it?"

"Yes, it has," he said. "It makes me love you more. Now I know that you need me as much as I need you."

31

October 3, 1952

When I came into the house tonight, Susanna told me I had a visitor in the parlor. I went into the parlor where Kyle was speaking with a young man I'd never seen before. They both stood up when I walked in.

"Here she is," Kyle said. "Seth, this is my sister, Katherine Swift. Kate, this is Seth Gallagher. Waverly Books sent him down here to take some publicity photographs of you."

Something happened to me when I looked at Seth Gallagher. It was as though the very sight of him made my knees go weak and my stomach do a somersault. I knew all at once why Matt and I have never been lovers. This feeling has to come first, and dear as Matt is, I feel nothing but friendship when I look at him.

Seth Gallagher is about Kyle's height and build. As a matter of fact, he reminds me of Kyle—he has the same straight-toothed smile, the same inquisitive look to his eyebrows. But his hair is a little bit darker than Kyle's and his eyes are a sparkling green. He looked surprised when he saw me. I had on a flannel shirt and my overalls, and my hair was tucked up under Daddy's old Stetson hat. I held out my hand to him and he shook it.

"You're Katherine Swift?" he asked.

"None other," I said.

He laughed. He has this great roar of a laugh that made Kyle and me smile at each other. "I expected someone . . . I expected . . . I don't know." Seth Gallagher was tripping all over his tongue. "I expected a lady. You know, Katherine Swift—the name sounds like it belongs to a real woman."

Kyle burst out laughing. He walked behind me toward the kitchen. "She is a real woman," he said and he flicked my hat off into his hand and my hair tumbled down over my shoulders. I was annoyed with him for doing that, for showing me off like I was a horse he was getting ready for the auction. But Seth's mouth dropped open and I felt the power of being female.

He stared at my hair. "Is the rest of you that beautiful?" he asked, straight out.

"Yes," I answered, just as boldly, and I knew right then I wanted this to be the man to put an end to my long, dreary years of virginity. I am sick to death of being a virgin.

Kyle leaned against the doorway, looking amused and amazed, with his arms folded over his chest.

"Seth is staying at the Coolbrook Hotel," he said. "He just stopped by to meet you tonight and tomorrow he'll be back to take pictures."

"Why don't you stay for dinner?" I said, and Seth did not need his arm twisted in the least.

I felt like a bitch in heat at the supper table as well as later on when Seth and Kyle and I played Monopoly. Seth is so nice-looking and his voice is real lively, though he sounds like a Yankee through and through and Kyle and I couldn't stop ourselves from teasing him about his accent. He is good-natured, though, and teased us back. Especially me. I wanted his attention worse than I've ever wanted anything in my life, and he was generous about giving it to me. His eyes never left me—I could feel him staring at me no matter what I was doing. I began to wish I had on something other than my dusty old overalls.

Seth is twenty-six. He's from Philadelphia, but he's lived in New York the past four years and he loves the city, which I cannot understand for the life of me, but at this moment I don't care. This has been the most exhilarating night of my life. I can't stop thinking about him.

Before Kyle went off to the parlor to sleep he stopped in my room. "That boy's going to have nasty dreams about you tonight, Kate, that's for sure," he said.

I told him I might have a few myself and chased him from my room. So tomorrow I will see Seth again. I'm so glad Matt picked this weekend to spend in New York. Otherwise he'd be moping around here moon-eyed and I'd feel funny being so brazen with Seth. Seth Gallagher. I love his name. I love his green eyes. I am acting like a love-struck fool.

October 4, 1952

I wore my hair in a long braid down my back this morning, and since it was warm, I put on khaki shorts and a white shirt. When Seth arrived with his cameras and tripod, he handed me a box filled with blood-red roses. I shook when I took them out and put them in a vase, they were so beautiful, so red.

"The only color I could even think of getting you," he said. He wanted to take my picture where I usually write, but that is either in the cavern or my bedroom. Tempted though I was to let him in my room, I couldn't do it with Susanna around, nor was I willing to let him see the cave. So I suggested the pits.

It was fun having my picture taken. Seth is so sure of himself and made me feel at ease. On the way back through the woods, he took my arm. "Kate," he said. "Will you go out with me tonight?"

I wanted to say yes so badly, but go out? I knew what would happen if I went out—I'd have one of my terrors and make a fool out of myself. "Maybe we could just stay here and play Monopoly again."

"No, I want to take you out to dinner and dancing afterwards. There's a band at the Coolbrook Hotel tonight."

So I agreed on the condition that Kyle could come too and bring a date. Kyle's not seeing anyone right now, so I wasn't sure he would agree to this, but he did. He's excited for me that I'm actually interested in someone. He can't believe it and neither can I.

"I want to look sexy tonight," I told him.

"You're the only woman in the Shenandoah Valley who can look sexy in overalls, Kate," Kyle said. We were in my room and he opened my closet and shook his head. "You don't own a single dress."

I suddenly wanted more than anything to wear a dress. I wanted to shave my legs and wear nylons.

Susanna spent the afternoon hemming one of her dresses for me to wear. Susanna is a quiet person who usually keeps her distance from me, but this afternoon she's been by my side every minute, helping me get ready for tonight. I'm even borrowing her nylons and garter belt and a special strapless brassiere that wraps around my ribs and makes it hard to breathe. Just what I need is to have more trouble breathing than usual.

The dress is beautiful. It is black and hugs my body and the long sleeves and yoke are made of a black lacy material. It's cut to a V in front and the tops of my breasts show.

"That dress looks better on you than it does on me," Susanna said as she fiddled with the neckline. "You have more cleavage than I do."

When I was completely dressed I stared at the stranger in the mirror. I tugged the dress a little lower, amazed by how voluptuous I looked. My legs were sleek and gorgeous. Susanna had parted my hair on the side and it looked like a golden waterfall. She put pencil and mascara on my eyes, rouge on my cheeks, and, despite my protests, lipstick on my lips.

Kyle came into the room, looking fine himself in his gray suit, and the expression on his face when he saw me made my getup worth it even if I didn't go anywhere except back to bed.

"Holy mother of Christ," he said. "Even I didn't know you could look this good." He took my hand and turned me around to get a view of me from every angle. Then he slipped the tips of his fingers under the neckline of my dress and tugged it up an inch or so.

"Kyle," I said, "I've spent the last hour getting it just right."

Kyle shook his head. "Do you want Seth to spend the entire evening with his eyes on your chest and his mind like oatmeal? Don't be cruel, Kate."

"I'm scared," I said. "I know what's going to happen the second I get there. I'll get dizzy and won't be able to breathe and . . ."

"Shh," he said. "You'll make it happen for sure if you keep thinking about it. I'll be right there with you. You'll be fine." He checked his watch. "I'd better go pick up Bess." He hugged me. "I'll be at the hotel by the time you arrive, beautiful lady," he said.

Seth picked me up at seven. He was shocked speechless by the way I looked and it wasn't until we were in his car and on the road that he told me I looked "like a movie star," and that he was "honored" to be with me.

I didn't feel at all nervous as we drove along and I know it's because he reminds me so much of Kyle. I was even fine when we got to the hotel. Kyle was waiting for us with a very pretty girl named Bess Donner. He was careful to sit next to me at the table in the hotel restaurant. The waitress took our orders and then I got the first little wave of breathlessness. It's hardest for me to just sit. My chest started tightening up like it does. I looked at Kyle and he leaned over and whispered in my ear, "You'll be fine, Kate."

Then Bess said, "It's rude to whisper," but I could tell she was teasing. Bess is the type of girl who teases a lot. She's confident about her prettiness. I'd never heard Kyle mention her before and wondered how he knew her. She has very straight light brown hair cut to her chin and big brown eyes. She's thin in an appealing, energetic way and was wearing a blue dress with lacy sleeves like mine, so I guess I am right in style.

Bess asked me questions about my writing and it put me back at ease to have something to talk about. Seth said I was one of the favorite children's authors at Waverly Books. He said they talk about how they'd love to get me up to New York to wine and dine me, but I always refuse their invitations. I'm viewed as something of a mystery, he said.

"Well, now you've met her," Bess said, "so the mystery must be gone."

Seth smiled at me. "Not at all. Meeting Kate has only added to the mystery. She's an enigma. I feel as though she must be a figment of my imagination. I expect to develop my film and find no one there."

Then our food was delivered which started my decline. When my nervousness comes on me, I cannot eat. The sight and smell of food makes me nauseous.

"Is something wrong with your food, Kate?" Seth looked at me from across the table. "You've barely touched it."

I'd been pushing the meat and potatoes and snap beans around on my plate, hoping that the fact that I was bringing none of it to my lips would not be noticed.

"That's Kate for you," Kyle said. "It's the creative mind. When she's working on a story, she gets a thought in her head and it absorbs all her concentration and she completely forgets what she's doing. It always happens at the table, doesn't it?" He looked at me and I nodded, his partner in this little ruse. "It's a wonder she has any flesh on her bones at all."

Seth once again buried his eyes in my flesh and I looked thankfully at my brother.

"What story are you thinking about now, Kate?" Bess asked.

I told them about Child of Sand and my words came out a little confused and breathy because of my nervousness, but I thought, what does it matter? I am a woman of mystery and peculiar eating habits. I can get away with just about anything.

Then the music started and Seth asked me to dance.

"I don't know how," I said. I couldn't go out there on that dance floor. I knew my fear would rise the moment I left Kyle's side. Seth was persistent and I was nearly sweating with terror by the time he finally gave up and took Bess out on the dance floor. I watched him pull Bess into his arms and felt a little jealous. I was starting to shake. Once I start to shake, it's hard for me to ever feel right again.

"Kyle," I said. "I'm going to have to leave." I was looking at him, pleading with him to save me somehow, save me from my own wretched self.

He took my hand under the table and squeezed it hard. "Relax, Kate. Think about something else." He looked around us. "You are easily the most beautiful woman in this room, do you know that?"

"Well, Bess is very pretty," I said. "How do you know her?"

Kyle looked toward the dance floor where Seth was turning Bess around and around in nauseating circles. I thought for a minute he wasn't going to answer me. Then he said, "Bess is the girl Matt sees in Luray."

"The hussy?"

"Shh." Kyle laughed. "She's a very nice girl, Kate. Be kind."

"Why, you've had her too," I said. I knew by the way he was so quick to take up for her and by the color in his face that I was right.

"That, sweetheart, is none of your business."

I felt triply jealous of this woman now. She was in the arms of the man I wanted, she was the occasional wanton lover of my dear friend Matt and she'd lain with my brother as well.

"Next dance is mine," Seth said when he returned to the table. "I won't take no for an answer."

On the dance floor I felt swoony in his arms, not so much from his touch as from my fear that I would pass out or upchuck down the front of his shirt at any moment. "I don't care if you step on my toes," he said cheerily. "I just needed to get you away from Kyle and Bess and all to myself for a while."

I barely heard a word he said as he danced me in circles, further from the door, further from Kyle.

"Kate," he said. "You're trembling. Are you cold?" *He pulled me closer, suffocating me, and I fought like an animal to escape his arms. I pushed away from him.*

"I'm sorry," *I said and I nearly ran back to the table, plowing through the mass of dancers to get there.* "I have to leave," *I said to Kyle.*

Bess stood up and touched my shoulder. She looked over at Seth who was trying to cut through the crowd more politely than I had. "Did he get fresh with you?" *she asked.*

"No." *I started crying, looking helplessly at my brother.* "Kyle," *I said. He lifted my coat from the back of my chair and put it over my shoulders.*

"What did I do?" *Seth asked when he reached the table.*

"Take her outside," *Kyle said to Seth.* "She'll be all right once she's outside. I'll take care of the bill."

People were looking up from their tables.

"Tell him the truth, Kate," *Kyle called after me.*

Outside, as Kyle had predicted, I felt better. I leaned against Seth's car while he asked me what was wrong. "What did your brother mean about telling me the truth?"

"Can we sit in your car?" *I asked. He opened the door and I got in. I felt sorry for him for thinking he must have brought this on somehow.*

"There's something wrong with me," *I said. I was still trembling and he held my hands.* "I've been this way a long time. Since I was a child. I get very nervous away from home. I was so excited about tonight and I hoped I could make it through somehow. I actually made it longer than I usually do. I'm so sorry, Seth."

"That's why you didn't eat."

"Yes."

He smiled, but it was a sad smile. "I had illusions of you visiting me in New York, me showing you around."

"I could try," I said, though a well of helplessness filled my chest. "I've never met anyone before that I wanted to try for."

"Does it make you nervous to be kissed?" he asked.

"No," I said, and he leaned over and kissed me, softly, once. "I'm not made of glass," I said. "You can really kiss me."

And he did, a long, hard kiss, and then he lowered his head to my breasts, buried his face there and I never felt happier to be a woman than I did at that moment.

Suddenly there was a knock on the window. I turned to see Kyle's face against the glass. "Is everything okay?" he asked through the window. He was holding Bess's hand behind his back and she was giggling.

"Yes, Kyle," I said. A minute ago I'd wanted him to save me; now I wanted him to leave me alone.

"I'm about to drive her home, big brother." Seth grinned. He is as handsome as all get-out.

As we drove toward Lynch Hollow, Seth said, "I'm staying over one more night, Kate. Will you see me again?"

"I'd love to." I was overjoyed that I had not completely ruined everything with him. When we pulled up in front of the house, he kissed me again, then stroked his fingertips along the neckline of Susanna's dress.

"We could spend tomorrow evening in my hotel room if you think you can manage that," he said.

I could see he was nervous about suggesting that to me, not sure how I'd take his forwardness. I guess I was seeming a mite unpredictable to him. "I'm a virgin, Seth," I said. "And I would like you to be the one to put an end to that condition for me."

He just stared at me for a moment. Then he smiled. "You're the strangest girl I've ever met." He kissed me again. "I'd be honored to help you out of that dilemma."

I waited up for Kyle to get home and when he finally came in my room to say good night, I told him our plan.

"Seth and I are going to make love in his hotel room tomorrow night," I said.

Kyle frowned at me. "I don't know, Kate. You don't know him very well and—"

"Kyle, don't you dare tell me I shouldn't do this. Don't you dare ruin it for me. You fuck everyone you meet."

"I do not. And clean up your mouth."

"I'm twenty-five years old and I've never made love." I felt so sorry for myself I thought I might cry. "I thought I never would. Then here comes this beautiful man just out of the blue, with his camera and his green eyes and his smile that's so much like yours. And for the first time I want somebody and I'll be damned if I'm going to wait until I know everything there is to know about him. I don't care what more there is. I want him now."

"All right," Kyle said. His voice was very quiet after my little scolding. "But Matt will die."

"Matt doesn't need to know all my business," I said. "I've known Matt for a thousand years and I've never felt the kind of attraction to him that I felt after one minute with Seth."

"All right, Kate. Sleep well." Kyle left my room and I threw my notebook at the door after he closed it. I wanted him to be happy for me. He's going to sap all the joy out of this.

October 5, 1952

I'm so excited. I took a long bath this afternoon with some of Susanna's bath crystals. I keep expecting to feel terrified each time I think of being in a hotel room so far from Lynch Hollow, but I'm pretty calm so far.

Kyle is repentant. He just came in my room, sat down on his old bed and told me he was sorry for trying to burst my bubble last night. Then he handed me a Trojan!! "Take this," he said, "in case Seth's fool enough not to have any." Then he reached into his back pocket and handed me another. "Better take two," he said.

I thanked him and slipped the Trojans deep in my purse.

"Listen, Kate," Kyle said. "Some men don't know the first thing about making sure a woman, you know, gets her pleasure when they make love. I don't know how much Seth has been around. You're the one who taught me, remember?"

I nodded, remembering how wonderfully drunk he was the night I drew him a picture of the workings of a woman's body.

"I don't know how long it would have taken me to learn that on my own," he said. "So if Seth wasn't lucky enough to have a sister who . . . I just don't want you to have high hopes and then be disappointed."

"I'll be fine," I said. I was beginning to feel embarrassed.

"It can hurt the first time, too."

"I know, Kyle. I read, you know."

"I'm irritating you," he said with a smile.

"Like salt on a wound." But I smiled back at him. I love Kyle so much. I'd miss it if he didn't worry about me. He said he'd sit in the lounge of the hotel tonight in case I need him, even though I'm sure I'll be fine. He has a book he wants to read, he said. He can read just as well at the hotel as he can here.

October 6, 1952

I'm sitting in my room. It's the middle of the afternoon and Kyle is asleep in the other bed, the bed he never sleeps in anymore. It is the first sleep he's had in two days and I am so relieved to finally see some peace in his face that I could cry.

My poor brother. His life changed overnight, and mine did not change at all. I am as much a virgin today as I was yesterday.

Seth picked me up at seven and we drove directly to his hotel. I wore my dungarees again and a wool sweater. "I've been thinking about last night," he said to me in the car. "The way you ran out of the restaurant and the things you told me about yourself."

"I'm sorry if I embarrassed you."

"No, that's not it. But it opened my eyes to how different you and I are." My heart sank to my feet.

"I love the city," he said. "I love to travel. You love staying home."

"I'm only twenty-five, Seth. I'm not a closed book. I can change."

He smiled and reached over to hold my hand. "Let's not talk about it now," he said. "We have a wonderful night ahead of us and even in pants you are the best-looking woman I've ever laid eyes on."

The lobby was empty when we got to the hotel. I knew Kyle had some errands to run before he'd get there and I was really sorry he was coming at all. It was unnecessary. I felt fine.

Seth's room was beautiful, one of the more expensive rooms in the hotel, I'm sure. The bed was a big four poster with a matching armoire and dresser. There was just one chair, so we sat on the bed to drink champagne and eat caviar on crackers. I'd never tasted caviar before and it was revolting and wonderful all at once. It seemed fitting to eat something new and wicked-tasting on the night I was to be deflowered. I said this out loud and Seth laughed his deep belly laugh. I had eaten quite a bit before I realized I was at ease. Looking back I think it was the champagne. I'll have to remember that. I can probably go places if I get rip-roaring drunk first.

I don't feel like writing much about what happened between us. We kissed a little. He asked me if I wanted the lamp on or off and when I said "On," he told me I was unusual, that most girls like the lights off. "Most girls are modest," he said, and I shrugged and said what I've been saying all my life: "I'm not like most girls."

It would have been good. I felt so at ease and so alive. He had taken my sweater and brassiere off and was kissing my breasts when a knock came at the door.

Seth drew back and looked up at me. "What timing. If that's your overprotective brother, I'll . . ."

The knock came again and Seth nodded toward the little alcove where I could stand without being seen while he opened the door. It was Warren Davison, one of the sheriff's deputies we've known forever, who had come to give me a message from Kyle. It seems that Kyle had been driving up Main Street toward the hotel when a little boy ran out in front of his car. Kyle hit him, and the boy was badly hurt.

"A lot of busted bones, but the worst is his head," Warren said, his cheeks aflame since I was standing in front of him holding my sweater to my chest. "Kyle says to tell you he's all right, but he wanted to go to the hospital with the boy so he won't be able to be here at the hotel like he said."

After Warren left, Seth asked, "What's that about Kyle coming to the hotel?"

"Nothing," I said.

Seth stared at me a moment before he shrugged and started kissing me again, but now I couldn't concentrate. I kept imagining how terrible Kyle must feel, and Seth's hands were starting to feel like sandpaper on my skin. Finally I stepped away from him.

"I can't do this now, Seth," I said. "I can't get my mind off Kyle."

Seth put his shirt back on. Any other man would have been angry, and maybe he was a little. He didn't say much as he dressed, but then he offered to take me to the hospital.

"No," I said. I knew I couldn't survive two minutes in the hospital. "Please just take me home."

Both of us were quiet on the ride home. I was feeling sorry for myself and for Kyle and for the little boy. I should have insisted Kyle not come to the hotel. There was no need at all.

"I'm sorry, Seth," I said when he stopped the car in front of my house.

"It's all right," he said. "I guess I'd feel the same way."

"I could come back tomorrow," I said.

"I'm leaving for New York tomorrow," he said, and I wanted to grab him and hold him and beg him to stay.

"Will I ever see you again?" I asked.

He nodded and leaned over to kiss me on the cheek. "I'll write to you very soon."

The sheriff brought Kyle home around midnight. Kyle headed directly for the outhouse and I forced myself to join him there, to hold his head while he vomited over and over again until there was nothing left to come up. When he could finally talk, he told me that the boy will live, but he is blinded for life and he'll have casts on his legs for a long time.

I heated him some milk and put him in his old bed in my room, but he couldn't sleep. He said he was afraid to go to sleep, that he was afraid he'd have nightmares about the accident. "He came out of nowhere," Kyle said. "He just flew up on the hood of my car. I could hear his bones breaking."

"None of it would have happened if you hadn't been coming to the hotel for me," I said.

Kyle sat up and looked at me directly as though he was noticing me for the first time that night. "How was it?" he asked. "You and Seth?"

"Once Warren told us what happened, I just couldn't go through with it," I said. "I made Seth drive me home."

Kyle sighed and lay down again. "I ruined your special night, Kate."

"Don't worry about it," I said. "I can lose my virginity any old time."

October 13, 1952

Kyle visits the little boy—Freddy Jenkins—every day. He reads to him from my books. Kyle is quieter than usual these days. I keep expecting him to cry, but he hasn't shed a tear. It's like something's hardened in him. He is scared and shaky and sick, but he doesn't weep.

I told Matt about Seth. He was real quiet at first and then he asked me if I planned to see him again. I told him I have no plans, which is unfortunately true. I want to see Seth so much. He said he'd write, but he's certainly taking his time about it. I've thought of calling Waverly Books to try to get his number. I never thought I would feel this way, like a typical female, pathetically pining for a man.

October 20, 1952

Today I received a big envelope from Waverly Books. In it was the photograph they're going to use on my book jackets. It's one that Seth took of me in the pits, with my hair braided over my shoulder. I look pretty and happy. I look like I'm falling in love with the photographer.

There was a letter from Seth, just one side of a page. He told me I am a special person. He will "always cherish" the time we had together, but it's just as well we didn't "finish what we started" that night because then I might have taken our relationship too seriously. "Our differences are insurmountable," he wrote. He said he smiled when he developed the pictures; he will always think of me fondly. He hopes Kyle is all right, and that the little boy in the accident is recovering. And that is the sum total of what Seth Gallagher had to say to me.

I won't cry over this although the tears are begging to come out. I still think of calling him, pleading with him to give me a chance to prove I can be different. But the truth is, I doubt it myself.

Kyle asked to hear Seth's letter and I finally read it to him. Kyle is so delicate these days, so full of hurt and guilt. He listened to the letter, put his arms around me, and did my crying for me.

32

"Whatever happened to that little boy you hit, Kyle?" Eden asked her uncle at lunch the next day. Lou was out once again with her painting friend from Georgia, and Eden was beginning to suspect that Lou's absences were designed to give her time alone with Kyle.

Kyle scooped a spoonful of potato salad onto his plate. "You've met him," he said.

"I have?"

"Fred Jenkins. He's head of the Children's Fund in Richmond."

Eden stared at her uncle, openmouthed. She had not made the connection between the victim of Kyle's accident and the dynamic blind director of the Children's Fund she'd had lunch with in Richmond. It sent a chill up her spine to see the course Kyle had set for this man so long ago. "God, that's ironic. He never mentioned a thing about it."

"No, he wouldn't."

She stood up and carried her plate to the sink, then leaned over to give Kyle a hug from behind, resting her cheek against his temple and, she knew, surprising him. "You had some terrible experiences, Kyle," she said.

He reached up to squeeze her hand. "I don't have much to complain about," he said.

She straightened up and faced him. "I'm ready for the next notebook," she said optimistically, but Kyle's eyes held the same reluctance she'd seen in them the night of her arrival.

"Soon," he said. "You can have it soon."

"All right. But after reading this notebook, there's one thing I have to know now. Did my mother ever take a lover before my father?"

Kyle looked surprised and then he smiled. "No, honey. Your father was Kate's first and only lover."

Ben drove into Coolbrook to pick up groceries for dinner. He was going to make pizza for himself and Eden tonight because it would be cheap. The trip to New York had nearly depleted his funds, but it had been worth it. Except for that mishap in the restaurant the last night, it had been a perfect trip. And that incident was a blessing in disguise because it led Eden to tell him everything she'd been holding inside half her life. She was lighter now. Freed up. And the bond between them was stronger because of what they knew about one another.

He bought mushrooms and green peppers in the little store on Main Street. He picked up a pepperoni at the last minute—an extravagance, but it matched his mood. He wondered how the pizza would turn out in his old oven. It didn't matter. He knew Eden would eat without complaint anything he made.

He stopped in the post office to check his mailbox. It was nearly always empty, so he was surprised to find a notice telling him he had a package. He turned the note over to the woman behind the counter and waited, wondering who could be sending him something. When he saw the package his heart sank. It was the box he'd sent to Kim Parrish, the dollhouse furniture. It had not been opened, the seal unbroken. Alex and Leslie's address had been crossed out with a red arrow pointing toward Ben's return address, along with the words Return to Sender. Damn!

*

There was a blue BMW in the dusty clearing in front of his cabin. Ben parked his pickup next to it just as a man stepped out of the car. Blond hair, wire-rimmed glasses. Sam.

Ben smiled as he jumped out of the pickup. "Sam!" He pulled his brother to him, felt Sam's damp cheek against his own.

"I was just about to leave you a note," Sam said. "I was afraid I was going to miss you."

Ben grinned at his brother. "New car?" He nodded toward the BMW.

"Yeah." Sam set a hand on the hood, casually, as if the car meant little to him. "Runs nice."

Ben couldn't stop grinning. "It's great to see you. What are you doing here?"

"I'm on my way to a conference in Charlottesville and I thought I'd stop in and see how you're getting along." Sam reached inside the car door and brought out his briefcase and a large tin which he handed to Ben. "Jen's macaroons. Your favorite. She made them for you last night. What's in the package?"

Ben thought of making something up. He hated Sam to know just how bad things were for him. But instead he shrugged. "A gift for Kim Parrish. I sent it to her but it came back unopened."

"Postal service is doing a great job these days, huh? I can take it—" Sam stopped in midsentence and looked Ben in the eye. "You mean Alex and Leslie sent it back to you?"

"Afraid so." Ben opened the cabin door and the stuffy hot air hit their faces. He set the package on his bed and walked across the room to turn on the fan.

Sam shook his head. "God, I can't believe they'd do that."

"No big deal. So. Did you have trouble finding this place?"

"It wasn't easy." Sam looked around the tiny cabin and Ben's cheeks reddened. He wouldn't be able to kid Sam into thinking he was living comfortably after today. He moved some pieces of dollhouse furniture from the sofa to the coffee table.

"Have a seat. Want some iced tea? Beer?"

"Beer," said Sam. "It's hot out there."

"It's hot in here, too. Sorry."

"You're making another dollhouse?"

"Yeah," Ben said from the kitchen. "For Eden's little girl."

"I hope our baby's a girl so we can get a dollhouse out of you."

"How are the adoption plans coming?"

"Great. January or February. We've got the nursery wallpapered and we're picking out a crib next weekend."

Ben handed Sam his beer and sat down on the other side of the coffee table, grinning again. "You look good," he said. Sam was one of those men whose looks only improved with age. He had their mother's coloring—blond hair, green eyes—while Ben favored their father. His mustache was fastidiously trimmed, his hairline just beginning to recede. The glasses brightened his eyes and gave him some credibility as a psychiatrist.

They had often been lumped together as kids. The Alexander boys. Sam had been a straight-A student in high school and a hard act to follow, but he never held his accomplishments over Ben. Ben was nearly as old, nearly as bright, nearly as handsome as Sam, but not quite. And though the rivalry was slight it was there nonetheless, so that when Sam announced he was going to major in premed in college Ben knew that was one major he could rule out for himself immediately.

The only thing Ben had ever beaten Sam at was fatherhood. The fertility tests had found Sam's low sperm count to be the cause of Jen's not getting pregnant, and he made it no secret to Ben that he'd trade in all his success for the chance to be a father. Ben took no pleasure in the fact that he'd finally done something better than his brother. He'd encouraged this adoption from the start.

"Have you seen this?" Sam opened his briefcase and pulled out a newspaper, the type you'd see in the grocery store checkout. On the cover was a picture of Ben and Eden.

The caption read: EDEN RILEY AND MYSTERY MAN PAINT BIG APPLE RED.

"Oh, shit," Ben held the paper on his knees. He looked up at Sam. "We went to New York with Kyle and Lou, and when we were leaving a restaurant some jerk sprang out of nowhere and took this picture."

"Well, I never would have recognized you, except for the fact that

I knew you were seeing her, so I gave the picture a second look. No one will know it's you without your beard. And the article doesn't say much. They don't have a clue who you are."

It was true that the picture didn't look like him. The angle of the camera threw his features off, made him look thinner, heavy-lidded. He shook his head. "She doesn't need this, though. She worries about her reputation."

Sam laughed. "So she takes up with you? She doesn't sound too bright."

"She is bright. And beautiful. And ambitious. A little screwed up, but who am I to talk?"

"Does she know?"

"Everything. And she believes me. She really does, Sam."

Sam smiled. "You've got it bad."

"Feels good to me."

Sam shook his head. "What happens when it's time for her to go back to Tinseltown?"

"We're not thinking that far ahead."

"You can tell her from me that if she does a number on you, I'll boycott her next movie."

"Sam. Chill out." Ben smiled, both amused and touched by his brother's concern.

Sam reached into his briefcase again. "Here's another journal article for you. And Winston will testify, if we can ever get a court date. I'd like to get some guys from the Accused Group to help us."

"No way," Ben said. The Accused Group was an organization of men who felt themselves wrongly accused of molesting their sons or daughters. They held workshops to learn ways to discredit their children's accusations, egging each other on. He'd gone to one meeting at Sam's insistence and came away repulsed. "They only care about what this has done to them," he'd said to Sam after the meeting. "Not one of them mentioned what their kids are going through." He'd left that meeting certain he was the only innocent man in the room.

"I really think they could help us, Ben. They have the contacts."

"Forget it."

Sam reached into his shirt pocket and handed a few photographs to Ben. "I brought some pictures of Bliss for you."

Bliss stood under an umbrella watching a fisherman weigh a small bluefish. "Where is this?" Ben asked.

"Saint Michaels. Remember, I told you Jen and I took her there a few weeks ago?"

Bliss was inches taller, her body stretching out, her pin-straight hair cut to the tops of her shoulders. She looked like a street urchin—beautiful, but lanky and underfed.

"I can't believe how much she's grown," Ben said. He looked through the pictures, all of them of Bliss on the waterfront. Her face was somber and unsmiling. In his memory, she smiled all the time. In the last picture she was waving at the camera, but still there was no smile.

"Doesn't she smile anymore?" he asked.

"Oh, sure. She was a little grumpy that day."

Ben sat back with a sigh. "I guess we'll be doing this until she's eighteen, huh? You sneaking me pictures?"

"I'll do it as long as you want me to."

"I know it puts you in an awkward position with Jen."

"Blood's thicker than marriage." Sam stretched, looked around him again. "Speaking of Jen, she wants me to talk you into coming for a visit. You can bring Eden, if you like. We miss you. We used to spend practically every weekend together, remember? Always had some project we were helping each other with."

"I'm not ready to go to Annapolis. I can't be that close to Bliss. I'd try to get a look at her."

"Mmm." Sam nodded. "By the way, did you know Sharon's father died?"

"No." Ben felt wounded, forgotten. "I thought he was doing better." Sharon should have called him. Regardless of what had happened this past year, she should have let him know. "I can't even call Sharon to . . . Do you have her new number?"

"Yeah, but Ben, I really can't."

"I just want to tell her I'm sorry about her dad. Come on."

Sam was easy on this one. He pulled out his wallet and read him

Sharon's number from a scrap of paper. "Don't tell them I gave it to you," he said. "By the way—I've found a couple of names of therapists up here. Why don't you let me . . . ?"

"Can't afford it."

"I'll take care of the cost."

"No, Sam. You know that's just not my way of dealing with things."

"Do you need a refill on the Valium?"

"I haven't taken any."

"Good. I really wish you wouldn't. You look like you've lost a little weight. Are you eating? How are you sleeping?"

Ben loved this side of Sam—the soft, concerned, nurturing side that was the reason for his success as a psychiatrist. He would make a wonderful father. "I'm fine. My best nights, though, are the nights I'm not sleeping because I have Eden with me. I've had some very sleepless nights lately."

Sam laughed. "My baby brother's sleeping with Eden Riley. Amazing." He swallowed the last of his beer and set the empty can on the coffee table. "There's just one more thing I have to tell you and then I've got to get back on the road."

"What's that?"

"Well." Sam took off his glasses and rubbed his eyes. "I hesitate to tell you because there's nothing we can do about it and I figure you're already feeling helpless enough."

Ben sat forward. "Tell me."

Sam looked him in the eye. "I think Sharon was seeing Jeff when you two were married."

Ben shook his head. "She barely knew him, if she knew him at all." Sharon didn't fit his image of a woman having an affair back then. "What makes you think that?"

"He slipped when Jen and I picked Bliss up to go to Saint Michaels. He said he and Sharon took Bliss to Wild World two summers ago. Sharon corrected him and he argued with her and then realized he was incriminating himself and shut up."

"Pretty slim evidence, Sam."

"Well, I asked Bliss about it and she thought it was two summers ago too."

"Bliss's memory is pretty unreliable."

"She calls him Daddy, Ben."

At first he didn't understand what Sam was suggesting. He only felt the sting of the word, remembering Eden's reaction when Cassie referred to her stepmother as Mommy. But then he caught on.

"Do you think . . . ?"

"I don't know. I know you didn't do it, and if Jeff was really around during that time . . ."

"But Bliss said it happened when she was in bed in her own room."

"Maybe when you were traveling."

"Christ, Sam, why don't you just punch me in the stomach and get it over with? Sharon wouldn't . . . You know her better than that."

Sam shrugged.

"She had back problems all that year. She wasn't even interested in sex."

"Maybe she just wasn't interested in sex with you. Or maybe not with Jeff either. Maybe she drove Jeff to Bliss or—"

"That's crazy," Ben said, but what he was remembering was the time he'd called home from Colorado and a man answered. Sharon had told him it was someone from school. She was having a meeting of some of the teachers. "Assuming it is true—what can we do about it?"

"That's just it." Sam put his glasses back on. "There's nothing we can do. I spoke with Barbara McKay and the social worker who investigated the case. They said there's nothing concrete to go on."

"I can't believe Sharon would let me go to jail for something Jeff might have done."

"You confessed, remember?" Sam had been furious with him for his incriminating outburst in the courtroom.

"I didn't feel as though I had a goddamned choice. They were going to torture Bliss."

"She's not as fragile as you think."

Ben set his beer down. He looked over at his brother. "Do you remember Randy?"

Sam frowned at him. "What are you dredging that up for now?"

"I've always wondered if you understood why I didn't want to let Bliss testify. I still remember what it was like having all those questions thrown at me."

"You really need to see someone, Ben. You should have put that stuff behind you a long time ago."

"It is behind me. Or it was until I saw that scared look on Bliss's face."

Sam stood up. "Maybe I shouldn't have said anything. Would you rather I just kept this sort of information to myself?"

"No." It took all Ben's strength to stand up himself. He didn't want Sam to leave. "Please don't start keeping things from me."

"Okay." Sam put his arm around his brother's shoulders and started toward the door.

"Thank Jen for the cookies."

"Sure." At the door Sam turned to face him. "I don't know how to say this other than just to say it." He pulled a check from his shirt pocket and pressed it into Ben's hand. "Use this for whatever you want. A better place to live, maybe. Or a trip for you and Eden. You should get away. Relax a—"

"Forget it." Ben's cheeks burned. He put the check back in Sam's pocket, but Sam extracted it again.

"Please, Ben, take it." There were tears in Sam's eyes, ready to spill over. Ben looked away, opened the door wider.

Sam set his hand on the doorknob. "I can't stand to see what's happened to you. This isn't right. It isn't fair. Please let me help with the money. It's the only way I can."

"No." Ben stared out at the BMW next to his pickup. He couldn't look at Sam's face, didn't want to see if the tears were making their way down his cheeks.

"You know how much we love you?"

Ben nodded. "Drive carefully, okay?"

He stared at the number for a long time before dialing the phone. He held his breath as it rang, grimaced when Jeff answered.

"This is Ben," he said. "I'd like to speak with Sharon." There was a moment's hesitation on the other end of the line.

"How did you get this number?"

"It doesn't matter. Is Sharon there?"

"She doesn't want to talk to you."

"Let her tell me that herself, okay?"

He heard Sharon's voice in the background, then Jeff growling, "You don't have to talk to him."

"Ben?" It was Sharon, and he felt an old rush of love for her.

"Sam just told me about Pop," he said. "I'm so sorry, Sharon."

She said nothing and he felt an aching in his chest.

"I wish you'd told me," he said. "He was a part of my life, too."

"I know." Her voice was husky. "I didn't know what I should . . ."

He heard Jeff bark something in the background. "Could you please ask Jeff to give you a few seconds' privacy?" To his surprise, she spoke to Jeff and Ben heard the slamming of a door. Poor Sharon. "I'm sorry," he said. "I don't want to create problems between you two."

"It's all right."

"How did Bliss take it about Pop?"

"I don't think we should talk about Bliss."

Ben closed his eyes, let the ache spread, fill him up. "She's my child, Sharon."

There was another long pause before Sharon spoke again. "She doesn't really understand," she said. "She keeps expecting him to show up at the door."

"Does she expect me to show up too?" He knew he'd overstepped himself the second the words were out of his mouth, but it was too late.

"Why should she?" Sharon snapped. "You made it very clear to her—and to me—that your pride was more important than your family when you refused counseling."

"Sharon, I was innocent. I couldn't go—"

"I'm getting off."

"Wait. Look. Just tell me how she is. How does she get along with Jeff? He sounds kind of gruff."

"At least he's not a wolf in sheep's clothing."

"Sharon, I want you to do something for me. Just entertain the thought that I might be innocent."

"I will not."

"You have to. Because if you truly believe something happened to Bliss and if I'm innocent, then someone else is guilty and . . . Sharon?" He dug his fingers into the quilt. "Were you seeing Jeff while we were married?"

Sharon drew in a sharp breath. "I can't believe you're asking me that."

"I'm sorry. But I—"

"Ben, don't call again, all right? There's no point to it. It upsets me and it upsets Jeff. And Bliss is never going to know you called, so don't imagine that she will. She's so much better now. She's finally starting to forget you, and the last thing we need is to have you harassing us again."

She hung up on him, and he slowly moved the phone from the bed to the apple crate. *She's finally starting to forget you.* Maybe it was best for her that she forget him, that he become one-dimensional in her mind. The bad daddy. Make it simple. Visitation was a poor idea, a terrible idea. Bliss's counselor was right. It could only confuse her.

He'd forgotten to ask Sharon if Bliss smiled anymore.

He'd promised her pizza, and she'd driven up to the cabin expecting to be greeted by the aroma of oregano and tomato sauce. Instead all she could smell as she neared the open cabin door was the heat.

He sat at the table in the center of the room, his back to her, and at first she thought he was working on the dollhouse. "Ben?"

He turned around, clearly startled. "I didn't hear your car."

She walked toward him. "You must be deep in thought." She put her hands on his shoulders, and as she bent down to kiss the top of his head she saw the photographs lined up on the table in front of him. "Are these new pictures of Bliss?"

"Sam brought them." His voice was flat.

"Sam was here?"

He nodded.

"I'm sorry I missed him."

Ben stared at the pictures in front of him and she felt the stiffness in his shoulders beneath her palms.

"She reminds me of you," she said. She was stunned again by the delicacy of this child. She looked as though a breeze might blow her away. "A blond version of you."

Ben suddenly jerked up his arms to throw off her hands. He stood up. "Sam thinks Jeff might have done it." He looked at her briefly, then looked away.

"But I didn't think he even knew—"

He waved his arms in the air. "Who the hell knows who knew whom when? What does it matter? I'm in prison here while my daughter's living with some creep who might have . . ." He shook his head. "I can't talk about this right now."

She sat down on the edge of one of the wooden chairs. "Ben . . ."

"Do you realize how pointless my life is?" he asked. "People either despise me or they feel sorry for me. What's my next job going to be? It'll be charity, whatever it is. Maybe I'll make just enough money to keep food in my stomach. That's a great life, isn't it? And the one thing I care about—my daughter—might still be in danger, and I'm as helpless to do anything about it as if I were dead."

"You're forgetting about people like me and Kyle and Lou and Sam. We're sticking by you because we care about you, not because we feel sorry for you."

He picked up a newspaper from the table and thrust it in front of her. "How about this? Great, huh? They don't know who I am now, but it's only a matter of time, isn't it?"

She looked at the picture of her and Ben on the cover and her stomach lurched.

"So how long are you going to stick by me now?"

She barely heard his question. "What does the article say?"

"Nothing." He paced halfway around the table and back again. "They don't know a damn thing. They just had the picture that guy took in the Village and had to do something with it. Had to wreck a life or two."

"It's not a big deal, Ben," she said, although the picture terrified her. "They publish stuff like this all the time. It'll blow over."

He stopped in front of her, dug his hands into his pants pockets. "Look, Eden, I need to be alone right now," he said. "I'm sorry. There's just too much on my mind."

"Ben." She set her hand on his arm. "Let me help."

He shook his head, led her to the door. "Give me some time alone, all right?"

She spotted the package to Kim Parrish on his bed. She'd thought he'd mailed it long ago. "Do you want me to take that to the post office?"

"It's already been. They sent it back. Didn't even open it. Maybe Cassie would like the furniture for her house."

"I'm sorry."

"Go."

She drove down the twisted road toward Lynch Hollow, her hands locked on the steering wheel. That tabloid. Had Wayne seen it? What price would she have to pay for that weekend in New York? What price would she have to pay for this relationship?

Ben was shutting her out. Worse, he seemed volatile and agitated. His life was pointless, he'd said. He was as good as dead. She pictured the bottle of Valium on the edge of his sink and stopped the car. She waited for a van to pass her before making a K-turn on the narrow road. Then she pressed the gas pedal to the floor. Please, Ben, don't. Her heart raced as she pulled up in front of the cabin. The front door was still open, but the cabin was empty. Then she saw the crack of light under the closed bathroom door.

She knocked on the door. "Ben?"

There was a second of silence. "I thought you'd left."

"What are you doing?"

"I'm getting ready to take a shower."

"Let me in please."

"Eden, I told you, I really want some time alone."

She turned the knob, pushed the door in. He stood in front of her in white boxer shorts, his hands on his hips and a scowl on his face. "What the hell are you doing?"

She looked at the sink. The bottle of Valium was still on the ledge. She could see the shadow of the pills inside. "I was afraid you'd try to hurt yourself."

He looked at the pills, so abruptly that she knew if he had not planned to use them at that moment, he had at some other time. He lost his scowl, and when he spoke his voice was soft. "I'm not going to hurt myself."

She drew in a breath and realized she was winded. "I'm sorry. I thought . . ."

He reached out his arms and pulled her against him. "Eden," he said.

"It scared me."

"I'm okay. I just had a rough afternoon." He let go of her. "Did you happen to notice that Bliss isn't smiling in any of those pictures? Does she look like a happy kid to you? I just wish I could see her for myself. I wish I could be a fly on the wall in her nursery school. I want to watch her with other kids, see her laugh a little. She looks so serious."

Eden had a sudden idea. "I could see her."

"What do you mean?"

"I visit schools sometimes. Usually kindergarten or first grade, but a nursery school would do. I read to the kids from my mother's books. It's publicity stuff and I haven't done it in a while. But I can fake it. I could see how she's doing and report back to you."

"I couldn't ask you to."

She walked back into the main room of the cabin and he followed. "Give me the name of her school," she said.

"Green Gables. In Annapolis."

She sat down on his bed and took the phone in her lap. She got through to Nina easily, as she'd expected. Nina was more than anxious to talk to her. She'd been calling her for a week now and Eden had returned none of her calls.

"What is it with you, Eden?" Nina asked. "Who is this guy you're with? Michael's moping around. He's not eating. Looks like a scarecrow. I'm afraid he's going to start using again, and—"

"Nina, shush for a second."

"Have you read the scripts?"

"No."

"Have you forgotten you have a career?"

"Look, Nina, I need you to set up a school visit for me."

"What? Now is not the time, Eden. We have to get you working again before—"

"Nina. Please. It's the Green Gables nursery school in Annapolis, Maryland." She looked up at Ben. "Teacher?"

"I think she has Joan Dove again this year."

She passed the name on to Nina, who was grumbling but writing down the information all the same.

"Bless you, Nina. Now listen and I'll tell you what's going on with me. I'm happy. I'm in love. I haven't forgotten you. I'm madly working on the screenplay. I'll call Michael to see how he's doing, but if he starts using again that's his decision. I'll tell him he won't have a role in *A Solitary Life*, though, if he does."

She got off the phone and looked at Ben, who was leaning against the table in his sparkling white boxer shorts.

"I'm going to see Bliss," she told him. "No doubt about it."

33

Eden knew Bliss the moment she stepped into the classroom at Green Gables, and now as she read *Child of Fountains* aloud, the other children were no more than a blur to her. This would have been true whether Bliss were Ben's daughter or not. Bliss stood out. She was taller than the others by a few inches and her thick, straight platinum hair was extraordinary. Eden sat in a low-to-the-ground beanbag chair with the children on the plush carpeted floor around her and their teacher, Joan Dove, in a chair nearby. Bliss sat immediately to Eden's left, as though she knew she should get as close to this stranger as she possibly could, and Eden could feel her fragility like something tangible in the air. She looked up from her book from time to time to see those enormous gray eyes watching her, alert and attentive. At one point during the story, Bliss asked a question—a serious, worried-sounding question about the welfare of the young heroine—and Eden reached down to touch her as she answered. She felt nothing but bone beneath her fingers. A knobby spine, ribs that could cut paper. The child was all bone and beauty.

She had selected *Child of Fountains* because it was the simplest of her mother's stories. She had often marveled at how Katherine Swift's books grasped the attention of even small children and held it fast. The stories were marked by wholesome adventure and a subtly delivered moral message, qualities that Eden viewed with some skepticism now that she was coming to know the real Katherine Swift. She had viewed her mother as something of a nonperson all these years. She'd thought Katherine's cloistered existence was the result of her having few needs as an adult or as a woman. But the truth was far more complicated, and it was up to Eden to interpret her mother's life on the screen in a way that would not lose her the sympathy and admiration of the people who put their trust in her—those parents who picked up a Katherine Swift book for their children with the certainty that it would be entertainment in the purest sense.

When she closed the book the children rushed her. She was accustomed to this, and she knew that these kids thought of her primarily as the beautiful witch from the film version of *Child of the North Star*.

"How did you turn from that ugly girl into the pretty one?" one child asked. "Are you a witch in real life?" asked another. "Where is your big furry cape?" She answered them all, and then the more personal questions began, as they always did.

"Do you have any little boys?" asked a freckle-faced boy.

"No, but I do have a little girl."

"What's her name?"

"Cassie."

"You should of brung her."

"Well, she's visiting her daddy right now."

"I visited my daddy in Charleston on Friday," said the freckle-faced boy.

"My daddy has come back to live with us," said a little girl.

And then Bliss spoke up. Although she'd been standing very close to Eden, she had been quiet since asking her question during the story. "My daddy is gone away," she said softly. "But he visits me at nighttime sometimes."

"Does he?" Eden asked her.

Joan Dove set her hands on Bliss's shoulders. "Her daddy's very far away, so sometimes she dreams he's visiting and it makes her feel happy—right, Bliss?"

"Mmm," Bliss said noncommittally, her eyes on Eden all the

while. Eden wondered if there was something in her own face that led Bliss to trust her, to lean forward and whisper, "He really does come sometimes." Her words sent a shiver up Eden's spine

She wanted to watch them play, wanted to be able to report back to Ben that she'd seen Bliss have fun. So she stayed for their recess, a disorganized free-for-all on the grassy Green Gables playground. She sat with Joan Dove on the steps.

"How did you happen to pick Green Gables?" Joan asked.

Eden shrugged and smiled. "My agent handles that end of things and I just show up."

"I'm so glad you did. The kids loved it."

Bliss was playing on a swing set. She climbed up on the support bar, hung by her knees, sat upright, jumped off, and sat down on one of the swings, all without saying a word to the other two girls who shared the swing set with her.

"The tall girl," Eden said to Joan. "She's striking."

"Yes. But she has a lot of problems."

"Really?"

"That stuff about her dad visiting her." Joan shook her head. "Her father abused her. Molested her. She's been through more hurt and trauma than anyone should have to go through in a lifetime."

Eden frowned. "That's horrible. How is she doing now?"

Joan sighed. "All right, I guess. She still talks about her father a lot. Her real daddy, she calls him. She has a stepfather now, who seems pretty nice, but I don't think she's really bonded to him yet. She's not allowed to see her real father, but she can't seem to get him out of her head. He was one of those guys who could really charm you—you know the type."

"Hollywood's full of them," Eden said, and then grimaced at herself in disgust.

"Even I thought he was the nicest guy before all this happened," Joan continued.

"You never can tell," Eden said.

"No, you sure can't. So Bliss, that little girl, lost a lot of weight she's never put back on. She's in counseling, but she's still not sleeping well and you can just tell she's got a heavy load she's lugging around with her. Even here at school she wakes up in the middle of her nap with a nightmare sometimes."

"Poor thing," Eden said. Joan began talking about some of the other children and Eden half listened, trying to make appropriate comments. But her eyes were on Bliss, who was now in competition with the girl next to her on the swings. She was trying to go higher, pumping her long, thin legs hard, her head thrown back and her mouth wide open. Was she laughing? From a distance her expression could have been either fear or joy, but Eden looked away before she knew for sure. She would tell Ben she'd seen his daughter laugh.

When she left Green Gables she followed the map Ben had drawn for her to Sam and Jen's. She'd told him she wanted to meet them, and now after listening to Joan Dove's description of Ben she was particularly desperate to be among his friends rather than his enemies.

Jen Alexander answered the door of the stately red brick colonial. She was a pretty woman who reminded Eden a little of Nina, with her shimmery dark hair and pixie face. She held out her hand with a smile. "Eden, I'm Jen. Please come in."

Eden stepped into a large foyer. The floor was green marble tile, and a huge crystal chandelier hung above their heads. She thought of Ben's cabin. No wonder he hadn't visited them since his move to the Shenandoah Valley.

"Sam will be home for lunch any minute." Jen led Eden toward the back of the house. "We've been looking forward so much to meeting you."

Eden sat on the sofa in the family room, which was an extension of the enormous kitchen. The shine from the hanging copper pans was nearly blinding. "I've wanted to meet you and Sam, too," she said. "Ben's so grateful for your faith in him."

"Well, I have to say, even I had a few moments of doubt in the beginning, but the bottom line is, that's just not Ben."

Eden moved to the table when Sam arrived. He wore a pale gray suit, and he took the jacket off and hung it up before shaking her hand. As he sat down he took off his glasses and put them in a case on the table. He was one of the best-looking men she'd ever seen, inside or out of Hollywood, but she would never have guessed he was Ben's brother. She struggled to find a resemblance. Sam was green-eyed, blond, and mustached, and he was impeccably groomed, every hair in place—no doubt kept there with spray. The man had found himself one hell of a barber. She wondered if this had always been the difference between the brothers, if Ben had always been the more casual of the two, the less vain, the brother who had elected to spend his life with his hands in the earth. She could not picture Sam on his knees in one of the pits.

"Did you get to see Bliss?" he asked as he took his seat at the table. Jen set their plates in front of them. She had made chicken salad with grapes and cold Oriental noodles, all beautifully arranged on the black square china.

"Yes. She's adorable." It was difficult for her to hold Sam's gaze for long because she was certain he was thinking, I am hot and you and I both know it. She wondered how his female patients managed to sit across from him week after week without drooling.

"She seems happy enough, don't you think?" he asked.

"Well, I didn't get to see her that long. She seems like a very serious child."

"There's nothing wrong with that." Sam smiled. "I was one myself."

Eden chewed on a grape. Perhaps she had to be careful what she said here. After all, she was a stranger to Sam and Jen, walking into their house, telling them she thought their niece was imperfect.

"She said something I thought was strange." Eden told them about Bliss saying her daddy still visited her sometimes.

Jen shuddered. "That's weird."

Sam frowned. "I keep in touch with her counselor and she's never told me that Bliss has said anything like that."

"Maybe someone should tell the counselor?" Eden asked.

Sam shrugged. "I'll mention it to her, but I think Joan Dove is probably right for the first time in her life. I think Bliss is dreaming—or maybe just fantasizing—that Ben's visiting. It's her way of coping with the loss. I think she's actually in good shape for all she's been through." He was obviously closing the subject.

They talked for a while about Ben, how they missed him, all the things they used to do together, and she became less and less comfortable with Sam. He was nice enough, but there was the subtlest bit of acid in his voice when he spoke to her, and finally she understood. He didn't trust her. When lunch was over and they leaned back in their chairs he looked her hard in the eye.

"Eden, I'd like to speak frankly to you," he said. "I can tell you care about Ben. I can tell you're sincere, and I'm glad of that because I was worried you might be using him somehow."

"How would I be using him?"

"Well, you're an actress, used to the excitement of Hollywood, and you're stuck in a rural area for the summer." Sam shrugged. "Ben's someone to do things with, someone to help you pass the time away."

"I'm not using him. I'm in love with him."

Sam smiled. "Yes, I can see you are. But I'm still concerned about what happens down the road. Ben says you worry about your image." He said the word "image" as though it tasted sour in his mouth. "At some point, Eden, the shit is going to hit the fan. What will you do then?"

She wanted to tell him it was none of his business, but thought better of it. "I don't see any point in worrying about what might happen in the future," she said.

Sam leaned toward her. "I'm not trying to put you on the spot. I'm just afraid Ben is going to get hurt. You're a nice person and I wish you all the best, but he's my first priority. What are you going to do when the media finds out that you're seeing a man who served time for molesting his daughter?"

"Sam." Jen put her hand on Sam's arm and looked apologetically at Eden.

"I'm hoping that never happens," Eden said. "If it does, I'll deal with it at the time. I love Ben. I'm happier with him than I've been in a long time and I'm not about to give that up without a fight."

Sam sighed and leaned back in his chair. "He's my little brother, you know?" He smiled again and she suddenly saw Ben in his smile.

"He always will be. All our lives I've tried to protect him, but this time I'm up against the wall. I haven't been able to do a damn thing for him. I apologize. I've overstepped my bounds. Ben would shoot me if he knew I was badgering you." He stood up and put his suit jacket back on. Then he turned to her once again. "Please don't hurt him, Eden," he said quietly, and she felt sorry for Sam, for the impotence she saw in his eyes. "He's taken just about all he can take."

She had intended to go straight to Ben's cabin after the three-hour drive from Annapolis, but she found herself turning down the road to Lynch Hollow instead. She needed to talk to Kyle and Lou first.

It was nearly six and she found them in the living room. Lou sat at her easel; Kyle was drinking coffee on the sofa, a fat book open on his lap.

"I need your advice," she said to them.

Lou set her paintbrush down and Kyle snapped his book shut. Eden smiled at the immediateness of their reaction. This was probably the first time in her life she'd asked them for advice.

She told them about seeing Bliss at Green Gables, about the little girl's worrisome thinness, the sober, adultlike expression on her face, the reported nightmares, the fantasy of her father's nocturnal visits.

"I don't know what to tell Ben," she said. "My idea in going to see Bliss was to be able to report back to him that she seems like a normal, happy kid. But she doesn't. Even if I hadn't known her, if I hadn't been looking for a problem, she would have stood out as being different from the others, disturbed in some way."

Lou shook her head. "That makes me very sad," she said. "I remember her as a happy, lively little girl. She always had a smile on her face."

"What should I tell him? Driving here, I was thinking I'll have to lie to him. What's the point in telling him the truth when there's nothing he can do about it?"

"If you were in his shoes," Kyle asked, "and a friend of yours had seen Cassie and discovered what you've discovered, would you want them to protect you from what they'd learned?"

Eden smiled. It was very clear. "No. But it's going to upset him because there's nothing he can do to help her."

"But he can tell his brother what you've observed, and maybe Sam can see that she gets more help than she's getting."

Eden groaned. "That man can't admit there's anything wrong." She told them about her visit with Sam and Jen.

"Well, he's in a bad spot too," Kyle said. "He's trying to help Ben, and trying to look out for Bliss, and he must have to watch his step around Sharon and her new husband. You probably just look like a major complication to him."

"I used to worry about Ben getting any more bad news," Lou said. "But I don't now, because you're here. You're a comfort to him, Eden. He'll be okay."

Ben met her at his door. "God, you're late," he said. "How did it go?"

She sat him down on the sofa and held his hand while she told him moment by moment and word for word about her morning at Green Gables. She presented it as fact, didn't color any of it with her own interpretation, because maybe she was wrong. Maybe he would see nothing worrisome in the way Bliss's ribs felt like carving knives beneath her fingers, and maybe Bliss had always awakened from her naps on the edge of a nightmare and that was nothing new, a symptom of absolutely nothing. He listened without comment, without change of expression, and when she was through he began to cry. She held him. "It's all right, Ben," she said, stroking his back, kissing his hair. "It's all right."

Sometime in the middle of the night he woke her up. His body was hot and damp next to her, and he had kicked the sheet off. It lay tangled over her legs and hips.

"You didn't tell me how it went at Sam and Jen's," he said. His voice was so clear that she knew he had not slept.

She put her arm across him, her head on his chest. She heard his heart beating and felt the softness of the hair on his chest beneath her cheek. "It was fine," she said. "I really liked Jen. And Sam thinks Bliss is doing well. So maybe this is an improvement over where she was."

"No," Ben said. "What you described is not a goddamned improvement. Did you tell Sam what you saw?"

"I think Sam thinks I caught Bliss on a bad day."

"Yeah, and he said those pictures of her at Saint Michaels were taken on a bad day too. I'll have to talk to him and—"

"Ben." She raised herself up on an elbow to look at him. "Please don't say anything to Sam that will make him think I'm interfering or being pushy or . . . Maybe you'd better not mention me to him at all."

"What are you saying?"

"He's worried I'll hurt you."

She could see his smile in the thin moonlight that filtered through his window. He reached up to touch her hair. "I'll tell him you're the only thing in my life that doesn't hurt at all."

She drove back to Lynch Hollow early the next morning. She had poured herself a cup of coffee from the pot in the kitchen and was about to take it upstairs with her when she heard Kyle's voice from his bedroom.

"I just read the notebook over and I don't see how I can possibly give it to her," he said.

Eden froze at the bottom of the stairs. She wondered if she should call out, let them know she was home. But before she could decide Kyle spoke again.

"Maybe I should just tell her about it instead of letting her read it."

There was no response from Lou, and for a moment Eden wondered if Kyle was talking on the phone. Or to himself. But then Lou spoke.

"You've brought her along this far with the journal, Ky," she said. "And you know it was what Kate wanted."

Eden was afraid to listen any longer. She walked quietly up the stairs to her room and sat down in front of the word processor. She hated hearing that worry in Kyle's voice. She hated that she was causing him any concern at all. She thought of telling him she'd overheard his conversation with Lou, that if he wanted to just tell her about the next notebook that was fine with her. He had shared so much of himself with her; she could ask no more of him. But she couldn't tell him she'd listened in. She would have to let him make his own decision on this.

She worked the entire day on the screenplay, except for a quick break for lunch and a long, satisfying phone call to Cassie. When she went downstairs for dinner she spotted the next notebook, black with age, on the counter and knew Kyle had made his decision. "Is that for me?" she asked as she took her seat.

"What are your plans tonight?" Kyle asked.

"Ben needs a good night's sleep after last night, so I'm going to stay home. Get a little more work done." She nodded in the direction of the notebook. "I could read that tonight if that's okay with you."

"Why don't the three of us go out?" Lou suggested.

"That's a good idea," said Kyle. "What movie's playing in town?"

"Well, I think I'll just—"

"Come with us, dear," Lou said. It was more of a command than an invitation.

So she rode into Coolbrook to watch a rerun of *Vertigo* at the renovated movie theater. The movie was so old it was lined and crackly on the screen—one of those movies that reminded her of the days when she longed to be an actress, when she thought that nothing else in life could ever satisfy her.

She sat next to Kyle in the theater. He'd put on a beige cardigan for the air-conditioning, and he smelled of Old Spice. She felt his presence like an old quilt, a comforter.

After the movie Kyle insisted they go to The Scoop Shoppe for ice cream sundaes, and after that Lou suggested they "stroll and roll" down Coolbrook's deserted Main Street. Anyone watching them would think they wanted to avoid going back to Lynch Hollow at all costs. So it was nearly eleven-thirty when they got home. Ben had left a message for her on Kyle's answering machine. Eden sat on the living room sofa, listening to him tell her that he felt better today and that he loved her.

She clicked off the machine just as Kyle walked into the room with the notebook. She stood to take it from him, and he wrapped his arms around her for a hug that lasted a long, long time.

34

August 2, 1954

Today is my 27th birthday. Daddy, Susanna, Kyle and I ate angel food cake with raspberries after dinner, and then Kyle said he wanted to take me for a drive. He said he needed to talk to me and I knew right away what he had to say. Dr. Latterly's at N.Y.U. now, and he has been after Kyle about going back to school. He wants him to go into a doctoral program in New York, and then later join him on an expedition to South America. Dr. Latterly thinks Kyle has enormous potential (so do I) and he wants to see him use it some place other than Lynch Hollow. Up 'til now, Kyle and I have just discussed the facts of the offer, the where, when and how. But we both know that if he accepts this route, he will be leaving Lynch Hollow for good.

So tonight we drove out to Coolbrook Park. We got out of the car because it was so hot and sat on the bank of the river. Kyle told me how badly he wants to go back to school. He apologized for feeling that way and I told him there was no need to apologize, that I thought he would be foolish to turn down this offer and I don't plan to give him anything other than encouragement. But as I said all this to him, like it wouldn't make a bit of difference to me if he was in Lynch Hollow or New York City, a numbness filled my heart.

"I'll miss it here," Kyle said. "This is the best place in the world, as far as I'm concerned, but I can't limit myself this way."

I started for the car. "Let's go tell Matt you've decided," I said, wanting to get away from Kyle. I won't cry about this in front of him. I am 27 years old! I've published 17 books, for pity's sake. I can stand on my own two feet.

September 5, 1954

Kyle is gone. Matt picked him up just an hour ago to drive him to the train. I couldn't go with them and I know Kyle didn't want me to. He didn't even touch me before he left, though he hugged Susanna and patted Daddy's shoulder. Then he said, "Bye, Kate," and got in the car. I couldn't get to the cave quickly enough to let out my tears.

Oh, Kyle.

Last night he came to the cavern while I was sorting papers on my mattress, nearly done for the night. He carefully piled up my papers, moved them to the table and sat down next to me on the mattress. He looked troubled and I asked him what was wrong.

"I hate leaving you," he said.

"I'll be fine."

"Maybe," he said. "But I'm not so sure that I'll be fine without you."

That surprised me. "You've never needed me," I said.

He shook his head. "You're so wrong, Kate." He leaned back on his hands and looked up at the ceiling of the great room high above us. "God, I wish things were different," he said.

"What things?" I asked. He was confusing me, though I think I understand now what he meant.

"A lot of things," he said. Then he looked at me. "There's so much about you I admire, but I worry about what you're missing in life."

"You mean a man," I said.

"Well, yes, partly. I mean closeness to other people. You keep yourself so isolated."

"There's Matt," I said.

"Yes," he said. "There's Matt. And you've overlooked him for so long, as though you think someone better will come along." He took my hand and held it on his knee. "I know Matt's not your idea of the perfect man for you, but nobody else is going to suddenly appear one day at the entrance to your cave."

"I'm not looking for anyone."

"But you want children, Kate. I know you do. Marry Matt. Even if he's not perfect for you, he can give you children."

I was startled by how desperate he sounded, but I laughed and told him I couldn't marry Matt because he would expect me to raise his children in a house, not a cave. I was trying to joke because Kyle was so horribly serious, but he didn't even smile. Instead, he started to cry, sending a terrible shiver through my body. I hugged him and he said, "Kate, I worry so much about you. I worry you'll end up like Mama."

I pulled away from him quickly. "Don't say that!" I said. "Don't ever say that."

His cheeks were wet and I tried to dry his tears with my fingertips, then with my lips. I was not thinking. I swear it was only instinct that made me try to kiss away the sadness in his face. I kissed his cheeks, his eyes, all the while aware of a powerful longing growing in my body while he sat perfectly still, barely breathing. His eyes were wide open, watching me. I knelt in front of him and pulled his head to my breasts as I kissed his hair and his forehead, and I could feel heat coming from him, pouring from him. I knew what he wanted even if he didn't know it himself.

He grabbed my hands. "Don't," he said, leaning away from me, but I bent my head low and kissed his neck, his jaw, his ear. "Kate!" he said. "Stop it."

I tried to stop then, to push myself away from him, but I just couldn't. Even so, I swear it was Kyle who set his mouth on mine first, whose tongue first played with mine. He pressed me back against the mattress, stealing my breath with his kisses. He kissed me furiously, like he was angry with me, but then his lips grew soft and tender against my mouth. After a while he sat back on his knees and I was afraid that he would stand up and walk out on me, but I could see by the look on his face that he had come to a decision, that he was determined to finish what he'd started, and I relaxed.

He began undressing me, very, very slowly, undoing the buttons of my shirt as though they might break if he hurried. He pulled my dungarees and drawers from my legs and then I sat up to take off my brassiere. My hair had fallen over my chest and he lifted it slowly while he lowered his head to my breast. He circled my nipple with his tongue before drawing it into his mouth. I think I said his name then, crying it out, but I'm not sure, because I lost every scrap of reasoning right then. Truly, to that point I felt as though I was in charge of what was happening, but suddenly everything changed and I was in his hands completely.

He laid me back on the mattress again. He was not shy about looking at me and I loved watching his face in the flickery yellow lantern light as his eyes moved over my body.

"You are the most beautiful woman I've ever seen, Kate." His voice was thick and his face so full of love and need that I started to weep. I knew right then that he was the only man I've ever wanted, that the only reason I'd been interested in Seth Gallagher was because he reminded me of Kyle. I was breathing deep and hard, and I gave a silent prayer of thanks that I'd never done this with Seth or Matt or anyone else, that I was a virgin, 27 years old, and that Kyle would be my first lover.

He let me undress him then, his hands touching me softly all the while. He had to help me with the buttons and the zipper because I was shaking so hard. I'd never seen a full-grown man in the flesh before, never seen a man's penis, and I was almost afraid to see Kyle's, but I needn't have been. It was as tempting as the rest of him. It felt like steel against my palm, satin beneath my lips.

He was a gentle lover, though I had guessed as much. I thought of the anatomy lesson I'd given him long ago, when we were teenagers. He has learned so much since then and I have learned next to nothing. He kissed the place I'd told him to touch so long ago and I loved that he would do that, bury himself that way in my most secret parts. His tongue was gentle but hot as flame, and the cavern echoed with my cries. He asked me if it hurt when he came into me. It didn't, but I wouldn't have cared if it did. I just wanted to hold him against me, inside me. I wanted to keep him there forever.

I will not marry Matt. I'll never let a man other than Kyle in this place he warmed. Never.

Kyle fell asleep quickly. I had a blanket in the chest and as I laid it over him I saw the long dark scars across his buttocks and the back of his thighs from the whippings. He will carry those scars forever, and I felt something I thought I'd stopped feeling a long time ago: a hatred for Mama. I covered

Kyle quickly and lay down next to him to hold him in my arms. "I am not like Mama, Kyle," I whispered. "I will never be like Mama."

I lay awake for much of the night, imagining going with him today. I thought I would be able to leave Lynch Hollow as long as I was with him. When we met people who didn't know us, we could tell them we were husband and wife. Or we could actually get married. For the first time ever, I was glad we were only cousins. Marriage is legal between cousins in Virginia, although I understand that's not so everywhere. We could hold each other like this night after night. My heart felt so warm and full at that thought. As Kyle slept, I assumed he could not imagine being apart from me any more than I could imagine being apart from him.

I planned to wake him early this morning and tell him I would go with him. I must have dozed off, and when I woke up it was still dark outside and he was already up and pulling his clothes on.

"Don't go yet," I said.

"Kate, I'm sorry. That was insane. It was a terrible thing to do." He began buttoning his shirt. He was cold. In the light from the lantern I could see that he was shaking all over.

I sat up. "I want to go with you," I said. "I've got to be with you."

"No, you don't. What you do have to do is put this out of your mind. And cover yourself up."

I had let the blanket slip to my waist, on purpose, I suppose. I wanted to see that look come into his face again, that look of love and longing, but I guess now I'll never see it again. I pulled the blanket around my shoulders. "We can get married," I said. "It's legal for cousins in Virginia."

He bent down to tie his shoe. "You've never called me your cousin in your life," he said.

I stood up then, holding the blanket to me. I tried to reach for him, but he brushed me aside.

"This never happened, Kate, do you understand?" And then he left, disappearing into the blackness outside my cave.

I am so angry with him, not for last night, but for this morning. I cannot believe his coldness to me as he left, the way he wouldn't look at me. I will never again be able to touch myself without imagining my hands are his. I will never again be able to lie on my mattress in the cave without hearing him whisper, "I love you, Kate," like he did when he was inside *me. I'll never be able to get his words from my head: "You'll end up like Mama."*

Eden turned the notebook facedown on her knees. Outside her bedroom window the air was black and still. She could hear no sound other than the dull thumping of her heartbeat. She remembered Kyle's words: "Your father was Kate's first and only lover." She raised her hands and counted on her fingers. October, November, December, January, February, March, April, May, June. Her hands trembled as she lifted the notebook and turned to the next page.

November 2, 1954

I am pregnant. There it is in writing. It was no shock to me when I missed my period. I knew within days of Kyle's departure that a new life had found its home in my body.

I have written eight letters to Kyle and received just three in return. His letters are cool, as though I am an acquaintance. He writes of the weather, his apartment, his classes. I read between the lines and see guilt, which I understand, and regret, which I loathe. He's learning so much, he says. He and Latterly are planning to go to South America in June. And he's met a woman who lives in the Greenwich Village area of New York. Her name is Louise and "She's an artist—very special and different from the rest." Does he know how those words hurt me? Would he still write them if he knew? For the first time in my life, I am unsure of Kyle's love. It's difficult for me to regret that night in the cavern but if it has cost me his love I will rue it 'til I die.

I am afraid to tell him about the baby because he will say I must get rid of it. He'll say it could be sickly or slow, like Ellie Miller, from us being so closely related. But I can just feel that this baby is all right. I think of little Ellie, who is seven years old now. She has a slow, shuffling walk, a constant smile because she is unable to learn that, for some, life bears more pain than joy. She has those little hands where her arms ought to be. The truth is, I would love this baby even if it came out with two heads and five feet. It would still be my baby. Mine and Kyle's.

I know I can't keep being pregnant from him, but I can't write about it in a letter. I will have to go to New York, although the thought overwhelms me. I can't go for a while yet, anyway. I've heard you're not supposed to travel by train in the first three months, and I'm not about to take any chances with my baby.

January 4, 1955

Maybe my mistake was not telling Kyle I was coming. He was unprepared to see me and that's why he acted as he did. Or am I fooling myself?

I got sick on the train. I always thought pregnant women got sick in the first few months. The early months of my pregnancy were glorious, but in the last week or so I've felt woozy much of the time.

New York was too much for me. I started feeling faint and having trouble breathing the moment I stepped out of the train station. I managed to get a cab and gave the driver Kyle's address. "That's in the Village," the driver said. "Your brother an artist or musician or something?"

I didn't understand what one thing had to do with the other. He started commenting on my accent and was being friendly, but I felt too sick to talk to him much.

The building was overheated and Kyle's apartment was up six flights of stairs. By the time I'd dragged myself and my suitcase up, I was sweating and out of breath and right close to retching again. I knocked on the door and a woman answered. She was tall with black hair and she was wearing a tight black sweater, black pants, and black boots. She held a cigarette in a carved ivory cigarette holder.

"I must have the wrong apartment," I said.

The woman smiled. "No, I think you've got the right one, judging by your accent. You must be a friend of Kyle's."

I knew immediately this was Louise. I was shocked. She looked far too old for Kyle. I had never seen anyone quite like her.

"I'm his sister."

"Kate?" The woman grinned and stepped back so I could walk into the room. "Come in. Kyle's just gone to the store. He's going to be so happy to see you."

Kyle's apartment is just one room with a little kitchen off to the side. In the main room, there's one of those couches that pulls out into a bed. It was open, made up with yellow sheets. I could see dents in both the pillows and I knew this skinny black-clad woman had slept there with my brother the night before.

Louise made me a cup of strong coffee and we sat in the tiny kitchen. I have to say she was very nice to me, talking about the train ride and all but I couldn't think of anything to say. I wanted to hate her. I looked at her skinny body in its black wrapping which left absolutely nothing to the imagination, and I could picture Kyle touching her as he had touched me, setting his mouth between her legs, and I went into the bathroom to get sick.

When I came out Kyle was in the kitchen talking to Louise. He hugged me quickly. "You should have told me you were coming," he scolded. There wasn't even the slightest smile on his face.

"I need to talk to you," I said. "Alone."

Louise hopped to her feet. "See you at my place later, Ky." She kissed Kyle on the cheek and after she left I saw the discomfort in Kyle's eyes at being alone with me. He poured us both more coffee.

"I can't believe you came up here," he said.

"That woman is wrong for you."

Kyle laughed. "You don't even know her."

"She's too old for you."

"She's only thirty-two."

"I think you're only with her to forget about me."

Kyle shook his head. "I'm with her because I love her."

I couldn't breathe. Didn't the night in my cavern mean anything to him? "Do you make love to her like you made love to me?" I asked.

Kyle looked worried that someone might hear me. He leaned towards me and practically whispered, "You have to forget that night ever happened, Kate. It was very wrong of me to give in to those feelings."

"Can you really forget how good it felt?"

Kyle stood up abruptly. "I don't let myself remember. I feel sick to my stomach when I do."

I knew I had to leave. I wasn't welcome here. Kyle had a new life and a new woman. The thought of me made him sick. I couldn't possibly tell him I was carrying his child.

I thought of New York waiting to swallow me up once I stepped outside his door. I'd have to find a cab, get back to the train station, stand in line. My heart pounded like it would burst just from thinking about it, but I forced myself to stand up.

"I shouldn't have come," I said, reaching for my suitcase.

Kyle looked confused about what to do. "Kate, you can stay. I mean, Lou has room at her place. I don't think you should stay here with me, though."

I left, closing the door on his insulting words. I walked slowly down the stairs, hoping he would come after me, but of course he didn't. He is through with me, through with Lynch Hollow, with his old life.

In a daze, I found a cab and rode back to the station. I wanted to die right then. The one person I could always count on no longer wanted to be a part of my life. I understood my real mama wanting to kill herself. I thought how easy it would be to jump in front of a train, how quickly it would be over. Then I thought of how strong my mama was to wait until after I was born to do herself in. I at least owed that much to my baby.

When my train arrived at the Winchester station, I called Matt and he came to pick me up. I was crying out of control by that time, so he drove me back to his house. He held me to comfort me and pried the story out of me. I told him Kyle and I had made love before he left for New York.

I have never seen Matt even close to anger, so I was shocked when he began storming around the living room, slamming his fist into the walls and kicking the furniture.

"How could he do that to you?"

I explained that I was as much to blame as Kyle, but Matt shook his head. "No, Kyle knows better. You don't have a normal sense of right and wrong."

I suppose I should have been insulted, but I couldn't argue with him. I could see nothing wrong with what Kyle and I had done, even though it's obvious to me now it was a mistake.

Finally Matt sat down on the sofa. His face was still red from his fit of temper. "I'll never forgive him for this," he said. "Never."

"I'm pregnant," I blurted out. It felt wonderful to say those words out loud for once.

Matt was quiet for a full minute. Then he laughed. "Looks like you have no choice but to marry me, Kate."

Well, I told him I wasn't about to marry him, but that he is the finest, sweetest man alive for asking. He said he'll help me any way he can. He offered to go to New York and "talk some sense" into Kyle, but I made him promise not to tell Kyle a thing. I don't want Kyle to be kind to me out of guilt or a sense of responsibility. I just want him to love me like he used to, before New York, and before Louise, and before September 5th, 1954.

January 20, 1955

I got a letter from Kyle today. He apologized for his "confusion" when I visited. He was "surprised" to see me and "not sure what to make of it." "Next time, write first." He hopes I got home all right, he hopes I am happy. He signed it, "Please write soon. Love, Kyle." I stared at the word "love" and tried to see in his handwriting if it is a mere word or something more.

I don't intend to write him. All he wants to hear about is the weather or Daddy's new car or Susanna's bout with bronchitis. He doesn't want to hear that I'm hurt and aching inside. I won't write to him ever again.

35

Eden didn't sleep. She barely shut her eyes the entire night. Sometime around three or four she got up and studied herself in the mirror. She couldn't shake the feeling that she was no longer physically normal, that she was a genetic anomaly, and surely if she stared long enough she would see it in the shape of her face, the lines of her palms. Her features were Kyle's. The blue eyes, the straight nose, the perfect teeth. Features she had always attributed to her mother.

Neither could she shake her sense of disgust. It consumed her, and no amount of logic freed her from its grasp. Her parents were good people, she told herself. Good people who for one moment lost control. But in her gut she was sickened by what she now knew about Kyle, about her mother, about herself.

Kyle had betrayed her all these years. Through cowardice, or trying to spare her feelings, or whatever. His motives didn't matter. She was furious when she thought of him withholding the truth from her. If she had not decided to research her mother's life would he ever have told her? Obviously, Lou knew as well. Both of them were watching her day by day, choreographing her discovery not only of her mother but of herself, and working hard to win her love in the process. Kyle had manipulated this whole charade very well.

She would go to Ben's for a few days to give herself time to think.

She'd have to leave Lynch Hollow before sunrise so there would be no chance of seeing either Lou or Kyle. Right now she couldn't face them.

At quarter to five she showered and dressed. She packed a few changes of clothing in her smaller suitcase, and started to close up the word processor to take with her but stopped herself. What was the point? She couldn't possibly put what she now knew about her mother into the screenplay.

She slipped the notebook into her purse and walked quietly down the stairs. The smell of coffee was strong, and she knew that she was already too late to escape. Lou was in the kitchen, sitting in her wheelchair at the table, reading yesterday's newspaper. She wore a pink robe and her hair looked as though it had been hurriedly gathered into place at the back of her neck. She looked up when Eden stepped into the room.

"You read the journal," she said.

Eden didn't answer her. She reached for her car keys hanging on the rack by the door.

"Where are you going?" Lou asked.

"I'm going to Ben's for a few days."

"Have a cup of coffee with me before you take off."

"No."

"Running away might have worked when you were nineteen, Eden, but it's not going to work now. Kyle wants to talk to you. He needs to talk to you."

Eden opened the door but turned to face Lou. "He's had my entire life to talk to me about this. And you did too." She closed the door behind her and walked across the dark yard to her car.

She knocked several times before Ben switched on the porch light and opened his cabin door. He'd pulled the sheet around his waist and he was sleepy-eyed. He looked at his watch.

"It's five-thirty in the morning," he said.

"Go back to bed," she said. "Just let me get in with you."

She fell asleep quickly. When she woke up, the smell of coffee greeted her for the second time that morning. He must have gotten up to make it, but he was still in bed with her, behind her and inside her. His arm was wrapped tightly below her breasts, his lips on her neck. He was moving slowly, gently. Cobwebby thoughts sifted through her mind. His daughter had awakened to find Daddy behind her, rubbing against her. She swept the image from her mind and began moving with him. He came quickly, and she wondered how long he'd been inside her while she slept. They lay still for a moment. She felt her pulse beating in her temple, her throat, low in her belly. Ben pulled out of her and leaned over her, spreading her legs with his hands. His unshaven cheek scratched softly against the inside of her thigh as he lowered his mouth to her. She thought of her mother and Kyle and tugged at his shoulder.

"I can't, Ben."

He lifted the sheet over her although she was drenched with perspiration and lay down again, his head next to hers on the pillow. "What is it?" he asked.

She got out of bed and handed him the notebook. Then she dressed and poured herself a cup of coffee and went outside. She sat on the wooden bench on the front porch, waiting.

Ben took a long time, longer than it would take to read the notebook. She finished her coffee, set the mug on the splintery wooden floor of the porch.

He finally came outside. He handed her the notebook and bent down to kiss her forehead, holding his cheek to her temple for a few seconds before letting go. "Wow," he said quietly.

"I feel so betrayed. He's known all these years and never told me."

Ben sat down next to her. "It would be a hard thing to tell."

She looked at him. "Aren't you completely disgusted?"

"Shocked, yes. Disgusted, no. I feel sorry for Kyle."

"Sorry for him?"

"You were his only child. At least I'm assuming you were. I'm sure he would have liked to have had a normal father–daughter relationship with you, and that was impossible."

"My heart bleeds for him."

"Would you rather he'd never told you? Or do you wish he'd told you years ago?"

"I wish he'd had a little self-control in the first place."

"Well, then you wouldn't be here to wish anything at all."

"He should have told me when I was eighteen." She remembered herself at eighteen, already slipping away from Lou and Kyle. If Kyle had told her then, she would have fled even more quickly than she had. He must have known that.

"He should have told me when I got married. This could have affected Cassie genetically, couldn't it? What gave him the right to keep that information from me?"

Ben had a faraway look in his eyes, and she knew that this revelation had a different meaning for him than it did for her. "So," he said. "Kyle Swift's not perfect after all. He screws up just like the rest of us. I always wondered."

She looked down at her hands. "He left me," she said. "He left me with Susanna and my grandfather. He left me to be sent away to the orphanage." She began to cry, like a child who'd had too much all at once and needed a nap.

Ben took her hand. "Did you get any sleep last night?"

She shook her head.

"Why don't you go back to bed?"

The thought of sleep was seductive. Ben walked her into the cabin and watched her crawl into his bed. He leaned over to kiss her. "Stick with me," he said. "I know all the tricks for escaping your emotions."

She woke up off and on during the morning, and each time she opened her eyes, Ben would leave the dollhouse and come over to sit next to her. He didn't say much, just held her hand until she lost herself in sleep again.

At noon he made her a cup of tomato soup, although it was at least eighty degrees in the cabin, and a grilled cheese sandwich. She sat up to eat, propping the one long pillow against the wall.

"I'm going to call Nina and tell her to forget about the screenplay," she said. "I can't write it. You don't make a biographical film and leave out a fact like this, something that shaped her life. But I can't put it in either."

He sat on the edge of the bed, balancing his own sandwich on his thigh. "I don't think you should do anything impulsive."

"I can't write this, Ben."

"Don't call Nina yet. Wait a few days so you can talk to her with a clear head." The phone rang as he spoke and he leaned toward the apple crate to answer it. "She's right here." He held the receiver out to her. "It's Kyle."

She shook her head. Ben hesitated a moment, then lifted the receiver back to his ear. "She's not ready to talk to you yet, Kyle." Ben kept his eyes on her as he listened. "I just don't know," he said into the phone. "Yes, all right. I will." He hung up the phone and set it back on the crate. "He really wants to talk with you."

She handed him her empty mug and lowered herself beneath the sheet. "And I just want to sleep."

Ben dragged her to the Dairy Queen for dinner that night. They sat at a sticky table, surrounded on all sides by Coolbrook's teenagers. Eden had been sullen and surly for much of the day, and now as she listened to the adolescent flirting and posturing from the other tables her irritation mounted.

When Ben had finished eating and she still hadn't touched the crab cake sandwich on her Styrofoam plate, he said, "I want to tell you something. Please don't take this the wrong way. I'm not saying you shouldn't feel hurt or betrayed or angry. But I want you to recognize that you've lost nothing here. You still have Kyle and Lou. You can have as little or as much of them as you choose. You still have me, for whatever I'm worth. You've got your life and your career. And your daughter."

There were fine lines around his gray eyes, muscles in his jaw that tensed as he spoke. Her eyes filled as she thought of what he'd endured this last year, what he endured every day as he pictured his daughter hurting and unhappy, knowing he could do nothing to help her. "I'm sorry." She squeezed his hand. "I am so sorry."

It was dusk when they pulled into the clearing in front of Ben's cabin, and she groaned when she saw Kyle's Jeep parked at the edge of the woods, Kyle himself sitting on Ben's front porch.

"He's holding your next notebook," Ben said.

"I don't want to talk to him."

"Come on." Ben walked around the truck and opened the door for her.

Kyle stood as they neared the porch, and Ben steered Eden toward the bench. "You two have a seat out here," he said. "I'll be inside."

Eden sat at the end of the bench, as far as she could get from Kyle. "I don't have anything to say to you," she said.

Kyle took his seat again. "I'm sorry, Eden. I never wanted you to be hurt by this."

She looked at him and could almost see him recoil under her glare. "Were you ever going to tell me?"

Kyle sighed. "I don't know. Lou and I talked about it many times. I expected when we took you in that I would tell you . . . but it never seemed like the right time. And later . . . I kept putting it off. I always hoped that one day the moment would be right. Then when you called about the movie, needing to do the research and all, I knew this was it. I thought of keeping the journals from you, but I knew that wouldn't be fair. And that's not what your mother wanted."

Eden sat forward. "Did you ever stop to think that I should have had this information for the sake of my children? What if something had been wrong with Cassie? You let me take that kind of risk with your niece."

"My granddaughter."

"Don't call her that! She's nothing more than your grandniece as far as I'm concerned. Or your cousin twice removed or whatever the hell it would be."

Kyle looked down at his hands. "After you wrote that you got married, I went to see a genetic specialist in New York. I told him the whole story because I was worried about what it could mean for your children. He told me the probability of anything being wrong with your children was minuscule. He said the probability of anything being wrong with you had been minuscule as well. It's not much of a concern with first cousins."

"You should have told me."

"You're right and I'm sorry." He stood up. "I brought the next notebook for you."

"The thought of reading any more of it makes me sick. I've decided I'm not going to make this film. I've been trying to write honestly and sympathetically about her life. If I'm honest now, I'll incriminate all of us."

"Well, I'll just leave it here for you, in case." Kyle set the notebook on the bench, and for a moment Eden was held fast by his eyes, eyes that in their shape, their color, the hurt they contained, were identical to her own. "I've always been proud to be your father, Eden." He stepped off the porch, and she watched him walk to his Jeep. There was the slightest limp in his gait, and it took him more than a few moments to get settled in behind the wheel. He had to start the Jeep twice before it turned over. She watched him make a tight turn in the clearing and pull out onto the road. And she felt a pang of worry, a feeling quick and hot that made her gasp, as if someone had squeezed her heart in his fist. Kyle was upset, it was growing dark, he was not as alert, as sharp as he'd once been. She knew what it was like driving down that steep, winding road to Lynch Hollow, the way gravity sucked at your car. It would be so easy for him to miss one of those hairpin turns, so easy for the Jeep to fly over the edge.

She sat in the darkness, ignoring the mosquitoes, until thirty minutes had passed and she felt sure in her heart he had made it home safely.

36

Eden took over the mornings in his cabin and that was fine with Ben. He'd wake to the sound of her in his kitchen, cutting fresh fruit, making coffee or, on one aromatic occasion, cinnamon rolls that came out doughy but delicious from his antiquated oven. He would set the pillow behind his back so he could sit up and watch her work. She'd be in her underwear, or sometimes in his. Her hair would be down, slipping over her shoulders and catching the sunlight from the little kitchen window, and on a couple of mornings, when the light hit her just right, he could see the blue of her eyes.

They made love every night, a feat he'd no longer thought himself capable of. The first night or two it had been a tender, needy lovemaking that ended with Eden in tears. They grew more playful as the days passed. She bought a chocolate-colored teddy to tease him with and read him provocative passages from some of her favorite books, and he thought, with great satisfaction, about what Michael Carey had missed.

There was no bickering between them. He was an easy person to live with, and she was surprisingly simple in her needs and demands. She seemed to have forgotten that she was an actress, a woman with a house on the ocean, with a face anyone would recognize on the street. She shopped for groceries, washed clothes by hand and hung them up to dry on the line he'd strung between two trees. She didn't complain about the minuscule bathroom or his lack of air-conditioning. She made tiny curtains for the dollhouse, little rag rugs. He'd watch her concentration, the slight squint in her eyes as she held the needle, the way she rested the tip of her tongue daintily between her lips. Everything about her charmed him, especially her contentment at living within his four close walls.

She no longer worked on the screenplay, but she had not yet made the call to Nina. He didn't badger her; she had to work this out on her own. The notebook Kyle had left with her a week earlier sat unopened on the coffee table. Sometimes in the evenings he'd catch her staring at it. They'd be sitting on the sofa, reading or playing backgammon, and she'd look over at it. Just once, on a night when she was losing badly and her concentration was off, he said, "Why don't you read it?" and she shook her head quickly and returned to the game.

Neither of them spoke about the fact that she was no longer working at the site. He tried to persuade her to see Kyle. He didn't like being caught between the two of them. Kyle called a few times, leaving messages for her that Michael or Nina had called, but she refused to speak to him and she never returned those calls to the West Coast.

Kyle was coming to the digs again, more than he had at any other time that summer. The only awkward moment had been that first morning after Eden moved into the cabin. Kyle arrived at the side of the pit where Ben was working around nine in the morning. Ben could see the high color in Kyle's cheeks as he slowly lowered himself down the ladder.

"Eden's not coming this morning?" Kyle asked. He looked around at the unimpressive pit walls rather than meet Ben's eyes, and Ben felt sorry for him. He wondered what he could say to put his old friend at ease.

"No. She wanted to do some shopping. And she's not up to seeing you yet. Give her some time, Kyle."

"I was hoping she would understand somehow. I guess it's a hard thing to understand." Kyle picked up the graph from the side of the pit. "So, what do we have here?"

Ben showed him the pieces he'd found the day before and their location on the graph, but Kyle wasn't following him.

"I shouldn't have told her," he said finally.

"You had to."

"She's so angry with me."

"Yeah, she is right now." He said it as though Eden's anger would pass, but he wasn't so sure.

Kyle looked over at him. "You angry with me too?"

"I'm not trying to keep her from you, Kyle. I wish she would talk to you."

Kyle reached into his shirt pocket. "Here's a couple of tickets to Wolf Trap for Sunday night. *Threepenny Opera*. I don't think Lou and I will be in the mood, so why don't you and Eden go?"

Ben closed his fingers around the tickets. He had a normal life. He could take a woman out, be around other people. Maybe by now things had blown over enough that he could start living again.

Eden was oddly quiet that Sunday morning. She sat on the sofa, an unopened book in her lap, her eyes staring into space.

Ben looked up from the dollhouse. "What are you thinking about?" he asked.

She looked over at him. "I have to figure out what to do." He leaned away from the table. "About?" He wasn't certain if she meant the screenplay or Kyle.

"Cassie's coming in another week," she said. "And I can't stay with you while she's here, which means I have to either go back to Kyle and Lou's or move into a hotel. But if I'm no longer working on the film, there's no real point to my being here at all. I should really pull myself together and go home. I need to find a new project to get involved in."

His heart contracted with such force that he thought it must show in his face. Her eyes were on him now, watching him.

"Is that what you want?" he asked.

"No."

"What do you want?"

"I want you," she said. "I'm so happy when I'm with you, Ben. I want you on whatever terms I can have you."

He was glad he was sitting at the table and she was on the couch. He couldn't touch her, couldn't cloud his mind with the feel of her under his fingertips.

"The price of being with me could be very high," he said.

"I don't care."

"I don't know where my next job will be. And I won't live off you."

"There must be something archaeological you can do in California. I have connections, Ben. I'm sure I could help you find something. But first we have to get you cleared on the molestation charge. My lawyer in—"

"Wait a minute." He put down the little scrap of wood he'd been working on. "Stop dreaming, Eden. You're not going to get me cleared. You've got to face that, okay? Because it has to be factored into your decision."

She dropped her eyes quickly and he saw her swallow hard. He pressed ahead, knowing he was pushing her now, testing her. "I know this doesn't make a whole lot of sense, since I can't see Bliss, but I don't like the idea of having the entire continent between her and me. And I'm afraid of L.A. I'm afraid of having strangers pop out of the woodwork to take my picture and plaster it all over creation."

She looked up at him. "Do you love me?" Her eyes were dry but he heard the threat of tears in her voice.

"You know I do. Very much."

"Then Cassie and I will go wherever you can find another job. It doesn't matter where I live, really. I'll have to travel a bit to work on the Children's Fund and when I get around to making another movie. But I would try to keep traveling to a minimum."

He told her there was no need to make decisions yet, that he didn't think either of them was thinking clearly enough to do a good job of it. But she'd lit such hope in him. They had played house in such an insulated and idyllic fashion that for the first time in over a year he felt certain of a future.

They talked about Cassie during the two-hour drive to Wolf Trap. The approaching visit of Eden's little girl made him anxious. He was afraid he would attach himself too strongly to her—he missed having a child in his life. On the other hand, he was afraid of feeling self-conscious around her. He was, after all, a convicted child molester.

He had reached that gratifying point with Eden where he could say all of this out loud to her. None of his fears seemed too great for her to handle. She wanted him and Cassie to be great friends, she said. He didn't need to worry about touching her; she knew he was innocent. He needed to keep that in mind himself.

The stage at Wolf Trap was set in the heart of an open-air theater. He and Eden had lawn tickets for the bowl of grass fanning out from the theater seats. They spread their blanket on the lawn, and Eden unpacked their picnic basket while Ben poured them each a glass of wine.

"Mommy, there's Ben!"

He turned at the sound of a child's voice. A couple of blankets away, Alex and Leslie Parrish were taking food from their own picnic basket, and their daughter, Kim, was running toward him, black hair bouncing around her face. Kim. His goddaughter who had never received her birthday gift.

He saw Alex and Leslie look up as Kim reached him and bent over for a hug. He hugged her stiffly. He knew his face was white.

"Kimmie, come back here!" Leslie snapped.

Kim looked at Eden, then back to Ben. "Where's Bliss?" she asked.

"She's not with me. Kim, this is. Eden. Kim's my goddaughter and an incredible soccer player. Best eight-year-old midfielder in Annapolis."

"I was goalie this year." Kim grinned.

"Yeah? How'd your team do?" He waved in Alex and Leslie's direction. They were talking to each other, probably trying to decide which of them should rescue Kim from him.

Alex finally stood up and started walking in their direction. He looked heavier than the last time Ben had seen him. His dark hair was splattered with gray.

"Hi, Alex," Ben said when Alex had nearly reached their blanket.

"Ben." Alex reached out a hand to Kim. "Come on, Kimmie."

"Sit down a minute," Ben said. "Eden, this is Alex Parrish. Alex, Eden Riley."

Eden smiled and lifted her hand to Alex, who shook it briefly. Ben could see the shock register in Alex's face at finding him here with Eden.

"I can't sit down." Alex looked over at Leslie. "I think Leslie wants to move the blanket—she wants to see if we can get a little closer."

And a little farther from me, Ben thought as he watched Alex and Kim walk away from him.

Eden laid her hand on his back and set her chin on his shoulder. "He was your best friend?"

"Yes."

"How can he treat you so coldly?"

Ben shrugged. "He thinks I'm guilty." He watched the Parrishes pick up their picnic basket and work their way through the crowd, stepping between blankets set close together on the lawn, finally settling down again a safe distance away from him.

He and Eden ate quietly, but Ben couldn't take his eyes off Alex and Leslie. How many dozens of picnic suppers had he and Sharon eaten with the Parrishes over the years? He even knew what would be in their basket: oven-fried chicken, three-bean salad with black olives, flan for dessert.

Leslie and Kim suddenly got up and headed toward the concession stand, and Ben stood up himself.

"I'll be back in a minute," he said to Eden. He walked through the crowd until he reached Alex's blanket, where he sat down without waiting for an invitation.

Alex looked over at him in surprise. "Ben, I don't think—"

"Do you have any idea how it feels to have your best friend cut you out of his life?" Ben interrupted him.

"Yeah, well, I lost my best friend in this whole mess too." Alex looked terrible. He was aging quickly, badly, as though this last year had taken a toll on him as well. His face was jowly, or maybe it was just that Ben was not accustomed to seeing him without a smile.

"You didn't have to lose me," Ben said.

Alex shook his head and looked at Ben with an acidic sneer. "Eden

Riley, Ben? Kyle gives you a job and throws in his niece as a bonus, huh? Christ. Maybe I ought to screw my daughter and see what I can get."

Ben wanted to hit him. "Fuck you. " He spoke through gritted teeth, painfully aware of the futility of his words.

Alex swirled the wine in his glass and looked toward the concession stand. "Look, we have nothing to talk about. You'd better get back to your blanket and your movie star."

Ben didn't move. He pulled a splinter of rattan from the open picnic basket. He could see the flan inside, uneaten. "Have you seen Bliss lately?" He had to know.

Alex hesitated a moment. "Yesterday. We spent the day out there at the pool."

Ben pictured the scene. His house, his pool, his wife and daughter and best friend, and the stranger who had walked in and taken his place. "Does she seem happy?" Ben asked.

"What do you want to hear, Ben? That she's miserable now that she's lost her abusive daddy? Yes, she's happy. She's just fine."

"What's Jeff like?"

Alex shrugged. "He's okay."

"Can you put yourself in my shoes for just a second?"

Alex laughed. "No, Ben, I cannot. I can't possibly imagine what it's like to feel an uncontrollable urge to molest my daughter."

"I'm innocent, Alex. The thing that bothers me the most is that you've never been willing to talk to me about this, to hear my side. All you know is what you read in the papers or heard through the grapevine."

"I was at the trial, Ben."

"You were?"

"Every day. I wanted to see for myself. I sat in the back. I heard the evidence. I saw you freak out when Bliss was about to testify against you. I heard you confess. What am I supposed to believe? So don't tell me I didn't try to see it your way. I wanted to hear you were innocent." He looked toward the concession stand again. "You'd better go back. Leslie doesn't even let me speak your name around the house."

Ben stood up.

"One more thing, Ben." Alex looked up at him. "I have to ask you this. Don't worry, I won't press charges or anything, but I need to know. Do you remember a couple of years ago when Kimmie stayed with you and Sharon while Leslie was visiting her mother?"

Ben nodded.

"Well, she started having horrendous nightmares after that. I have to know. Did you do anything to her back then?"

Ben swallowed the bile rising in his throat. He turned his back on Alex and walked across the lawn to Eden as quickly, as proudly, as he could.

The show was lost on him. He told Eden about his conversation with Alex, but then fell quiet for the rest of the evening while Eden held his hand, stroked his back. He said little on the long drive home. When they pulled into the clearing by his cabin, he turned to her.

"I'm glad tonight happened," he said. "This is reality. You needed to see it. I needed to see it. We have to stop pretending. All the talk about us having a normal life together is fantasy, Eden. You need to think long and hard about what you're getting yourself and Cassie into. And I have a favor to ask. If you don't think you can handle it, please leave me now? Don't wait until I'm so full of hope about us that I—"

"Shush." She turned in the seat and put her arms around him. "I love you. And I'm in way too deep to get out now, even if I wanted to."

Once in the steamy darkness of his cabin, she sat him down on the bed and undressed him, her fingers cool and silky where they met his skin. He thought he would be unable to make love to her, but she was patient and persistent. And he thought he would be unable to sleep, but his dreams came quickly and they were safe dreams, easy dreams. Just once did he wake up in the middle of the night. He could see the light on by the sofa, could see Eden curled up there in his boxer shorts and T-shirt, the notebook open on her knees. He heard her sniffling, saw the crumpled tissue in her hand, and let her be.

37

All the world thinks the baby I'm carrying is Matt's. Only Matt and I know the truth. It's odd how people just assume things about me. I never announced my pregnancy, and no one ever asked me, "Are you pregnant?" But Susanna and Daddy gradually noticed the change in my shape and Susanna bought me a couple of maternity dresses without ever commenting on how it is I came to be this way. So now I wear dresses, which are not as uncomfortable as I recall dresses being, but maybe it's just that my middle enjoys feeling untethered for a while.

Daddy says I have to marry Matt, and Matt is begging. I think Matt has actually started to believe this baby is his. I don't want to marry him, but last night Susanna gave me a long lecture about how every baby deserves two parents. "Think of the child," she said. She is right. I don't want my baby to grow up a bastard, feeling different from other children. I know what it's like to be set apart, and I don't want that for my baby. I have such hopes for this little one. So I've decided to tell Matt yes, so long as we can stay here near the cave. I could not move into his house, so far from Lynch Hollow.

I'm thinking about my own mama again, my real mama. I don't feel at all disgraced, like she did. I wish she could have had a man like Matt to save her from her shame.

March 22, 1955

We were married quickly by a judge friend of Matt's on the nineteenth of March. I think it was the right thing to do. We didn't take a honeymoon or any of that nonsense. Instead, we spent our wedding night at his house, talking about the details of this marriage. I was nervous, spending the night away from Lynch Hollow, and Matt just held me the night through. He is so dear, and he understands my feelings well. He said that he will sell his house and that he has spoken to Daddy about building a second story onto our house for us to live in. He asked me what I want to do about sex. I felt shy all of a sudden, but told him I would like to wait to make love until after the baby's born. I pretended it was that I am uncomfortable with my expanding belly, but really I am not yet ready to let him erase Kyle's mark on my body. Matt agreed to this without hesitation, although he was quick to say he is not at all put off by my pregnancy and if I should change my mind before the baby comes, to let him know.

I do plan to let Matt make love to me after the baby's born. I couldn't marry him and then cruelly turn him away. And it will be worth it if it means more children.

I wrote to Kyle about the marriage but still have said nothing about the baby.

May 1, 1955

I've been sitting here in the cave for the last hour, just staring at this blank page, trying to think of words to describe my terrible sadness.

Matt died yesterday. He was working on the second story of the house when he fell, breaking his neck. I was here in the cave when Daddy came to tell me and I wept until I was sick. Why such a good man? Why not me instead? I am selfish and demanding and obstinate. Matt should have married Delores Winthrop. He would have had his nice, settled-down sort of life. He should have told me—like any other man would tell his wife—"I've got a perfectly fine house and you're going to live in it with me."

Instead he was building that second story. For me and for Kyle's child. If taking my own life would give his back to him, I would do it in an instant. I loathe myself right now. I wish that we had made love, that I had given him that. I wish he had not been so quick to put up with me, that he had demanded more of me. I wouldn't have loved him less.

Daddy has sent word to Kyle.

May 4, 1955

We still had heard nothing from Kyle by the time the funeral started yesterday. Naylor's Funeral Parlor was packed with the staff from Matt's paper and community people who'd come to know and respect him. I sat up front, with Daddy and Susanna. Susanna had somehow found a black maternity dress for me. I could hardly sit still, hardly breathe. My belly is so big it's left no room for any air in my lungs. I felt sweat rolling down my back and between my breasts. And I could feel all the people behind me, staring at me, whispering about me.

When the preacher started talking, I spotted Kyle at the side door. He walked towards us quickly, his shoes clicking too loudly on the floor, and slipped into the seat between Daddy and me. He kissed my cheek and held my hand. I had to breathe through my mouth to keep from crying.

The preacher said some nice things about Matt, but he went on too long and I could feel Kyle's eyes on my belly. Then I knew he was doing the arithmetic in his head, ticking back the months. His hand squeezed mine hard and he said in a whisper only I could hear, "Oh my God, Kate." Both of us stared at the preacher, not hearing a word the man said.

In the graveyard, Kyle literally held me up. When it was over and Matt was in the ground, Kyle told Daddy he would bring me home. We waited 'til the crowd left and then sat at the side of Matt's new grave.

"Why didn't you tell me?" he asked. "I know people in New York who could have taken care of it."

"That's why I didn't tell you."

"It might have terrible problems because of us being related."

"I don't care."

"Did Matt think it was his?"

"Matt and I never made love. He knew the baby was yours."

Kyle put his head in his hands and sat that way for a long time. Finally he raised his head up and said he would leave school and move back to Lynch Hollow. He wouldn't go to South America. He could work in our digs and take care of me and the baby.

I told him I didn't want that. One man had already sacrificed his life for me and I wasn't about to let Kyle do the same.

"Then I'll get a job and send you money."

I shook my head. Matt had plenty of money and I have some from my books. I don't need Kyle's money. "If you really want to do something for me you can promise you'll never again write me cold and hurtful letters that make me feel like you don't love me anymore."

He looked truly surprised. "I love you more than I'll ever love anyone else," he said. "But I can't write that in a letter. I can't commit that sort of thing to writing. What if the letters were found?"

I shrugged. "I write far worse in my journal all the time."

Kyle looked pale. "You've written about the baby in your journal? About us?"

"Don't worry, they're well hidden." I told him where they were and he seemed reassured.

Kyle left again this morning. He promised to write more often and to try to get back here as much as he can. That's all I want, all I would ever ask of him.

May 22, 1955

I miss Matt. I cannot even write my stories, I'm so preoccupied with thoughts of him. Friends of Daddy's have finished the second story and I'm moving the bed that belonged to Matt's parents into the big bedroom that was meant for both of us.

June 12, 1955

Last night, Eden Swift Riley made her journey into the world. My labor was long ("Swift is the wrong middle name for her," said the midwife), but hardly worth writing about now that she's here. She is beautiful and perfect, as I was certain she would be. She has white fuzz on her head and big blue eyes. She is delicate and dainty—not quite seven pounds, with skin as white as sugar. Her head is nearly perfectly round, which the midwife says is a miracle, since my labor was so long. I can't wait for Kyle to see her. We had a phone put in just last week and Daddy called and left a message with the manager at Kyle's apartment house.

June 18, 1955

Kyle and Louise arrived late last night. They will stay several weeks, then join Professor Latterly in Colombia.

I was sleeping when they arrived and Kyle woke me up and sat next to me on the big bed. He took Eden on his knees and just stared into her little face.

"I can't believe it," he said over and over again. He was smiling. We were both smiling and I thought of how long it's been since there was happiness between us. Kyle looked for all the world like a proud daddy and Eden played her role well, yawning and gurgling, looking up at him as if she knew that no matter what anyone told her from this day forward, this man was her father.

We talked a long time, like we used to. He told me he will marry Lou, that he knows he's found the right woman for him and the reason he knows that is because she reminds him of me! I thought of the skinny, cigarette-smoking woman I met in his apartment and asked him what he meant.

"Not physically," he said. "But she's the type of person who pays no attention to the rules of society if she doesn't agree with them. She doesn't care what anyone thinks of her. She's creative, like you are, though she's an artist and dancer rather than a writer. She's not reclusive, but in other ways she's very much like you. She knows Eden is mine," he said. "After Matt's funeral I told her everything."

"What did she say?"

Kyle shrugged. "She wasn't the least bit shocked. She cried a little. She said I should be the best uncle I can possibly be."

At first I wished he hadn't brought Louise with him. I didn't want to share him for these two weeks. But this morning I was sitting in the rocker on the front porch when Lou came and sat down next to me. She looks completely different to me now, although I know she actually looks the same. She had on dungarees and a black sleeveless shirt and she smoked one cigarette after another while we talked. Her face is pretty—very thin, with pointed cheekbones and round blue eyes. When she speaks, her accent is hard, but her voice soft.

"I love your brother, and he loves me," she began. "But nobody in the world, including me, is going to take your place in his heart. If you had not been raised as brother and sister, there's no doubt in my mind that he would choose you over me or anyone else."

I thanked her for telling me that. It was a generous thing to say, and I can see now why Kyle is in love with her. I told her I wasn't sure she was right, though. I said Kyle was always bothered by the fact that I preferred to be alone than to be out among people. I told her that my greatest fear is that I might turn Eden into a hermit as well.

Lou suggested I learn how to drive, that I buy a car with some of the money from the sale of Matt's house so I could get out more. Ha! That's quite a joke. I figure that no matter how well Kyle described me to her, she doesn't quite have the picture of me yet.

This afternoon Kyle, Lou and I walked Eden in her carriage over to the cavern. Lou was fascinated and wanted a geological description of the tites and mites, which I provided while Kyle sat on the sunlit ground outside the cave holding—and staring at—his daughter. He cannot take his eyes off her and I don't blame him.

June 23, 1955

Daddy and Susanna dislike Lou and they do not hide their feelings well. She talks about the plight of poor people (she means city poor, not like the poor we used to be) and of colored people. She speaks of Mozart and Picasso. She is too worldly for the likes of Daddy and Susanna. I enjoy listening to her though. She is not at all afraid to speak her mind.

June 24, 1955

Daddy told Kyle he'd like Lou out of the house, that she is upsetting Susanna. I think it is more Daddy that's upset. He's grown irritable this *last year and he spends too much time with the bottle. I am afraid Kyle and Lou will leave early and I've begged Daddy not to make a fuss.*

June 27, 1955

Lou asked me last night if she could hold Eden and only then did I realize she had not yet held her. I thought maybe she was just not the mothering type, but after I watched her and Kyle cooing and clucking over Eden, I realized she had just not wanted to step in too soon. She and Kyle told me they don't plan on having children because they'll be traveling too much. Watching them with Eden I knew what a loss that will be for them. It makes Eden even more important for Kyle, for both of them, I guess. I'm more than willing to share her. After all, he is her father.

I'm not jealous of Lou, except sometimes when I see Kyle touch her and feel that old longing leap up inside me before I can check it. I think Kyle is very careful not to touch her around me. They are both careful not to hurt me.

June 28, 1955

We are getting indoor plumbing with some of the money from Matt's house. Luxury! Kyle is putting the rest in a special bank account for Eden to use when she's ready for college. He says she won't be a charity case like we were, thanks to Matt. Kyle and Lou are leaving on Friday for New York and Sunday for Colombia. Colombia is a painful distance from Lynch Hollow.

July 6, 1955

I can write again! For the first time since Matt died, I want to get back to the book I was working on. Eden is in her little bassinet with cotton in her teensy ears so the typing doesn't bother her too much. It's hot outside, but cool in here. I'm so grateful I have Eden. I would be very lonely without her. I want to be a good mother. Kyle gave me a camera before he left for Colombia. He doesn't want to miss out on seeing Eden grow up, and I take one picture after another of her. Daddy says I give her too much attention,

I hold her too much, I'm going to spoil her. I told him that's my intention: I plan to spoil her rotten.

August 15, 1955

Kyle and Lou were married on my birthday. It was a Tuesday and people thought they were odd to get married midweek, but they were set on my birthday. I can't believe my good fortune that Kyle met a woman like Lou. Imagine how different things would be if she were the type of woman (like most women) who he could not tell about Eden. Instead, his letters are warm and loving, never mentioning the ultimate secret of course, but everything I read between the lines these days is good.

38

When she woke up, she was half lying, half sitting on the sofa, the notebook clutched to her chest, and Ben was gently shaking her shoulder. It was still dark outside and the only light in the cabin was from the moon. Her head was foggy, but the journal came back to her like bits and pieces of a dream as Ben walked her across the floor to his bed. She slipped between the sheets and settled into his arms.

"I don't want her to die," she said.

"Who?"

"My mother. I want to change the ending. I don't want her to leave me." She felt him tighten his arms around her, pull her closer. "The end is so close," she said. "I'm going to lose her all over again."

When she woke up a second time, she was alone in the bed and the smell of bacon was in the air. Ben looked over at her from the kitchen.

"Get dressed," he said. "I'm making our cholesterol fix for the week."

Her head felt very clear. She took a shower, put on her white shorts and a white T-shirt, and joined Ben at the table. "Charlotte's gone," she said.

He nodded. "I noticed yesterday. I think she figured you were here for the duration and I don't need her anymore."

She set her bare foot on his knee under the table. "I have to go over to Kyle and Lou's," she said. "I need to ask them if Cassie and I can stay with them until your job here is up and you've got something else to go to. Then I'm going to call Nina to tell her I'm putting the film on the shelf indefinitely. I'll read the scripts she sent. Get back on track."

He stared at her while she spoke, a chunk of omelet balanced on the tines of his fork. When she was finished he smiled. "I guess I'd better get serious about looking for a new job."

"If you insist on working, yes, you'd better."

"Where would you like me to look? Geographically, I mean. Florida? New England?"

"It doesn't matter, Ben." She wondered how long it would take him to realize that she truly didn't care at all.

"You have got to be kidding me," Nina said, slowly, biting off each word. Eden could picture her at the other end of the line, gnashing her teeth, pulling her hair. "You were all gung ho on this thing and now you're quitting?"

"That's right. So which script is best? Which do you want me to look at first?"

"Look, kiddo, we need to have a long talk. Do you have reservations for your flight back? I'll pick you up and we can—".

"I'm not coming back, Nina. I'm staying here until Ben finds another job, and then I'm going with him, wherever that is."

There was silence on Nina's end.

"Nina?"

"This guy have you drugged or what?"

"Just tell me which script to start with."

Nina sighed. "Read *Treasure House*. It's written for you. I mean literally. John Packwood said he had you in mind the whole time. I don't think he'll do it without you."

"I'll let you know what I think."

*

She drove to Lynch Hollow that afternoon. It was not the first time she'd seen Kyle and Lou since moving in with Ben, but it was the first time she intended to hold a conversation with them. She found them sitting on the back deck.

"I just wanted to clear my plans with you," she said, sitting on the edge of one of the redwood lounge chairs. It was hard for her to look Kyle in the eye. "I've made some decisions. I'm not moving back to California. I'll have to go back to sell the house and work on the Children's Fund and maybe do a movie from time to time. But I'll live wherever Ben can find another job." She brushed a ladybug from her shorts and said, almost as an afterthought, "And I'm not going to make the film about my mother."

Lou glanced at Kyle, but neither of them spoke, and Eden continued.

"Cassie will be here next week," she said. "I'd like to stay here with her at Lynch Hollow, but if you'd rather, she and I can find a place in Coolbrook." Coolbrook would have been her first choice, but she'd already spoken to a realtor and learned it would be difficult to find a rental for just a few months.

"Of course you'll stay here," Lou said.

Eden looked at Kyle. "Kyle?"

"We want you here, Eden. I would hope you'd know that by now."

"There's a foldaway bed you can set up for Cassie in the little room upstairs," said Lou.

"That'll be great," Eden said. "She has a kitten. Ben said he can keep it at his cabin if you'd rather not . . ."

"A kitten is fine." Lou smiled.

Eden stood up. "Okay. Thanks."

"I'll walk you out." Kyle stood up and followed her into the house. At the front door he set his hand on her elbow and she turned to face him. "A few things worry me, honey," he said. "Just let an old man say his piece, all right?"

She folded her arms across her chest like armor.

"I'm worried about you rushing into something permanent with Ben when you're upset."

"I'm not upset. And I'm not rushing."

"He may never be able to get another job, and that is the honest truth. I've called people, tried to drum something up for him, but no one wants anything to do with him. I mention his name and they laugh out loud."

She winced.

"Have you thought about what you'll do with Cassie when you have to travel to California or wherever? You could leave her home with Wayne with no problem, but with Ben?"

"What are you insinuating, Kyle? He's innocent. You said so yourself."

"I know that, and you know that, but the rest of the world is pretty convinced otherwise and you'll be putting him in a very awkward position. People will be watching Cassie for a sign that he's hurt her."

"Are you trying to split us up?"

"I'm just not sure you know what you're getting yourself into."

"I'm fine, Kyle. I haven't jumped into this blindly." She opened the screen door and stepped onto the porch.

"I'm very disappointed about the film, Eden," Kyle said from behind the screen. "I think you would have done an excellent job with it."

Over the next few days she bought clothes and toys for Cassie, kitty litter and food for the kitten, jeans and tennis shoes for Ben. "Don't think of this as charity," she said when she handed him the clothes. "I'm enjoying myself."

She made up the folding bed in the little room next to her mother's old room and filled the small pine dresser with the clothes she'd bought. She ate a few meals with Lou and Kyle and slept at Lynch Hollow on a couple of nights, trying to ease the tension of being with them so it wouldn't overwhelm Cassie on her arrival. Staying here again would not be difficult. She'd had years of practice relating to Kyle and Lou on a purely superficial level. She knew how to keep her distance from them.

She missed Ben on those nights at Lynch Hollow. In the middle of one particularly hot night she threw on her robe, drove the winding black road up to his cabin, and climbed into his bed. They made love in the breathless air of the cabin, the damp sheet twisting around their bare legs. Afterward he told her she was crazy to leave an air-conditioned house on a ninety-five-degree night just so she could sleep with a man already on the verge of heat prostration. And she replied that soon Cassie would come, soon she wouldn't be able to sleep with him at all, and they both grew very quiet. When Cassie arrived, everything would change.

One night while she was at Lynch Hollow, Michael called. At first she thought he was stoned. He was so low-key, so soft and slow. But after speaking to him for a few minutes she knew it was acceptance she heard in his voice. He was no longer on, no longer trying hard to win her affection. He asked her questions about Ben, questions to help him understand her attraction to him, and she was careful to be honest in her answers without revealing Ben's past. He was glad she was happy, he said, and with a pang of guilt she knew he cared about her enough to mean it.

"Nina's furious," he said. "But I told her it's your life and she should butt out. But God, when I think of you not living down the street from me anymore . . . I miss you, Eden. I'm lonely as hell without you. Can I still call you every once in a while?"

"I'd like you to."

"Ben won't get jealous?"

"He's not the jealous type," she said, although she realized she had no way of knowing that for certain. She had lived with Ben in a cocoon, not in the real world.

When she got off the phone she sat still for a long time. That had been the first real conversation she'd ever had with Michael. The first one in which she felt like they were two people talking with one another, rather than two characters rehearsing their lines. His bravado, his slick, masculine image was no more real than the character he'd played in Heart of Winter. She felt a tenderness for him that was new. The next time she spoke to him she would tell him to nurture that soft, open part of himself, to let the women he met see it. He wouldn't be lonely for long.

*

Wayne arrived with Cassie that Friday evening. All day Eden had felt an anxiety she couldn't label. She'd had lunch with Ben on the footbridge over Ferry Creek and had not been able to eat.

"You're not in competition with Wayne," he'd said. "This isn't a popularity contest."

She nodded, knowing Ben had zeroed in on the source of her nervousness.

"I won't plan on seeing you for a couple of days," he said.

"Why not?"

"You and Cassie need some time to get to know each other again without a stranger around."

She hadn't thought of that, but once he said it she knew he was right. She wanted Cassie all to herself for a while.

Cassie was sick when she arrived. Wayne carried her out of the car just as dusk was falling. Her hair was longer, a dark patch of silk on Wayne's shoulder. She looked limp and liquid in his arms.

"Hi, Mommy," she said in her sick-little-girl voice.

"Hi, baby." Eden kissed her cheek. It was hot.

"She hasn't felt too well the past couple of days," Wayne said as he carried her into the house. Eden trotted alongside, lugging the kitten in its little kennel and trying to make out Cassie's features in the dim light. "April and Lindy had a stomach thing and I guess she has a touch of it. The mountain roads didn't help."

He carried Cassie upstairs, where a stuffed koala bear perched on the pillow of the folding bed. Kyle must have put it there before he and Lou went out for the evening. Eden moved it to the dresser and pulled down the covers.

"Her pajamas are right on top in her suitcase," Wayne said, but Cassie had already tugged the covers to her chin, and her eyes were closed. Eden felt a stab of worry, followed by disappointment that this evening would not go as she had planned. There would be no long and loving talk with Cassie tonight.

"Sorry to bring you a sick kid," Wayne said. "She's been fine all summer."

She took his words personally—Cassie was fine as long as she was with Wayne. But when Wayne bent down to kiss his sleeping daughter good-bye, when he stroked Cassie's hair and whispered, "I love you, sweetheart. I'll miss you," she felt a little twist of love for him.

He stood up again and looked around him. "This is where you grew up?"

"Yes. Well, downstairs. It was different then. Not nearly so nice." She walked him downstairs and showed him around the house. When they reached the kitchen, she poured him a glass of iced tea and they sat at the table.

Wayne looked good. He had a sunburn across the bridge of his nose, a little more gray at his temples.

"So." He grinned. "Who's the guy you painted the Big Apple red with?"

He'd seen the tabloid. "He's a friend of Kyle's."

"Are you . . . Do you have something going with him?" She nodded and couldn't help her smile. He smiled back.

"Is he an archaeologist?"

"Yes."

"What's he like? Is he divorced or what?"

"Now you're getting nosy."

"Well, I think I have a right to know something about him if he's going to be around Cassie."

"I don't recall you asking my permission before you started sleeping with Pam." She was immediately contrite. She lowered her eyes. "I'm sorry."

"No, I'm sorry." Wayne set down his glass. "I'm not proud of how I handled things back then. And I didn't mean to be intrusive just now. If he's a friend of Kyle's, that says enough. I was never really comfortable knowing Cassie was hanging around Michael Carey." He stood up. "When do you go back to Santa Monica?"

"I don't think I will. Ben needs to stay on the East Coast, so I'll be staying myself for a while."

Wayne's jaw dropped; then he smiled. "I like this guy better all the time. If you're living here I could see Cassie more often, couldn't I?"

"We can probably arrange that."

"What about your career?"

"I'll work it out."

She walked him out to his car. He looked up at the dark bedroom window before getting in. "She's been afraid of the dark lately. Maybe you could get a night-light for her? She's been looking forward to seeing you. The important thing is for us to keep telling her we both want her, we'll both always be there for her."

"Of course." Eden hurt for him. She knew how it felt to drop Cassie off and drive away.

"She might be a little homesick for a few days," Wayne continued. "Let her call if she wants to. You can use my work number during the day."

"I'll let her call all she wants. And Wayne?" She set her hand on his arm as he slid behind the wheel. He looked up at her. "I think Cassie's lucky to have you as her father."

He stared at her a moment before he smiled. "You've changed," he said.

"I know."

She lay in her mother's old bed, the bed she had been born in, worrying that Cassie might wake up in the middle of the night to find herself alone in a strange room. Finally she got up and brought Cassie and the stuffed koala into bed with her. Cassie's forehead was cool now, and she drifted in and out of sleep as Eden changed her into her pajamas. Cassie settled into the pillow, clutching the koala as though it had been hers for a long time. Eden drew the covers over both of them and was immediately enveloped in Cassie's scent, subtle yet unmistakable, and she pulled her daughter closer to breathe her in.

39

In the morning Eden sat in the wicker rocker and studied her daughter. Cassie slept heavily, compressing the pillow and mattress as though she weighed two hundred pounds instead of forty-one. She was not a classic beauty and probably never would be. Not like Bliss who, if only for a few seconds, stole your breath away. But Cassie was irrepressibly cute. Even asleep there was an impishness in her turned-up nose and full cheeks, the suggestion of a smile at the corners of her mouth. Her dark bangs were spiky and short, and Eden recalled Wayne telling her that Cassie had taken it upon herself to cut her own hair the week before. For the first time, Eden was grateful Cassie resembled Wayne and not herself. She didn't have to wonder where Cassie got her nose or her eyes. She wanted no reminders of Cassie's ancestry or her own.

Eden walked over to her closet and took a pair of shorts off their hanger. Her back was turned on her daughter for just an instant, so she was startled when Cassie said, "Whoever is this?"

She turned to see Cassie sitting up in the bed, grinning, holding the koala up for inspection. Her hair was a mass of wispy brown tangles except for the bangs that stood straight up above her big brown eyes. She was beautiful. Eden climbed back on the bed and hugged her.

"It's from Uncle Kyle." She tried to comb Cassie's bangs into place with her fingers, but it was hopeless.

"Is Daddy still here?"

"No, honey, he had to leave last night."

Cassie jumped out of the bed and ran to the window. She gnawed at her lower lip with her small front teeth as she looked outside. "I thought I heared his car."

Eden felt a flash of insecurity, as though she wasn't at all certain she could remember how to take care of a child by herself. "It must have been your imagination. He said to tell you he loves you and he'll miss you and he can't wait until the next time he gets to see you. We can call him later if you like." She walked over to the window and laid her hand on Cassie's cool forehead. "Are you feeling better this morning? Do you want some breakfast?"

"Yes." Cassie marched around the room in her yellow shorty pajamas, examining everything, touching Eden's familiar comb and brush set on the dresser, taking a few seconds to look at her own picture on the night table. She'd always awakened this way, immediately alert, exploratory, checking out her world. It reassured Eden. She knew this child.

"Where's Stuart?"

"Stuart?"

"My kitten."

"Oh. I left him in the kitchen for the night. But we can move his litter box up here today. What will you name your koala?"

Cassie looked at the koala lying on the bed.

"April," she said. "It's from Uncle Kyle?"

"Uh huh. Do you remember Uncle Kyle and Aunt Lou?"

"Sure, silly. Aunt Lou rides in a wheelchair."

"Great, that's right. You have a good memory." She pointed Cassie in the direction of the bathroom. "Come on, let's get dressed and go down to breakfast."

The table in the kitchen was set for four and laden with pancakes and blueberries, fresh-squeezed orange juice, and wedges of cantaloupe. Cassie had seen Lou and Kyle only three times in her life—two brief visits in New York and once last year in California. Eden imagined that the visit last year could be the only one clear in Cassie's memory. Cassie had been distressed by Lou's missing leg, which she'd searched for under the furniture and in the closets, making Eden extremely uncomfortable, although Lou herself seemed amused.

Once Cassie was born, the obligatory visits with Lou and Kyle became more tolerable. Cassie provided the entertainment, something for the four adults to focus on other than the strain that existed between them. Now at the breakfast table Eden knew this would be the case once again. The tension that had filled the house since she'd learned Kyle was her father floated high above them, too high to be much of a threat. It lost its charge with Cassie in the room. Eden felt it up there, a good, safe distance above her.

Cassie seemed to have adjusted easily to the overnight upheaval in her life. She was her usual, unshy self, fully aware of her ability to charm. She relished being the center of attention, and Lou and Kyle made an appreciative audience. She babbled about her month in Pennsylvania, April and Lindy, the swimming pool, and Stuart, the plump gray kitten. She was an expressive child, her face a mirror for her words, and Eden watched her from a new perspective—one born of a month's deprivation.

Lou leaned close to Eden. "She's going to be an actress for sure."

Eden felt deflated by the idea. Wearing the mask was not the life she would choose for her daughter.

Cassie looked up at the shelf above the sink. "What's that?" she asked, her eyes so huge that the whites showed all around the nearly black irises.

Eden looked up to see a ceramic plate in the shape of a flounder.

"It's a serving plate for fish," Lou said.

"Why, it's exquisite," Cassie said and they all laughed. She was definitely on this morning.

"I was hoping that you and I could go fishing one day while you're here," Kyle said.

Eden had a sudden memory of Kyle taking her fishing. She must have been no more than Cassie's age, and she remembered sitting with him on the bank of the Shenandoah, the fishing line damp and taut beneath her fingers.

"Today?" Cassie asked.

"That's up to your mother." Kyle looked at Eden.

Eden had wanted Cassie to herself today, but they would have plenty of time together over the next few weeks. "That would be fine," she said.

"Hooray!" Cassie raised herself to her knees to dig deeper into her cantaloupe.

"How do you feel about worms?" Kyle asked.

"Oh, worms, yummy, I love them." She giggled ridiculously.

"That's good," Kyle said. "If we don't catch any fish we can eat the worms for supper."

Cassie rolled her eyes. "Silly."

Kyle took Cassie out to the shed to find a pole she could manage, and with her daughter's departure Eden felt the tension drop from the ceiling to her shoulders.

"He used to take you fishing," Lou said. "Do you remember?"

Eden stood up and began clearing the table. "No. Not really."

Lou set her napkin on the table. "How long are you going to stay angry with us?"

Eden turned from the sink to look at her aunt. "You ask that question as though it's something I have control over, as though I can choose my emotions."

"It's eating away at Kyle," Lou said quietly.

"He seems fine to me." Eden faced the sink again and turned on the faucet full force. The hot water spiked against the frying pan in the sink, blocking out any other sound in the room, anything Lou might have left to say. From the corner of her eye Eden watched Lou stack the plates on the edge of the table and then slowly wheel her chair toward the door. And only when the handles of the chair had disappeared into the living room did she turn the water off. Suds filled the sink to the rim; the hot water burned her hands and wrists. She pressed one soapy fist to her mouth. Damn. She was not handling this well. She was acting like an adolescent, like herself at seventeen.

Only she'd been tougher as a teenager. A puny little scene like this would never have been enough to make her cry.

*

There were catfish for dinner that night, breaded and pan-fried and, at Cassie's insistence, served on the flounder platter.

"Uncle Kyle caught the big ones and I caught the little one," Cassie said. Eden had never seen Cassie eat fish and she watched as her daughter struggled gamely to get some of it down. She managed two mouthfuls before requesting a peanut butter and jelly sandwich.

Cassie had come home exhausted after her morning with Kyle. Her shorts were wet, her arms and cheeks were streaked with dirt, and a layer of black grime was embedded beneath her fingernails. She smelled of fish and worms, earth and river. Smells that filled the tiny upstairs bathroom as Eden ran water for her bath, that hung in the air an hour later when she cleaned the tub. Smells of Eden's own childhood that she couldn't shake, that left her with a painful mixture of comfort and yearning. But the smell she longed to remember most was missing. The cavern. She couldn't remember, couldn't even begin to conjure up the texture and scent of the air in the cave.

Now as she slipped a bone out of the catfish on her plate she looked at Kyle. "How did the cave smell?" she asked.

Kyle raised his eyes from his plate. "Like a tomb," he said bluntly, closing the subject with the tone of his voice, and she knew all at once that he was angry with her too.

The following day she and Cassie returned from a matinee at the Coolbrook theater to find Ben sitting at the kitchen table. She wasn't surprised to see him there. They had spoken the night before and decided that at some point today he would come over. Yet after two days of not seeing him her immediate reaction was visceral—a rush of adrenaline, a fire low in her gut—as if he were an alluring stranger she'd caught a glimpse of on the street. She smiled at her response, at the satisfying knowledge that this stranger was hers.

He was drinking apple juice and reading the newspaper, and he didn't stand when they walked in. Instead he stayed in the chair, at Cassie's level, and Eden thought how smart he was, how accustomed to a child.

"Cassie, this is a friend of mine, Ben," Eden said.

Cassie leaned hard against Eden's leg, looking at Ben from beneath a furrowed brow. She'd acted this way when she first met Michael, too, sizing him up, holding back. She'd never really warmed to Michael.

"I heard there was a kitten over here and I wanted to meet it," Ben said.

Cassie eyed him suspiciously.

"Does it belong to you, Eden?" Ben asked, his gray eyes innocent.

"It's mine," Cassie said.

"Can I see it?"

Cassie ran off in the direction of the living room and Ben smiled up at Eden. "She's great," he said.

Eden leaned over to kiss him. "I miss you."

Cassie returned with the kitten cuddled in her arms. She handed it to Ben, the guard in her eyes lifting a little. "Is it a boy or a girl?" Ben asked.

"A boy. His name is Stuart."

"Stuart?" Ben's eyes were amused. "He looks very well cared for."

"He is." Cassie told him about Stuart's diet and how she cleaned the poop out of his litter box every day. Stuart stretched out his fat little body, his rear paws on Ben's thigh, his front paws kneading the shirt above Ben's ribs. Eden was jealous of the cat.

Cassie edged nearer to Ben until she was close enough to scratch Stuart's head. She was on a roll now, telling Ben about the vitamins cats require, how to prevent fur balls, the merits of various forms of flea control products. Eden had no idea Cassie knew about such things. Ben asked questions and listened closely to her answers. He didn't tease, didn't talk down to her, and Cassie swelled with pride at being taken seriously by this man who had an insatiable curiosity about cat care.

Ben kept his visit short, but the next afternoon he invited Eden and Cassie up to his cabin, and it was then that he won Cassie over completely. Cassie was awestruck by the dollhouse. "It's for me?" she said, her eyes wide. She had to be wondering why this stranger would give her something so resplendent. She walked in a circle around the yellow and blue Victorian house where it rested on the table. "It's exquisite," she breathed. Ben, hearing her use this word for the first time, laughed with pleasure.

They took her to the dollhouse store in Belhurst to buy dolls for the house. She selected a tiny woman in a housedress, a clean-cut man with a briefcase, and two little blond girls. Eden gave her the money to pay the cashier, and she and Ben waited at the door while Cassie made her purchase.

"Do you think she sees that mother doll as me or Pam?" she asked.

"She probably just sees it as a mother doll."

As they walked back to the truck Ben took Eden's hand. Cassie plowed between them, grabbing their hands and pulling them apart. "Don't hold his hand, Mommy," she said.

"Why not?" Eden asked. "I like holding his hand."

"'Cause he's not Daddy. You're only allowed to hold Daddy's hand." She watched Eden carefully for another few steps and when she was satisfied her mother was not going to take Ben's hand again, she ran on ahead of them, rubber-soled heels flashing behind her. Ben looked at Eden with raised eyebrows.

"I'd better have a talk with her," Eden said.

"Yeah," he said. "You'd better if you ever want to hold my hand again."

"That's not all I want to hold."

He groaned. "Don't talk dirty to me when you can't follow through." He put his arm around her but dropped it quickly. "Are we ever going to make love again?"

"God, I hope so."

That was the only drawback to having Cassie with her: there was no place, no time to be alone with Ben.

Eden began checking into day-care for Cassie for the fall. Maggie DeMarco, Sara Jane Miller's younger daughter, ran a small program out of her home. Eden and Cassie spent an afternoon with Maggie and her little girls, and Cassie was thrilled beyond measure at being around other children. She used to prefer the company of adults, but Eden could see the difference the month with April and Lindy had made. Eden herself felt comfortable with Maggie, who treated her like any other mother. She seemed neither impressed nor intimidated at having Eden Riley in her house. Maggie had that lazy, almost bored smile that Eden remembered from their meeting at

Sara Jane's apartment. She looked like a woman whose nerves never frayed.

"You know," Maggie said over a glass of iced tea, "that time at my mother's was not the first time we've met. You and I were buddies when we were little, before your mother died. I don't remember it, but that's what my mother says."

Eden was stunned. "I didn't think I had any playmates at all back then."

Maggie shrugged. "I couldn't swear to it, but Mama claims it's true."

Eden signed Cassie up to start day-care in September. Maggie said she'd be happy to take her for the rest of the summer, but Eden wasn't ready to give Cassie up just yet.

Besides, Cassie was being well entertained at home. She helped Lou bake cookies and pies, and Kyle set up a little music stand she could use as an easel right next to Lou's easel. Cassie loved slapping the paint on her "canvas," although her short attention span hardly allowed for the production of great art.

In the evenings she sat on Kyle's lap while he read her *The Lazy Lizard* or *Soup for Seven*, and Eden watched them, feeling once more that eerie nostalgia. Surely he'd once read to her that way, with her nestled in his arms, his bearded cheek resting against her temple. She could very nearly remember it.

She took Cassie to the site on a couple of mornings, and Ben buried arrowheads for her to dig up. He'd treat her discoveries with great sobriety, pretending to chart them and telling her about the people who'd made them thousands of years ago. What Cassie understood of his explanations Eden wasn't sure. But she'd listen with complete attention and take great care with her little artifacts.

By the end of that week Eden and Ben could hold hands without protest from Cassie. Cassie liked Ben, but liking Ben came with a little confusion and guilt. She would occasionally parrot things Eden had said to her, suddenly, out of context. Once she looked up from a book Kyle was reading her to say, "It's perfectly okay that I like Ben," and Kyle, masking his surprise, said, "Sure it is, honey. You can like anyone you want."

One night Ben bought a giant bubble wand, and he and Cassie spent most of the evening blowing huge iridescent bubbles that floated and bounced on the hot air of the cabin. Eden sat on the bed, watching Ben create bubbles the size of beach balls, then bubbles inside bubbles. Cassie giggled and screamed and begged for more. Suddenly she ran up to Ben where he sat on the sofa. She set her hands on his knees and looked him squarely in the eye.

"My daddy is always going to be my daddy," she said, letting him know that all this fun could never change that fact.

"Oh, yes," Ben said, his face very serious. "He absolutely is."

When Cassie finally tired of chasing bubbles, Eden laid her down on the bed, on top of the blue-and-white quilt, and joined Ben on the sofa.

"She's an extremely precocious kid," Ben said.

"Is that an insult or a compliment?"

"In this case, a compliment. I wish Bliss had more of Cassie's spunk. Cassie's very sure of herself. I can't imagine anyone ever hurting her and her not telling. Have you talked to her about it? Good touching and bad touching and all that?"

"Yes. She has a book about it, though it's in Santa Monica. I don't know how often you have to reinforce that kind of message. I don't want to make her paranoid."

"I think you can't reinforce it enough, but then my whole perspective on the subject is skewed. Sharon and I talked to Bliss any number of times, but apparently we screwed up somewhere along the way. We told her if anyone hurt her to come to us, never to keep it a secret no matter what that person told her. And still she didn't tell. I think it was because she was so convinced it was me. If I told her to keep it a secret, of course she would. If you can't trust your own dad, who can you trust?"

He would have moments like these from time to time, when Eden could feel him sinking, when his arm around her shoulders felt like lead. But they were becoming less frequent, less extreme, and she knew having Cassie around gave him more pleasure than pain.

She and Ben spent little time these days with Kyle and Lou. The pleasure the four of them had experienced together only a few weeks earlier—the tramposo, the easy conversations—had died a sudden death. Eden knew she was the only person who could lift the pall that had settled over Lynch Hollow, but she had no intention of doing so. She was content to let Cassie take responsibility for lightening the mood.

She missed the sexual side of her relationship with Ben more than she would have guessed. For over a year she had not cared about sex and had had no difficulty turning it down when it was offered to her, but that was before she met Ben, before her body had grown accustomed to the solid feel of him next to her in his narrow bed. She was all right when she wasn't around him, but seeing him without being able to hold him felt like a cruel sort of punishment. She didn't feel free to show him physical affection in front of Cassie, and he agreed it would be premature. One evening when he was leaving the house at Lynch Hollow, he took Eden in his arms to kiss her but pulled away abruptly when Cassie walked in the room.

"'Bye," he said instead of a kiss and, with a doleful smile on his forbidden lips, walked out the door.

Lou, who had witnessed the scene and must have read the frustration in Eden's face, said, "Now you have the tiniest sense of how your mother felt."

"What do you mean?" Eden asked.

"Being in love with someone you can't touch."

Eden scowled. "Stop it, Lou. There's no comparison."

But that night she lay in bed feeling renewed sympathy for her mother. Kate had loved a man as deeply as a woman could. She'd had him just once, and then suffered the pain of knowing she could never have him again.

The following day Kyle suggested they visit the caverns in Luray. She had been intending to go to the caverns since the day she arrived, but as she got Cassie ready for the forty-minute drive she felt apprehensive and knew why she'd been putting off the trip. She had not been in a cave since the day of her mother's death. No matter how lightly she had spoken of the cavern while working on the screenplay, she could not deny her uneasiness at the thought of stepping inside a limestone cave.

Lou said she wanted to stay home to paint, but as Eden climbed down the never-ending steps into the caverns she knew that Lou had not mentioned the real reason for not coming along: the caverns were not equipped for a wheelchair.

Once down in the bowels of the cavern, surrounded on all sides by curtains of stalactites and the cool, damp air, Eden felt trapped. The air seemed thin; she found herself breathing faster to pull in more oxygen. Her heart pounded against her ribs. Their guide was giving them his well-rehearsed talk about the cauliflower-shaped quartz deposits, the one hundred and twenty years it took for an inch of calcite to form on the stalactites, the blind albino shrimp that lived in the quiet pools of the caverns. How long had he said this tour would last? She craned her neck to see the way out of this massive cave.

"I can't see, Mommy," Cassie whined from somewhere in the region of Eden's hipbone.

"Come here, Cass." Ben bent down and picked Cassie up. He lifted her neatly onto his shoulders and she wrapped her hands around his forehead to hang on.

They moved into the next cave, Eden forcing one foot in front of the next. Though the air was cool, she felt perspiration dampen the hair at her temples.

"Isn't that amazing?" Ben said in her ear, and she realized she had heard nothing the guide had said. Then she felt Kyle's hand on her back.

"Are you all right, honey?" he asked.

"A little dizzy."

"Can you make it through the tour?"

She looked at Kyle's concerned blue eyes, looked away. "I'm not sure."

"Stay here." Kyle walked through the group of people to the guide and waited until his spiel in this cave was over. Eden saw him whisper something to the young man, saw the guide nod and speak into the walkie-talkie in his hand. Then Kyle spoke with Ben, who looked over at her briefly and nodded. Cassie leaned her chest against Ben's head, cupped her little fingers over his chin like the strap of a helmet.

Eden felt embarrassed as Kyle walked back to her.

"He's calling for another guide to come take you out. I'll go with you, and Ben and Cassie can go on with the tour."

The rest of the tour group disappeared into the next cavern. Eden watched Ben duck to avoid hitting Cassie's head in the low-ceilinged passageway before they were swallowed up by the earth. Then she was alone with Kyle, standing in a circle of stalactites that made her think of bat's teeth.

"I'm sorry," she said. "I just felt weak all of a sudden."

Kyle sat down on a rocky ledge. "I know what you mean," he said. "I felt the same way the first time I went into a cave after I sealed up the one at Lynch Hollow. It was years later, but the memories all came back." He took his camera case from his shoulder and set it next to him on the ledge. "The last time you and I were in that cave was pretty unpleasant. You were so little—just Cassie's age. I guess you don't remember much. The river was—"

"Kyle, don't, please. I don't want to talk about it." She thought she might get sick. She gripped the peak of the stalagmite next to her and let go of it quickly, recoiling from the cold, smooth, familiar feel of it. She remembered nothing of that last time in the cave. But afterward—she could see this very clearly—afterward the insides of Kyle's arms were scratched and raw. She remembered sitting next to him at the dinner table with her grandfather and some neighbors on a night when everyone was still and sad. She'd stared at Kyle's arms as he reached for something on the table, the cabbage or the sweet potato biscuits. She could see the pattern of those cuts, the long, jagged streaks of dried blood on the tanned skin of his arms. He'd seemed so old to her then. Actually, he'd been younger than she was now.

"A fellow called me last night," Kyle said. "From Hollywood. Said he'd heard you decided not to make the film about Kate, so he wants to do it. He asked if I'd be willing to talk with him."

"What?" Eden forgot her nausea. "Who was it?"

"William Crisper, Crispin, something like that."

Bill Crispin. "He does glitzy stuff, Kyle. He can sensationalize a day in the life of a carnation. Please don't talk to him."

"I don't intend to, although he was willing to pay me plenty to act as a consultant. Enough to save the site and then some. He said there'd be others interested in doing the film now that you've pulled out and he'd beat any other offer I got, but I told him the only person I'd help was you."

"Hellooo!" A smiling young woman suddenly appeared at the cave entrance and motioned them to follow her. "This happens all the time," she said, patting Eden's shoulder. "Don't give it a thought."

As they started out of the cave the guide suddenly gasped and stood back to take a good look at Eden. "Good Lord. You're Eden Riley."

Eden donned a smile. "Can we keep that just between us, please?" She could see the headline now: EDEN RILEY COLLAPSES IN CAVERN.

"Of course we can." The young woman led Eden and Kyle back up the stairs and outside into the hot August air. She took Eden's elbow and pointed her toward a bench. "You're all right now. Just have a seat and get your wind back."

"Thank you." Eden sat down next to Kyle as the guide walked back to the caverns.

"Ironic, isn't it?" Kyle said. "That a cave was the only place your mother felt comfortable?"

"Mmm." Eden's legs still felt rubbery, and she thought once again about Bill Crispin. It was unthinkable that he'd write the screenplay for a film on Katherine Swift. He'd turn out a piece of trash. Anyone besides herself who made that film would do it wrong. They'd distort Katherine Swift as she'd been distorted in the past. But at least they would never be able to learn what Eden had learned. Her heartbeat quickened. They couldn't, could they?

She looked at Kyle. "Who knows that you're my . . . not my uncle?"

"Just the four of us. You, me, Lou, and Ben. That genetic specialist I spoke with in New York died a year or so ago."

"So there's no way anyone could possibly learn the truth, right?"

Kyle sighed, and when he spoke she heard a tinge of sarcasm in his voice. "No, Eden. There's no way. Your reputation is safe."

The doors of the cavern exit opened and their tour group emerged. Eden felt cool air brush past her face and arms. Ben stepped out of the door holding Cassie's hand. Cassie was speaking to him in her usual animated style, and he leaned down to listen to her.

"Ben and Cassie seem to be getting along fine," Kyle said.

"I think she keeps him from missing Bliss so much."

"Well, I doubt that." Kyle lifted his camera case and slung it over his shoulder as he stood up. "It doesn't matter who you're with or what you're doing, you always miss your own child. Even when she's sitting right next to you."

40

King's Dominion amusement park had been too much for Cassie, and Ben was certain it was his fault. He'd worn her out. Eden had let him, of course. Not once did she say, "She's had enough, Ben." Eden seemed to know he needed this day to make up for the childless existence of the past year. But now both he and Eden would pay for their indulgence.

Cassie whined for the entire first hour of the drive back to the Valley—something he had not seen her do before. She'd finally reduced it to a whimper, and now she was slumped over her seat belt, sound asleep in the backseat of Eden's car.

Eden unfastened her own seat belt and got to her knees to reach into the backseat. "Can I use your sweatshirt to make a pillow for her?" she asked.

"Sure." Eden was wearing shorts, and he took his hand from the steering wheel to run his fingers up the inside of her thigh. Her body quivered perceptibly beneath his hand. "I'd forgotten how good you feel," he said.

"I hate this." She sat down again. "I'm going to get a house of my own in Coolbrook even if I have to pay for the entire year."

He knew having a place of her own where they could more easily be together was only one of her reasons for wanting to leave Lynch

Hollow. She was anxious to get away from Kyle and Lou, whom she was treating with a distance they didn't deserve.

She took his hand and held it on her thigh. "Have I told you today that I love you?" she asked.

"Not in words," he said. "But I could tell." He'd caught her eyes on him a few times that day, watching him through the sunglasses she'd worn to keep from being recognized. Every time he found her looking at him, there was a smile on her face. Approving. Accepting. She'd bought him a sweatshirt, taken a dozen pictures of him, locked her fingers in his as they walked. He knew very well that she loved him.

They stopped at the small supermarket on the edge of Coolbrook to pick up something for dinner. They had to wake Cassie from a deep sleep to take her into the store with them, and she was pouty and mean. They bought lettuce, a loaf of Italian bread, spaghetti sauce. Cassie dragged her feet after them, wailing, "I want Reese's Pieces, Mom. I want Magic Middles."

She stood between them in the checkout line, slumping dramatically against the counter. "Mom, I need them. Please may I have Reese's Pieces? Please, please, please?"

"You've had more than your share of junk today, Cassie," Eden said.

Ben pulled a ten out of his wallet, but Eden shook her head as she reached into her purse. He put his money away quietly, gratefully. She started to take a bill from her wallet, but her hand froze. He followed her eyes to the rack of tabloids above the counter and saw immediately what had caught her eye. There was a huge picture of Eden and Michael Carey, a wide black slash drawn between them, separating them. The headline proclaimed simply, unequivocally: EDEN DUMPS MICHAEL FOR CONVICTED SEX OFFENDER.

He touched Eden's arm and felt the stiffness in her body as she lifted the paper off the rack and set it upside down on the counter with their groceries. Then she slipped her sunglasses from her purse and put them on, although she was inside and it was nearly seven o'clock in the evening.

"Mom, I need them." Cassie's eyes were on the candy display next to them.

Eden spun around. "Cassie, I said no, damn it!"

It was the first time he'd heard her speak to Cassie in anything other than a loving tone. But his surprise was nothing compared to Cassie's, who shut up quickly and whose eyes filled from exhaustion and the sting of her mother's words. He set his hand on her little shoulder and squeezed.

Once in the car, Cassie began to cry. It was a whining cry, grating in its insistence as it filled the ominous silence between him and Eden. The tabloid rested on Eden's thighs. The picture—Eden in a clingy, low-cut dress and Michael in a white tuxedo—was barely visible in the dim light, and she wasn't looking at it. She stared out the window at the darkening cornfields as he drove.

"I want Reese's," Cassie crabbed, and then with a manipulative little catch to her voice, "I want my daddy."

"Cassie," Ben said, "would you please stop whining?"

Eden snapped her head toward him. "Don't yell at her!"

He felt as if she'd slapped him. He tightened his hands on the steering wheel and kept his eyes on the winding road.

He pulled into the clearing in front of his cabin and turned off the ignition. For a moment the three of them sat in the dark car, listening to the rise and fall of the cicadas' song, unable to summon the energy to unfasten a seat belt or open a door.

After a few minutes Eden looked over at him. "I'm sorry I yelled at you."

He tried to see her face, but it was too dark. "You knew this had to happen at some point," he said.

"No," she said quietly, reaching for the clasp of her seat belt. "I guess I didn't."

Inside the cabin he melted butter and chopped garlic for the bread while Eden made up the couch for Cassie, who was too wiped out to protest any longer. She climbed between the sheets and was asleep by the time Eden sat down at the table and opened the newspaper. He was annoyed at himself for the guilt he felt. He had kept nothing from her. He hadn't betrayed her, but her silence felt like an accusation.

He tore a head of iceberg lettuce apart and began slicing a tomato. Eden glanced over at Cassie before reading him the lead-in to the article.

"Head of Handicapped Children's Fund takes child molester as her lover."

He snapped the knife through the tomato and seeds flew, landing on the wall, on his shirt.

"Do they refer to me by name?" he asked.

"Yes. Someone really did his homework." She read a bit of the article to herself, then made a sound of disgust. "Sue Shepherd," she read, "president of the Handicapped Children's Fund, which was founded by Ms. Riley, said, 'If it's true, we certainly would no longer want her representing our organization.'" Eden's face was white, her chest rising and falling rapidly as she continued reading out loud. "A close friend stated, 'It's hard to believe Eden would get herself mixed up with someone like that, but her divorce left her pretty messed up, so who can say? They'll ban her children's films, no doubt about it. I can't believe she'd put her career in that sort of jeopardy.'

"Ironically, Michael Carey, who stands to lose the most by this turn of events, says he bears Eden no grudge. 'If it's true, then I'm worried for her. That's all I have to say on the subject.'"

It was worse, far worse than he'd imagined. He walked over to the table and set a tentative hand on her shoulder. "Eden, I don't know what to say."

She raised her hand until her fingers grasped his, and he was relieved by her touch. She looked up at him, her eyes huge and clear. "Make love to me," she said.

"Now?"

"Yes."

He looked at Cassie asleep on the sofa. "Where?"

Eden glanced at her daughter, then looked around the four dismal walls of the cabin until her eyes lit on the only possible source of privacy. "The bathroom."

He followed her into the bathroom, aware of his own raw need for her. But it was the sex of a pornographic movie, the kind of sex he thought a child molester might have. Neither of them felt tender.

The moment the door was closed behind them, Eden reached for the snap on his shorts and he pushed her T-shirt above her breasts. She leaned over the sink and he pounded into her, her own body hammering back at him with an anger he hoped was not meant for him. He came with a swiftness that shamed him, leaving her far behind. The cold white light of the bathroom suddenly hurt his eyes and he closed them to shut out the pain. He was breathing hard as he rested his cheek on Eden's back and slipped his hand between her legs.

"No." She brushed his fingers away and stood up. "I don't care." She pulled her T-shirt down over her breasts and lowered herself to his dingy bathroom floor, where she set her head on her arms and began to cry. Her weeping echoed in the cold metal and graying porcelain of the bathroom, and the walls tightened around him. He pulled up his shorts and sat next to her, trying to take her in his arms, but she was rigid—a jutting mass of elbows, knees, shoulders—and impossible to get close to. He stroked her hair, hunting for softness, then rested his hand on her hip where her warm bare skin met the wretched linoleum of the floor.

"Eden, please. Let's go in the other room."

She shook her head without lifting it from her knees. "It's not fair," she said.

"I know."

"Everything was so good. I'd finally gotten close to Lou and Kyle, I had a wonderful film to work on. I'd fallen in love. Now it's all coming apart at the seams." Her words were muffled. He had to lean close to hear her.

He sat back with a sigh. "Here's what I think you should do," he said. She didn't raise her head, and he continued. "Call this garbage pail newspaper. Give them an interview. Tell them you had seen me briefly and I'd kept my past from you. Once you found out, you were shocked and outraged. You dropped me like a hot potato."

She raised her face slowly and he was unsettled by the hurt in her eyes. "Could you let go of me that easily?" she asked.

"You've worked so hard to get where you are, Eden. I don't want you to lose all that—your career, the Children's Fund, the fans that love and respect you. There's no reason you should have to pay for my problems."

She leaned her head back against the wall and he saw determination replace the pain in her eyes. "I'm not going to let the media run my life, Ben." She wiped her cheeks with the back of her hand. "I've had a good career. I've had fame and money. I've had the Children's Fund. But what I've never had"—she reached out and touched his cheek, let her fingers linger there for a moment—"is someone like you."

41

She refused to take any phone calls the next day at Lynch Hollow, and Kyle finally asked Michael and Nina not to call again. "Eden will call you when she wants to talk," he said, and she was grateful and guilty for his intervention.

But then Wayne called. It was ten o'clock, too late for him to be calling to speak with Cassie. Eden took the phone from Kyle's hand and waited until he had left the kitchen before sitting down at the table, steeling herself for whatever the next few minutes would bring.

"Hi, Wayne," she said.

"Eden. What the hell have you gotten yourself into?"

She sighed. "He's innocent, Wayne. The paper blew the whole thing out of proportion."

"Look, Eden, I'm trying to stay calm about this. I'm trying to stay rational. But I did some checking on this guy. I have a friend who knew the prosecuting attorney on his case. The man's an abomination, Eden. What he put his kid through . . . Are you letting Cassie around him?"

"Cassie is fine. She's having a great time."

"Do you know what that pig did to his daughter?"

"His name is Ben, Wayne. And I know what he was accused of doing. I also know he didn't do it."

"Oh, I see. You know more than the judge and jury. Eden, please listen to me. My friend says Alexander is a pathological liar. On the surface he comes across like a great guy. Sincere. Honest as the day is long. But he has no morals. He's not capable of caring about anyone but himself."

"You wouldn't say that if you knew him and knew how much he loves his daughter."

"Eden, Jesus Christ! He abused his daughter. Not just once, either."

"I don't see the point in continuing this conversation."

Wayne was quiet for a moment. "I think this is all my fault somehow. I didn't handle the divorce very well and I guess it was harder for you than I realized. Maybe you're desperate or—"

"Don't flatter yourself, Wayne. I'm not desperate."

"Well, my main concern—and I hope yours as well—is Cassie's welfare. If you insist on seeing this jerk you'll have to send her back to me."

"Forget it. You had her for an entire month. She's mine now. And she's perfectly happy here."

"I don't want her around him, Eden. If you don't send her back voluntarily I'll go back to court. I'll get her easily—you can see that, can't you? Your judgment is obviously out of line."

She squeezed the phone cord between her fingers as though she could shut him up if she pressed hard enough.

"Does Kyle condone you seeing this guy?"

"Kyle knows he's innocent."

"You've all lost your minds. Let me talk to Kyle."

"No. I don't want to drag him into—"

"Look, Eden, I'll give you the weekend to think about this before I do anything. But keep him away from Cassie, do you hear me?"

"Yes."

She hung up and within a few seconds the phone rang again. She heard Kyle pick it up in the living room, heard his muffled end of the conversation and knew he was talking to Wayne. She went upstairs to check on Cassie, who was smiling in her sleep. Eden sat on the edge of the folding bed and smoothed the hair back from her daughter's cheek. If she thought for an instant Cassie was at risk, she would never see Ben again. Never. Surely Wayne knew that.

She met Kyle in the kitchen. "I hate to ask you to do this, Kyle, but could you keep an eye on Cassie? She's sound asleep and I need to see Ben. I won't be long."

"All right." Kyle switched on the porch light and walked her outside. "That was Wayne on the phone. He's very serious, Eden. I wish I could say you should stick by Ben, but he's going to cost you, honey. He's going to cost you a lot."

Eden spun around to face him. "And what do you think it would cost me to make a movie about my mother screwing her brother?"

Kyle looked as though he'd been stung. "We were cousins," he said, quietly, weakly, and he turned to walk back into the house.

She took a step after him. "Kyle, I'm sorry. I—" She jumped as the screen door slammed closed on her apology.

Ben was nearly asleep when his phone rang.

"Is this Ben Alexander?" It was a male voice, sharp and unfamiliar.

"Yes."

"This is Wayne Cramer. Eden Riley's ex-husband."

Ben sat up. He had not expected this phone call. Perhaps he should have. "Yes?"

"I just spoke with Eden. I explained to her that if she intends to continue seeing you, I'll fight to get our daughter back. And I'll win."

Ben shut his eyes. No doubt he would win. No doubt at all. "Well," he said, "I guess if I knew the little about me that you know, I'd feel the same way," he said. "But I can assure you Cassie's safe. She's a wonderful kid and—"

"Oh, Christ, don't you fucking dare tell me about my daughter. If you touch her, I swear I'll kill you."

Ben knew this man's anguish. He knew his fear. "Wayne, I know you think I'm guilty, but I'm not. I understand how you feel because I feel the same way. I worry that someone else might have hurt my daughter and I think about that day and night. That person might still be around her and I can't—"

"Look, I just want you to know that Eden's going to lose Cassie along with everything else. Are you worth that?"

Ben swallowed. "No one's worth that," he said, but he heard the phone slam down at the other end as Wayne Cramer hung up on him.

He was sitting on his porch when Eden pulled into the clearing.

"What are you doing here?" he asked as she sat down next to him on the bench.

"I needed to see you, but I thought you'd be asleep. Why are you outside?"

"Thinking." He set his hand on her back, played with the ends of her hair. "You asked Kyle and Lou to sit?"

"I had to. Wayne just called me." She sounded disgusted. "He read the paper, I guess, and he's worried about Cassie."

"He'd be a lousy father if he weren't." He wrapped a strand of her hair around his finger, watched how it caught the glow of his porch light. "He called me, too, Eden."

"Oh, no." She turned to look at him. "I'm sorry, Ben."

"He's going to try to get Cassie back."

"Let him try. I have a wonderful lawyer."

"Listen to me, Eden. I know from experience that this is a very difficult thing to fight."

She shook her head. "I think he's bluffing. He's just all wound up right now. He talked to someone close to the case who said you were a pathological liar and a horrendous human being, so he's convinced that's what you are. The fact that I know different means nothing to him."

"No. I'm sure it doesn't."

She sighed. "For the moment, I'd like to pretend there's nothing wrong."

"I'm not sure I can do that."

"Please, Ben? Could we dance?"

He laughed. "Dance?"

"Are you too tired?"

"No." He stood up. He would go along with her, whatever she wanted.

Once he was holding her, moving to the music, he understood

what she was trying to do. She wanted to recapture the early moments of their relationship when there had been so little to worry about, but she couldn't relax. He felt her agitation beneath his arms.

"Let's just make love," she said, pulling away from him. She took his hand and led him to the bed. He let her undress him, let her discover for herself that his body could offer her no escape tonight. "Oh Ben," she nearly wailed in her disappointment. "I need to feel connected to you."

"Come here." He pulled her down into his arms and she wrapped her leg over him as if she was struggling to get as close to him as she could.

"Ben?"

"Yes?" Her hair brushed against his cheek as she raised her head to look at him.

"Have you ever lied to me?" she asked.

He thought for a moment. "Maybe through omission, in those days after we first met and I didn't want to tell you about Bliss. I might have told a few white lies then for the same reason. I don't remember."

She sighed and shifted closer to him as though satisfied by his answer, but he was disturbed. Have you ever lied to me? It was the first seed of doubt he'd seen in her. Creeping in. Creeping between them. She no longer completely trusted him.

42

Kyle and Lou left for New York the following day. Kyle didn't bother to say good-bye to Eden as he got behind the wheel of the Jeep, and his wordless anger, his wounded pride, felt like a weight on her chest as she watched them pull out of the Lynch Hollow driveway.

She and Ben—and Cassie—had the house to themselves for two days and one night. They spent the morning cleaning the downstairs and weeding the garden, avoiding any discussion about Wayne and the problem that loomed over them.

In the afternoon they drove to Coolbrook Park to let Cassie ride the ponies that had suddenly appeared in town. Cassie barely waited for Ben to park the car before she flew out the door and over to the makeshift ring someone had set up next to the parking lot. There were three ponies. Horses, actually. Tired-looking. Swaybacked and thin. They tromped around in a circle led by glassy-eyed teenagers.

Cassie was jumping up and down by the time Eden and Ben caught up with her. "Can I go on the yellow one?" she asked.

"Sure." Ben took a bill out of his pocket and gave it to the girl holding the reins of the aging blond stallion. Eden sat down on a bench to watch as Ben lifted Cassie onto the horse, and she knew she was seeing her entire world in that moment. The smile on Ben's face as he raised Cassie into the air and the excitement in Cassie's eyes as she hugged the saddle with her little nut-brown legs filled the universe. She could not live without either of these things.

Wayne, please, please don't do this.

Cassie clung to the horse with great concentration and an uncertain grin. When the horse started to move, she let out a little scream. She looked wobbly in the saddle and Ben walked next to her, steadying her with his hand on the seat of her pink shorts. Eden's smile faded. She wished he'd move that hand. He could achieve the same result with his hand on her back, couldn't he? He was talking to Cassie, looking up at her as they trudged slowly around the dirt track. When they returned to the ring entrance, Ben lifted Cassie off the horse and his hands slipped under her shirt as he set her on the ground.

You're being paranoid, she told herself as Cassie ran toward her.

"Did you see me, Mom? Did you see how high up I was? His name is Dusty. He's my favorite horse in the whole world."

"Do you want to go again?" Ben asked.

"Yes!"

Eden started to say no but caught herself. She would not give credibility to an irrational fear. She reached into her wallet and handed Ben a dollar bill.

"Are you all right?" he asked. "You look a little pale."

"I'm fine."

This time when Ben lifted Cassie onto Dusty's arthritic-looking back, Eden turned away.

On the drive home Cassie and Ben talked about Dusty. Ben told Cassie about his first horseback ride, something about Sam and their grandparents, and Eden felt apart from the two of them, as if a glass shield divided the car in two. She could barely make out their words.

Once they reached Lynch Hollow, Ben cornered Eden in the kitchen.

"What is it?" he asked.

"What's what?"

"Something's got you upset."

"I can't imagine what," she snapped. "My ex-husband's only trying to take my daughter away from me. What the hell do I have to be upset about?"

He stared at her for a moment before he caught her shoulders and drew her toward him. He kissed her, slowly, deeply, and she felt her fear disintegrate with his touch. When he started to pull away from her, she wouldn't let him go.

"I'm sorry, Ben," she said. "I'm acting crazy. I'm thinking crazy things. I'm just scared."

She felt better by evening. They played board games with Cassie, ancient ones like Uncle Wiggly and Candyland they found tucked away in the hall closet. Her paranoia from that morning's pony ride seemed ridiculous by dinnertime. She put fresh sheets on Lou and Kyle's bed while Ben barbecued chicken. They would have a good night tonight.

"Do you still need to connect to me?" he'd asked her earlier, in the middle of Candyland.

"Yeah." She'd smiled at him over Cassie's head. "What are my chances?"

"I'd say the probability of a mutually satisfying connection is good to excellent."

Cassie stood up and clapped her hand over Ben's mouth. "Stop using those big words!" she demanded.

After dinner Eden did the dishes while Ben played cards with Cassie at the kitchen table. She was putting away the last plate when the phone rang. She considered letting the machine pick it up but thought better of it. It might be Lou or Kyle.

"Hello?"

"My God. Is that Eden Riley answering the phone herself?"

"Nina."

"Well, I have a surprise for you, kiddo. Michael and I are in a little hamlet called Coolbrook. Ever hear of it?"

"You're not."

"Yes, indeed we are. We figured if you refused to take our calls, we'd just have to force ourselves on you. So please tell us how to get from here to there. Lynch Hollow, right? I'm sure someone around here can give us directions if you choose not to."

"Nina." She ran a hand through her hair and looked helplessly at Ben. "Please don't come here. There's a hotel in Coolbrook. Why don't the two of you stay there tonight and I'll meet you for lunch tomorrow?"

"No way, Eden. We're here because we care about you and we're scared shitless by what's going on with you. You're going to see us tonight if we have to kidnap you."

"All right. There's a restaurant just outside Coolbrook." She gave them directions to Sugar Hill. "I'll meet you there in an hour."

"Michael's with her?" Ben asked when she got off the phone.

"Yes. Cassie, would you go watch TV for a little bit?"

"But, Mom, it's my turn to say 'Go Fish.'"

"Come on." She scooted Cassie out of the room. "I need to talk to Ben."

Ben waited until he heard Cassie switch on the TV in the living room. "Do you want me to go with you?" he asked.

Eden laughed. "That would certainly foil their plan," she said. "They're here to tell me what a fool I am to be seeing you. They could hardly do that with you sitting right there."

"You are a fool to be seeing me."

"Please don't say that. And thanks for offering, but I don't want you to come with me. We'd both be very uncomfortable. Do you mind watching Cassie? It's almost her bedtime."

"No, I don't mind." He picked up the cards from the table. "But would you please get her ready for bed before you go? Into her pajamas, I mean?"

"Of course." She understood. He wanted to protect himself from anything she might imagine.

It was a Friday night and Sugar Hill was packed. She should have suggested someplace less popular. But she found Michael and Nina easily, sitting at a corner table far from the bar. They greeted her quietly, not wanting to attract attention.

Michael squeezed her hand and grinned at her. He had on a blue shirt open at the neck, and his hair was swept back from his face and longer than she'd ever seen it. Still, he was so unmistakably Michael Carey that she wondered how he'd gotten in here without all the women recognizing him.

"You look beautiful," he said, "but awfully white. You need some California sunshine, doesn't she, Nina?"

"She needs some common sense," Nina said.

"Look, guys, I'm here because you've given me no choice. But if you intend to insult me and rip me apart, just tell me now so I can leave and save you the trouble."

"We're not here to insult you, are we, Michael? We just need to see with our own eyes that you're okay."

"Well, you can see that, can't you? I'm just fine. I've had a good summer and everything's—"

"Eden, slow down," Michael said. "Relax. You don't need to be so defensive. I have something to say to you, okay? Let me just get it out." He took in a big breath, and she knew he had rehearsed this. "I've been in love with you for a long time, but I have no reason to believe you'll ever feel the same about me. I tried to make you fall for me, but it didn't work, did it?" He smiled. "So I know that most likely you and I will never end up together. I'm just telling you I know that so you won't think that's what's motivating me here. It's not." He took a sip of his drink and held the glass up to her nose. "Plain orange juice," he said. "A.A. says one substance is as bad as the next, so I've quit them all. All those wonderful mind-altering, pain-dulling substances. I'm clean now, Eden. I've been clean since before you left and sometimes I hate it but I know it's best in the long run. I know the stuff was destroying me. It was going to ruin my career. Thanks to you I saw that in time, before I went down the tubes. So what I'm saying is, what you're doing is not that different. If you keep seeing Ben Alexander, it's going to destroy you. It—"

"Michael . . ." she said.

"Shh." He set his finger to her lips. "Let me finish. I don't think you realize how nasty this thing has gotten already. You're very isolated out here, so you don't know what people are saying and—"

"You're going to be blackballed, Eden," Nina cut in.

"It wouldn't be so bad if you were a different sort of actress with a different sort of image," Michael said. "But you've built your career around children. You're the daughter of the loco but lily-white Katherine Swift. You've done more single-handedly to help handicapped kids than any other actress around. Do you remember how worried you were when *Heart of Winter* came out? Remember how you worried you'd lose your fans? Well, Christ, Eden, if you'd gone out and looked for a way to lose your fans, you couldn't have done a better job of it than taking up with this guy."

Hopelessness hit her, dragged her down like an undertow. She looked at her own drink, studied the rim of the glass. She wouldn't let herself cry in front of them. "But he's innocent." The words came out in a whisper. "He really is. And I'm in love with him and I think it's terribly unfair that I should have to give him up just because the rest of the world thinks he's guilty."

Nina covered her hand, and when she spoke her voice was soft, laced with pity. "Sweetie, what in the world makes you so sure he's innocent?"

"I know him."

Nina looked at Michael, who, on cue, lifted a manila folder from his lap to the table. "I've been doing a little research." He opened the folder and pulled out a stack of photocopied newspaper articles. "Have you seen any of this stuff from his trial, or do you only know what he's told you?"

"Just what he's told me," she admitted. She felt like a child, sinking lower in her chair while the two of them grew in stature. She looked at the article on the top of the stack. Michael had marked certain paragraphs with a yellow marker, and there was a picture of Ben. Michael turned the article toward her so she could see the picture.

"Is that him?" he asked.

The black-and-white photograph was so unflattering that in and of itself it was incriminating. Ben looked swarthy, his beard jet black against white skin, and he stared unsmilingly into a space somewhere above the camera.

"I would barely recognize him," she said. She was embarrassed. Michael, with his beautiful black hair, his huge, clear dark eyes, asking her if this ruined-looking man was her lover.

Michael set the article in front of him again and began reading the marked portions. He had the articles in chronological order and she followed Ben's ordeal from arrest to conviction. The outburst of his guilty plea had made the headline for two days straight. Bliss was described as "the star of the show" by one reporter. "She had most of the courtroom, her father included, in tears," Michael read. "The poised and lucid four-year-old identified the defendant, Ben Alexander, as her father and clearly stated that it was her 'daddy' who hurt her. After his daughter's testimony, Alexander became ill and had to be escorted from the courtroom."

There were other pictures of Ben and one of Sharon, dabbing her eyes with a tissue. And finally a quote from the prosecuting attorney: "I'm proud of this jury. I've never been more certain of a verdict in my entire career." Michael closed the folder and looked at her.

Eden was shaken. If she had not known Ben, if she had been one of the hordes of people following his trial, she would have thought far beyond a shadow of a doubt that he was guilty. She would have wanted him hanged. She shook her head. "I still can't imagine that the Ben Alexander I know . . ." She saw his hand on the seat of Cassie's shorts and remembered Wayne's words, Alexander is a pathological liar.

"Are you one hundred percent certain he's innocent?" Nina asked.

Eden hesitated just long enough to let herself know that, no, she was no longer one hundred percent certain.

"Because if you're not, Eden," Nina said, "you can't take that kind of risk with Cassie."

Cassie was with him. Eden looked at her watch and saw that her hand was trembling. Right this minute he'd be putting her to bed. She let out a small, audible gasp.

Michael leaned toward her. "You've lost your objectivity, Eden."

"You're in love with him." Nina put her hand on Eden's shoulder. "You've slept with him. So you had to make him innocent in your own mind."

"Right," Michael said. "You had to justify your feelings somehow."

"And it's one thing for you to be involved with him." Nina was so close that Eden smelled the alcohol on her breath. "It's entirely another for you to involve your daughter."

"Cassie's with him right now," Eden said.

Michael leaned back so suddenly she jumped. "You left this guy"—he held up the stack of papers—"with your four-year-old daughter?"

"He cares about her," she said. "I know he does."

"I'm sure he cared about his own daughter, too." Michael leafed through the articles and then read her a quote from a psychiatrist. "Men like Ben Alexander can't help themselves. Their behavior is out of their control. Even with treatment, the prognosis isn't good. Those men who are aware of their problem will struggle to keep themselves out of trouble by avoiding temptation whenever possible, but it's often a losing battle."

She thought of Ben asking her to change Cassie into her pajamas before she left. Was he trying to avoid temptation? "Oh, God." She reached for her purse. "I'd better go."

"One more thing, sweetie." Nina grabbed her arm. "You have to rethink your decision on the Katherine Swift film."

"Christ, Nina." Michael glowered at her. "Not now."

But Nina ignored him. "Bill Crispin's gearing up to do it and I hate to see that cretin make a mint off your idea."

"I can't do it, Nina."

Nina stood up and grabbed the check from the table. "Let me pay this and then we can all leave. Talk some sense into her, Michael."

Michael pulled his chair closer to Eden's and put his arm around her protectively. "Ignore her," he said as Nina walked toward the cashier. "You don't need to think about the film right now."

She leaned against him. He smelled good. He smelled safe. "I found out something while I was doing the research, Michael." She looked at him, felt his hand soft on her arm. "Don't tell this to a soul. Not Nina. Not anyone. I found out that my uncle—the one I'm staying with—is actually my father. He and my mother were cousins, but his parents adopted her, so they were raised as brother and sister. They were lovers."

Michael's eyes widened as her words began to make sense to him. "Katherine Swift had sex with her brother?"

"Shh. Yes. How can I possibly write the screenplay knowing that?"

Michael looked toward the front of Sugar Hill where Nina was paying the bill. "Leave it out," he said. "Forget you know it. Write the screenplay with Matthew Riley as your father. No one will be any the wiser."

She looked at Michael. He had Matthew Riley's warm brown eyes, she was certain of it. "I miss you," she said. "I miss my house and the ocean and L.A."

"Everybody misses you, Eden. Everybody's worried sick about you. Come home, please. I'll help you with the film." He drew away from her as Nina returned to the table.

"All set," Nina said. "We're out of here."

Eden stood up. "I'll do the film, Nina," she said. "Tell Crispin to find something else to sink his fangs into."

"Hurray!" Nina said, too loudly, and some of the diners looked up from their tables and stared.

Michael walked her to her car. "Take this." He handed her the manila folder through the window. "Read it when you start losing perspective."

She set it next to her on the seat and looked up at him.

"If I call you tomorrow, will you speak to me?" he asked.

"Yes."

He squeezed her shoulder, then let her go.

The house was quiet when she reached Lynch Hollow. She forced herself to calmly turn on the kitchen light, calmly set her purse and the folder on the table. "Ben?"

"In here."

He was in the living room working on a broken table lamp Kyle had been trying to repair. He looked up when she walked into the room. "How'd it go?"

"All right. Is Cassie asleep?"

"Yeah, just. After two stories, five glasses of water, and three kisses. Manipulative kid you've got there."

"I'll go check on her."

"Why don't you tell me what happened with Michael and Nina first?" He patted the sofa next to him.

"I'll be back in a second."

She felt breathless, nauseated, as she sat on the edge of Cassie's bed. She watched her sleep in the light from the hallway until she could stand it no longer. "Cassie?" She shook her shoulder.

Cassie rolled onto her back and opened her eyes.

"Hi, baby," Eden said.

"You're supposed to be out."

"I just got home. Did you have fun tonight?"

Cassie closed her eyes again and nodded and within seconds had fallen back to sleep. Eden lowered the sheet and studied Cassie's yellow shorty pajamas and long brown legs. What was she looking for? A mark? A clue? She covered her daughter again and walked downstairs.

Ben was in the kitchen. He stood above the table, leafing through the articles Michael had given her. He looked up at her, his eyes very gray, very cool.

"You woke her up," he said.

"Yes."

"Did you check her over real carefully, Eden? Because we child molesters are pretty sneaky. We know how to cover our tracks."

"Don't talk that way, Ben, please."

"Looks like you've got your reading cut out for you." He nodded toward the articles.

She shivered. "I'm mixed up, Ben. I don't know what to do. I love you, but . . ."

"But what? Let me finish your sentence, all right? I love you, Ben, but I can't take the chance that you just might be guilty after all." He stepped closer to her. "I could handle it if you said you loved me, but Wayne would get Cassie if you stayed with me. Or even, you love me, but it would ruin your career if you stayed with me. But I can't take your suspicions. You know me as well as I can let anyone know me and you're still not convinced, are you?" He grabbed her shoulders. "Are you?"

"In my heart I am, Ben, but . . ."

He let go of her and walked to the door. "I'll make it easy for you, Eden. It's over. That's what all this is leading up to, anyway, isn't it?

If not today, then tomorrow or the next day. Because your suspicions are multiplying by the minute. I know how it works. Once you start doubting me, there's not a thing I can do or say that will make a difference." He reached for the door, then turned to face her again, and this time his eyes were furious. "God damn you for trusting me as long as you did."

43

She wanted to wait until morning to call him. She moved through the house, through the rooms, like a sleepwalker, watching the windows for the first hint of dawn. When it was still black out she sat down on Lou and Kyle's bed and stared at the phone. If Michael and Nina had not come, she and Ben would be in this bed right now. Maybe sleeping, maybe not. But she would be with him. She drew her knees up, hugging them with her arms. Her stomach ached from uncertainty and doubt, from not knowing, never being able to know, the truth about Ben. He had ended it last night. He'd made the decision for her, but he was right. If she had not found the strength to end their relationship last night, she would have today or tomorrow. She had to. She could not allow Cassie to be the victim of his past, or God forbid, his present.

Was he able to sleep tonight? Or was he lying awake wondering, as he used to, what he had to live for? Was he thinking about the Valium?

She dialed the phone and clutched the receiver as it rang at his end. Five rings. Ten. Maybe she'd misdialed. She hung up, dialed again. If he didn't answer she would put Cassie in the car and drive up there. She would—

"Hello." His voice was flat and controlled. He was wide awake and he knew who was calling.

"I just wanted to be sure you're all right." She braced herself for his sarcasm or his wrath.

"Thank you." The sincerity in his voice started her tears again and for a moment she couldn't speak.

"I'm sitting on Lou and Kyle's bed," she said finally. "I wish you could be here next to me."

Another long silence stretched between them. She could hear a radio playing softly at his end. The oldies station, no doubt.

"You should call Wayne tomorrow," Ben said. "Save him the trouble of getting a lawyer."

"Ben, I want to see you."

"There's no point to it, Eden."

She shut her eyes. "I love you but I can't have you. Just like my mother."

"What do you mean, like your mother?"

"Nothing. Ben, promise me you won't hurt yourself."

"If you think I'm so dishonest, why would you think I'd keep a promise?"

"Ben . . ."

"Go back to bed, Eden." He hung up, so quietly that she thought he was still on the line, and it wasn't until she heard the dial tone that she hung up herself.

Kyle and Lou returned the following day, and she waited until they'd unpacked and settled in the living room with the newspaper before telling them that she and Ben had split up. They didn't seem surprised, and she guessed her swollen eyes and red nose had given her away.

She sat down on the hassock near Lou's chair and told them about the articles Michael had brought her. "I found myself doubting him," she said. "How could I justify having him around Cassie if I'm not absolutely positive about him?"

Lou nodded. "I'm sorry, dear."

"Is Ben all right?" Kyle asked.

"I'm worried about him," she said.

Kyle looked at his watch. "I'll take a drive up there in a bit and see how he's doing."

Eden flattened her damp palms against her thighs. "Cassie and I have reservations to go back to L.A. next Monday," she said. "We'll fly out of National."

Lou glanced at Kyle, who was toying with the lamp Ben had been working on. He turned the switch and light filled the shade.

"Ben fixed it," Eden said.

"I can see that," said Kyle.

Eden licked her lips. "I've also decided to go back to work on the film," she said. "Only I'm going to leave it with Matt Riley as my father."

Kyle switched the lamp off and turned it upside down to study the base.

"Well," Lou said. "You've made a lot of decisions this weekend."

Kyle set the lamp back on the table and stood up. "Need anything from the kitchen, Lou?" he asked.

"Kyle," Eden said, and this time her voice shook. "Since I'm working on the screenplay again, could I please see the next notebook?"

Kyle frowned at her. "Why bother when you can just make up the past to suit yourself?"

"Ky," Lou chided.

"The journals are yours, Eden." Kyle turned his back on her as he headed for the kitchen.

For the rest of the day she felt alone despite Cassie's constant entertainment and the phone calls from Michael and Nina. Michael was saintly in his low-pressure support, but Nina wanted her to make a statement to the press.

"You have to, Eden. It'll be short and simple. He seduced you. You were vulnerable, being away from Michael all those weeks. You fell for his charm, never knowing his sordid, odious crime."

"Nina, no," she said. "I can't say any of that."

"You have no choice, kiddo. We have major damage to undo."

"I don't care."

"Well, I care. And you will too as soon as you get your head out of the clouds and start thinking like yourself again. Even if you don't care about what this will do to yourself, Eden, think of the Children's Fund."

"I'm not the only person in the world who can represent the Children's Fund."

"Will you please think, Eden? You're being so dense you're driving me crazy. The Children's Fund is already suffering because of this. It's losing its support base. You know how quickly something like that can happen. People start to think that Eden Riley isn't the wonderful person they thought she was. If she's capable of poor judgment in one area, she's capable of it in others. She's probably embezzling the money she's taking in, or—"

"Oh Nina, for heaven's sake, shut up. You're getting carried away."

"I am not. Look, I didn't want to tell you this, but Sue Shepherd is fit to be tied. She said some of the Fund's biggest contributors have already pulled out."

Eden closed her eyes. "Isn't it enough that I've broken up with him?"

"No, sweetie, it's not enough. We need a statement."

"Can't I at least say that I think he may be innocent?" she asked.

"No, Eden. He was convicted. Besides, we have to convince everyone you're over him."

"Let me work on it awhile," Eden said. She needed a reprieve.

She called Ben that evening with the intention of telling him about the statement. It would be all right. After all, Ben himself had suggested she go to the press after they'd first seen the tabloid. Still, she wanted to let him know how public it would be, how sorry she was that she had to do it. But he gave her no chance.

"Eden, don't call me, all right?" he said the moment he heard her voice. "It makes it harder." He told her he wanted to bring the dollhouse over the following day but would do it at a time when she was out, and she realized how serious he was about not wanting to see her or speak to her. She was not being fair. Calling him was selfish. Asking for his blessing on a statement that was going to add to his grief was cruel, a way to ease her guilt.

"Call when you want to come over," she said. "And I'll leave."

When Nina called back, Eden read her the statement. She had

avoided the word "seduced" and any reference to Michael Carey, but the statement was still ugly and self-serving. And Nina wanted it uglier.

"You don't sound repulsed enough," Nina said.

Eden argued with her for another hour over the wording, and then over the insertion of commas—anything to put off the release of the statement.

"Okay," Nina said. "Are we finally ready to go on this?"

Eden was drained by the last hour, the last few days. "I can't do this to him," she said.

"This is self-defense, kiddo. It's either you or him. Okay?"

Eden looked down at the handwritten statement on her lap. It was not much, just a few blue scribbles on white lined paper.

"Eden?"

"Okay."

Her regret was immediate. She tried to call Nina back the second she hung up the phone but the line was busy. What had she done? She'd rushed into this, let herself be coerced.

She sent Cassie down to dinner without her, and an hour later Kyle knocked on her door. She sat up against the headboard of her bed as he lowered himself into the rocker. He was holding one of the notebooks.

"Cassie said you were crying," he said.

"Have you seen Ben today?"

Kyle nodded. "He's mechanical. Withdrawn. Doesn't want to talk."

"I have to make a statement to the press denouncing him. I'm going to betray him." The tears threatened again as she waited for Kyle to berate her. She wanted to be scolded, but Kyle looked as though he hadn't heard her. He held the notebook up.

"Just one more after this," he said. Then he sighed. "I wish you wouldn't leave so soon, Eden. I'm afraid it will be like it was before, with us hardly ever getting to see you."

"I have to go, Kyle. I was crazy to think I could live outside L.A. It's the only place I feel secure."

"Like an animal in a zoo, huh? You know someone will feed you and clean up after you and you never have to worry about the real world outside your cage." He stood up and put the notebook on her bed. "But it's a cage just the same, Eden."

She didn't read the journal that night, and once again she slept poorly. In the morning Lou returned from town with muffins and the *Washington Post*. The statement was in the Style section, and in black and white it took on a disturbing credibility. No one would doubt her sincerity. No one would doubt Ben's devious nature and irrefutable guilt. Eden read the statement twice and went into the bathroom to throw up.

She walked to the site later that morning. Ben was crouched in the third pit, dusting the earth. He looked up as she neared him but lowered his eyes again quickly.

"Leave me alone, Eden," he said.

"You saw the paper?"

He sat back on his heels and looked up at her again. "I went into Miller's Bakery this morning and Sara Jane Miller wouldn't sell me a doughnut. 'We reserve the right to refuse to serve scum,' she said. 'How could you deceive a sweet girl like Eden Riley?' she said."

"Ben, I'm so sorry."

"So am I."

She took a step closer to the pit.

"Look, Eden." He stood up. "This is the one place where I can lose myself and I don't have to think about anything. This goddamned hole in the ground is it, okay? The least you can do is let me work here in peace."

She turned and walked back across the field and into the woods. She stopped at the entrance to the cavern and set her hands on the cool surface of the huge boulder Kyle had rolled into place. She looked up at the dark triangular opening above the boulder and shuddered. Her mother's world had been inside this cave. Her life and her death. The journal was almost finished. Everything was coming to an end.

January 5, 1956

I love the word "sacrifice." I love the hard and soft sound of it, the hard and soft meaning. Making it is the hard part, feeling good afterwards is the soft. Motherhood is like that, always having to put Eden's needs ahead of my own. I haven't had time to write more than a word or two since she was born, but I'm not complaining. The reward is great, because she is truly a beautiful, flowering little child. I like knowing that I'm absolutely necessary to someone else.

For Christmas, Kyle and Lou sent Eden a wonderful rocking horse carved from wood and painted a shiny gold with real horsehair for its mane and tail. Eden is seven months old now and not yet too impressed with any of her gifts, but I held her on the horse and Susanna took pictures we can send to Kyle.

He and Lou sent pictures of Machu Picchu and the other incredible archaeological sites in Peru. I'm a little envious of their work, but I know I could never go someplace like that. Even little trips to Coolbrook terrify me these days. It scares me sometimes. I cannot raise a child in a cave.

May 22, 1956

Kyle and Lou just left to return to Peru after a wonderful three-week visit. Kyle had a hard time tearing himself away from Eden. He adores her. I've tried hard over the past year to let him feel as though he knows her. I've sent pictures each week, and letters describing every new tooth, every cute little thing she does. Some men—most, I guess—would be bored by this. But Kyle writes back asking for more. He doesn't want Eden to feel like a stranger to him.

I offered them my big bedroom and double bed on the second floor but they refused to put me out. Instead they slept in my old room, the one Kyle and I used to share.

We spent much of their visit in the cavern where I've moved my typewriter again now that the weather's warmer. I see a difference in the way Kyle acts with Eden in the house, where Daddy and Susanna are around, and in the cave, where he is free to act more like a father than an uncle. Eden says da-da-da-da all the time—it is about all she can say so far—and I loved hearing her say that to Kyle. It made him nervous though. "Say Uncle Kyle, Eden," he'd say to her, and Eden would respond "Da-da-da-da."

She took her first steps right into his arms. For months now, she's been walking by holding on to my hands. I was walking her around the cave one day when Kyle crouched down and said, "Come to me, Eden," and stretched out his arms. I let go of her hands and she staggered over to him, giggling all the way. That led Kyle to believe that she will never learn a thing unless he's around. He's taken to telling me how to raise her now, which amuses me and makes Lou roll her eyes.

They brought me a copy of one of my books, Child of the North Star, that had been translated into Spanish! I knew my books were in other languages, but I had never actually seen one. It was amazing, and what is even more amazing is that Kyle and Lou can read it.

A few nights before they left, they gave me a dance lesson in the cave. They'd brought a Victrola and some records with them and first Lou put on some Spanish music and danced by herself. She studied dance when she was in her teens and twenties. She is a very good and very sexy dancer. She wore a black top and skirt and she danced around the cave looking like she should be in the movies, kicking her leg up next to her head and letting it down real slowly, her head tossed back and one arm cutting through the air. Then she danced with Kyle, and I have to admit they look wonderful together.

I just watched them at first while Eden fell asleep in my arms. Then I took Eden back to the house and by the time I'd returned to the cave, Kyle had poured us each a glass of wine and said it was time for my lesson. First, Lou showed me the woman's steps, and then I tried to dance with Kyle. I don't know if it was the wine or just my natural poor coordination, but I could not master the steps and we got to laughing so hard we couldn't hear the music. Then Lou got behind me so she could guide me and we were both dancing with Kyle, me pressed between them, and suddenly none of us were laughing. I felt Lou's breasts warm against my back, one of her hands light on my waist, guiding me. Kyle held both of us against him with his arm. He's grown a beard and I liked the way it felt against my forehead. At first we followed the steps, and then we shifted into a tight circle, arms around each other and swaying to the music, rather drunkenly, I suppose. It had been so long since I felt the touch of adult human beings. I didn't want to breathe or speak for fear of breaking the spell. I felt enormous desire for the first time in a long time and I'm certain they felt it as well. But I knew none of us would give in to it. It seemed an unspoken rule between *us, that we would enjoy this moment but carry it no further. So it seemed safe to rub my brother's back as we stood there, and he must have felt safe as well, because he rested his hand on the side of my breast and nuzzled my forehead with his lips. My body was so full of life. I felt drawn even to Lou, and I let my imagination dream for just a moment of the three of us undressing one another, making love on the cold floor of the cavern. I don't know how long we stood there like that, aware only of touching and being touched. The needle of the Victrola had been at the end of the record for many minutes by the time Kyle chuckled and said, "Lord, are we drunk."*

Lou lifted her head to kiss him. "We're smashed all right," she said.

"I think we're stuck like this forever," I said, pleased by the thought. "If any one of us lets go, the other two will topple over."

"We'll have to move as a unit back to the house," Kyle slurred, and that brought me to my senses. We would have to go back to the house, back to our separate rooms. I knew I would lie awake with that longing in my body, knowing that sometime during the night Kyle would leave his bed and join Lou in hers. He would make love to her in the bed that used to be mine.

I pulled myself gently from the circle. "I'd better get back to look in on Eden," I said. That brought Lou and Kyle back to life and within seconds we had the Victrola turned off, the glasses picked up, and were heading through the dark forest to the house.

April 10, 1957

Eden is nearly two. She has loads of energy and it is a scramble to keep up with her. She will sit still for a picture book, though. Last night I was thinking about an old picture book Daddy used to read to Kyle and me when we were little. I went down to our old room and hunted in the bottom drawer of Kyle's dresser where the books Daddy used to hide for us are still kept. I found the book, but I couldn't get the drawer back in, so I pulled it all the way out and peered inside the dresser. Wedged into the back of the dresser I saw a long white box. I pulled it out, opened it and nearly screamed when I saw what was inside. My hair! The hair Mama lopped off for some misdeed I can't even recall now. I'd never thought about it or wondered what had become of it. Obviously Kyle had saved it. He'd tied a blue ribbon around one end and found this box somewhere. I sat and stared at the hair for a long time. It is blond, a dozen shades blonder than my hair is now, though not quite as blond as Eden's. The texture too is somewhere between my daughter's and my own. I wonder if Kyle remembers he squirreled this away. I managed to get it back in place in the dresser. I took the book I'd found into the parlor and settled down to read it to Eden, but my mind was in Peru. After I put Eden to bed I wrote Kyle a long letter. I didn't mention the hair. I don't want to embarrass him. I just wanted to feel close to him.

I try hard not to wish things were different. When the fantasy of being with Kyle tries to come into my mind, I push it out. On the back of my ledge in the cavern, I have dozens of stories I wrote long ago in which I imagined being with him, being his lover. Sometimes still I let those fantasies blossom to full flower. I think of Kyle being with Eden and me every day, working here by my side, sleeping with me at night. But thinking about it makes reality unendurable. So I try to put those thoughts aside and attend to the business of being a mother, a writer, an archaeologist. And a sister. That should be a full enough life for anyone.

Eden was making Cassie's bed in the morning when she noticed the long white box resting on the little dresser by the door. She knew what was in it immediately, although the box was larger than she had imagined it to be from the journal. Kyle must have set it there when he came up to kiss Cassie good night the night before.

She finished making the bed while Cassie struggled to dress herself. Then she slowly, deliberately walked over to the dresser and lifted the top from the box. She gasped as the shiny gold tresses sprang free. She had expected something less, a few locks, perhaps, a hundred strands tied with ribbon. But the box overflowed with glittery blond hair.

She held the end tied with blue ribbon and lifted the hair from the box. "Look, Cassie," she said. The hair was at least a foot and a half long and nearly too thick to get her hand around. Kyle must have scraped every strand from the kitchen floor on that morning fifty years ago.

"What's that?" Cassie looked up from the floor where she was fighting with her sandals.

"Your grandmother's hair. It was cut off when she was thirteen. Isn't it beautiful?"

"My grandma in the picture?"

"That's right. Grandma Riley."

Cassie stood up and touched the hair, softly, the way she would stroke her kitten. "It's exquisite," she said, and then sat down to resume dressing.

Eden set the hair back in the box, but first she checked the ribbon to make sure it was still holding. It was. The ribbon was tied in a series of double knots that would last forever, the meticulous handiwork of a devoted fourteen-year-old boy.

44

She was standing in the kitchen watching the rain spike against the driveway when the car pulled up in front of the house. The rain was so fierce she couldn't tell the color or make. Lou and Kyle were out for the afternoon and Eden hoped one of their older friends had not driven through this storm for a visit.

A man got out of the car, his face obscured by a large black umbrella, and it wasn't until she opened the kitchen door that she recognized Sam Alexander.

"Come in, Sam," she said, as if she'd been expecting him. In a way she had. She'd thought he might call to tell her exactly what he thought of her now.

Sam left his umbrella on the porch and stepped into the kitchen, shaking off the rain. "Incredible storm," he said. His blue shirt was damp, but every hair was still in place.

"This is my daughter, Cassie," Eden said as Cassie emerged from the living room.

Sam reached his hand toward Cassie as though the little girl were an adult. Cassie took a step backward and gave him that hooded look she reserved for strangers.

"Cassie, Sam is Ben's brother."

"No he's not," Cassie said. "Ben's too old to have a brother."

Sam smiled and Cassie grinned back, pleased that she'd amused him. "Ben built me a dollhouse," she said.

"Yes, I know."

"Do you want to see it?" Cassie asked.

"I'll take a look at it before I go, Cassie." Sam looked at Eden. "But right now, I'd like to talk with your mother."

Eden sent Cassie back to the living room and Sam sat down at the table. He refused her offer of something to drink. She sat across from him. "You're angry with me," she said.

He took off his gold-rimmed glasses and began cleaning them with his handkerchief, his green eyes never leaving Eden's face. "I'm way beyond anger, Eden. Anger's what I felt when Ben told me the two of you split up. What I felt after I read your quote in the paper was closer to rage. Closer to disgust."

"I know," she said. "I'm not proud of it."

"Then why the hell did you do it?"

"Circumstances," she said weakly. "Nothing I can really defend."

He slipped his glasses into his shirt pocket. "You kick a man when he's down, Eden, you'd better be able to defend it."

She leaned forward. "Sam, I'm worried about him. He has that Valium you prescribed. I know in the past he's thought of killing himself."

Sam frowned. "He's always denied feeling suicidal."

"He told me he considered it at one time."

Sam stared at her. "God, if he ever . . ." He closed his eyes and covered his face with his hands, and Eden hurt for him.

She leaned forward, touched his arm. "Sam?"

He slowly lowered his hands to the table and she wasn't surprised at the tears in his eyes. "This has gone too far," he said. "It's gone on too long. He's suffered more than . . ." He looked up at her, his eyes piercing. "Eden, I know for a fact that Ben is innocent."

"How can anyone besides Ben know that?"

"Because I'm a psychiatrist. I understand human behavior. He didn't ever hurt your little girl, did he?"

"No."

"See? If he were a child molester, he wouldn't be able to help himself. If the opportunity is there, he has to take it." Sam's voice rose and beads of perspiration dotted his forehead. He stood up abruptly and paced to the sink and back again. "It's like a drug addict. A force outside himself takes over and he's helpless to stop it."

"But there can be isolated incidents, can't there? I mean, he may have hurt Bliss but would never—"

Sam slammed his fist into the table and she jumped. "He did not hurt Bliss."

Eden leaned away from him. She felt a little fear. Irrational. Still, she wished Kyle and Lou were home.

"I've got to be everything to Bliss now," Sam said, pacing again. "Uncle and father. Jeff is useless. I can't stand the sight of him. He and Sharon include us in a lot of things for Bliss's sake—we're going over there for a barbecue tomorrow night—and I have to sit there and watch his smug face as he enjoys everything Ben worked for and no longer has." Sam pulled his handkerchief from his pants pocket again and mopped at his forehead. Then he turned to face Eden, hands on his hips. "And you've certainly done a lot for Ben, haven't you? With your goddamned public condemnation of him?"

"Please lower your voice. I don't want Cassie to—"

Sam's face was flushed; the tendons stood out in his neck. "It would have been bad enough if you'd just broken up with him. He was so hung up on you that that would have devastated him quite enough. But to make him look like a liar, a user, when the truth is, you used him, right? I had your number all along. The superstar needed some entertainment while she was stuck out here in the country. He was good-looking, good in bed. You could—"

She stood up quickly, nearly knocking over her chair. "I think you'd better go."

He looked at her, stunned, as though he'd surprised himself with his words. "God, I'm sorry." He shook his head tiredly. "I'm very sorry. It's just that I don't see what's left for him."

She thought of telling him he'd better worry about himself for a while. He seemed close to breaking point. But she knew her concern would not be welcome.

He glanced toward the living room. "Let me see that dollhouse before I go," he said.

She stood trembling against the sink, listening to Sam chat with Cassie. Hearing his voice from the next room, she would have sworn he was Ben. In a moment he was back in the kitchen. He opened the door for himself, and the sound of driving rain filled the room. He turned to look at her one last time.

"I'm angry with you because I'm angry with myself, Eden. You're not the only person in this room who's betrayed Ben. Think about that, will you?"

She frowned as she watched his car disappear behind the curtain of rain. Then she walked into the living room, where Cassie had every stick of furniture out of the dollhouse and on the floor.

"Let's put this away, Cassie," she said. "We need to straighten up before Aunt Lou and Uncle Kyle get home."

Cassie was quiet as she knelt in front of the dollhouse, helping Eden move the furniture inside the little rooms. "I don't like Ben's brother," she said after a few minutes of silence.

Eden could certainly understand that. Sam was more than a little scary. She wondered what he was like with a fragile child like Bliss. "Why not, honey?" she asked.

"He's creepy. And he touched me in a bad way, Mom."

She looked up indignantly and Eden's hands turned to ice.

"What do you mean, he touched you in a bad way?"

"He pinched my bottom."

"He did?" Calm, Eden, calm. "When did he do that?"

Cassie pushed the little sofa against the back wall of the living room, the room Ben had wallpapered with tiny yellow daisies. "When he was going away he did it with his stupid old hand."

Eden clapped her hand over her own mouth. "Oh my God," she said. "Oh my God."

Cassie looked frightened. She leaned over to hug her mother. "I'm sorry, Mommy."

"No," Eden said. "You have nothing to be sorry about. You're such a good girl to tell me."

You're not the only person in this room who's betrayed Ben.

"You're so smart to know a bad touch from a good one."

Think about that, will you?

She called Maggie Demarco to ask her to watch Cassie for a while. Then she looked up the address she needed in Kyle's phone book. She left a note for Lou and Kyle, ran with Cassie through the rain to her car, and headed out of Lynch Hollow.

It was dark and the rain had finally let up by the time she found the house. She recognized it from the picture Ben had shown her, but it was more imposing in reality, with its long, clean lines and huge angular windows. She parked the car in the street and walked up the curved sidewalk to the front door. Although she'd spent the last few hours rehearsing what she would say, she was nervous.

She knew that the woman who answered her knock was Sharon, although her hair was shorter and blonder than in the pictures Eden had seen of her. Sharon obviously recognized her as well. She stood behind the screen door, lips pursed.

"What are you doing here?" she asked.

"I need to talk to you, Sharon."

"You've been intrusive enough already. That whole ruse about visiting Bliss's classroom—I thought that was so nice, Eden Riley taking time out to read to a bunch of little kids—until I found out that you were seeing Ben. He put you up to it, didn't he? Sent you to spy on her? He just can't leave her alone."

"No, Sharon, it was my idea. Please give me a few minutes. It's very important."

Sharon glanced behind her, then opened the screen door and stepped out onto the front steps. She was very pretty, her skin pale and lightly freckled. She folded her arms across her chest and looked stonily at Eden.

"I may be out of place," Eden began, "but I have to tell you that I think it was Sam who hurt Bliss."

Sharon laughed. "Oh, brother. Now you're really reaching. I thought you were through with Ben? The paper said he lied to you and—"

"I'm the one who lied. I lied to the press to save my own skin. And I was beginning to worry that he might be guilty. But today Sam came to see me."

"Does Sam really strike you as an abuser?"

"Did Ben strike you as one?"

Sharon's expression flattened. "I've gotten used to thinking of him that way."

"Sam touched my daughter."

"What do you mean?"

"She told me he pinched her bottom."

"Maybe she . . . misinterpreted."

"Maybe Bliss misinterpreted."

Sharon was quiet and Eden continued. "He told me he's betrayed Ben. What else could he mean?"

"He means he feels guilty he hasn't been able to help him. It plagues him that he can't do more."

"Maybe that's not all he feels guilty about, Sharon. I think he wanted me to figure this out. He gave me enough clues, and he said he was absolutely certain it wasn't Ben. How else could he be so sure?"

Sharon shrugged. "He adores Ben. He's never been able to accept the fact that his own brother could do something like that."

"When I saw Bliss at Green Gables she told me her daddy still visits her at night sometimes."

"She's dreaming."

"I think Sam is still abusing her."

Even in the dim light, Eden could see Sharon's cheeks flame. "You really have no right to come here and . . ." Sharon brushed her hair from her forehead and looked out toward the street. Eden could see her mind working. "Ben has got to be guilty," Sharon said. "If he's not . . . I couldn't live with the knowledge that he's paid so much for something he didn't do."

A man appeared at the screen door. He was very tall and broad and his hair was red, something Eden had not expected in Jeff. "Everything all right out here?" he asked.

"Yes, Jeff. I'll be in in a minute." Sharon waited until Jeff had walked away from the door. "How is Ben?" she asked, and the tone of her voice told Eden that she had once loved Ben very much. Eden felt like crying again. Everyone had lost something in this game, not just Ben and his daughter.

"I haven't seen him in a few days," she said. "But my uncle says he's not good. He's depressed." Eden looked up at the house. "He told me the two of you designed this house."

"Yes."

"Right now he lives in a cabin about the size of your garage. With no air-conditioning or—"

Sharon narrowed her eyes. "Did he ask you to come here?"

"He doesn't know any of this, Sharon. He doesn't want to see me. This really has nothing to do with Ben. I'm here because I'm a mother too and if someone thought my child was in danger, I'd want them to tell me. Sam said he was coming over here tomorrow night. If I were you, I wouldn't leave him alone with Bliss."

45

Ben was just outside Annapolis and no closer to figuring out why Sharon wanted to see him than he'd been when he left the cabin. She'd called him just as he got in from the site to eat lunch. She was crying on the phone, crying so hard he could barely understand her, and he thought something must have happened to Bliss. "Bliss is all right," she reassured him. "That isn't it." But she needed to see him. Right away. He told her he could be there by three—it was nearly that now—and asked where he should meet her. He tensed when she said to come to the house.

"Will Bliss be there?" he asked.

"No. I'll make sure she's out."

He was afraid to see the house, afraid of the feelings it would elicit in him. He turned now onto Gracey Court and pulled over to the side of the road. He could see the house from here, set in a curve about a quarter mile from his truck. They'd looked for that lot for over a year. He could still remember their excitement when they first set eyes on the long, gentle arc of land backing to the thick blue-green forest and the river beyond. The house looked the same, the natural wood a rich brown. Sharon's blue Accord was in the driveway. He turned his pickup back onto the road and drove slowly toward his old home.

Sharon answered the door. Her eyes were puffy, cheeks wet. She was a reluctant weeper and it frightened him to see this much pain in her face.

She reached for him. "Ben." Her arms circled his neck and he held her, his heart pounding. It was Bliss. It had to be Bliss. Something horrible had happened that Sharon hadn't wanted to tell him over the phone.

"Is she alive?" he asked. "Sharon, please, just tell me she's alive."

"Yes, yes, she's all right." She moved away from him and in that moment he saw the stretch of his pool in the backyard through the glassed living room wall, the lush curtain of pines behind it.

"Sit down, Ben. Do you want something to drink?"

"No. I want you to talk to me."

She sat at the opposite end of the sofa, as pale, as fragile-looking as he'd ever seen her. She put her hand over her mouth. "I know you're innocent," she said.

"It was Jeff," he said, feeling a surge of fresh hatred for the man who'd taken his place.

"No." She shook her head and one tear, then another, slipped down her cheek. "I don't know how to tell you this, but . . . It was Sam, Ben."

Ben laughed. "Oh, come on."

Sharon moved closer to him and rested a cold hand on his arm. "We set him up last night," she said. "He and Jen came over for the evening, and after Bliss went to bed Jen and I went shopping for baby clothes. Jeff told Sam he had to run to the store. But he didn't go. Instead he watched Bliss's room through her window, and when Sam went in Jeff went back in the house and confronted him. At first Sam said he was just checking on her, but then he broke down and admitted it had been him all along. The police took him in last night."

Ben stared at her as an icy chill settled into his blood. "There must be a mistake," he said.

Sharon kneaded her long pale hands together in her lap. "I'm the one who made the mistake when I didn't believe you. Oh God, Ben, I'm so sorry."

"This is crazy." He stood up, running his hands through his hair.

"Why would you suspect him in the first place? Why would you even think to set him up?"

"Eden Riley figured it out."

"What?"

"Something Sam said to her made her suspicious. She thought he wanted to get caught. She came to warn me. I thought at first that you'd put her up to it."

Ben closed his eyes, pressed his fingers to his temples. Eden had come here. She'd seen his house, talked to Sharon. But she hadn't spoken to him.

"Maybe Sam just said he did it to get the heat off me," he said.

Sharon shook her head. "He's sick, Ben. Jen is devastated. The baby would have been here in a few months, and this will put an end to that."

Ben sat down again. He'd thought he knew his small world and all its players, whom he could trust and whom he couldn't. This made no sense at all.

"I can't believe Sam would let me go through all this. He let me go to jail and lose my job." He looked at Sharon. "And my marriage." He knew he sounded childlike, hurt and bewildered, and when Sharon moved next to him and wrapped her arms around him he couldn't stop himself from letting out the tears.

"All this morning I've been thinking about what you've lost," Sharon said. "I can't stand it, Ben. I don't know how I can ever make it up to you. I never stopped loving you, though I felt guilty. I thought, what's wrong with me that I can still love this man who hurt my daughter?"

He pulled away from her. "Our daughter, and I never hurt her. I want to see her. Where is she?"

"They won't let you see her yet. She went to her counselor this morning, who said they have to prepare her a little more before she sees you."

"I don't give a damn what her counselor says. I'm sick of other people running my life. Where is she?"

Sharon hesitated. "She's next door at Mary's. But Ben, listen to me. We have to do this carefully. She's been told for the past year and a half that you did bad things to her and had to stay away from her for her own protection. They have to clear the way for you a little."

Bliss was next door, a few yards from where he sat. He stood up. "I want to see her now."

Sharon rose and put her hand on his. "All right. But calm down first, Ben. Please." She squeezed his hand. "You'll scare her. Everyone's told her now that it was Sam. He called her himself this morning after he was released on his own recognizance. But she's still confused."

Ben clenched his teeth together, determined to stay calm. "Please get her, Sharon, or I'll go over there myself."

Sharon was gone for a long time. Ben sat numbly on the sofa at first, then walked into the kitchen and leaned over the sink because he thought he was going to be sick.

Sam.

No, he wouldn't think about Sam right now. He was going to see Bliss. One trauma at a time. Would she be afraid of him? He couldn't stand that thought. He splashed cold water on his face and returned to the living room just as Sharon and Bliss walked in the door.

Bliss was taller, her arms and legs long and far too thin. She held Sharon's hand and looked at him, uncertain and unsmiling, and his heart cracked in two. He walked over to her and knelt down to take her in his arms while Sharon let go of her hand and stepped into the kitchen. He could hear Sharon crying while he held his daughter, who was so stiff and delicate that she felt brittle beneath his arms. He leaned back to look at her. Her big gray eyes were clear. "Don't cry," she said.

"I can't help it. I'm so happy to see you. I've missed you very, very much."

Bliss looked anxiously toward the kitchen. "Mama?"

"I'm right here, Bliss." Sharon appeared in the doorway, gamely smiling, clutching a tissue.

Bliss looked back at Ben. "Where did your beard go?"

She had never seen him without his beard. He must seem even more of a stranger to her. "I shaved it off. Do you think I look better or worse?"

"Worse," she said, and he thought he detected the hint of a smile.

He sat back on his heels. "Do you understand what's going on?"

Bliss nodded. Her bangs were too long and caught on her pale eyelashes when she blinked. "Sam said you never did bad things to me. He make-believed he was you."

"That's right," Ben said, although he still did not believe it himself. "And then I had to go away because the police thought I hurt you and they wanted to protect you. But now they know I didn't do it and I can see you anytime I want." He looked up at Sharon and she nodded.

"Do you want to see my new Barbie?" Bliss asked.

Barbie dolls? Bliss? He would have to get to know this strange little girl all over again. "Yes, I would." He stood up and started toward her room, but she held back.

"Mama has to come too," she said, and as Sharon joined them in the hallway he wondered how long it would be before Bliss felt comfortable with him alone. He would be patient. He would regain her trust bit by bit. And she would put on weight and lose that gaunt, frightened look. She would start to smile again. But it tore him up inside to know that she would be haunted by the demons of this last year for the rest of her life.

Sam himself opened the door and Ben immediately saw the effects of a night in jail on his brother's features. His hair was uncombed, the lines in his face deep and dark, his eyes red. He looked older, beaten down. The transition was frightening and seeing it allayed some of Ben's anger.

Sam stood back to let him in.

"Where's Jen?" Ben asked.

"Gone to her parents."

Sam walked into the kitchen and Ben followed. "I didn't know if you'd come over or not," Sam said. He took two beers from the refrigerator, set one on the breakfast bar for Ben, and popped the other open for himself. He took a long drink and Ben marveled at his own reaction to this man. Driving over here, he'd pictured himself bursting through the door in a rage, pummeling his brother into the carpet. But now he felt calm. He had a sense of being outside himself, watching this scene unfold.

"How could you do it?" he asked.

Sam sat on one of the barstools and looked Ben in the eye. He let out a long sigh. "Do you mean, how could I fondle Bliss or how could I let you take the rap for it?"

"Everything." Ben felt the anger rising and worked to keep it down. "And skip the euphemisms, okay? You didn't fondle Bliss, you molested her. Jesus, Sam." He shook his head. "I feel as though I don't know you at all."

"There's a lot about me nobody knows." Sam set his beer on the counter. "I love Bliss," he said. "I was jealous of you—it was so easy for you and Sharon. One day you decide to try to have a baby and the next day Sharon's pregnant. And Bliss was so beautiful. I never hurt her, Ben, you've got to believe that. I mean, I was always very gentle with her."

Ben slammed his own beer down on the counter. "How can you say that? You're a psychiatrist, for Christ's sake. You know the toll this is taking on her."

Sam shook his head. "I was gentle. And I never meant for you to get the blame. The first night I was with her, she was so sleepy and out of it, she assumed I was you and I just played along with it. I didn't let her get a look at me. Then when the shit hit the fan, I thought for sure you'd get off and it would all blow over. When it didn't, I just gave in. Learned to live with the guilt, I suppose. I'm sorry, Ben. There's no way I can tell you how sorry I am." He looked at his brother. "You don't know what it's like to be this way. I can't control it. I'd be at your house and picture Bliss asleep in her bed and I just couldn't help myself."

Ben stared at the stranger in front of him. "Have there been others?"

Sam looked down at the bar. "A few over the years." He sighed, rubbed his eyes. "It's probably best they lock me up."

"I don't understand when you did it."

"When we'd be at your house and I could figure out a way . . . like one night when we were all in the pool and Bliss was already in bed and I said I wasn't feeling well and went into the guest room to lie down. Only I never went to the guest room."

Ben remembered that particular night. Poor Bliss. He'd been laughing in the pool with Sharon and Jen and she'd been completely vulnerable in her bedroom. And then the scene formed in his mind. The image he'd been avoiding slipped in so fast he couldn't stop it. He saw Sam behind his daughter, saw him undressing her, touching her, and he began to shake with rage. He stood up and grabbed Sam by the collar, yanking him off the stool and pressing him up against the bar.

"I hate you for this," he said. He pulled back his fist and let it fly. Sam's head snapped to the side and blood pooled at the corner of his lip. He shut his eyes, waiting for the next blow, waiting as though he knew he deserved it, as though he welcomed it. He looked wretched, pitiful. And ruined.

Ben let go of him and went into the kitchen. He wrapped a few cubes of ice in a dish towel and leaned across the bar to press it into Sam's hand. Then he walked to the door, but before he left he turned to take one last look at his brother. Sam was leaning against the wall, eyes closed, holding the dish towel to the side of his face. Two round red drops of blood sat like rubies on his collar.

"Maybe someday I can forgive you for what you've done to me," Ben said. "But I'll never forgive you for what you've done to my daughter."

He spent the next morning at the university, negotiating his reinstatement for the spring semester. He thought of calling Alex Parrish, but he was still too angry with his old friend. Let Alex learn about it through the grapevine and wallow in guilt for a few days. Let Alex be the one to call him.

He spent the afternoon with Bliss and Sharon before heading back to Virginia. Once on the road, though, it was not Bliss who filled his thoughts but Eden. Insane. He'd been given back his daughter, his job, his life. Yet he wasn't satisfied. He'd lost Eden in all of this. He'd call her to thank her, but he wouldn't see her. In that statement to the press she'd said she was looking forward to returning to California. "I want to put this past summer behind me," she'd said. Fine. He would do the same.

When he reached the Shenandoah Valley, he turned onto the back roads running through the string of small towns. The first little village was Gloverton, just four blocks long. When he reached its west end, he spotted the marquee on the tiny movie theater. *Heart of Winter*. He pulled over to the side of the road and stared at the sign, feeling as though he'd driven into the Twilight Zone. *Heart of Winter* had long been out of the major theaters. This sign was only here to torment him.

He got out of his truck and checked the time of the movie. Seven o'clock. He had an hour to kill. He ate a hamburger and fries at a little cafe and walked the length of Gloverton, four blocks east and four west. Then he settled down in one of the theater's hard vinyl seats and waited.

The opening music was powerful. He hadn't noticed it before, but now he felt moved by it to the point of pain. Then the movie began and he wondered why he was torturing himself, watching Eden with Michael Carey. She was different on the screen; her voice, her expressions were not her own. This was Eden Riley the actress. He knew the real woman. Did Carey? With increasing agitation he watched the relationship grow between the two actors, and he left before the hotel room scene. He'd gotten back in his truck and was out on the road before he realized how fast his heart was beating, as though he'd escaped from a great danger just in time. It would have done him no good at all to watch that scene, to see her blouse fall open for the camera, to see Carey plunge his hands beneath her skirt, to see her toss her head back with a shower of blond hair. He didn't need to see it to remember it.

46

Every morning she rose from sleep with the certainty that Ben was beside her. Her hand rested on his stomach, just below his navel, his penis stiff and ready above her fingers. Or she had the taste of him in her mouth, or his scent on her pillow. Only when her eyes were fully open and the sun had swept the shadows from the room would she admit to herself that her hand rested only on the firm surface of her mattress, that the taste in her mouth was nothing more than the stale taste of a poor night's sleep.

If it were not for Cassie chattering to herself in the next room while waiting for Eden to get up, she would roll over and go back to sleep so she could see Ben again, talk to him, touch him. She thought of calling him but couldn't face the hurt and anger in his voice. She thought of telling him her suspicions about Sam. But what if she was wrong?

In a few days she would no longer have the temptation of knowing he was nearby. The Santa Monica house was waiting for her. She would be fine once she got there. She'd throw herself into the film, force herself to read the script for *Treasure House*. And she'd let Michael's new sober, tender side fill the emptiness Ben had left her.

She spent her waking hours either with Cassie or at work on the screenplay. She was determined to have the first draft completed by the time she left on Monday, and it was going extremely well now that she was free to change her mother's history. She was good at fiction, at making up characters to suit the story, and the work kept her from thinking about Ben, about California.

On Friday afternoon she wrote the scene of her own conception, with Kate finally yielding to the gently persuasive, sweetly sensual Matthew Riley. It was a beautiful scene that nearly wrote itself. Eden felt no guilt over the lie she was telling on the screen. She had come to believe it herself.

She was nearly dizzy with fatigue by the time she went downstairs Friday evening. She had promised Cassie she'd play a game with her, but except for Kyle and herself the house was empty.

"I sent Cassie and Lou to the store for ice cream," Kyle said. He was sitting on the sofa, a clipboard on his lap and a pencil in his hand. "I wanted a moment alone with you."

Here it comes, Eden thought. Kyle wouldn't let her go back to California without first trying to settle their differences. She leaned against the wall instead of sitting down, waiting.

"Ben called me from Annapolis a while ago," Kyle said. "He's been cleared. His brother confessed to everything."

Tears quickly filled her eyes and she blinked them back. "That's wonderful," she said.

"He said he was grateful to you for going up to see Sharon."

She shook her head. "It doesn't seem like much compared to the grief I caused him."

"He's also gotten his job back for the spring and he talked them into providing funding and a supply of graduate students for the Lynch Hollow site—if he can produce one of the skeletons from the cavern."

She frowned, amazed that Ben had dared to suggest opening the cavern to Kyle.

"I'm going to let him do it. I won't go in myself, but if he wants to . . ." Kyle shrugged. "He's right. It's the one thing that will save the site. The only thing. I've arranged to have a work crew out there tomorrow afternoon to move the boulders."

"How will he know where to look?"

"I'm making him a map from memory." Kyle lifted the clipboard in the air. "The main cavern shouldn't be a problem. It's that maze room that can turn you around."

The cave would be open. She could step inside it if she liked. She shuddered, and Kyle didn't miss it.

"Do you want to go in?" he asked.

"No," she said quickly. "No, I couldn't." She took a few steps toward the stairs. "Will you let me know when Cassie gets home?"

"Sure. And Eden?"

She turned to look at him.

"That was a nice thing you did for Ben," he said.

She nodded. "I only wish I could have done it before I lost him."

Upstairs she sat in front of the word processor and composed a statement for the press. This one took no time at all. It flowed from her fingertips, despite the fact that it would incriminate her rather than Ben.

"No way," Nina said when Eden read it to her over the phone. "Your first statement was very well received, Eden. Let's just let it lie."

"I can't, Nina. He's innocent."

"So let him make his own statement."

"Nina, either you take this to the press or I will."

Nina sighed. "All right. Read it to me one more time."

The rain had settled into a steady gray drizzle by the next morning, but the downpour of the past few days was taking its toll.

"The Shenandoah broke its banks last night," Kyle said at breakfast. "Even Ferry Creek's about to spill over."

Cassie looked up at Eden. "What broke, Mom?"

"The river broke its banks," Eden said. "The water's gone up on the land." She found herself avoiding the word "flood." That word had always gotten stuck in her throat.

"You're not eating, Ky," Lou said.

"I'm not hungry this morning." Kyle tapped his toast on the side of his plate. Every once in a while he'd glance out the window. She understood his apprehension, maybe even shared it. Today the cavern would be opened, a gaping reminder of the past on his land. "Once that cave is open, Ben will have to work fast in case the creek gets high enough to be a threat."

"What time is the work crew coming?" Eden asked.

"One. Ben will meet with them. I'm staying here."

She worked on the screenplay most of the morning, taking a break to drive out to Coolbrook Park with Cassie to watch the swollen Shenandoah whip through the forest. The water was frothy and white. It swept entire trees downstream, tossing them into the air like toothpicks. The other spectators standing nearby talked excitedly about the possibility of a flood. Some of them stood around the tall slender marker at the corner of the parking lot, pointing to the yellow line a foot or so above their heads. There was a date below the line and Eden didn't bother to get close enough to see it. She knew what it said. The last time the water had reached that mark had been on May 29, 1959. She had been Cassie's age. She had very nearly drowned.

She dropped Cassie off at Maggie DeMarco's for the afternoon and returned to Lynch Hollow and the screenplay, but as she sat in front of her word processor her concentration sagged and she found herself staring out the window as Kyle had that morning.

Finally she put on her waterproof duck shoes, took Lou's enormous green umbrella from the hall closet, and left the house. Kyle had told her that the trail down to the cavern and the site had been washed out by the rain, so she walked down the driveway and out to the road.

When she reached the field she was a fair distance from the site, and she saw three men standing in the trees by the cave. She walked forward a few steps until she was close enough to see that one of the men was Ben. She decided to watch from here. This was close enough.

The men emerged from the woods and one of them picked up a sheet of paper from the ground near the second pit. They huddled around it, gesturing toward the cave as they spoke. And then Ben caught sight of her. He looked in her direction for a few seconds and then back to the paper. Did he think she had come to see him? Well, hadn't she? She had known he'd be here.

After a moment the two workmen picked up a chain from the

ground and headed back into the woods while Ben walked across the field toward her. She felt her heart kick up, her hand tighten around the stem of the umbrella. His hair looked a few shades darker from the rain and his shirt was soaked. She wanted to cry, wanted to throw her arms around him and tell him how happy she was for him, how sad for herself. But she stood still, clutching the umbrella, uncertain of what expression to put on her face, what mask to wear.

"Hi," he said when he was next to her. He put his hands in his pockets and turned to look back to the woods.

"Do you want to share?" She held the umbrella toward him and he slipped under it. Their arms touched, their shoulders. She could smell his after-shave.

"Do you believe Kyle is letting this happen?" Ben nodded toward the cavern. "They're having some trouble figuring out how to move the boulders. Crowbars are useless. We're going to try to wrap chains around them and then hook them up to my truck. If that doesn't work, we'll have to get a backhoe in here. When Kyle sealed that cave he was counting on it being sealed forever."

"Yes, I'm sure he was. Will those guys go in with you?"

"No."

It seemed unwise for Ben to go in alone, yet she was relieved. She didn't like to think of strangers inside her mother's cavern.

"Eden." Ben sank his hands lower in his pockets. "Thanks for what you did. You've turned everything around for me."

"I'm sorry I ever doubted you."

"Well, you had plenty of company, but it's over. All I care about now is finishing up my work here and moving back to Annapolis to start my life over. I want to make up to Bliss for the past year."

"How is she?"

"Mixed up." The muscles in his jaw tightened. "Maybe I'm wrong, but I feel as though I'm the only one who can heal her."

"I bet that's true."

Ben looked behind them. "I wonder how much higher the creek's going to rise."

"Cassie and I went to Coolbrook Park this morning. The river's really up and wild and people were talking about . . . flooding. Maybe you should wait till this blows over before you go in the cave." Her throat felt tight. They were speaking to each other as though they were acquaintances, nothing more. She wanted to say, I dream about you every night. I wake up wishing you were next to me. But his coolness, his distance did not invite her to share her private thoughts.

He shook his head. "If the water gets into that cave where the skeletons are, it could ruin them."

"Maybe they're already ruined from the last flood."

"No. Kyle said it never reached the maze room."

For a few minutes neither of them spoke. They stared at the woods, although there was nothing to see. The workmen were barely visible as they struggled to fit the chains over the boulders.

Finally Ben drew in his breath. "I'm sorry Sam touched Cassie, Eden. Really."

"She's okay. I'm sure he thought that was the only way he could get me to figure out what was going on without actually telling me."

"I know." There was another short silence before he spoke again. "So Monday's the big day, huh? Back to the land of alfalfa sprouts and glitter?"

"Yes."

"Where you can put this summer behind you."

She cringed. She'd said that in the first statement. She turned her head to look at him. "Ben, I'm sorry I ever—"

"Don't apologize. I understand the feeling completely. I can't wait to have this past year and a half behind me." He looked toward the cavern. "I'd better get the pickup over there and see what we can do."

Eden moved nearer to the cavern as the men attached the chains to the bumper of Ben's truck. Ben got in behind the wheel and slowly fed the truck gas. It moved a few feet along the side of the third pit before the chain slipped from the boulder. One of the men let out a string of expletives. After two more attempts the huge boulder tipped out of the opening, teetered precariously for a few seconds on its rounded stem, and began to roll, flattening several saplings in its path and stopping just short of the third pit.

A cheer went up from the men, and Eden stared at the narrow black opening in the hillside. How many times had she stepped into that blackness as a child? How could it look so unfamiliar? It struck her how extraordinarily peculiar her mother had been to have made this forbidding hole in the earth her second home, to have made it the playground for her child.

Ben knelt near the cave entrance, checking the wiring on his headlamp, and Eden turned and headed back to the road. She had seen all she cared to see of the cave and she did not want to watch Ben disappear inside it. She would go home and lose herself once more in the screenplay.

But the screenplay offered her no refuge that afternoon. She thought of picking Cassie up early, taking her somewhere for the rest of the day and letting her daughter keep her mind occupied. Cassie would be disappointed, though, if her afternoon with Maggie's kids was cut short.

She wandered down to the kitchen where Kyle was peeling apples and Lou was rolling out piecrust on the low, pullout counter. "Let me do that, Kyle," Eden said. Kyle offered no resistance as she took the peeler from his hand and sat down at the table.

"Thanks." He looked at his watch. "I want to go have a look at Ferry Creek. I thought you were hard at work on the screenplay."

"I need a break."

"How's it coming, dear?" Lou asked.

"Much better now that I've left it with Matthew Riley as my father. It's all falling into place."

A silence followed her words, and she knew she should have found a different way to tell them that things were going well.

"I'll be back in a while," Kyle said as he took the umbrella from the coatrack and stepped outside.

Eden began peeling a small red apple.

"Eden," Lou said. "Set down that apple for a minute."

Eden looked up at her aunt.

"Set it down. I want your full attention."

Eden set the apple and peeler on the table.

"I can't take this anymore," Lou said.

"Take what?" Eden asked, although she was certain she knew.

"Your attitude. Kyle will put up with it. He'll let you go back to

California, let you run away again, but I won't. I can't. Not without a fight. Kyle will tolerate anything from you because he's so afraid of . . . Eden, think back. Remember the night of the accident?"

Eden stiffened. "Yes," she said.

"You know, they say when you're in shock, when you go through something traumatic, you develop amnesia for it. You can't remember it. But I remember everything about that night. I remember following you and that boy who was bound and determined to take you away from us. I remember being scared for you—you were so young and so desperate. I remember thinking that Kyle would die if he came home and found you'd gone like that, without a word." Lou's chin quivered and Eden dropped her eyes.

"I remember seeing that car slide into me," Lou continued. "Feeling it slide into me. My leg's been gone for seventeen years and sometimes I can still feel the pain. You tried to get me out. You were screaming and sobbing. I knew right then that you loved me. I actually thought that. Part of my mind was afraid I was going to die, another part was thinking: Why, this child loves me. She never says it, but I know she does."

Eden stood up. She walked to the counter and stared out the window. She could see the springhouse, the path into the woods that led down to the cavern.

"I don't remember much about the ride in the ambulance," Lou said, "except for you holding my hand and begging me not to tell Kyle your part in all of it, and a couple of days later I helped you concoct that story that you were in the car with me so he'd never know what really happened."

"I'm sorry I did that, Lou. I wish I could take it back. I wish I could take back that entire night." She looked at her aunt. "You never did tell Kyle the truth, did you?"

"No. It's the only lie there's ever been between us. Eden, I want you to remember something. Why didn't you want Kyle to know the truth about the accident? What were you afraid of?"

Eden shrugged. "I didn't want to get in trouble."

Lou rejected her explanation with a wave of her hand. "You'd been in trouble before," she said. "You knew Kyle wasn't much of a disciplinarian."

Eden thought back to that night and immediately knew the answer to Lou's question. She remembered how she'd felt at nineteen, how she'd felt through most of her teenage years. "I was afraid he would hate me if he knew the truth. I was always afraid of that, that he would stop loving me."

Lou nodded. "Yes. And that's exactly the reason he's never told you he's your father. He was afraid you'd stop loving him. That's why he'll put up with anything from you. He was so happy the first part of the summer when you were finally starting to relax around us, when you seemed to want to be with us. He began to think you could accept the truth about him. Now he's afraid he's lost you for good."

"He hasn't."

"You need to let him know that."

Eden sat down again and picked up the apple she'd been working on. "I'm not sure how to do that."

"Don't leave on Monday."

Eden's eyes filled. "I have to. I have to get away from Ben."

Lou reached over and took the apple out of Eden's hand. "You're not only running away from the family who loves you, but from the man you're in love with as well. Does that make any sense, Eden? It seems to me you have two men to make your peace with before you can leave Lynch Hollow." Lou looked up as they heard Kyle's footsteps on the porch. He opened the door and turned to set the umbrella on the stoop.

"Ferry Creek's rising fast," he said. "It's nearly to the pits. If it keeps rising at this rate, it could be just a couple hours from the cavern. I have to go into the cave and tell Ben that if he can't find one of the skeletons within the next hour to forget it. It's not worth the risk."

Kyle was winded and red-faced. Perspiration dampened the gray hair at his temples. He couldn't possibly go into the cavern.

"I'll tell him," Eden said.

Kyle frowned at her. "You can't go into a cave."

"Well, you can't either."

"You'll pass out."

"You'll fall and break your neck."

"All right, all right," Lou said. "I'll go."

Kyle laughed and looked at Eden. "Are you sure?"

"Yes."

"You just need to get to the tunnel entrance and call to him. Your voice should carry, though you might have to go in a ways."

Her heart started thumping. "How long is the tunnel?"

"Thirty yards or so." He looked at her doubtfully. "Remember, honey, it's not going to be like it was when you were little. There won't be any light other than what you take in with you."

She went to her room to get a sweater and when she returned to the kitchen Kyle handed her a green helmet with a headlamp attached to the front. She put it on. It was a little loose. "How do I look?" she asked.

"That helmet's proof that you'd look good in anything," Kyle said as he handed her a flashlight. "I'll walk over with you. If I think the creek's getting too close I'll call you out."

He told her about the maze room as they walked out to the road. "I tried to tell Ben where to look," he said, "but my memory's not that clear on it, and that part of the cave is a spelunker's nightmare."

"My God," she said when they'd reached the field. Ben's truck was parked up on the road, and that was fortunate because Ferry Creek had devoured much of the field. The turbulent green water clawed at the rim of the first pit. "It can't possibly get higher than this," she said.

"You don't remember, huh? It can and it might."

As they neared the cavern entrance the enormity of what she'd agreed to do struck her. She looked into the black wound in the side of the hill and steadied herself against the entryway.

"You don't have to do this, honey," Kyle said.

"I want to. I'm all right."

She turned on her flashlight and headlamp and stepped inside. Almost immediately the floor tipped beneath her feet, and her heart rocketed. She had forgotten this descent. God, how the water would pour in here. She turned to look back at the entrance, but already the walls of the cave hid Ferry Creek from her view.

She stepped forward, the beams of her headlamp and flashlight illuminating the long, narrow wonderland of stalactites and stalagmites in front of her. The floor began to level out slowly until she no longer felt as though she might fall with each step. The cavern smelled musty after being closed up all these years. Her lights were bright, but the glow they cast was foreign. The cave had taken much of its personality from Katherine's lighting, from the lanterns and candles she'd strewn around its walls and ledges.

After a few more steps the narrow cave suddenly opened into the great room, and she had to clutch a stalagmite to keep her balance. She felt the jolt of the familiar. She knew where she was. All around her the tites and mites formed walls of orange curtains and fountains of frothy rock.

She continued walking, looking up into the great vaulted ceiling where she could see the spiky stalactites captured in her headlamp. Her toe caught on something and she nearly tripped. She looked down and caught her breath. The typewriter. She knelt next to it. It was on its side, rusted nearly beyond recognition. She touched the keys and her fingers came away covered with orange dust. The lid was thin and crusty and gave way beneath her fingertips.

She stood up again and looked around her. This was the level area where the furniture had been. Kate's desk had been to her right, and Eden could see the ledge where she'd hidden her journal and, deep in the crevice, her wistful stories of herself and Kyle, the stories he'd found and burned although Lou had called them Kate's best work.

Eden turned and looked back the way she'd come, but the darkness had swallowed any light from the entrance. She wasn't sure she could go on. She was gulping air, breathing so deeply that the cool air seared her lungs. Kyle is out there, she reminded herself. He's sitting just outside the cave, waiting for you, and Ben is in here somewhere. All around her she felt the benevolent ghosts of the past. Her mother. Matthew Riley. Kyle. She pictured them sitting on the settee and the rocker, reading by yellow lantern light as though they were in someone's living room. She imagined how Kyle's Spanish music would have echoed in here, how it would have filled this room as Lou danced among the rocks.

She walked on, finally reaching the back of the cave, where she saw the still, black water of the reflecting pool. The pool was carved into the rock at the height of her waist, the ceiling just a yard or so above it so that the thousands of tiny stalactites were reflected in the water. In front of her, jammed against the wall that formed the pool, was the old furniture. The frame of the settee was nearly intact, the upholstery completely rotted—or eaten—away from it. It was tipped on its back, its rusted springs exposed. Her mother's desk lay on its side, the wood dry and cracked. A chair lay in splinters nearby.

She knew that the tunnel was to her right. She found it quickly and stood at the entrance. The ceiling was low, nearly to her head. Ben would have had to stoop to get through it. She cupped her hands around her mouth and called, "Ben!" She cocked her head to listen but heard nothing in response. Thirty yards, Kyle had said. She'd need to get a little closer.

She ducked her head and started walking through the tunnel. After she had gone several yards the walls began to close in around her. The ceiling was lower. She couldn't stand up straight without hitting her head, or unfold her arms without scraping them on the walls. She stopped and tried to calm her breathing.

"Ben!"

There was still no response and she felt she had no choice now but to go on. She would rather find herself at the end of this tunnel with Ben than back in the blackness of the cave with the entire length of the great room to walk before she reached daylight. She concentrated on setting one foot in front of the other. The ceiling dropped lower still, the floor rose, and she was nearly crouching. She turned a corner and a huge rocky protrusion blocked most of the passage in front of her. She felt paralyzed, afraid to try to squeeze past the craggy rock and afraid to turn back. She dropped to her knees, unable to hold her stooped position any longer.

"Ben! Ben!"

"Eden?" His voice sounded far away, but she could hear him clearly. "What the hell are you doing in there?"

"I have a message from Kyle. But I'm stuck. It's so narrow."

"It gets wider," he called. "Keep coming."

She tried to stand again and remembered to hunch over just in time to prevent herself from hitting her head on the ceiling. She slipped past the protruding rock and let out her breath.

"Eden? Are you still there?"

"Yes." She walked on, stooped and shivery-kneed, and soon saw a pale yellow light against the rocks up ahead. She turned another corner and was nearly blinded by Ben's headlamp.

"Just another few yards," he said as he backed out of the tunnel ahead of her. She followed him into the maze room. She wanted to fall into his arms with relief, but he just touched her shoulder, lightly, briefly, while she leaned against the wall and gasped for breath.

"Are you okay?" he asked.

"Yes, but Ferry Creek is nearly to the pits. Kyle says you have less than an hour left. He says to forget the skeleton if you can't find it soon, and get out of here."

Ben nodded. "It's slow going in here. Look at this place." He waved the beam of his flashlight around the room. It was indeed a maze, a never-ending dense forest of stone columns. "I haven't been able to go in too far because I've stayed tied to the entrance so I can find my way out again." She saw the rope tied from a column near the entrance to his belt. "But since you're here, I can leave my flashlight to mark the exit and we can both look."

She nodded and started snaking her way through the maze as silence fell between them. She wanted to speak to him. She needed to. She could start with something safe.

"It was a strange feeling to walk through the cavern after all these years," she said.

For a moment he said nothing. She heard him moving through the other side of the maze room, saw the shadows shift around her as the beam of his headlamp bounced around the walls. "Let's just work, Eden," he said finally. "We don't have time to shoot the breeze."

Her cheeks burned. A dozen responses came to mind but she said none of them. She would let him have his silence.

She angled her body back and forth to walk between the columns and within a very short time found herself in a more open area. She knew even before she examined the floor that she'd found Rosie's resting place, and sure enough, the skeleton lay no more than a yard from her feet. She called to Ben and knelt down to look at the skeleton. It was small. A child. Not much bigger than Cassie.

Ben stood above her and shook his head. "I've been scouring this place for over an hour and you walk right to it. Spooky." He lifted his camera and took a few pictures, then laid a sheet on the ground as close to the skeleton as he could. The skeleton was embedded in an inch or so of earth. Ben pulled a brush from his jeans pocket and cleared the loose dust away. Then he dug carefully at the dirt with his pocketknife, and as always, Eden felt electrified watching his hands. They were strong hands, well shaped and efficient. He touched these bones as though they offered him clues to their existence, as though he felt something with his fingertips that she could never hope to feel.

She helped him lift the skeleton onto the sheet. He wrapped it up and slipped a black plastic bag over it, all without saying a word. Eden was afraid to say anything herself for fear of being reprimanded again.

It took them a few minutes to work their way back to the exit. He went into the tunnel first, pulling the skeleton behind him as delicately as he could. She followed, stooping awkwardly, lifting the bag as they turned corners and stepped over rocky patches in the earth. The stooping was taking its toll, and her shoulders ached along with the muscles in her thighs and the small of her back. But she felt no apprehension this time. There was no longer any unknown here. And she was with Ben.

Once they were in the great room, Ben lifted the bag into his arms and carried it like a child. She walked on ahead, lighting their way.

"Your mother was a strange duck for thinking this was a hospitable place," Ben said.

"Imagine how inhospitable her own home felt to her that she preferred being here," Eden replied.

Kyle was waiting for them under Lou's big green umbrella just outside the cave entrance. "I'm glad to see the two of you," he said.

"Holy shit," Ben said as he watched the water of Ferry Creek pour into the pits. It had nearly filled them to the top. "If I'd known the water was this high, I don't think I would have been all that relaxed in there." He started toward the truck. "I'll take this back to the cabin, Kyle, and up to the university on Monday."

"Can you use some help?" Eden offered. She needed to talk to him. *You're running away from the man you love.*

"No," Ben said without turning around. "I'll be fine."

She walked up to the road while Kyle helped Ben put the skeleton in the truck. They set it on the front seat, out of the rain. She didn't watch. Ben wanted nothing more from her. They were finished and he was willing to let it go. Anxious to let it go and get on with his life. And what did she want? Not this. Not this achingly cold good-bye. Yet she had lost him all on her own. There was no one else to blame. She had mistrusted him; she had maligned him. How could she expect anything from him now?

Kyle started walking toward her and she lifted her face fully to the rain to erase any trace of emotion. They were up on the road when she heard Ben start the ignition in the truck. He would have to drive past them. She would lift her hand and wave. It would be simple.

"You want to be with him," Kyle said as they started walking.

"He doesn't want to be with me."

"Bull," Kyle said.

Ben drove past with a couple of taps on his horn and she raised her hand without looking up from the road. She and Kyle walked back to the house in silence, but once they were inside, surrounded by the smell of apples and cinnamon, he turned to her.

"I'll pick up Cassie at Maggie DeMarco's," he said. "You go on up to Ben's." He took her car keys from the rack by the door and pressed them into her hand, then opened a drawer in the hutch and handed her a darkened notebook. "The last one," he said.

47

By the time she reached the cabin, the rain had stopped. The gray clouds split open above her head, revealing a deep blue-violet sky as evening settled over the Valley.

Ben opened the door before she'd had a chance to knock. He had showered and changed into a pair of faded jeans and a blue chambray shirt she had never seen on him before.

"May I come in?" Her voice sounded timid to her ears. There was nothing welcoming in his face.

He let go of the door and walked into the kitchen, poured himself a glass of orange juice.

"Want some?" he asked.

She shook her head and looked around the cabin. The skeleton in its black plastic bag rested on the table in the center of the room, but something else was different.

"It's cool in here," she said, and then she noticed the air-conditioning unit where the fan used to be. "An air conditioner!"

He leaned against the counter. "I brought it from home. Along with a VCR and an upgrade on the stereo. I could have taken anything I wanted. Sharon is a very guilt-ridden woman."

"So am I."

He sighed and set his glass down on the counter. "Look, Eden. I guess you think we need some sort of resolution to this whole mess, that we need to talk it out or something, but I'm not interested in doing that. I've accepted the fact that you and I are through, and now I want to think about the future. It's been a long time since I felt as though I had one."

She shouldn't have come. Kyle had been wrong about Ben wanting to see her. She felt as though she was in a strange cabin, talking to a man she didn't know, who wore clothes she'd never seen. She looked out the window where the sky was quickly turning black. "Do you want me to leave?"

"I really don't see much point in you staying."

"You're still furious with me."

"No, I'm not."

She hugged her arms across her chest. "You must be to be treating me so coldly."

"I just don't want to feel close to you again. I'd like to barely notice that you've left on Monday. I've reached my limit on suffering. I'd like to be able to wake up Tuesday morning and say to myself, 'Eden's gone. Big deal.'"

She winced, and he looked away from her.

"That wasn't too nice," he said. "I'm sorry. I guess I am still angry. I want to hurt you. I want to hurt everybody, but I shouldn't have said that."

"I still love you, Ben."

He laughed. "You know what? I don't think I believe you. I don't trust you. You said you were in love with me, and then you spent one lousy hour with Michael Carey and suddenly you're treating me like I'm Jack the Ripper. Next thing I know, people on the street are calling me scum, and I read in the paper that I mean nothing to you. I was a mistake, a lapse in judgment. I was convenient, wasn't I? Good enough for you in private, but God forbid anyone might see you with me." He walked over to the door and pulled it open. "How does it feel not to be trusted?"

She swallowed hard. She walked to the door and turned to face him. "I wish only the best for you, Ben." She walked across the clearing, got into her car, and pulled it out on the road before she let herself cry.

Ben left his cabin shortly after Eden. It was nearly nine and he was hungry—he'd had nothing to eat since lunch. He drove the few miles to Sugar Hill, wishing the last half hour had not happened. That battered look on Eden's face when she left his cabin was going to haunt him all night. He'd hurt her all right. She shouldn't have come over. It would have been better if she'd left the Valley without any words passing between them at all.

Sugar Hill was surprisingly quiet for a Saturday night and he had no trouble finding a table. Ruth walked toward him carrying the unnecessary menu and he braced himself for her snarly greeting, but she surprised him.

"May I sit down for a minute?" she asked.

He looked up, stunned. "Yes."

She sat across from him, licked at her orange lips. "I owe you one hell of an apology," she said.

"What for?"

"For thinking all those months that you'd hurt your little girl. We all thought that, and we treated you like we thought you deserved to be treated. Now that we know different, we feel right small, I can tell you."

He narrowed his eyes at her. "How do you know I didn't do it?"

"That article in the paper."

"What article?"

"You haven't seen it? Well, I don't suppose you would of. It's tomorrow's paper, the Sunday, but my boy gets a big hunk of it in the city on Saturday and brings it up here when he comes for the weekend."

He frowned, trying to follow her. "There's an article about me in tomorrow's paper?"

"Wait a minute." She got up and returned in a minute with the Style section of Sunday's *Post*. "Here it is." She opened the paper to page three and set it in front of him. "You want your regular, hon?"

Hon? "Yes, please."

There was that picture of him and Eden taken in the Village, and several quotes from Eden that not only exonerated him but indicted herself for her denunciation of him. "I made a mistake," she said in closing. "I was frightened for my daughter and my career and I protected myself the only way I knew how at the time. As a result, I hurt someone I love very much."

The words blurred on the paper in front of him. He stood up and found Ruth. "I need to leave, Ruth." He set his hand on her shoulder, a shoulder he wouldn't have dared touch an hour ago. "Is it too late to cancel my order?"

"No problem, hon. Come back tomorrow night. It'll be on the house."

She read Cassie a story, the words pouring mechanically from her lips. She kissed her good night, closed the door, and walked across the hall to her own room, where she changed from her jeans and T-shirt to her white satin nightgown and climbed beneath the covers. It was early, but she was exhausted from her work in the cave and from the confrontation with Ben. Her shoulders ached from stooping in the tunnel, the muscles in her thighs burned.

She lay still for a few minutes, staring at the black ceiling. Finally she switched on the lamp on her night table and pulled her purse from the floor to the bed. She would read the journal Kyle had given her. The last one.

She reached into her purse, but her hand froze as she heard the slamming of a car door in the driveway. She held still, listening to the knock at the kitchen door, to the quiet murmur of Kyle's voice, to the footsteps on the stairs. Ben.

She set her purse back on the floor and folded her hands in her lap.

He knocked softly on the door. "Eden?"

"Come in," she said.

He opened the door and shut it softly behind him. He sat down on her bed and pried one of her hands loose from the other so he could hold it on his knee.

"I was a jerk earlier," he said. "I'm sorry."

"It's all right."

"Ruth had a copy of tomorrow's paper. Your retraction is in it."

"Good." She was relieved he had seen it. She might leave Monday a miserable woman, but at least her conscience would be clear.

"You didn't need to be so hard on yourself," he said.

"Yes," she said, "I did."

He looked down at her hand, stroked his thumb across its smooth surface. "Did you mean it earlier when you said you still love me?"

"Yes."

He smiled, a bit wistfully, and squeezed her hand. "I saw *Heart of Winter* last night. It's playing in Gloverton. I stopped on my way back from Annapolis."

"But you'd already seen it twice."

"I know," he said quietly. "But I had to see you, and that was a safe way to do it. I could watch you without . . . being tempted by you. Without any danger of making a fool out of myself, or . . . I was so grateful to you for helping me get out of the mess I was in, but I didn't want to forget what you'd done to me." He shrugged. "It wasn't very satisfying, seeing you up on the screen. It wasn't you up there. You were the woman in the movie, Lily whatever-her-name-was. You were her completely. You're an excellent actress, Eden, but it still irked the hell out of me seeing Michael Carey paw at you, watching you kiss him." Ben shuddered. "I left before the climax, so to speak."

She smiled, raised her hand to touch his cheek.

"I love you too, Eden," he said.

"Then tell me you don't want me to leave on Monday."

"Please don't leave."

She rose to her knees to kiss him, but the pain in her shoulders and legs made her cringe.

"You're sore from the tunnel?" he asked.

She nodded.

"I'd offer to give you a massage but I'm afraid once I touch you I won't be able to stop."

"Touch me, then. Please."

He stood up and hit the lock on her door and returned once again to her bed. "This is beautiful." He stroked the back of his fingers down the white satin between her breasts. "How come I've never seen it before?"

"I never needed it at your cabin. We just went from dressed to undressed."

"Well, I think we'll have to take it off you in order for me to rub your shoulders properly."

She felt suddenly shy at the thought of pulling her nightgown over her head, sitting naked and vulnerable in front of him, but he leaned over to switch off the lamp on the night table and the darkness filled her with longing. He slid the gown up her body and over her head and set it behind him on the bed. "Lie on your stomach," he said.

She lay down willingly, her head resting on her arms, and waited while he took off his shoes. He straddled her and his first warm touch on her shoulders brought tears to her eyes. It had been too long since she'd felt his hands on her, since she'd felt any love from him at all.

"You're tense," he said, gently pressing, kneading. And then his hands stopped, rested flat against her back, and she knew he could feel the spasms as she tried not to cry. She felt his lips on her back. "No," he said. "Please don't cry." He pulled her into his arms and she clung to him.

"I was afraid I'd never get to see you again," she said. "Or talk to you, or hold you. I'm not used to caring that much. I figured I'd be okay once I was back in California where I could pretend everything is all right. I don't feel pain there, but I never really feel happiness either. This summer's been different. I've felt everything. My emotions have been all over the map—up and down, back and forth—but they're my emotions. They belong to me, not to some character I'm playing. Not to some plastic Eden Riley."

He kissed her shoulder. "Lie back again," he said.

She lay on her back as he set his hands on her thighs. "Show me where it hurts," he said.

She guided his hands to the line of fire in her thighs. He ran his thumbs along the bruised muscles and she gripped the sheet in her fists and tensed against the pain.

"Try to relax," he said.

He was good at this. She let go of the sheet and closed her eyes, and gradually her muscles loosened beneath his hands.

She knew he was through with the business end of this massage when his thumbs slipped from her burning muscles to the inside of her thighs. And she knew she was through with the pain when her legs parted of their own accord.

She remembered suddenly where she was, with her daughter next door and Kyle and Lou downstairs.

"We have to be quiet," she whispered, but what she was thinking was that she was safe. Safe and happy, surrounded by the people she loved.

"Please come back to the cabin with me tonight," he said one long amazing hour later, when the room was still and her heartbeat had slipped back to normal.

"All right. Only I'd like to be back early in the morning, before Cassie wakes up."

But Lou and Kyle told them not to worry about Cassie. "We'll take her in our bed with us in the morning," Lou said. "Go on now. She'll be fine."

Although it was that hour in her bed that Eden would remember best, she knew it was the rest of the night spent in Ben's cabin—the hours of talk and reconnection—that bound them together, that set their future course.

He told her about his few days in Annapolis, the nearly unbearable roller coaster of emotions, the mix of wild anger toward Sam and pure love for his daughter.

"Are you still in love with Sharon?" she asked. They were in his bed, under a blanket to keep off the chill of the air conditioner.

"No. I could never recapture the feelings I had for her and I have no interest in trying. I feel terrible for her, though. She's really been through hell."

"Did you see Sam?"

"Oh, yeah." Ben's body stiffened next to her. "My incredible brother. The one person in the world I thought I could always count on. Parents die, friends come and go, spouses might come and go. But your brother. Sam was someone I thought I couldn't lose."

He told her about his meeting with Sam, the satisfaction he took in hitting him. She had difficulty picturing Ben hurting anyone, although wasn't that what he had done to her earlier that evening when she'd stopped by his cabin? He hadn't used his fists then, but she had felt the force of his attack all the same.

"I have so much fury in me," he said. "I know it's meant for Sam, but it's coming out all over the place. I don't know how I'll ever deal with him. One minute I want to kill him, the next I want to hold him and tell him I'll do absolutely anything in the world to help him. What I really can't stand is imagining him with Bliss."

"What was it like seeing her?"

"Terrific, although you were right about her being way too thin and fragile. She looks haunted to me. And she's into Barbie dolls." He laughed. "Five years old. I was hoping it would never happen. I feel like it's my fault. If I'd been there I could have somehow protected her from the influence of her misguided peers."

She smiled. "It's so good to hear you laugh."

He pulled her closer, and his voice softened. "One day Bliss is going to realize what happened—that because she thought Sam was me, her parents split up and her father went to jail. How do I protect her from that, from blaming herself?"

"You'll find a way," she said. "Something that always touched me about you was the way you put Bliss ahead of yourself. Even when things were at their worst for you."

"You would do the same. As a matter of fact, you did, and I've never held that against you, your wanting to protect Cassie."

They were quiet for a minute and then she asked, "What's Annapolis like?"

"To visit or to live in?" He was smiling. She could hear it in his voice.

"To live in."

"It's quaint." He kissed the top of her head. "It has a lot of charm, yet everything you could possibly need or want is close by. Unless you happen to need or want a movie studio."

She laughed. "I will want a movie studio." For the first time in a long time she knew that was true. She wanted to read the script for *Treasure House*. She wanted to get her career back on track. She felt an energy inside her that was new and real. "I'll have to travel from time to time," she said. "But I'll work it out."

"We'll work it out," Ben said.

In the morning she dressed in Ben's underwear, made coffee, and carried two mugs of it along with her mother's notebook back to bed. Ben propped the pillow up against the wall and she settled in next to him, the notebook resting on her lap.

"It's the last one," she said, and he must have seen the apprehension in her eyes.

"Read it to me." He put his arm around her shoulders. "Read it out loud."

And with reluctant fingers she opened the stiff, water-stained cover and began to read.

48

November 5, 1957

Last Friday a friend of Susanna's came to the house. She is an older woman, about fifty, who knew Susanna when she was small and just stopped by to chat. She and Susanna were sitting in the living room and I had just fed Eden lunch in the kitchen when Susanna called me in to introduce Eden to Mrs. So-and-So. I led Eden in by the hand, but when she spotted the woman she hid behind my legs and no amount of reassurance would bring her out.

"Why, she's afraid of her own shadow," the woman said.

This has happened a few other times recently. Once with Reverend Caper, another time with Susanna's mother, who said she never saw a child so afraid of people. I'm certain I'm responsible for this fear in her. How can a child raised by a recluse like me come up normal? She never sees other children. She barely sees anyone but me and Daddy and Susanna. Susanna says she's too quiet; Daddy says she's too pale. What am I doing to my child?

December 29, 1957

Kyle and Lou are here for two weeks. So far it has not been a good visit. It's been horrid in fact, at least as far as I'm concerned. They arrived two days before Christmas bearing their usual bounty of gifts. Kyle was very anxious to see Eden. But she shrank from him and cried when he reached out for her. He looked so disappointed and I felt guilty, responsible for what's happened to my daughter. "The shy stage," Lou said. "That happens around this age." Daddy and Susanna piped in that they're worried about Eden, that she's so shy with everyone. "She's not a normal two-and-a-half-year-old," Susanna said. Soon even Lou was saying there seems to be something wrong, and Kyle grew quiet around me. I read his silence as anger, and I felt I deserved it.

I barely noticed the festivities on Christmas Day, I was so caught up in studying Eden. She clings to me. She wanted me to unwrap her presents for her, and after the third or fourth one Kyle said, "Let her do it herself, Kate. You do everything for her." His tone was so reproachful that it was all I could do not to cry.

Last night, I was in the kitchen and Lou and Kyle were in the living room. They must have thought I was upstairs, because they were talking about me and Eden and I'm sure their conversation was not meant for my ears.

"By some miracle we managed to create a healthy child," Kyle said, "and now she's being ruined."

"You're making too much out of it," Lou said.

"I don't want her to turn out like Kate."

"Kate's happy in her own way."

Kyle made a disgusted noise. "You can say the same about a pig in a pigsty," he said. His exact words. I will never forget them, or forgive them. "Eden looks sickly," he said. "She's white as a ghost."

"Do you want to take her with us?"

My heart nearly leapt from my chest. My baby. I would never let them take my baby.

"I couldn't do that to Kate," Kyle said. "Besides, the way we move around would be even worse for her."

Lou sighed. "I don't know what else to suggest, Kyle."

"I've been thinking that maybe I—we—should stay here for a while."

I felt a tremendous joy, but then I heard sniffling and knew Lou was crying.

"Don't," Kyle said, in the tender voice I know well. "Please, Lou."

"Is that what you want to do?" She sounded very hurt.

"No, it's not what I want to do!" Kyle was nearly yelling. "But I brought a life into the world and I'm not going to let it rot in a goddamned cave."

"Shhh."

"There's craziness in this family and the chain's got to break somewhere."

"But you're talking about your life, Ky," Lou said. "Your career. You just have another year on your doctorate. You can't give it all up."

"I'm not talking about forever. But Eden's my daughter. If I were here I could take her places, get her away from the house and the cave. What difference does it make if I get my doctorate next year or in five years?"

There was a long silence. Then Lou said, "I don't think I could live here. It's stifling. It's backwards. Besides, your father and Susanna despise me."

"Are you saying you wouldn't stay with me?"

I could hear Lou crying. There is something horrible about Lou's tears. She has such a tough shell around her that it almost scares me to see her weaker side.

I decided to put an end to this problem right then. I gathered up my pride and went into the living room, where they both looked shocked to see me.

"I heard everything you said," I began, as I took a seat on the sofa. "I'm not blind or stupid. I know my isolation is hurting Eden. It worries me too and I'd like your help. But talking about me behind my back isn't the way to go about it."

Kyle was up in an instant and sat next to me on the sofa, taking my hand. "Kate, I'm sorry," he said. It was hard for me to let him comfort me after the things he said. A pig in a pigsty. "I'll move back here for a while."

"No, you won't," I said, though it took every speck of my strength to say that. I could see the relief in Lou's face. She wiped at her eyes with the back of her hand. "You've got a career and a wife and a whole life to tend to," I said. "So moving back here is out."

"I'll teach you to drive," Lou said. "Then you can borrow your daddy's car and visit friends."

"I don't have any friends," I said, and I missed Matt all of a sudden.

"It'd be easier to make friends if you could drive," Kyle said.

"All right." I figure I can probably learn how to drive the damn car. It's going anyplace that I'm not sure I can do.

"You can go to church with Susanna on Sundays," Kyle said. "That's the best way around here to socialize."

I rolled my eyes. "All right," I said, though I can't picture myself actually doing it.

"And don't go back to the cavern in the spring," Kyle said. "Stay here in the house to do your writing."

"All right," I said again, although I know when the weather warms up I'll start pining for the cavern. Well, at the very least I'll go there less.

So, the three of us made our little plan to save Eden and I guess it's up to me to make it work.

January 5, 1958

Lou taught me to drive this afternoon. No one was more surprised than me at how easy it was for me to learn. I have a feel for it. "You're a natural," Lou said. I actually drove us into Coolbrook and back, which was fine since we didn't have to go into any shops.

Lou and Kyle are leaving tomorrow. Tonight, when I was putting Eden to bed, Kyle came into the room. He read her a story, all three of us snuggling on the twin bed I slept in as a child. He held my hand the whole time. I loved watching Eden look up at him with those big blue eyes that are very much like his. He's won Eden over with his stories, his presents and his gentleness.

There will be these little moments in my life for me to treasure. Once a year, more or less. My hand in the hand of the man I love, our child warm and sleepy-eyed against his chest, his voice—Oh, damn. I want more than this! I want more than I can ever, ever have.

April 8, 1958

I made promises to Kyle that I have not kept. I tried going to church with Susanna, but my terrors overcame me and all I could hear in there was my heart pounding. I had to leave in the middle of the service. I left as quietly as I could, but I created a stir nonetheless and I will not go back. I don't want all of Coolbrook to see me look the fool and hold it against Eden while she's growing up. That thought terrifies me. I remember better than I care to what it was like being the daughter of a woman everyone thought was batty. How can I protect Eden from that? The chain has to break somewhere, Kyle said. I'm trying, Kyle, but I just don't know how to break it.

As for driving, I can manage to get to Coolbrook but I can't do a thing once I'm there. I can no longer even set foot in a shop without feeling like I'm going to fall over any minute. Once I managed to get into the butcher's, but while I was in line the dizziness set in and I had to leave, returning home empty-handed, which peeved Susanna no end.

I spend far less time in the cavern, although I am in it more than Kyle would like, I'm sure. I've tried not to make it Eden's home. My typewriter remains in the house and I just come to the cave to write by hand or to sit and think.

Despite all this, Eden is just fine. Sara Jane Miller has a little girl named Maggie who is a few months younger than Eden. Susanna's driven Eden over there a few times and Maggie's come here. She's a child with the devil in her, but she plays well with Eden and I can see Eden come to life when she's with her. This little girl can do far more than I can to help Eden over her shyness.

August 2, 1958

Today is my thirty-first birthday and I've given myself a present—moving my typewriter into the cavern. What joy to be working in the cool of the cave again, surrounded by the mites and tites! Tonight I will write a letter of apology to Kyle. I'll tell him how well Eden is doing, that if I really felt working in the cave was harming her I wouldn't do it. She loves the cavern too. Yesterday she and Maggie spent the entire afternoon playing in it while I wrote.

September 1, 1958

Daddy says I have created a monster in Eden. He says she is "brassy" and "bratty," all because she took a handful of peas off his dinner plate. I laughed when she did it. I would rather see her be demanding and pushy than cowering and shy any day. But Daddy was furious. He gets angry so easy these days and he cannot leave the bottle alone. He pulled Eden out of her chair by the arm and whacked her across her bottom. He might as well have hit me in the face with the razor strap. I jumped up and started beating on him with my fists, screaming at him never to hit her again. This was the first time Eden's been struck and I had vowed to myself she never would be. I was crazy with anger and Susanna had to pull me off Daddy. He sat down again, all red in the face, and that's when he said Eden was a monster. I told him I would move out (ha!) and he said to stop talking nonsense, that he would never hit her again.

December 3, 1958

Kyle and Lou can't make it home for Christmas this year. Kyle is now Kyle Charles Swift, Ph.D. Doctor Kyle Swift! He and Lou need a few more months to finish their work in Peru before Kyle takes his very own expedition to Argentina in June. He said he and Lou will come back to Lynch Hollow for a full month in the spring, before they leave for Argentina. He also said he would like to take a bone from old Rosie in the maze room to send to New York for "carbon dating," a process that would figure just how old she is. He explained this process in great detail in his letter, but I really don't understand it or believe it works. I am curious to know Rosie's age, but I hate to tamper with her when she's rested peacefully in the cave for hundreds of years. What right do we have to disturb her?

April 1, 1959

Well, I guess poor Eden has lost her little friend Maggie on account of me. Sara Jane called Susanna all in a snit that I'd let Maggie play in the cavern. Maggie's come down with pneumonia or worse, Sara Jane says. She's wheezing from bat dung or cave dust or some such nonsense. She said Maggie can't play here anymore, though I hope Sara Jane will still let Eden come over there once Maggie's feeling better.

Eden has no lack of playmates though. Only thing is, they're all in her mind. I am proud to be the mother of a child with an imagination that rivals my own. She and I are terrific buddies. She talks non-stop these days. There is nothing she doesn't want to discuss. She is so smart. She could give tours of the cave, I believe.

Kyle and Lou will be here next week for more than a month! Eden doesn't remember them, but she has a thousand pictures of them and shares my excitement when she says, "Unka Kyle and Auntie Lou are coming."

April 10, 1959

Eden was shy with Kyle and Lou but not for long. They arrived the night before last and they had so many presents for her that they were difficult people for my greedy little daughter to resist.

I insisted that Kyle and Lou take my big double bed this time. I'd made the arrangements in advance so they couldn't argue about it. They'll be here for so long that it's ridiculous for them to have to sleep in those little separate beds down in Eden's room. So I'll sleep down there with Eden which is fine with me. I know she'll end up in my bed every night. Sometimes she tiptoes up the stairs and sneaks into my bed and only if I wake in the middle of the night do I know she's done it. I love finding her there, all sweet-smelling and warm. I wonder then if she comes to me because she needs me or because she knows I need her?

April 16, 1959

Saturday, Lou took Eden shopping in town. Eden cried a little when she left me, but she did go, to my relief. When the car pulled away, Kyle put his arm around me and aimed me in the direction of the cavern and I knew then that he and Lou had planned the shopping trip to give Kyle and me a chance to talk.

It's funny. I rarely think anymore about desire or my needs as a woman. I put all my energy into writing or the digs or mostly, into Eden, and it seems enough to satisfy me. But when Kyle put his arm around me it was as if I was one enormous aching need.

I sat in the rocker with my hands folded and he sat on the settee.

"You've done such a good job with Eden, Kate," he said. "I can see the shyness is much better. I know it hasn't been easy raising her without a father."

"She's just fine," I said, though I was feeling a little guilty since I didn't have much to do with it.

"I'm still concerned, though," Kyle said. "I don't think you can see a problem with her because you see her every day. But she's got dark circles around her eyes and her skin is so white. Her nose is always running. The cave is no good for a child, Kate. It's no good."

My hands started fidgeting in my lap. I was nervous, not knowing what he was leading up to.

"I can't let it continue," he said. "We have to work out a way I can help. It's going to be even worse the next few years because I'll be responsible for an expedition. I don't know when I'll be able to get away. So, I want you to come to Argentina with Lou and me for a visit—I mean a long visit. Several months. Maybe you could come again next spring before Eden has to start school. And then again every summer."

I was shocked, my mouth hanging open to my knees. "Go to Argentina?" I said. "I couldn't go to Argentina for an afternoon, much less several months."

"You made it to New York when you were motivated enough."

"That was years ago, Kyle, and I was desperate." I could see that Kyle had no idea how bad things have gotten for me. I would have to tell him. "I can't even go into Coolbrook anymore," I said.

He frowned. "Not at all?"

I shook my head. I felt so ashamed.

"Kate, do you understand how important this is for Eden?"

"Yes." I knew he was right. She needs sunshine, she needs to meet people. She needs a different mother. I started to cry because I thought I would have to send her with Kyle and Lou, with me staying behind.

"Kate." Kyle reached his hand toward me and I moved over to the settee and sat down next to him. He put his arm around me. "It will be so good for both of you," he said. "You can even bring your typewriter, if you like."

"I can't do it, Kyle. A plane ride. Hours and hours in the air?" I trembled just to think of it. "Kyle, I'll die."

"No, you won't." He smiled, not taking me at all seriously. "You'll have Eden with you and you'll have to be strong for her. And you'll be with me. And with Lou. When have you ever felt unsafe with us?"

"When I'm with you, I want you." Only as the words came out of my mouth did I know how true they were. I realized just at that moment that I always hope he will be overcome by his longing for me, that he will make love to me again. As I sat there looking at him, his skin so dark, his hair and beard sun-bleached, his eyes Eden's shade of blue, I felt such an ache inside me. I just needed to hold him. I would settle for that.

I turned and put my arms around him and felt his own arms lock tight around me. His hands pressed against my back and he kissed my neck, then gently pushed me away.

"Katie." He shook his head at me.

"I know," I said. "Lou."

"No, it's not Lou. Lou would understand. It's me. In spite of the fact that we got a beautiful daughter out of making love, it was a terrible thing to do. Please don't try to tempt me. Don't make me have to say no to you. I want you to come to Argentina, but I don't want you to come with any expectation of getting more from me than a brother can give."

"All right," I said. "We'll come." I don't know how I will do it, but I know he is right. I'm not sure which will be harder for me: leaving Lynch Hollow or living close to Kyle without ever touching him.

May 1, 1959

Ever since I made the decision to go to Argentina I have seen my little daughter in a new light. For the first time I can see the circles under her eyes, the whiteness of her skin. She is a daily reminder that my decision is the right one. The only one. That's what I tell myself when I start getting scared.

Kyle took a bone from Rosie's toe yesterday to send to New York, and while he was in the maze room he discovered two other skeletons! He is ecstatic and says someday he'll be working in the Lynch Hollow site again.

May 9, 1959

Last night Kyle, Lou, Eden and I sat for hours in the cave talking and listening to a record Kyle had of some Peruvian songs. It was pouring outside and has been for several days. Kyle and Lou have Eden all fired up *about visiting Argentina. She is a chatterbox around them now and Kyle said we have to do something about her accent.*

"It's hard to get by in the world when you sound like you're half asleep all the time," he said.

Kyle has completely changed the way he talks. He sounds more like Lou now, though his words fortunately still have a softness to them, while Lou always sounds hard to me.

"I think she speaks just fine," I said.

"The word is *f-i-n-e*, not *f-a-h-n*," he said.

"She'd sound pretty strange talking that way around here," I said.

"Well, she's not going to live around here forever."

I could see the future laid out in front of me all of a sudden. Kyle would never cruelly take Eden away from me, but he will always be able to offer her something more exciting, something better, than I can. Maybe someday she'll choose to stay with him. The thought made my heart ache and it must have shown in my face because Kyle said softly, "Just take things a day at a time, Kate. Don't worry about tomorrow."

Eden was sleepy and he lifted her onto the settee where she quickly fell asleep, her head nestled in the crook of his arm. We were quiet for a long time. I was thinking that in three short weeks I would leave my cavern for good.

"We have to close it up real well," I said. "We have to make it impossible for me to get into, otherwise I'll be right back in here when we get home from Argentina." I know this is true. When it comes to the cavern I am as weak as Daddy is around the bottle.

"We'll use rocks," Kyle said. "Boulders. Don't worry. You'll never be able to get in again."

I fastened my eyes on Eden, all flaxen-haired and sleeping like a princess in Kyle's arms. It's for her, I reminded myself. I've got to do this for her.

The record had stopped and we listened to the rain splattering the ground outside the cave. Then Lou said, speaking to both of us: "Will you ever tell her the truth?"

Kyle and I looked at each other. I've thought about this often. It always hurt me that I didn't know about my real mama. If it were me in Eden's place, I would want to know who my parents were. Yet I cannot imagine actually saying those words to her: "Your Uncle Kyle is really your daddy."

"I'd like her to know the truth one day," Kyle said.

"Yes," I said. "I would too."

"She has the right to know," Kyle continued. "But how old should she be when we tell her? I'm thirty-two and I still wouldn't be ready to hear that kind of news about myself." Kyle stroked Eden's long hair. "Maybe when she's old enough to understand how much I love her. Maybe then she'll be ready to hear it."

"My journal," I said. "Someday I'll give her my journal and then surely she'll understand." I felt joy and relief that I'd kept these notebooks all these years. It seems to me they explain it all. And I'll know when to give them to her. She and I will be so close that I'll know the right moment. I won't have to guess.

May 29, 1959

The storms have finally let up after toppling trees and swelling the river. Even Ferry Creek has crossed the field and is creeping up on the pits. Kyle and Daddy have gone to Coolbrook to lay sandbags in front of the fire station and library because the Shenandoah's expected to flood by nightfall.

In two days Kyle, Lou, Eden and I will leave for Argentina. We have to take three planes to get us there, not just one. I can't picture me walking up the steps to a plane no matter how hard I try. Usually I can imagine anything I want, but this picture refuses to form in my head.

I've broken new ground in the art of being terrified. I can feel my heart beating clear through my back to the mattress when I'm in bed at night. I am always trembling and I can't stand the sight of food. I am quiet about my nervousness, but Kyle doesn't miss it. He strokes my back and tells me how beautiful the view is from the sky, how warm the sun is in Argentina.

I am in my beloved cavern for the last time. Tomorrow Kyle will fill the entrance with rocks. He asked me last night if I am still sure I want him to do this. He is having second thoughts, feeling guilty for pushing me into this decision. But I tell him not to talk about it, just to do it. When Eden and I come back from Argentina, I won't need this cave any longer. I will be a different person. After six plane rides and two months in a new place where no one speaks English, I will either be different or I'll be dead! Eden is in here with me. She is so excited about the trip. She's on the *settee right now, playing with little wooden dolls Kyle and Lou brought her that fit one inside the other. She's talking to them and to herself. What changes there are in store for her. What adventure! It makes me smile to think of what the next two months will be like for her. In no time at all, she'll have roses in her cheeks, Kyle says. And he says that children pick up foreign languages quickly. She'll be teaching me Spanish in a few weeks.*

I'm watching my wan-faced angel entertaining herself on the old settee and thinking she deserves far better than this and she will have it. Oh Kyle, slap those rocks against the entrance to this cave and push me on that plane! It will all be worth it. There's no sacrifice too great for someone you love.

"Mama," Eden just said to me. "I don't steal."

Her forehead had a little crease across it and I could tell she's been fretting about this for a while now.

"I know you don't steal," I said. "You're an honest girl."

"But Uncle Kyle says I'll steal everybody's heart in Argentina."

I laughed. "He just means that everybody in Argentina is going to love you."

"Oh," she said. "Does Uncle Kyle steal everybody's heart too?"

"I don't know about that," I said. "But he stole mine a long time ago."

"Mine too," she said, and went back to her dolls. I can't help but wonder if she has any idea how.

Eden turned the page, but it was blank. She leafed through the rest of the notebook, but the pages were yellowed and empty.

"Oh, Ben." She buried her head against his neck and felt the warmth of his arms around her, but he was quiet and she imagined that the picture in his mind was the same as in hers: Kate stopping her pen in midsentence, looking up from her notebook, startled, as she heard the water break over the entrance to the cave. She must have gone to look, must have seen the water pouring in, rushing at her, rushing . . .

"Eden," Ben said. "I'm sorry."

She raised her head to look at him. "I have to see Kyle," she said, and he nodded.

"You don't need me there," he said. "Take the truck." She got out of bed and pulled on her jeans, and when she leaned over to kiss him he caught her hand and sat her down next to him.

"Go see Kyle," he said. "But then come back to me, okay?"

"Yes." She lifted his hand to her lips.

"We've both been hurt too much by the past, Eden," he said. "It's time to put the suffering behind us."

49

Lou and Cassie were already at their easels when she reached Lynch Hollow. Lou looked up from her work and without even waiting for Eden's question said, "He's at Ferry Creek."

She drove the truck back out to the road and down to Ferry Creek. The field was gone, buried beneath the deepening waters of the once docile creek. She saw Kyle sitting on the top step of the footbridge, watching the angry sea below him.

The water lapped at both sides of the road as she parked the truck and got out. She felt as though she was on a long, narrow island as she walked toward the bridge. Kyle hung on to the wires to keep his balance as she climbed the steps, the bridge swaying gently beneath her weight. At the top step she turned and sat next to him. Across the field, directly in front of them, the water poured into the entrance of the cavern.

They watched in silence for a few minutes. Then Kyle said, "When it flooded in 1959, everyone said it was a once-in-a-hundred-years flood. Hard to believe it's happening again."

Eden stared at the cave, mesmerized. It was as though the entire field of water was being sucked into the earth through that black hole in the hillside.

"What was it like inside yesterday?" Kyle asked. "Was it familiar to you?"

"The great room was. But it was much darker than I remember."

"Kate always had those lanterns burning."

"I nearly fell over the typewriter."

"Was any of the furniture left?"

She told him about the settee, the desk, the chair. "Everything was against that back wall by the reflecting pool."

Kyle nodded. "That's where they found Kate. You don't remember it at all, do you? The flood?"

"No." She turned her head toward him and asked him almost shyly, "Can you tell me?"

Kyle looked toward the cavern. "My father and I were sandbagging the fire station in Coolbrook and suddenly it occurred to me—I don't know why so late—that if the flood could get as high as the fire station, it could get as high as the ground here by the cave. I left to come back here, thinking at first that I was overreacting. So I forced myself to walk slowly, but as I got closer I could see how high and wild the creek was and I started running. I pictured you and your mother in the cavern with cotton in your ears, not able to hear the water coming. By the time I got here, sure enough the water was pouring through the entrance. Not as quickly as it is now, but quick enough. It was only up to my ankles at the entrance but it was much deeper inside. Deep enough to put out most of Kate's lanterns. Just two were still burning.

"I couldn't see her at first. I called to her from the entrance to the great room and she called back to me, and after a minute I could see her as my eyes adjusted to the darkness. She was holding you in her arms and trying to fight her way to the entrance, but the water was coming in so fast she couldn't make any headway. She said, 'Take Eden,' and she was holding you out to me. You were screaming your little head off." He smiled. "Trying to hang on to your mama, not making it easy for her to hand you over. I went in as far as I dared and she nearly had to toss you to me. You latched onto me like a monkey, and I managed to get you back out here. I set you up there on the road." He pointed to where the truck was parked. "It was just a dirt road then. I told you to stay there. I remember thinking that without being weighed down by you, Kate could probably get out on her own, but by the time I got in again, she was pushed back even further. The water was to her waist and she was holding on to a stalagmite, trying to keep from being pulled deeper into the cave."

Eden hugged her knees, queasy from the images forming in her head.

"I got closer," Kyle said. "I was scared we'd both drown. I kept looking back toward the entrance and could see the space between the water and the ceiling getting smaller and smaller. And I kept thinking about you out there alone on the road. I was afraid maybe you'd try to get back into the cave, or maybe get swept into the creek.

"I was holding on to the stalagmites, trying to work my way toward Kate, when suddenly it went dark. The last lantern went out. It was black as pitch in there. Kate screamed out my name. 'Kyle!' she screamed. Her voice bounced off the walls loud enough to hurt my ears. I called to her. I called and called but . . ." He shook his head. His eyes had filled and Eden slipped her arm through his and set her head on his shoulder.

"Sometimes I still think about it," Kyle said. "That maybe if I'd had a rope . . . Maybe if I'd run from Coolbrook instead of walked . . ."

"Maybe if you didn't have to get me out first," Eden said.

"No." He touched her hand where it rested on his arm. "No, that's one thought I've never had."

"All I remember from that whole episode is that your hands and arms were scraped up."

He smiled slightly. "You remember that?" He turned his hands palm side up in his lap, but the scars were gone. "I guess from the tites and mites. Your mother's arms were covered with scrapes too when they found her."

"Who found her?"

"Daddy and a neighbor. They went in the next day after the waters went down. I couldn't go in. Not until after she was out. Then I went in for the journals, and when the water was completely gone I sealed the goddamned hole in the ground—for eternity, I thought."

He let out a long sigh. "Poor Eden," he said. "You kept asking for your mama, and we'd explain the best we could that she was dead, and I thought you finally understood. But then the next year when I came to visit, you asked if Kate was with me. You said you wished she'd come back."

They were quiet for many minutes, watching the savage waters churn below them.

"I loved her so much, Eden," Kyle said. "When I look back, it's amazing that we didn't make love much sooner than we did. We had so many opportunities, we were so close, and I certainly wanted to, but I knew it could only hurt her, someone who already lived on the edge of reality. I only gave in to it that once and I regretted it. I can't tell you how ashamed and filled with remorse I was. I regretted it until the day you were born. Once I looked at you, once I held you, I stopped regretting."

"I love you, Kyle," she said.

He put his arm around her, kissed her temple. "I love you too, sweetheart."

For a moment neither of them spoke. A sense of contentment, half formed and fragmentary, fell over her and she knew what she needed to do to make it complete.

"There's something I have to tell you." She lifted her head from his shoulder. "About Lou's accident."

He dismissed her with a wave of his hand. "I know all about Lou's accident."

"No," she said. "You don't know what really happened that night."

"Yes, I do."

"How could you? Lou said she never told you."

"She didn't. She wouldn't betray you. But that boy you were running off with—Tex?—wrote me a letter shortly after the accident. He was in a drug program and his counselor made him write to me. He pretty much spelled out what happened."

Eden pulled away from him. "You've known all these years?"

"Yes."

"Weren't you furious with me?"

Kyle sighed again. "I was furious with myself, Eden. I failed you somehow that you wanted to run away, that you couldn't tell me the truth. I always felt as though I failed you, right from the start. I couldn't be a real father to you. I should have fought to take you after Kate died, and I should have told you I was your father long, long before I did."

She left Kyle sitting on the bridge and drove to the Lynch Hollow house. She should get the truck back to Ben, but there was one thing she needed to do that couldn't wait.

She sat down in front of her word processor and opened the screenplay. She scrolled through the pages until she found the love scene she'd written between Kate and Matthew. She read a few lines. It was a beautiful scene. Wrenchingly lovely. The dialogue rich, the sensual tension compelling. She pressed the button that would delete the scene in its entirety and smiled at the blank screen left in its wake. Later today she would fill that screen with something even richer, something real. But not right now.

She pulled up the title page and changed the title from *A Solitary Life* to *A Secret Life*, then scrolled to the very end of the document, where she wrote:

THIS FILM IS DEDICATED TO MY FATHER, KYLE SWIFT

She put paper in her printer, centered the lines on the screen, and hit the print button. Then she sat back to watch the letters take shape on the clean, white paper.

The End

Author's Note

Even though I've written eighteen novels since *Secret Lives*, it will always hold a special place in my heart and I'd like to tell you why.

Although I love my first two novels, *Private Relations* and *Lovers and Strangers*, I don't feel as though I truly discovered my "voice" as a novelist until *Secret Lives*. With this book, I began to understand how important structure, pacing and revelations are to a story. They can make the difference between a slow-moving novel and a book that's hard to put down.

As is often the case with my books, this story has its roots in several different areas. First, I read a newspaper article about an old acquaintance who had been accused of molesting his young daughter. Having worked professionally with him as a social worker, I couldn't imagine the accusations were true and I assumed he was being set up by an angry ex-wife. But it started me thinking. How could you ever be sure about a man like that? How could a woman—a woman with a young child—ever trust him? I knew that dilemma would be part of my story.

Around the same time, I visited the Shenandoah Valley in Virginia. On a hike, I stumbled across an archeological dig and was quickly caught up in the tales the archeologist told me about his findings. The characters of Kyle and Ben and the connection between them began to take shape as I listened to that archeologist speak. On that same trip, I visited the Luray Caverns and was mesmerized by their beauty and mystery. I knew from the moment I set foot in the caverns that I wanted to use them in the book. I wanted the setting—Kate's beloved cavern—to become a character in its own right.

I spent days in the library in Winchester, Virginia listening to oral histories of people who'd lived in the hollows of the Valley after World War II, and I interviewed a couple of women in person to learn more about their lives so that I could paint Kate and Kyle's world as accurately as possible.

I fell deeply in love with my characters, particularly Kate. Kate's chapters are, of course, written in first person, since they're all in the form of journal entries. I'd never written in first person before and I discovered how incredibly close I could feel to a character by putting myself inside her heart and mind in that way.

Another reason *Secret Lives* touched me was Kate's agoraphobia. I didn't set out to make her agoraphobic—she simply became that way over the course of the book. I, too, suffered from agoraphobia as a child and young adult, which is another reason why I related to her so strongly. I understand Kate very well.

I chose not to update this book because Kate and her journal belong in a specific era. The contemporary portion of the story takes place around 1990, which is why there are no cell phones or personal computers or iPods . . . and definitely no e-book readers!

I hope you enjoyed this tale of love and family . . . and one very special woman.

Diane Chamberlain, 2011

For the first time in print,
read Diane Chamberlain's short story

The First Lie

1958

I leaned my bike against our lopsided porch and tiptoed up the steps, still real shaky from the last few hours. It had to be four in the morning by now and I'd be in deep trouble if I got caught sneaking in, so I pushed the front door open as soft as I could. I knew right away I was doomed. From our bedroom, I heard Mary Ella yelling, "Mama! Mama!" Something terrible was happening for her to yell like that. Our mama's been gone for a long time, locked up with the other crazy people at Dix Hospital. I called out for her myself sometimes when I was scared or hurt, even if it did no good. Even if I couldn't really remember Mama at all.

Mary Ella must have been having a bad dream. I stood still as a statue in the darkness, wondering if I could quiet her before Nonnie woke up and caught me sneaking in, but I was too late. My eyes was getting used to the dark and I could see the couch was empty, the sheets half off the cushions; Nonnie was already up. Usually I could sneak past her while she snored. But there wasn't nothing usual about tonight.

I heard Nonnie talking to Mary Ella in the bedroom. "It's all right, child," she said. "Everything'll be all right." But I could tell by the way Mary Ella was hollerin' that nothing was all right. I wanted to turn around and run back outside again, even though it was cold and windy and pitch black. Instead, I tore off my scarf and the old coat that used to belong to Daddy and ran across the living room to the bedroom. The best I could hope for was that Nonnie'd be thinking so much about Mary Ella that she didn't care I'd been out all night.

Mary Ella was propped up against the headboard, her wild yellow hair lit up by the lamp on the dresser. The ratty blanket covered her big belly like she was trying to hide a pumpkin, and her face, usually so pale this wintry time of year, was red from her screaming. Nonnie pressed a damp rag to her forehead, but when she spotted me, she let the rag drop to the bed and the next thing I knew, she was swatting my arms with her swole-up hands.

"Where've you been, you little tramp?" she shouted.

"I ain't a tramp!" I yelled back. I didn't think you could be a tramp at thirteen. Mary Ella, now, she was a different story. Having a baby at fifteen pretty much made her one for sure, even though I defended her to anyone at school who said a word against her after she got kicked out for being in the family way.

There was no time for bickering, and I was glad when Nonnie stopped hitting me and sat down on the bed, wiping Mary Ella's face with the rag again.

"It *hurts*!" Mary Ella shouted. She hardly seemed to see either of us while she hollered and cried out for Mama and gripped the blanket in her fists. I didn't know what to do. I pried loose one of her hands to try to hold it, but she pulled it away. We wasn't the kind of sisters that held hands, anyway. We might of slept in the same bed every night, but we didn't talk much or share no secrets. And Mary Ella had plenty of them, for sure.

"What's wrong with her?" I asked Nonnie. "It's too soon for the baby, ain't it?"

"The baby don't seem to know it," Nonnie said.

That scared me. Things could go wrong when you had a baby, and Mary Ella sounded for all the world like she could die. I remembered she said that when our daddy died in the tractor accident, she saw his spirit go up in the sky. The way she looked right now, I was afraid I could see hers heading in the same direction, but I think it was just all that yellow hair looking like a halo around her head.

"There, there, child," Nonnie said, her voice nearly swallowed up by Mary Ella's screams. Nonnie looked up at me. "You need to run to the Gardiners' and call Mrs. Werkman," she said.

"Now?" I said. "It's four in the morning!"

"And don't I know it!" Nonnie smacked my arm again. "Four in the morning and my granddaughter's out there running wild. That's just what I need. Another Mary Ella."

"I ain't nothing like her." I couldn't be like Mary Ella if I tried. She was the kind of girl that made boys lose their minds when she walked past, even though she didn't dress trampy or do nothing to tease them. It was just something about her that made boys crazy. I might of had hair almost the same color and eyes almost the same blue, but I was pretty sure the day would never come when a boy lost his mind over wanting me.

"Go call Mrs. Werkman!" Nonnie said again.

I thought she was so upset, she wasn't thinking straight. "Nonnie, it's the middle of the night," I said, like I was talking to a five-year-old. "She won't be in her office yet, and anyway, it's Nurse Ann we need right now, not a social worker."

"Don't you argue with me, missy," she said. "Mrs. Werkman wrote her home phone number on the back of her card. Why'd she do that if she didn't want us to use it? You know which cabinet it's in, right? Go call her."

"But we need *Nurse Ann*. You're not making any sense!" The older I got, the more I realized Nonnie wasn't real smart.

She tried to hit me again, but I ducked out of the way and almost knocked over the lamp.

"Do as I say." She pointed to Mary Ella, whose face was tightened up with pain. "Do you see your sister here? She's a right mess, and you already made us wait too long. I couldn't leave her alone to go and call myself. You get over there right now!"

I left the bedroom and ran to the kitchen, honestly glad to get out of that room and all the shouting. I found two little white cards in the cabinet with the Ball jars of tomatoes that Nonnie put up last summer. One card was Mrs. Werkman's, the other was Nurse Ann's. I threw on Daddy's coat again as I ran outside, sticking the cards in my pocket. I got back on the bike and rode through the woods, heading for the Gardiners' house. I wondered if Henry Allen would be in bed by the time I got there. It seemed like no more than a minute had passed since I left him on Deaf Mule Road after our crazy adventure tonight.

Me and him had talked a lot about Mary Ella while we was together tonight, and now I wondered if that was a coincidence or if I somehow knew she was in trouble. Usually when we snuck out, we'd do something fun, maybe go to the pond that was froze over and skate on it on the soles of our shoes, since we didn't have no skates. Henry Allen actually did have some—his daddy owned the farm where me and Nonnie and Mary Ella lived in one of the old tenants' houses—and he had lots of things I couldn't never dream of having. But he never brung his skates, so I didn't feel bad about having none of my own. Sometimes me and him would meet up in one of the tobacco barns, empty now since it was winter, and just talk, or we'd ride our bikes through the woods, pretending we was cowboys on our horses. Sometimes we'd go to the graveyard and ride between the headstones like it was an obstacle course. I really didn't like it when we did that on account of Daddy being there, but I went along with it anyway.

Even though I knew we was wrong to sneak out at night like we did, we usually did no harm. I couldn't say that about tonight, though. Tonight we done two things that was flat-out wrong: We broke into our little Baptist church and we messed with a Ouija board.

The Ouija board belonged to the Gardiners' maid, Desiree. Them boards was evil—everybody knew that, including Desiree, who never let nobody know she had one, but Henry Allen saw it one day when he was helping her move the dresser in her room. He was only about ten then and when he asked her about it, she said it was the work of the devil and she was going to throw it away. She never did, though, and he'd been waiting all this time to get his hands on it but couldn't till tonight, when Desiree was off visiting her sister for the weekend. So I guess we could add stealing to all the things we done wrong, even though it was really just borrowing. Henry Allen was probably putting it back in Desiree's room right this minute.

I'm not sure why we ended up in the church. We was going to use the Ouija board at the graveyard, but it was so cold and windy that we decided to try the church doors and one was open, like it was inviting us to come in. The church is teeny tiny and I know it like I know our own kitchen. I been going there my whole life, though Nonnie and Mary Ella stopped going because of the shame when Mary Ella started getting big, and then I had to get a ride with the Gardiners. I'd sit in the pew next to Henry Allen and we'd try not to laugh at Pastor Kett's bushy eyebrows or the way Mrs. Patrick sang louder than anybody with her squeaky high voice. We didn't want his mama and daddy to get mad. I tried never to make the Gardiners mad, because we owed them so much. *Without their Christian kindness,* Nonnie always said, *we'd be out on the street.*

"We shouldn't be here," I whispered to Henry Allen as we walked inside. The church seemed really different from a Sunday morning when it was filled with light and people dressed in their finest and music from the little organ and Pastor Kett's booming voice. Now it was quiet and pitch dark and just plain spooky. Me and Henry Allen both had lanterns and we put them on the floor between the pews, hoping they didn't give off enough light that somebody could see us. By that point, though, it wasn't people I was scared of. I worried we brung the devil into the church along with that board.

"Let's set it up on the altar," Henry Allen said.

"No," I said. That would be carrying our evil too far.

"Chicken." He laughed. The lantern light from the floor turned his face into a mask of creepy shadows, and I couldn't look at him for long. Usually I liked looking at him. He had blue eyes the same color as mine but his hair was dark and straight, always flopping down in his eyes. He was a nice-looking boy except with them shadows on his face.

"Let's put it here on the floor so we'll be hid by the pews if anyone looks in the windows," I said.

"Nobody's around to look," he said, but he got down on the floor with me and set up the board between us, the light flickering across the letters and numbers.

"How's this work?" I asked, shivering. I wasn't sure if I was shaking all over from the cold or my nerves.

"We put our hands—just our fingertips—on this here thing—

it's called a 'plancher' or something like that—and ask the spirits questions and it moves around and gives us answers." He showed me where he'd put his fingers and where I should put mine. "We got to take off our gloves," he said, peeling his off. My fingers already poked out of my gloves in a couple of places, but I took them off anyway to do it right. I set my fingertips on the plancher thing.

"I think messing with this in a church is the worst way of doing it," I whispered.

"Don't worry about it," he said. "Just concentrate. Don't think about anything except talking to the spirits."

I felt like everyone buried in the graveyard was out there waiting for us to get started. I pictured them like a big wall of ghosts ready to have their day, and I wondered if Daddy was one of them. I remembered him real well even though I was only five when he got killed. Him being Nonnie's son, she always talked about him and kept him alive in my head. He was a real good man.

"Can we talk to my daddy?" I asked.

"I don't think we have a say over it," Henry Allen said. "Whoever comes is who we get. Hush now." He shut his eyes, frowning, and we both got real quiet. I didn't like how the lantern light made his face look and wondered if my own face was just as craggy and scary.

"Is anybody here?" Henry Allen asked quietly.

For a moment, nothing happened. Then the plancher thing started moving slowly. "You're moving it!" I said.

"Shh! I'm not."

The plancher went right up to the YES on the board. I could of sworn a cold finger ran up my spine. I even turned my head to look behind me, but no one was there.

"What's your name?" Henry Allen asked.

The plancher started moving again. "Are you moving it?" I whispered, and he shook his head. I believed him. My whole life, there was one person I knew I could trust and it was Henry Allen Gardiner. The plancher spelled out R-U-B-Y so fast, our fingers could hardly keep up. I couldn't breathe. This was real! We was in touch with a real spirit.

"You know anybody named Ruby?" I asked. Henry Allen shook his head again.

"Thanks for coming to visit with us, Ruby," Henry Allen said, real polite, like he wanted to keep on her good side. "Can you answer some questions?"

YES, she said.

"How old are you?" he asked. "I mean, when you died. How old was you?"

The plancher flew to the 2, then the 7.

"Are you buried out here in the graveyard?"

NO.

"How did you die?" Henry Allen asked.

The plancher just sat there. My fingertips was hardly touching it, and I could see Henry Allen's hands was shaking.

"Maybe that's too personal," I said, but then the plancher started moving again.

R-I-F-L-E, it spelled, and I shuddered. I glanced at Henry Allen. He was chewing his lip.

"Who shot you?" Henry Allen asked.

I-N-B-E-D.

"Who's that?" I whispered to Henry Allen.

"She must mean it happened in her bed."

I pictured a lady with her head blown off, blood all over her sheets. Before I could get that picture out of my mind, something hit one of the church windows with a *bonk!* We both jumped.

"What was that?" I whispered.

Henry Allen leaned forward, talking so quiet, I could hardly hear him. "I forgot something," he said.

"What?"

"We was supposed to say a prayer first. To protect us."

"Is it too late?" My arms was shaking from holding my fingertips steady on the plancher.

"You have to say it before you start," Henry Allen said. "That's what Desiree told me."

"Well . . . maybe we can change the subject?" I spoke real quietly. "Maybe we can ask her other things, just not about herself. So we don't upset her."

"Okay," Henry Allen said. He glanced toward the window, where the sound had come from, then back at the board. "What do you want to ask?"

I wanted to know if she knew Daddy in the spirit world and how he was doing, but I was scared of the answer.

"I don't know," I said. "You ask her something."

Henry Allen thought for a minute. "Who's going to win the World Series this year?" he asked finally, and I laughed.

"How's she supposed to know that?"

"Shh."

I was glad he asked something silly that would clear them R-I-F-L-E and I-N-B-E-D answers out of my head. We watched as the plancher slipped around the board, spelling out Y-A-N-K-E-E-S, which happened to be Henry Allen's favorite team. I glanced at his face and saw he was grinning, but the shadows made him look evil, so I quickly looked at the board again.

"Will I ever get to play for them?" he asked. The plancher went right to the NO. "Aww," he said, "dang it." He loved baseball. Every boy I knew loved it.

"Your turn," he said to me. "You ask her something."

"Okay." I concentrated hard on the board. "How many kids am I gonna have, Ruby?" I asked.

The plancher moved between the 3 and the 4. "What's that mean?" I asked Henry Allen.

"Don't know," he said. "Maybe one of your kids'll be a half-wit." He laughed and I was glad he didn't add nothing about Mary Ella. Some kids called her a half-wit or worse. I hated when they did that, even though it was mostly true.

"Ruby," I said, "is Mary Ella's baby a girl or a boy?"

"She don't know that!" Henry Allen said.

"How do you know what she knows? She told you about the World Series."

"Everybody knows about baseball," he said, "but she don't even know who Mary Ella is."

"It's moving!" I said, and we watched as the plancher spelled out B-O-Y plain as day and right fast.

"See?" I said. "She *does* know." I thought I'd try another question. "Ruby," I said, "how many kids is Mary Ella going to have?"

The plancher didn't move right away. Then slowly, very slowly, it slipped across the board to the 0.

"Well, that sure ain't right." I laughed. "She don't know what she's talking about."

"Don't laugh at her," Henry Allen said. "You'll make her mad. She's already peeved 'cause someone killed her in her bed."

"Shh! Don't talk about it."

"You got any more questions?" he asked.

I nodded. I had one more that I was almost afraid to ask—the question that had been making me and Nonnie crazy for months and months. "Ruby," I said, "who's the daddy of Mary Ella's baby?"

"Don't keep asking about Mary Ella," Henry Allen said.

But the plancher thing started moving. It went to the E, the exact place I didn't want it to go. When it headed toward the L, I jerked my hands off it before it could get there.

"You're not supposed to take your hands off!" Henry Allen hissed at me. "The spirit'll get stuck here if you do that and she'll haunt us forever."

I was too shook up to care. "You was right." I folded my arms across my chest. "She don't know nothing about Mary Ella."

"Come on. Put your fingers back on. We won't ask her no more about things like that. Do you want to know anything about your Daddy?"

Henry Allen could always talk me into things. I put my fingertips on the plancher again. "Let's just ask her more questions about herself, only not about the . . . you know"—I lowered my voice—"the dying part."

So we asked her about her people and where she grew up, but the plancher didn't budge. Ruby was done talking to us. It was worse than when she told us about getting killed, because every time we asked a question and waited for her answer, something brushed against the windows and it started to sound like ghosts to me. Like they was trying to get in.

"I think when you took your hands off, she got mad," Henry Allen whispered. "You asked a question and then didn't listen to her answer and instead got her stuck here forever. And now we're doomed."

"Don't say that!" I leaned across the board to hit his arm. I was afraid he was right. I felt Ruby inside the church with us, swooping around our shoulders. I felt her brush past my hair. Our lanterns flickered and the darkness was like a thick black blanket coming down over us. "How can we get her back where she belongs?"

"I don't know," he said. "Put your fingers on it again."

I did.

"Ruby," Henry Allen said, "we're right sorry we messed you up. We didn't mean nothing by it. Can we help you get back where you belong?"

The plancher didn't move at all and the dark blanket fell tighter over us, making it hard to breathe. All of a sudden, for no reason at all, Henry Allen's lantern blew out.

"Shit!" he said, scrambling to his feet. "Let's get out of here!" He grabbed the board and the plancher and I grabbed my lantern and we ran for the door and out into the graveyard, heading for our bikes.

"Pray!" he said as he jumped on his bike. "Pray real hard!"

I rode after him, saying the Lord's Prayer over and over again, but I could still feel Ruby swooping around me, her breath, hot and damp and nasty on my neck, and I started to cry.

We didn't stop pedaling till we got to Deaf Mule Road where it ran through the Gardiners' farm. I wiped the back of my hand over my eyes as we got off our bikes. My heart was still pounding hard and I had no wind at all, but moonlight rested on the empty brown fields and they looked beautiful to me. They looked like home.

Henry Allen laughed. "We just scared ourselves silly for no good reason," he said, like he didn't believe anything that had just happened.

"What do you mean, 'no good reason'?" I asked. "What do you think made your light go out?"

"Gust of wind."

"A gust of wind inside the church?"

"I'm just saying it was all our imagination, what happened back there," he said, though he didn't sound convinced. "Look how windy it is tonight. The door was unlocked, so maybe a window was part open, too. Who knows?" We started walking our bikes up the road so we could talk. It was real dark out, but I could still see the outline of his face. He'd been my best friend my whole entire life, but every once in a while, I'd catch a look at him and see him like he was new to me and it would make me feel shy all of sudden. Lately, I'd been wondering how it would feel to kiss him. I was sure he wasn't thinking no such thing himself.

We was quiet for a bit and I felt like maybe we lost Ruby somewhere on our wild bike ride. All that praying we did probably got rid of her. I never prayed that hard in my life.

"You know it *could* be Eli," Henry Allen said as we walked. "You got to face that fact."

I shook my head. "If that baby comes out colored . . . I don't know what'll happen. Mary Ella will ruin everything. Your daddy'll kick us off the farm, just for starters."

"No, he wouldn't."

It was amazing Mr. Gardiner hadn't kicked us out of the tenants' house already. An old lady and two girls wasn't much use on the farm, and soon one of them girls would have a baby to take care of. We wasn't like Eli Jordan and his family that lived in the other tenants' house. They was a hardworking bunch of boys, for sure. We all used to play together—me and Henry Allen and Mary Ella and all the Jordan kids. We'd fish or play tag or ball. That was before we got old enough that "mixing the races," as Nonnie called it, wasn't right. I had the feeling Mary Ella never got that message.

"It could be anybody's baby," Henry Allen said. "You know how Mary Ella is."

"But Ruby said . . ." I shut up, worried that if she was still around us, she might perk up at the mention of her name. "Never mind," I said. "Let's not talk about it no more."

We split up then, him riding to his house, me riding to mine, and by the time I got home, I'd nearly forgotten about Ruby altogether, especially when I heard Mary Ella screaming for Mama and Nonnie shouting at me to call Mrs. Werkman. Now, as I rode my bike to the Gardiners' house, the wind howling around my head, I wasn't thinking about anything other than my sister, all tore up with pain. What Mrs. Werkman could do for her, I couldn't figure, but we needed some kind of help, for sure.

The Gardiners' farmhouse was dark. Even the little stuck-on room at the back—Desiree's room—was dark, and I guessed Henry Allen had already got the Ouija board back where it belonged and was up in bed. As I got closer, though, I could see a flickering light coming from one of his windows and knew he hadn't got into bed quite yet.

You could fit about six of our little houses into the Gardiners' house. I dropped my bike in the dirt, then ran up the front steps to the big porch and rang the bell. It made a buzzer sound that I could hear through the door. I pressed it twice but no one came. Then I knocked and waited another minute before I finally started pounding on the glass window in the door. I'd never done nothing like that before— wake the Gardiners up in the middle of the night. Mr. Gardiner being a farmer and all, he'd be getting up soon anyway, but not this early.

Through the glass, I saw Henry Allen coming down the stairs in the same overalls he'd had on when I left him. His mother was right behind him. Henry Allen gave me a panicky look when Mrs. Gardiner opened the door, like he was worried I'd gone crazy and was going to say something about the Ouija board and get us both into trouble.

"Ivy!" his mother said. "What's the matter?" She had on a blue robe and her dark hair was loose around her shoulders instead of in the bun she always wore.

"I think Mary Ella's going to have the baby." I was winded from the ride and the words came out in a rush. "And Nonnie told me to come over to call Mrs. Werkman, but I think she's confused and I should really call Nurse Ann, don't you think?" The Gardiners knew Mrs. Werkman and Nurse Ann. They knew pretty much all there was to know about my family. We'd lived on their farm since Daddy was a little boy.

"Come in, dear." She reached for my hand and drew me into the house. "You're ice cold!" she said, wrapping both her hands around mine. I'd forgotten my gloves. "Henry Allen, you put some milk on to heat. This girl needs something to warm her up."

"Yes, ma'am," Henry Allen said, but before he walked away, he gave me a look that said *Don't say a thing about tonight,* like I might of. It made me mad he thought I was that stupid.

"How close is she?" Mrs. Gardiner asked. "Mary Ella? How close to having the baby?"

I shivered. "I don't know how to tell, ma'am," I said. "But she's hollerin' a lot and—" I thought of how Mary Ella's hair looked like a halo, how her spirit might be leaving her body right this minute, and my voice closed up. "Nonnie said to come over here fast," I said. "But she said to call Mrs. Werk—"

"Yes," Mrs. Gardiner said. "I believe she's right, except that Mrs. Werkman's office will be closed until morning, so—"

"I have the number for her house," I said, pulling the card from my coat pocket. "But she ain't no nurse. Nurse Ann always said she'd come when it was time for the baby."

"Don't be troubled, dear." Mrs. Gardiner smiled one of them *I'm a grown-up and I know what's best* smiles. "Come into the kitchen." She wrapped her robe closed tight and led me toward their kitchen, an arm across my back. Henry Allen already had the milk heating in a pan on the stove. He glanced at me, looking less nervous than before, now that he knew I wasn't there to get us in trouble.

Mrs. Gardiner sat me down at the table and put the phone in front of me. "Nurse Ann is in agreement," she said. "Mr. Gardiner and I spoke to her and your grandmother and we all feel that Mrs. Werkman can arrange Mary Ella's care best."

I shook my head. "She ain't no nurse!" I felt like everybody except me had lost their minds. "This is an emergency. Mary Ella needs a nurse!"

Henry Allen poured the milk into a mug and put it on the table in front of me. I could smell the night on him—the wintry air and the scent of the church—but Mrs. Gardiner didn't seem to notice.

"Would you like me to make the call for you?" she asked.

Again, I shook my head. I felt funny calling Mrs. Werkman in the middle of the night, but I was afraid Mrs. Gardiner couldn't explain it good enough. She was acting way too calm to describe the mess Mary Ella was in. I dialed the phone—it was only the third time I'd used a phone in my life. It rang for a long time. Nine or ten rings, and Mrs. Werkman sounded half asleep when she answered.

"This is Ivy Hart," I said.

"Ivy!" she sounded awake all of a sudden. "Is it Mary Ella?"

"Yes, ma'am. I think she's having the baby soon. She's hollerin' something awful. Should I call Nurse Ann to come over? I don't have a number for—"

"No, you don't need to call her," she said. "She won't be delivering the baby. Mary Ella needs to go to the hospital, instead—"

"Why?" What was going on? All along, the plan was for Nurse Ann to come when it was time. She was supposed to deliver the baby right in our house.

"Mary Ella needs to have her appendix out after the baby's born," Mrs. Werkman said, "so she has to be in the hospital for them to be able to—"

"What?" I shouted. "Nobody said nothing about her 'pendix!"

"Well, the last time I spoke with Mary Ella, I could tell she needed to have an appendectomy—have her appendix removed."

I was too shocked to speak. When I was eight years old, a girl in my school died of a busted appendix. I'd never forget the terribleness of it. What if the same thing happened to Mary Ella?

Mrs. Werkman kept talking. "I've been in touch with Nurse Ann so she knows, and Mary Ella'll be well taken care of at the hospital," she said. "I'll call over there right now so they'll be waiting for her. I'm sure Mr. Gardiner can take her. All right?"

"All right." I hung up the phone and looked at Mrs. Gardiner. "She said Mr. Gardiner should take her to the hospital."

Mrs. Gardiner turned to Henry Allen. "Run and fetch Eli," she said.

"No!" I stood up so fast, some of the milk sloshed onto the table. "Can't Mr. Gardiner take us?"

"He's got a chest cold," Mrs. Gardiner said. "Took him half the night to get to sleep. Eli can drive the truck just fine."

"But it's almost morning!" I said. "Mr. Gardiner'll be getting up soon, won't he? Please?" I didn't usually push like that. Not with the Gardiners, who held our past, present, and future in their hands. I didn't have no right to push, but I didn't want Eli Jordan anywhere near Mary Ella right then.

Henry Allen stood at the kitchen door, one hand on the knob, waiting to hear what to do. "Go, son," Mrs. Gardiner said to him, and he didn't look at me as he grabbed his jacket from the hook next to the door and headed outside. "And you, Ivy," she said. "Go home and get Mary Ella ready. Hurry now!" She gave me a little shove toward the door.

"Nonnie won't like it," I said, more to myself than to Mrs. Gardiner as I ran out of the room, but I knew we had no choice. We hardly ever did.

I raced out of the Gardiners' house and headed back down Deaf Mule Road on my bike. On the other side of the field, I saw a small white light bouncing through the darkness and knew Henry Allen took his bicycle to get to the Jordans' house quicker. I pictured him pounding on their door, waking up Lita Jordan and her boys.

I rushed into our house. Nothing was any different from when I left. Mary Ella was still shouting and hollering, sometimes calling out for Mama, and Nonnie was still trying to calm her down and mopping her forehead with the rag.

"You talked to Mrs. Werkman?" Nonnie asked when I ran into the bedroom.

"I did." I had to bend over to catch my breath. "She said for somebody to drive Mary Ella to the hospital. That she needs her 'pendix out! How can she know—?"

"Who?" Nonnie interrupted me. "Who can drive her? Is Mr. Gardiner coming?"

"He's sick," I said. "Henry Allen's gone to get Eli."

Nonnie's eyes got real big. "Oh, Lord," she said. "Now, ain't that just perfect."

Mary Ella moaned and I didn't know if she was in pain or upset about Eli. Nonnie looked over at me where I stood in the doorway. "Get some things ready for her to take to the hospital," she said.

"What kind of things?"

"Nightie. Clean underwear. Toothbrush. You know. Use your head!"

I gathered up everything I could think she might need, but I'd never spent the night at a hospital so I didn't really know what to pack. I put her things in our clothespin bag; we didn't have no suitcase. Back in the bedroom, Nonnie tried to get Mary Ella to sit up, but she kept saying "It hurts! It hurts!"

"She'll never be able to walk through the woods to the truck," Nonnie said.

"Maybe Henry Allen could get the wheelbarrow and we could move her that way?" I looked through the bedroom window. The sun was starting to light up the sky a little, and I saw Henry Allen and Eli coming out of the woods. I ran through the living room and out to the porch.

"She can't walk to the truck!" I shouted to them. "Henry Allen, what about the wheelbarrow?"

Henry Allen stopped walking, but Eli kept right on coming. "I can carry her," he said. I thought he could do it. He was so big. Nothing like the boy that played with us when we was kids. He climbed onto the porch in one big step. He was at least five inches taller than me and brawny and dark, except for his eyes, which was the color of honey. "Where's she at?" he asked, but he didn't need me to answer, because her hollering told him the way to the bedroom.

I ran into the house after him.

"You can't come in here!" Nonnie shouted when he reached the bedroom.

"Excuse me, ma'am, but does she need to get to the truck or not?" Eli asked.

Nonnie stood up and tried to neaten the mussed-up housedress Mary Ella was wearing, tugging it as low on her legs as she could get it. Eli waited till she stepped aside; then he moved next to the bed and reached down for my sister. Mary Ella didn't look at him the way I did—like he'd turned into a stranger since we was kids. She raised her arms to him so he could lift her up, her eyes never leaving his.

"It hurts, Eli," she said. They was the first calm and quiet words I'd heard out of her mouth all night.

"She got a coat?" he asked as he lifted her from the bed.

"I'll bring it!" I said, relieved to have something to do. Me and Nonnie gathered up her coat and the clothespin bag and Nonnie's purse and hustled out of the house after him.

Henry Allen tried to help Eli as they walked toward the woods, but anyone could tell Eli didn't need no help. He carried Mary Ella like she weighed no more than a feather pillow, her yellow hair spilling over his arm, me and Nonnie scrambling to keep up.

Eli had to put her in the truck bed so me and Nonnie could sit with her. Eli took off his jacket to put under her head and Nonnie and me spread her coat out on top of her. Henry Allen waved to us and we was off. Me and Nonnie held Mary Ella's hands while she cried and shouted words that made no sense except for every once in a while, that "mama" that made my heart ache. I thought about how much she must be hurting, with the baby getting ready to come out, plus her appendix being sickly.

Eli drove quick except where there was bumps in the road. He seemed to know where they was and slowed down to go over them as careful as he could.

"There, there, child," Nonnie kept saying over and over to Mary Ella, her voice shivery in a way I never heard before. I didn't know what to say myself.

"You'll be okay," I tried. "Everything'll be okay." But I was getting more and more scared.

We was halfway to the hospital when Mary Ella started going real quiet, which was worse in a way than all the hollering. Daylight was on us now, and she stared straight up at the sky.

"She don't look right," Nonnie said, leaning over Mary Ella to peer into her face.

She didn't. She kept staring at the sky. I could see the feathery white clouds in the blue of her eyes and it was like looking into the sky myself. It was like looking at heaven. Mary Ella stopped blinking. She was real still, just staring that faraway stare, going quiet, and I thought, *She's dying*. All of a sudden, I felt Ruby in the truck with us. I remembered what she said. Mary Ella would have 0 children. *Zero*. Ruby floated around me the way she did in the church. I felt her around my neck and in my hair, and I waved my arms to get her away from me.

"Get out of this truck!" I shouted at her. I pressed my body over my sister's to keep the evil away. If Mary Ella died, it was my fault for taking my fingers off that plancher thing. For messing with a Ouija board to begin with. For sneaking out with Henry Allen. My fault, all of it. She was all I had left of my family, besides Nonnie. We was night and day different, but right then I would of killed to protect her. Right then, I felt all that love for her that went missing sometimes.

"What are you doing?" Nonnie tugged at my shoulder. "Who are you talking to?"

I shook my sister's arm. "Mary Ella!" I shouted, but she still stared at the sky like she was already in heaven herself. I couldn't lose her. I was sure the baby was already lost. *Zero*, Ruby'd said. *Zero*.

Mary Ella suddenly squeezed her eyes shut and let out a scream like somebody struck her with a knife.

"Oh, Lord!" Nonnie said, smoothing Mary Ella's hair back from her forehead. "You poor, poor baby!"

As terrible as the scream was, I was so glad to hear it. She was alive! I wanted to hug her and kiss her cheeks, but she would of thought I'd lost my mind.

We pulled into the hospital parking lot and stopped right under the emergency sign. Eli got out of the cab and jumped into the truck bed to lift Mary Ella into his arms again. He climbed out of the truck, fast but careful. Me and him and Nonnie was walking to the entrance when a nurse came out of the building pushing a wheelchair. She stopped when she saw Eli.

"You can't come in here, boy," she said.

He nodded like that was no surprise and set Mary Ella, moaning and scared looking, down in the wheelchair.

Nonnie turned to Eli. "You better pray to God she's okay," she snapped.

Eli shrugged and stuck his hands in his pockets. "Don't seem like God's done much for her so far," he said, and I thought Nonnie would of hit him if he hadn't turned so fast to go back to the truck.

*

They put me and Nonnie in a waiting room. We felt right out of place sitting there with three men who was waiting for their babies to be born. One of them read a book, one flipped the pages of a *Life* magazine, and the third just sat and stared into space. Me and Nonnie didn't say a word to each other. She pretended like she was looking at a *Good Housekeeping*, but I knew she wasn't seeing nothing on the pages. I didn't even bother pretending. I was too nervous about what was happening on the other side of the waiting room door.

I felt like I already knew what Nonnie didn't know: Mary Ella's baby wasn't going to make it. My eyes kept filling up with tears while we sat there and I brushed them away as quiet as I could because I didn't want her to see.

After a long while, a doctor came through the door wearing a white coat and a big smile. He walked straight over to the man who was reading the book and held out his hand.

"You have a fine son!" He pumped the man's hand up and down.

"A son!" The man jumped to his feet. "Finally!"

"Everyone's doing well," the doctor said. "You can see your baby in the nursery in a few minutes."

The man grinned as he watched the doctor leave the room. Then he reached into his jacket pocket and pulled out a handful of cigars. It was just like you always hear about. He handed the cigars to the other two men in the room and they told him, "Congratulations!" Then he turned toward me and Nonnie. He looked straight through us like we wasn't there. His smile disappeared for a minute, but he was whistling as he walked out of the room.

"Guess we don't get no cigar," Nonnie muttered so only I could hear.

I didn't say nothing. Inside my head, though, I was plenty busy. I was praying to God to let my sister live.

After a while, a nurse came into the room and walked over to us. I could tell she wasn't going to make no big loud announcement like the doctor done with the cigar man, and I tensed up. She sat in the chair next to Nonnie and leaned close.

"She had a boy," she said. "She had a difficult time and lost a lot of blood, but she's going to be okay."

Nonnie closed her eyes. "Thank you, Jesus," she said.

I clutched the arms of my chair. "The baby—?" I asked.

"He's doing just fine." She smiled.

I could hardly believe it! Nonnie grabbed my hand and squeezed it. It felt like the happiest moment we had in a long time.

"Did they take out her appendix?" I asked.

The nurse raised her eyebrows at Nonnie, who nodded like she was giving permission to talk to me.

"Not yet, honey," the nurse said. "They'll do that later today or maybe tomorrow."

"But it could bust!" I said.

She chuckled, winking at Nonnie. "I promise you we'll keep an eye on it," she said, like it was no big deal. Then she turned all serious. "Is your granddaughter keeping the baby?" she asked Nonnie.

Nonnie looked shocked by the question. "Of course!" she said.

"You want to see him, then?" the nurse asked. "The girl's still asleep, but the baby's in the nursery."

Nonnie hesitated so long, I had to answer for us. "Yes, ma'am," I said. "We want to see him."

We followed her down a long hallway to where some windows was cut into the wall. The man with the cigars stood there, puffing away, grinning. "That's my son there." He pointed through the glass. There was a bunch of little metal cribs in the room and I followed his finger to a baby I could hardly see, he was in a crib so far from the window. "He's cute," I said, trying to be polite, but I hardly noticed his baby. I was too busy looking for ours.

The nurse went into the nursery and put a white mask over her face. She reached into one of the cribs, lifted a tiny bundle into her arms, and brung him over to the window. I couldn't get a real good look at him, he was so bundled up, but I could see his face was pink and his head was covered with lots of dark curls. I forgot all about worrying what color he was. He was the cutest baby ever. That was all I saw. The cutest baby ever.

I looked at Nonnie and she was smiling wider than I ever seen before. She pressed her hand to the window, her lower lip shivering and her eyes filling up. She could surprise me sometimes. She acted mean, but maybe she was just scared. Scared this new baby would be half colored and no one would want it around. Scared we'd get kicked out of our house and have nowhere to live. Scared, like I was, that Mary Ella would die.

"Well," she said after looking at him for a minute, "I reckon I ain't never seen a baby so handsome."

Five whole days passed before Mary Ella came home, on account of her losing a lot of blood. They even had to give her somebody else's blood, but the doctor said she'd be fine. She was alive; that was the important thing. I couldn't wait to see the baby again. I hadn't seen him since that first day in the nursery when all I got was a peek. Nonnie'd seen him again when he was three days old, though. She got a ride to the hospital from one of her old church friends while I was at school.

"What's he look like now?" I'd asked when I got home from school that afternoon. She was scrubbing the kitchen counter and I watched her face carefully for the answer.

"Like a baby," she said. *Scrub, scrub.*

"Did they take a picture?" One of my friends said the hospital always took pictures of new babies.

"They don't take no pictures of bastard babies," Nonnie said, working the sponge into the corner.

I wasn't sure what that word meant but I knew it wasn't good. I worried it was another word for Negro. The same friend who told me about the pictures also told me colored babies could come out light and then darken up. "But," I said to Nonnie, "you saw him, right?"

"Of course I saw him." She was in a right awful mood and she went on talking, but not really to me. "More curly black hair than a baby has a right to, but he's okay. Ain't nobody going to know."

"*We* don't even know, Nonnie," I said, trying to get her to look at me. "It might not of been . . . what you're thinking."

She glanced up from the counter to give me a look like I was living in a fairy tale, then went on with her work. "She named him William. You know anybody with that name?"

I thought about it. There was a real short boy named Bill in my class at school, but I was a thousand percent sure he didn't have nothing to do with Mary Ella's baby. I thought of all the day laborers Mr. Gardiner brung into the fields over the last year. I didn't know most of their names. Any one of them could be a William.

"I don't know no William," I said. "Maybe she just likes that name."

The day Mary Ella was coming home, I tried to fix up the bedroom real nice for her. Eli's mama, Lita, had a baby last year and she brung over a bassinet she didn't need no more and I made it up with little sheets and blankets Mrs. Werkman brung us, then set it up next to Mary Ella's side of the bed. I'd washed our own sheets and then worried they'd freeze on the line, it was so cold out. My hands went numb making up the bed with them. I hoped they'd warm up some before Mary Ella got home.

I put away all the baby clothes Mrs. Werkman brung us and all the little diapers and pins that had blue and yellow ducks on them. That was my favorite thing, them little ducks. She brung us bottles and formula and a big box of sanitary napkins. She said Mary Ella would need a lot of them when she got home. I was only getting used to using them things myself, since I just started my monthlies around Christmas. I wouldn't of known what was happening if I didn't have an older sister. Not that Mary Ella exactly explained it to me, but I knew how every month she used them napkins. At least, until the month she didn't need them no more. That's when Nonnie figured out she was going to have a baby.

"You go wait by the road now," Nonnie said after we fixed the house up as good as we could. "They'll need help coming through the woods, what with Mary Ella still healing up and trying to carry a baby."

I walked through the woods, feeling excited. I knew it was a terrible thing, Mary Ella having a baby, but we needed something good to happen in our lives and a little kid was always a good thing.

I sat down on the scrubby dirt at the end of Deaf Mule Road, right near the spot Mrs. Werkman always parked her car when she came to see us. I could feel the cold ground through my dungarees and I buttoned Daddy's coat up to my neck. I looked out over the fields. It wouldn't be long before we'd all be working out there again, getting the earth ready for the tobacco plants. I hoped Mary Ella could still help even though she had a baby to watch over.

From where I sat, I could see the Gardiners' house down the road, Henry Allen's bicycle leaning against the tree in the side yard. On the school bus that morning, he said he talked Desiree into getting rid of the Ouija board.

"You told her we used it?" I asked, shocked.

"Nah," he said. "I couldn't tell her I took it. I just told her a friend used one and let a spirit loose and he's had no end of bad luck since. House burned down. Father died. Dog got run over." He laughed. "I almost overdone it," he said. "But her eyes got big and she said she was going to get rid of that thing. She always knew Lucifer was inside it, she said. I don't know what she done with it, but it's gone. I checked when she was hanging up the wash."

"Good riddance," I'd said. I knew he was still shook up about what happened in the church, but I wasn't afraid of Ruby no more. Mary Ella and her baby was both alive, and whoever Ruby was, she was dead and gone.

I must of sat there a half hour before I saw Mrs. Werkman's car coming down the road in a cloud of dust. I got to my feet and brushed off the back of my coat and my dungarees. Mrs. Werkman stopped the car close to me and got out.

"Happy to see you here, Ivy," she said. Even though her car was a dusty mess, Mrs. Werkman always looked perfect. She had real pale-colored hair tied back at her neck and she wore pants, but they was always clean and pressed. Nonnie said she looked like a movie star. She was probably the same age my mama would be by now, though I had the feeling my mama, locked up in a mental hospital, didn't look like no movie star.

I took a few steps toward the car, weeds crackling beneath my feet. I couldn't see Mary Ella real good behind the window.

"You can carry William while I help your sister," Mrs. Werkman said. "She's still a bit sore." She opened the door and I watched Mary Ella turn her body carefully till her feet was on the ground. The baby was in her arms and before she stood up, she pressed her cheek to his little forehead. I'd never seen that softness in her before. That love. I could feel the power of it. I didn't know this new part of my sister, but it choked me up.

"Hey, Mary Ella," I said. "Glad you're home."

She raised her head from her baby to look at me. Her face was whiter than I'd ever seen it. White as bone. It gave me a chill, but then she smiled the most beautiful smile ever. "You want to get a look at him?" she asked.

I nodded, and she moved aside the blanket where it covered his face. His eyes blinked open, squinting a little, and I figured the sun was too bright for him. He had really long black eyelashes that was stuck together in little points, like he'd been crying. "I ain't never seen nothing so tiny," I said. He didn't look a thing like Mary Ella, but he didn't make me think of Eli either. He didn't make me think of nobody I knew and that was a good thing. He'd just be his own little self.

"Give him to Ivy to carry, Mary Ella," Mrs. Werkman said. She'd strung the old clothespin bag over her shoulder along with her purse.

I reached toward Mary Ella and for a moment I thought she wasn't going to hand him over, but then she set him softly in my arms. He weighed next to nothing and the clean smell of him filled me up.

Mary Ella leaned on Mrs. Werkman's arm and we walked real slow and careful through the woods. I watched out for roots and stones on the path, not wanting to fall with that sweet bundle in my arms.

Nonnie stood on our porch in her raggedy old housedress, but she'd put her pink "special occasion" sweater over her apron. She looked right old standing there, hugging her arms because of the chill, or maybe because of nerves. All morning she'd been fretting about how long it'd been since she took care of a baby.

"He's so perfect, Nonnie," I said when I got near the porch, but I kept my voice hushed. I didn't want to stir him up when he was being so good. I wanted her to love him.

Mrs. Werkman helped us get settled in. She made everything smooth and easy and I was nervous about her leaving. Mary Ella sat on the sofa to give William—she called him Baby William—a bottle, while me and Nonnie and Mrs. Werkman sat nearby, watching like we was seeing the most amazing thing in the world. To me, it really was. My sister a mama. It was hard to believe.

Mary Ella was real tired, though, and after she fed him, we put her to bed on those fresh sheets that had warmed up good.

"Remember you have to eat, Mary Ella," Mrs. Werkman said from the foot of the bed as Nonnie raised the blanket to Mary Ella's chin.

I didn't think my sister even heard her. She was too busy watching me tuck William into his bassinet.

"I'll make sure Nurse Ann stops by in the next day or so to check on William and take a look at your incision," Mrs. Werkman said to Mary Ella. She let go of the footboard and turned to the door. "She can take the stitches out when it's time," she added.

"It'd be good if she could come tomorrow," Nonnie said as she followed Mrs. Werkman out of the room.

I sat down on the bed facing my sister. I wanted to tell her I was happy she was healthy and had a perfect baby, but me and Mary Ella didn't talk that way to each other, so I just smiled at her and she smiled back with her nearly white lips. I wondered how long it would take to get her blood built back up. I didn't know if it was the appendix operation or having the baby that made her go white like that. Probably both.

Then I asked her the question I couldn't figure out no matter how I tried or how many times I asked Nonnie about it.

"How did Mrs. Werkman know you needed your 'pendix out?" I asked. "Did you tell her it was hurting you?" Mary Ella must of been so scared when she found out her appendix was sick. She knew all about that girl at our school who died when her appendix burst.

Mary Ella lowered the blanket and lifted her nightgown so I could see where the doctor cut her. It was a puckery-looking line by her belly button, and it was sewed up with black thread that stuck up at the end. "It didn't hurt me at all," she said. "Mrs. Werkman just knew somehow."

I admired Mrs. Werkman so much. "I think she saved your life," I said.

Mary Ella nodded. "She's like God," she said. "God's the only one who knows things like that." She shut her eyes and I knew she would fall asleep any minute. I leaned over and wrapped one of her crazy curls around my finger. "I'm glad you're still here, Mary Ella," I whispered.

She smiled but kept her eyes shut. "I got the most beautiful baby," she said.

"Yes, you do," I said.

I sat with her and the baby until I was sure they was both asleep. Our bedroom door never quite shut all the way and I could hear Nonnie and Mrs. Werkman talking by the front door as I pulled down the shades at the windows and started to leave the room. My hand was on the doorknob when something made me stop moving, and I stood there listening to them through the crack in the door.

"And I know you feel overwhelmed right now with a new baby to look after," Mrs. Werkman was saying. From the sound of her voice, I thought she was halfway out the door already. I couldn't quite make out what Nonnie said back to her. It sounded more like a mutter than actual words.

"Well," Mrs. Werkman said, "Mary Ella will be up and around and able to take over much of the care soon enough."

"Oh, she don't know nothing about taking care of a baby," Nonnie said.

"Nurse Ann can teach her what she needs to know," Mrs. Werkman said. "And the best part is, you won't ever need to worry about this happening to her again. I'm sure that's a relief."

"Thank the good Lord for that!" Nonnie said.

They was crazy if they thought this could never happen to Mary Ella again. Not unless they locked her up.

"I'm sure Ivy will help out, too," Mrs. Werkman said.

"Ha!" Nonnie snorted. "That one's a baby herself. Ornery. Does whatever she wants. She just makes more work for me."

My cheeks burned. Was I that useless? I thought of all the nights I snuck out with Henry Allen doing stupid things like messing with the Ouija board or riding our bikes through the woods pretending we was cowboys.

"Oh, she's growing up," Mrs. Werkman said. "I think Ivy might surprise you."

I was grateful for her faith in me. I wasn't sure I deserved it.

I walked away from the door and sat down on the edge of the bed again. The room was real dim now with the shades pulled down, and I couldn't see Mary Ella or her baby too clear, but I felt them there. I felt the weight of them on my shoulders. Nonnie was right: You couldn't trust Mary Ella to take good care of herself, much less a little baby. Even Nonnie wasn't that good at taking care of things. She got upset if one of us even sneezed or tore a hole in a dress. *Ivy might surprise you,* Mrs. Werkman had said. It was up to me now. I'd do my part. I'd stay home at night. Take care of my nephew. My sister. Take care of everything.

I leaned over the bassinet and kissed William on his forehead. Oh, that clean, sweet baby smell! I stood up, feeling like a different person than I'd been an hour ago. It was like I was starting a new chapter in a book. A real good book.

I'd make sure it had a happy ending.

Discover more gripping novels from

DIANE CHAMBERLAIN

Available now from

To discover more about your favourite author

DIANE CHAMBERLAIN

visit

www.dianechamberlain.com

You can also find her on

Facebook at www.facebook.com/
Diane.Chamberlain.Readers.Page

Instagram @diane.chamberlain.author

Twitter @D_Chamberlain